Praise for Bar
JAPAN

One of *Suspense Magazine*'s Best of 2013 Thrillers
Shortlisted for the Barry Award for Best First Novel

"[A] sophisticated international thriller . . . Having lived and worked in Japan for more than 25 years, Lancet brings an impressive breadth of knowledge to the historical aspects of the mystery and a sharp sense of immediacy to its action."

—*The New York Times Book Review*

"The first book in what will likely be a long and successful series."

—*San Francisco* magazine

"One of the hottest debut authors of 2013 . . . [a] taut international thriller that races from San Francisco to Lancet's adopted hometown of Tokyo. . . . J. J. Abrams of *Lost* fame recently bought the TV rights to the book."

—*Suspense Magazine*

"Engrossing . . . *Japantown* is full of action and surprises . . . an extremely impressive debut that is almost sure to be short-listed for any number of awards next year. Pick it up now to see what all the excitement will be about."

—Bookreporter.com

"Is the 21st century ready for multinational ninja MBAs who hack computer networks instead of flinging poisoned darts, and who surgically take out business rivals instead of whacking feudal lords? More important, does Jim Brodie have the brains and fortitude to save his young daughter and himself from these cold-blooded modern-day predators? Read *Japantown* and you'll find out."

—Mark Schreiber, *The Japan Times*

"Lancet, an American who has lived and worked in Japan for decades . . . commands a much stronger knowledge of the culture than his predecessors and . . . provide[s] a deep and easy familiarity with the dilemmas that his protagonist faces trying to bridge the gap between two vastly different cultures. . . . Strong writing and deep passion for the material carry the story and characters far enough to hold the interest of any reader who enjoys this sort of story."

—*Pittsburgh Post-Gazette*

"The debut novel by a 25-year resident of Japan is a zippy page-turner set in San Francisco's Japantown, Tokyo and a remote Japanese village."

—SFExaminer.com

"A fine thriller filled with satisfying mystery, solid characterization and high drama."

—*California Bookwatch*

"Lancet's fluency in the Japanese language, extensive knowledge of, and empathy with, the culture from which it is inseparable, and gift for creating likable (as well as despicable) characters add depth and authenticity to this captivating thriller that other non-Japanese authors rarely attain. . . . Far from a mere mouthpiece for multiculturalism, [Lancet's hero, Brodie,] comes across as a complex figure with a genuine personal history, at once blessed with extensive expertise in his chosen fields and dogged by the kind of emotional conflicts common to the human experience. . . . I was kept guessing until the very end."

—*Washington Independent Review of Books*

"Lancet successfully places a PI in an international thriller plot in his highly entertaining debut. . . . Readers will want to see more of the talented Jim Brodie, with his expertise in Japanese culture, history, and martial arts."

—*Publishers Weekly* (starred review)

"Engrossing debut thriller. . . . Lancet has a gift for pacing and keeps the reader engaged and guessing 'til the very end."

—*Library Journal*

JAPANTOWN

A Thriller

BARRY LANCET

SIMON & SCHUSTER PAPERBACKS

New York   London   Toronto   Sydney   New Delhi

Simon & Schuster Paperbacks
A Division of Simon & Schuster, Inc.
1230 Avenue of the Americas
New York, NY 10020

First Simon & Schuster trade paperback edition July 2014

SIMON & SCHUSTER PAPERBACKS and colophon are registered
trademarks of Simon & Schuster, Inc.

For information about special discounts for bulk purchases,
please contact Simon & Schuster Special Sales at
1-866-506-1949 or business@simonandschuster.com.

The Simon & Schuster Speakers Bureau can bring authors
to your live event. For more information or to book an event,
contact the Simon & Schuster Speakers Bureau at
1-866-248-3049 or visit our website at www.simonspeakers.com.

Designed by Kyoko Watanabe

Manufactured in the United States of America

10 9 8 7 6 5 4 3 2 1

The Library of Congress has cataloged the hardcover edition as follows:
Lancet, Barry.
Japantown / Barry Lancet—First Simon & Schuster hardcover edition.
p. cm.
1. Antique dealers—California—San Francisco—Fiction.
2. Japanese—California—San Francisco—Fiction.
3. Murder investigation—San Francisco (Calif.)—Fiction.
4. Murder investigation—Japan—Fiction. 5. Japantown
(San Francisco, Calif.)—Fiction. 6. Mystery fiction. I. Title.
PS3612.A547486J37 2013
813'.6—dc23   2012049519
ISBN 978-1-4516-9169-6
ISBN 978-1-4516-9170-2 (pbk)
ISBN 978-1-4516-9171-9 (ebook)

The translation of Rengetsu's "The Thief," as found in *Lotus Moon: The Poetry of the Buddhist
Nun Rengetsu* (Weatherhill, 1994), is reprinted with the permission of John Stevens.

*To my parents, Bob and Lenny, for their unflagging support,
and to those of my Japanese friends who have always felt "hemmed in"*

A wise man hears what makes no sound and sees what has no shape.

ZEN PROVERB

JAPANTOWN

JAPANTOWN

DAY 1

NOT A TRACE OF THE THIEF

SAN FRANCISCO

TWO shades of red darkened the Japantown concourse by the time I arrived. One belonged to a little girl's scarlet party dress. The other was liquid and far too human. City officials would evince a third shade once reports of the carnage hit the airwaves.

But long before the news jockeys began grappling with the Japantown slaughter, the problem landed on my doorstep.

Minutes after receiving an urgent summons, I was charging down Fillmore in a classic maroon Cutlass convertible. Before the midnight call had interrupted my evening's work, I'd been repairing an eighteenth-century Japanese tea bowl, a skill I'd picked up in the pottery town of Shigaraki, an hour outside of Kyoto. Now, even with the top down on the Cutlass, I could still smell the stringent lacquer used to fix the thumbnail-size chip on the bowl's rim. Once the lacquer dried I'd apply the final flourish—a trail of liquid gold powder. A repair was still a repair, but if done right, it restored a piece's dignity.

I swung left on Post hard enough to leave rubber and cut off two gangbangers tooling uphill in a flame-red Mazda Miata. A crisp night breeze swirled around my face and hair and wiped away every last trace of drowsiness. The gangbangers had their top down, too, apparently the better to scope out a clear shot.

They slithered in behind me, swearing in booming voices I could hear over the screech of their tires, and in my rearview mirror, angry fists shot into the air as the sleek sports car crept up on my bumper.

A pistol appeared next, followed by a man's torso, both etched in ominous shadow against the night sky. Then the driver caught sight of a police blockade up ahead, slammed on his brakes, and snaked into a U-turn. The drastic change in direction flung the shooter against the side of the car, and nearly into the street. Arms flailing, he just managed to grab the frame of the windshield and drop back into the Miata's cushioned bucket seat as the car peeled away with a throttled roar of frustration.

I knew the feeling. If I hadn't received a personal invitation, I'd have done the same. But I had no choice. A marker had been called in.

———

When the phone rang, I'd peeled off the rubber gloves, careful not to let remnants of the poisonous lacquer touch my skin. With my days filled to overflowing at the shop, I tackled repairs in the darker hours, after putting my daughter to bed. Tonight it was the tea bowl.

Lieutenant Frank Renna of the San Francisco Police Department wasted no time on pleasantries. "I need a favor. A big one this time."

I glanced at the pale green digits of the clock. 12:24 a.m. "And a fine time it is."

On the other end of the line, Renna gave a grunt of apology. "You'll get your usual consultant fee. Might not be enough, though."

"I'll survive."

"Keep thinking that way. I need you to come look at something. You got a baseball cap?"

"Yeah."

"Wear it low over your eyes. Cap, sneakers, jeans. Then get down here asap."

"Down where?"

"Japantown. The outdoor mall."

I was silent, knowing that except for a couple of bars and the Denny's coffee shop, J-town was bottled up for the night.

Renna said, "How soon can you get here?"

"Fifteen minutes if I break a few laws."

"Make it ten."

Nine minutes on, I found myself speeding toward the blockade, an impromptu cluster of rolling police steel parked haphazardly across the road where the pedestrian shopping mall on Buchanan came to an abrupt end at Post. Beyond the barricade I spotted a coroner's wagon and three ambulances, doors flung open, interiors dark and cavernous.

A hundred yards short of the barrier, I eased over in front of the Japan Center and cut the engine. I slid off tucked black leather seats and walked toward the commotion. Grim and unshaven, Frank Renna separated himself from a crowd of local badges and intercepted me halfway. Behind his approaching bulk, the rotating red and blue lights of the prowl cars silhouetted him against the night.

"The whole force out here tonight?"

He scowled. "Could be."

I was the go-to guy for the SFPD on anything Japanese—even though my name is Jim Brodie, I'm six-one, a hundred-ninety pounds, and have black hair and blue eyes. And I'm Caucasian.

The connection? I'd spent the first seventeen years of my life in Tokyo, where I was born to a rugged Irish-American father, who lived and breathed law enforcement, and a more delicate American mother, who loved art. Money was tight, so I attended local schools instead of one of the exorbitant American international facilities and absorbed the language and culture like a sponge.

Along the way, I picked up karate and judo from two of the top masters in the Japanese capital, and thanks to my mother got my first peek at the fascinating world of Japanese art.

What drew my parents to the far side of the Pacific was the U.S. Army. Jake, my father, headed up a squad of MPs in charge of security for Western Tokyo, then worked for the LAPD. But he took orders badly so he eventually returned to Tokyo, where he set up the city's first American-style PI/security firm.

He began grooming me for a position at Brodie Security a week after my twelfth birthday. I accompanied him and other detectives on interviews, stakeouts, and research trips as an observer. In the office I pored over old files when I wasn't listening to the staff speculate about cases involving blackmail, adultery, kidnapping, and more. Their conversations were gritty and real and a thousand times better than a night out at a Roppongi disco or an ultracheap Harajuku *izakaya,* though I managed to work those in too, four years later, with a fake ID.

Three weeks after my seventeenth birthday, Shig Narazaki—Jake's partner and "Uncle Shig" when he visited our home for dinner—took me on a "watch-and-see." It was a simple information-gathering stakeout for an extortion case involving the vice president of a major electronics firm and a local gang of yakuza wannabes. Japanese mafia. Just a recon trip. No action, no approach. I'd been on dozens like it.

We sat for an hour in a car tucked up an alley watching a neighborhood yakitori shop long closed for the night.

"I don't know," Shig said. "I may have the wrong place." And he left to take a look.

He did one circuit around the restaurant and was heading back when a street thug sprang from a side door and clubbed him with a Japanese fighting stick while the rest of the gang escaped out another exit.

Shig collapsed and I leapt from the car and yelled. The attacker zeroed in on me, glaring and cocking the stick like a baseball bat, which told me he had no training in the art of bojutsu. Then he charged. Luckily, the stick was the short version, so the instant his front foot shifted, I rammed my shoe into his kneecap. He went down with a howl—enough time for Shig to recover, snag the guy, and take me home with a story that made my father proud.

Unhappily, the incident demolished what was left of my parents' rocky marriage. While Jake loved his adopted country, my mother never really took to it. She felt like the perpetual outsider, a pale-faced Caucasian in a size fourteen dress surrounded by a sea of eternal size sixes. "Putting me at risk" was the last straw in a precariously high haystack. We flew to Los Angeles, and Jake stayed in Tokyo. The arrangement became permanent.

But that was fifteen years ago. A lot had happened in between: my mother passed away, I moved to San Francisco, and I got a handle on the art trade—soft work, according to Jake, but a world I found as fascinating as my mom had, though it was filled with its own brand of shark.

Then nine months ago, not a word between us in years, Jake died suddenly, and when I flew to Japan to attend the funeral, I landed in the path of real yakuza this time, not Uncle Shig's cheeseball yaki hopefuls. I managed to hold my own against them—barely—in the process tracking down a long-lost tea bowl that belonged to the legendary tea master Sen no Rikyu. The events made the headlines and I became something of a local hero.

Which was another reason I'd been invited to Japantown. That, and the fact that I had resources the SFPD did not: Jake had left me half of his agency, despite our estrangement.

Both my parents were gone, and I was being sucked into the life that had driven them apart. Which is how, at the age of thirty-two, I found myself juggling an art store and a detective agency. Refined on the one hand, brutish on the other.

In short, I was the bull in the china shop—except I owned the shop. And tonight I had a very bad feeling about where that might lead.

SHIELDING me from the curious looks of his colleagues, Renna clipped a police ID to the lip of my shirt pocket, then pulled the pocket flap over the photograph. With his barnlike mass, the lieutenant could have blocked out a whole squadron. Even my tallish frame and broad shoulders were smothered in the shadow of his looming six-four brawn with an upper trunk wider than that of most NFL defensive linemen. When he pointed a gun and yelled halt, sensible people did.

"There," he said, inspecting his work. "No one will look twice."

"Reassuring."

Renna took in my jeans and lightweight flannel shirt, then squinted at the lettering on my baseball cap. "What's the *HT* stand for?"

"Hanshin Tigers."

"Who the hell are they?"

"Japanese ball club out of Osaka."

"I tell you wear a cap, you give me exotic? Why can't you do anything like normal people?"

"Part of my charm."

"Someone somewhere probably thinks so." Renna jerked his head at the badge. "Says you're undercover. Means you're here but you're not. Means no one expects you to talk much." Renna's steady gray eyes looked weary. This was going to be bad.

"Got it."

Dropping back a step, the lieutenant favored me with another thoughtful inspection.

"There a problem?" I said.

"This is . . . different from your usual stuff. It's not, uh, stolen goods."

Behind his words I heard doubt: he was wondering if I could make the leap from things people created to things they destroyed. Lately, I'd been wondering the same thing.

I'd met Renna years ago when he and his wife had walked into Bristol's Antiques in the Outer Richmond, near the end of Geary. They'd come for the English walnut lowboy in the show window. As soon as Miriam Renna pointed to the piece, her husband had grown unnaturally still and glanced my way. The sparkle in Mrs. Renna's eye told me the piece had caught her. She'd probably dreamed about it. Lost sleep over it. Begged and wheedled until her husband had caved, helpless to curb her compulsion. When a good piece of art grabs you, that's how it works. And it was a good piece.

I could have closed the sale with a few choice comments about the quality of the inlay and the elegance of the cross-banding. I knew it and Renna knew it. But his expression and her modest jewelry told me the purchase would be a painful one, so I guided her toward an equally elegant nineteenth-century Pembroke table a century newer and a quarter of the price. With time, I told her, the piece would appreciate.

On that day, a bond of trust was born between the Rennas and myself that has deepened over the years, not unlike the patina of their Pembroke. Back then I was winding up my apprenticeship as an art dealer with old Jonathan Bristol, who specialized in European antiques. These days I had my own place out on Lombard, with a strong focus on Japanese artifacts and a scattering of Chinese, Korean, and European. After our first meeting, Renna had taken to swinging by on occasion to ask my opinion about some Asian aspect of one of his cases, usually in the evenings over a pint of Anchor Steam or a good single malt. But this was the first time he'd invited me to a crime scene.

Renna said, "This is going to get grisly. You want, tomorrow I could bring snapshots. You wouldn't have to look at the rest. None of the guys you know are around, so you can still walk."

"I'm here. Might as well do it."

"You sure? This is leagues away from inlay and filigree."

"I'm sure."

"Don't say I didn't warn you."

"Fair enough," I said, squinting into the glare of the flashing police lights.

"Nothing fair about it," Renna muttered under his breath, and I understood he was referring to whatever lay beyond the barricade.

Far above our heads, a chilly gale bullied a dense fog bank past, smothering the city's loftier peaks in brooding billows but leaving the flatlands, where we stood, bare and exposed to capricious wildcat winds.

"Awful big turnout this late at night," I said, speculating about the crowd of uniformed and plainclothes cops milling about the mall entrance. "Any particular reason?"

"Everyone wants a look-see."

This is going to be real bad, I thought as Renna led me toward the kill zone.

On a rooftop two hundred yards away, a man who used the name Dermott Summers when he traveled lay flat on his stomach and watched Lieutenant Frank Renna walk toward ground zero with a recent arrival.

Summers sharpened the focus of his night-vision binoculars and frowned. Jeans, flannel shirt, hat, an obscured badge. No city official would show up dressed like that.

Undercover cop? Maybe. But then why did the lieutenant go over to greet him?

Summers zoomed in on the newcomer. There was something in his stride, but no, he wasn't law enforcement. Summers set down the binoculars and picked up his camera. He adjusted the range of the telephoto lens and captured several shots of the new guy.

This time he noticed the *HT,* and the hairs on the back of his neck rose. Japanese ball cap? Bad news. But just the kind of news he was charged with discovering—and defusing. That was the beauty of Soga. With deep-cover surveillance on site *after* the kill, no one could trip them up.

Summers trained his camera on the new man's car and snapped a close-up of the license plate, several of the Cutlass, then called in the number. He'd have name and vitals inside thirty minutes.

At the thought, Summers's trigger finger twitched. The takedown had been perfect. He'd brooded over being sidelined during the kill, but here was a bonus straight from heaven. He might see some action yet.

T HE kill zone fell midway between the rest areas.

The one-block stretch on Buchanan between Post and Sutter had been converted to a pedestrian mall long ago. Soft red brick replaced cold black pavement, and a sushi shop, shiatsu parlor, and a few dozen other shops sprang up along the concourse. Two rest areas provided benches and sculpture and were originally designed to allow shoppers a place to pause and refresh body and mind. Now they framed a scene I would never forget.

As we approached, portable klieg lights brought the victims into focus: three adults and two children.

Children?

My abdominals tensed and something in my stomach began to curdle. Inside a circle of yellow crime-scene tape was a parent's worst nightmare. I could make out the small neat bodies of a boy and a girl. *Someone's daughter*—and the same age as my Jenny, give or take. Nearby lay two men and a woman. A family. And a Japanese one at that. Tourists. This wasn't a murder scene. This was sacrilege.

"Hell, Frank."

"I know. You gonna be okay with this?"

Why did there have to be children?

Renna said, "You can still opt out. Last chance."

I waved the suggestion away. Someone had decimated what had once been a vital, functioning household, leaving in the wake of their attack with high-powered weaponry a tossed salad of shredded flesh, frayed garments, and clotted blood.

The sourness stirred in the pit of my stomach. "This has got to be the work of a psycho. No sane person would do this."

"You been around any gang action lately?"

"Good point."

When my parents' divorce flung me back to Los Angeles, I'd spent five years on the cusp of South Central in a gang-infested neighborhood, then put in two more here in the Mission District grunge before I could afford decent quarters in the Sunset and, after marriage, in my present cupboard apartment in East Pacific Heights. I'd seen my share of corpses, but this outdid nearly any scenario gangland could summon up. Slick purple-red pools of blood had collected in the spaces between the bodies, and viscous streams threaded their way through the brickwork.

I took a deep breath to settle my nerves.

Then I saw the mother's death mask. A tortured face. Despairing. Aware, in the last seconds of life, of the horror playing out around her.

The sight left me breathless and depleted. Maybe I *wasn't* up to this. My limbs grew leaden. Ramming my fists into the pockets of my jeans, I gritted my teeth to restrain my fury.

One minute the family was strolling through Japantown, the next they faced darkness and death in a foreign land.

> *Not a trace of the thief*
> *but he left behind*
> *the peaceful stillness*
> *of the Okazaki Hills*

Years ago, long before we married, Mieko had whispered those words in my ear to ease the pain of my own mother's passing, my second encounter with the poem. Unbidden, it came to mind a third time when Mieko was killed, leaving Jenny and me to struggle on without her. Now the verse made its presence felt once more and I knew why. Embedded in those four lines was the balm of a larger truth, a comforting kernel of wisdom stretching back generations.

"You still with me?"

I dragged myself away from personal demons. "Yeah."

Renna rolled a couple of imaginary marbles around in his mouth as he considered my answer. A full head of black hair capped deadpan cop eyes and rugged features. He had a hard face with deep lines, but the lines had soft edges. If his face were a catcher's mitt, you'd say it was broken in just right.

Renna stepped up to the crime scene tape and said, "How's it going, Todd?"

Inside the tape, a forensic tech scraped up a blood sample. His hair was clipped short and his ears were large and pink. "Some good, mostly bad. This was late night in a commercial district, so we have an uncontaminated site. That's the good news. Other side is, Henderson was grumbling louder than usual. He's saying nothing we got is gonna tell us squat even though he's fast-tracking it. He gathered debris, fibers, and prints and rushed back to the lab but did a lot of frowning. Fiber's old. Doesn't think it's from the shooter."

"What kind of prints?" Renna asked.

Todd glanced my way, then with a look queried Renna, who said, "Todd Wheeler, Jim Brodie. Brodie's consulting on this one but keep it to yourself for now."

We exchanged nods.

Todd angled his head at an alley. "Hasn't rained for a while so we got footprints in the passageway alongside the restaurant. Soft and padded and probably silent. A treadless loafer or moccasin-type shoe. Probably the shooter waiting."

Renna and I looked at the alley. An unlit walkway ran between a Japanese restaurant and a kimono shop to public parking in the rear. With a balcony extension overhead, the lane was steeped in shade. I scanned the shops to the left and the right. On the other side of the mall was a second alley, but it offered less cover.

My stomach muscles twitched and I returned my attention to the victims. They lay in a close-knit cluster, arms and legs crisscrossing in places like some grotesque game of pickup sticks. In the brittle white glare of the kliegs, eye ridges cast dark shadows over sinking sockets and highlighted round cheekbones, chic haircuts, stylish clothing. A look I saw three times a year when I flew across the Pacific.

These Japanese were from Tokyo.

In fact, if this were old Japan, the scene might have found its way into a woodblock print when the genre veered away from the "floating world" and other lighter subjects. I had clients who snapped up the more grotesque *ukiyo-e* prints with ghosts and goblins and gore. The pictures weren't as graphic as the spectacle before me, but some came close, for in the old days before photography ukiyo-e, and variations of the art, served a secondary purpose of reporting the events of the day. They functioned more as a premodern data stream than art, which is why they made their way west to Europe as disposable wrapping material for breakables, much as newspaper is used today.

Renna spoke in a low growl. "The kill went down fast. Automatic at close range. Maybe four-five rounds a second. Ejected casings scattered like peanut shells. Bastard didn't care too much about leaving them."

"Awfully arrogant," I said. "Add high-level firepower, what's that say? Psycho or gang?"

"Could be either. Come take a look at this."

Shoving his hands in his pockets, Renna ambled around to the far side of the scene. I trailed after him until we stood at the point closest to the mother, which also gave us a different angle on the children. The boy's mouth was slack, his lips ice blue and parted. The girl's long black hair fanned across the brickwork. She wore a glistening red dress under a pink coat. The dress looked new and very much like the kind of thing my daughter might dream of wearing.

I raised my hand to block the glare. The girl's fingers were plump with baby fat and curled around a furry lump matted with blood. I thought I recognized the lump. "That a Pooh bear?"

"Yeah."

I was suddenly aware of the frigid night air coursing through my lungs. Aware that tonight only a thin yellow band of tape separated the living from the dead. That the frail girl on the cobblestones, clutching a favorite toy, resembled my Jenny to an uncomfortable degree.

Renna thrust his chin at the mother. "That look familiar?"

My eyes swept over the scene from our new position. About six feet from where we stood, a scrap of paper floated in a pool of blood near the mother. On it was a kanji character, which crawled over the note's fiber-rich white surface with the jagged, free-form sprawl of a giant spider.

Kanji were the basic building blocks of the Japanese writing system—complex, multistroke ideographs borrowed from the Chinese hundreds of years ago. Blood had seeped into the paper and dried to the brownish purple of old liver, obscuring the lower portion of the character.

"Does it?" Renna prodded.

I shifted to the left to cut the glare of the kliegs—and froze.

Illuminated in the unforgiving white light was what looked to be the same kanji I'd found the morning after my wife died.

CHAPTER 4

M OSTLY, I remember the bones.

The inspector and his team had spread black plastic tarp across my in-laws' front lawn and were laying ash-covered debris out in a grid as they reclaimed items from the rubble. Shapeless blocks of melted metal. Scorched slabs of cement. And, in a discreet corner behind a freestanding screen, a mounting collection of charred bones.

Over the next two months I spent all my time attempting to track down the kanji spray-painted on the sidewalk. It had given me purpose, a way to attack my grief. If there was a message to be had about Mieko's death, I wanted to find it.

Calling in a pile of markers, I received introductions to experts all over the United States and Japan. But no one could read the kanji. No one had ever seen it. The damn thing didn't exist. Not in the multi-volume kanji dictionaries. Not in linguistic databases. Not in regional records dating back centuries.

But I'd laid eyes on it myself, so I dug deeper. I applied the same techniques I used to trace an elusive piece of art, and eventually I unearthed a lead. In a musty corner of a mildew-laden university library in Kagoshima, a wizened old man approached me. He had heard of my inquiries and asked to see the kanji, then insisted on anonymity before he would speak. I consented. Three years ago, he told me, he had seen the same kanji next to a body in a suburban park in Hiroshima, and it had also been found at another murder site in Fukuoka fifteen years earlier. But my only witness was clearly terrified of something and vanished before I could drag any further details out of him.

Renna knew about my hunt for the kanji—he and Miriam had watched Jenny during my crazed string of trips to Japan, comforting her while her father communed more with the dead than with the living.

I said to the lieutenant, "Is a closer look possible?"

He shook his head. "Can't move it yet. Can't allow you inside the tape. But from here, you think it's the same?"

"Ninety percent chance."

"What'll close the deal?"

"Need to see it without the blood."

Before Renna could reply, someone near the patrol cars shouted for him. Muttering under his breath, Renna stalked off and dove into a huddle with a plainclothes detective. They exchanged some words I couldn't hear, after which Renna signaled to a female detective with cinnamon-brown hair, good muscle tone, and no makeup. She separated from the crowd.

"Sir?"

"Corelli," Renna said, "have you done this before?"

"Twice, sir."

"Okay. Listen up. I want teams of two knocking on any door with lights. As soon as it's decent, say six, hit the rest. Get warm bodies up Buchanan checking the apartment complexes on both sides of the mall for witnesses. Hit anyplace on the hill that overlooks the crime scene. Send two teams to rip apart the Miyako Inn, where the vics were staying. Find out if anyone saw or heard anything and if any members of the family had contact with the staff. Talk to all shifts. Drag them out of bed if you have to. Got that?"

"Yes, sir."

I wondered if the police footwork would ferret out any useful information. Should the killer prove to be even half as elusive as the kanji, Renna's efforts would lead nowhere.

"Good. Next, bring me the hotel bill, luggage, and a computer printout of any calls in or out. Order a full workup on the rooms for prints and fiber and get onto the Japanese consulate for a list of any friends the vics might have in town, the state, the country. In that order."

"Okay."

"You find any walk-by witness yet?"

"No, sir."

"Anyone in the coffee shop?"

"No, but that's where the deceased last ate. Tea and cake for the adults, sundaes for the kids. Third night running. They were on their way back to their rooms when they got hit." She pointed to the Miyako Inn's blue sign beyond the far end of the pedestrian mall, glowing benignly behind the towering twin pillars of a red torii gateway designating the northern edge of the concourse.

Torii were most often composed of two red, inward-leaning columns surging up into the sky and topped by a pair of horizontal rails. They were symbolic structures from Shinto, Japan's indigenous religion, and usually mark the approach to a shrine, where sacred ground begins. This one was decorative and marked the north face of the Japantown mall, its placement at the boundary of a commercial district faintly sacrilegious.

Renna pursed his lips. "But no witnesses?"

"No."

"Who heard it?"

"Most of the people in Denny's, for starters. But this close to the projects, they either thought it was gangs or firecrackers."

In other words, no one was willing to venture into the night to confirm the source of the noise.

"Okay, close off the area. Don't let anyone out until our boys have their vitals and don't let anyone in unless they have a note from God. Got it?"

"Yes, sir."

"And Corelli?"

"Sir?"

"Did you call Bryant HQ for the rest of my people?"

"That's next on my list but—"

Renna's eyes narrowed. "What?"

"It's a lot of manpower. Are you expecting heat on this one, sir?"

"I'm expecting it to rain large political turds—why?"

"Never mind."

Corelli bolted with newfound motivation and Renna stomped back to my bench. "We got computer-confirmed IDs off the family's passports. Hiroshi and Eiko Nakamura, kids Miki and Ken. Mean anything?"

"No. But there's probably a million Nakamuras in Japan."

"Smith and Jones?"

"Yeah. You have a Tokyo address for them, right?"

"Not yet."

"It'll be Tokyo."

"You sure?"

"Yeah. Grooming, clothing, they're from the capital."

"Good to know. How about Kozo Yoshida? The second male."

I shrugged.

Renna's eyes roamed the mall. "Not unexpected. Now, refresh my memory. Tell me everything about the kanji and why you still can't read the goddamned thing. And make it simple."

———

Two miles off the California coast, a man in his early thirties sat at the stern of a thirty-six-foot Sports Fisherman with twin Volvo engines piloted by Captain Joseph Frey. The boat chugged doggedly through rolling Pacific swells, navigating a course for Humboldt Bay, two hundred fifty miles north of San Francisco. The passenger and his three companions posed as affluent Asian businessmen wanting to fish the Northern Californian seaboard. Tackle was hooked and oiled. Live bait swarmed at the bottom of a steel tank, blue slivers darting in the moonlight.

This was their third excursion in the last two weeks with Captain Frey, who hoped they would become regular customers. The previous weekend, they'd trolled south of San Francisco, laying line at three lively locations between the city and Santa Cruz, where the four men had deboarded for an IT convention due to start the following day. The weekend before, they'd headed three miles straight out for some serious deep-sea fishing. On this trip, the captain's prized customers wanted to drop line at a string of favored sites on the way north, then disembark at Humboldt and catch an evening plane to Portland for a regional company conference.

What Captain Frey didn't know was that this would be their final trip together. In fact, it would be the last time his passengers would set foot in the Bay Area for at least five years.

The rules of Soga forbade it.

At the front of the craft, one of the men engaged Frey in conversation, asking about the best place to lay for lingcod. While holding a steady northerly course, the captain described the sweet spots he would hit on the seaboard, gesturing with enthusiasm to unseen fishing grounds beyond the bow. Unobserved by Captain Frey, the man in the stern unzipped a black sports bag at his feet, extracted the Uzi submachine gun used for Japantown, and dropped it overboard into the frothy chop, where the weapon began a journey to the murky floor forty-five hundred feet below.

CHAPTER 5

MY nightmare was beginning again.

I looked over at a clutch of uniformed cops huddled at the barricade. To fight off the sea-chill, many of the patrol boys wore black leather jackets over their summer blues while the detectives hunkered down in trench coats or heavy-duty parkas. Some talked, some listened, and more than a few fired quick glances down the corridor of shops toward us.

No, that wasn't right.

Toward the bodies.

Uncertainty was the prevailing emotion. It spoke of violation and despair in a way you rarely saw in officers of the law, but this was the unhealthy mix I'd lived with every day since my wife's death four years ago, when she flew to L.A. to help her parents with some immigration papers.

The call woke me at 6:49 a.m., the police having gotten my number from a neighbor. I grabbed the next commuter flight to LAX and pulled up in a rental car while the fire inspector was still working the site.

When I introduced myself, he gave me a sympathetic look. "These cases, what can you do? With your older homes, you get slippage. Say you have substandard electrical, or it stresses during a strong quake or punchy aftershock. A conduit tube might pop from its power box, taking the wires with it. If they connect to an unused outlet, it goes unnoticed. Then your years of hot L.A. weather parch the two-by-fours, and when the exposed wire eventually droops and comes in contact with a beam—up she goes. Unless any of the victims were a smoker, that'll probably be our culprit."

"None of them smoked."

"Well, there you go, then."

I stood on the sidewalk in a daze, watching absently as the excavation continued. My wife, her parents, and a visiting uncle had slept in the house the night before.

It was while waiting for the fact-finding exercise to wind down that I noticed the kanji. Mieko's parents lived five blocks from my old place, so I knew the neighborhood well. The area was integrated and gang infested, with the typical graffiti eyesores. Much to my surprise, embedded in the territorial markings of the local Salvadoran gang was a Japanese character. It was sprayed on the sidewalk in the same black, red, and green, intentionally mimicking the gang's highly abstract hieroglyphics. To the uninitiated it blended in, just another gratuitous defacement. However, if you could read Japanese, it sprang out at you with the aggressiveness of a 3-D graphic. And the paint looked newer.

Asian gangs cruised the area, so the kanji's presence was not unusual. But because I found it outside the house where my wife had just died, and because old friends in the neighborhood told me they hadn't seen the marking before, I became suspicious.

Once I confirmed that the kanji hadn't shown up elsewhere in the area and wasn't listed in any dictionary, I headed to Japan, where the old man cornered me in the library and divulged his secret. Seemingly fearful for his life, he disappeared the second I turned my back. But the fact that someone else had actually seen the kanji—and, shockingly, only at murder scenes—was a godsend.

But only to me.

Those who should care didn't.

When I approached the Japanese police in Hiroshima, I received a sympathetic but condescending reception. No one could recall such an incident or had heard of an unreadable kanji. Besides, they told me, hundreds of parks dotted the suburban landscape. Reluctantly, they allowed me to fill out the appropriate paperwork, then quietly ushered me to the exit with endless bows and an assurance that they would be in touch if something turned up. Nothing turned up. The LAPD didn't bother with paperwork; they just laughed me out the door. Two weeks later the fire inspector's office declared the blaze accidental and the police closed the case.

"Simple," Renna reminded me.

I raked my fingers through my hair. "After the fire, I talked to everyone, Frank. I went everywhere, even Taiwan, Singapore, and Shanghai, on the chance the kanji was a Chinese offshoot. I got nothing. No one's *ever* seen it. If it weren't for that old man in Kagoshima, I'd have lost my mind."

Renna rolled his marbles as he listened. "But you did have *something*. And if this turns out to be the same, we've got another shot at it."

"I can't imagine it being different."

"All right. You know the M&N Tavern on Fifth?"

"Sure."

"Early dinner around four? I'll bring you the kanji after the labbies run it under the scope."

"Works for me."

"Think it'll clean up?"

I nodded. "If standard calligraphy ink was used, it'll come through undamaged. Once the ink dries, it resists most liquids. That's why so many old scroll paintings have come down intact."

Renna's eyes sparkled at what I imagined was the first encouraging news of the night. "Good to hear," he said.

"Good and bad. If we get a match, we get big trouble."

He nodded unhappily. "You're talking about the multiple vics in both places, right?"

"Yeah."

"Not promising, I know. But I signed on for the full tour. The old guy let slip about a body count at either of the Japan sites?"

"No. But he did have his suspicions."

"Which were?"

"A very methodical serial killer."

CHAPTER 6

6:38 A.M.

WHEN the knock came, I was whipping up some scrambled eggs and toast while listening to *Zen II*, an early album by Katsuya Yokoyama, one of Japan's bamboo flute virtuosos. In this piece he played soulful tunes with a knowing calm. In others he stretched his notes to the throaty hoarseness of a mountain wind. He could make the *shakuhachi* wail or mourn, his inflection teetering on the edge, straining for a hard truth. All things I knew something about.

I unlocked the door and Jennifer Yumiko Brodie, my six-year-old daughter, skipped into the room with a "Morning, Daddy," and reached out toward me expectantly. She was returning from a sleepover with Lisa Meyers, a classmate who lived upstairs.

I scooped her up in a swift hug, then raced back to the kitchen, cradling her in the crook of one arm while I attended the eggs with my free hand. Jenny kissed my cheek. As her long black pigtails swung across her face, she yawned and gave me a sleepy grin. Looking longingly at the gap where her central incisors would emerge and fill out the smile, I wished she could stay six forever. If not for her sake, then for mine.

Wrinkling her nose Jenny said, "What's that smell?"

"Lacquer from a tea bowl I'm repairing."

The lacquer build on the bowl needed two more days to dry before I applied the gold finish, so I left it on the mantel under an impromptu tent of plastic wrap to keep dust off.

Jenny was looking at me strangely. "Daddy, are you okay?"

My daughter didn't miss much. After Japantown, I'd worked my way through the remaining bottles of Anchor Steam in the fridge, then topped them off with a good measure of a Niigata saké brewed with some of the best rice in Japan. I drank long and hard to my utter failure to decipher the kanji that most likely put my wife in the ground—and now an entire Japanese family in the city morgue. Japantown should have scared the hell out of me, but instead it fueled a dormant rage that uncoiled from the darker regions of my mind like a snake unwinding itself after an overlong hibernation.

I set my daughter down. "Sorry, Jen. I didn't sleep much."

She pointed at the kitchen wall. "What's that hole?"

Somewhere between the third or fourth shot of saké, I'd cursed the kanji and slammed my fist through solid plaster. Only my martial arts training prevented me from pulverizing a dozen bones in my hand with the stunt. But none of my defensive skills equipped me to deal with the sharp mind of my daughter.

I colored slightly. "My anger got away from me last night."

"Why?"

"It's hard to explain."

"I'm six, Daddy. I can understand."

"I know you can, Jen, but later, okay?"

"Okay, but I won't forget," she said, and gave me her I'm-not-a-little-kid-anymore look, then ceremoniously handed over the *Chronicle* before flopping down on her pink- and yellow-striped monstrosity of a beanbag, webbing her hands behind her head, shutting her eyes, and sighing in pleasure. Bliss in my daughter's universe.

I scanned the front page for news of the killings. Nothing. To give the SFPD time to work the case without the pressure of public scrutiny, city officials had clamped the lid down tight. Amazingly, they'd managed to dodge the newshounds. The reprieve wouldn't last long, but even a few hours without the dogs snapping was a blessing.

Behind closed eyes, Jenny said, "I wish I could see Mommy like I can see the China guy."

I stopped reading. "What China guy?"

"The funny man in the hallway with the twitchy eye. I think he was gonna steal our paper but I surprised him."

After one of the residents complained about Jenny's constant pounding up and down the stairs between our place and Lisa's, my daughter had perfected the art of navigating the route in silence. Obviously, her sudden appearance had startled someone. While I didn't think anyone was out to spirit away our newspaper, the "funny" part raised my parental antennae.

"Did he say anything?"

"He asked my name."

A coldness surged through me. "Did you tell him?"

"Sure."

My whole body turned to ice. "And?"

"He said my name was pretty and asked if I knew whatever floor Ms. Colton lived on."

Mental alarms blared. No one by the name of Colton lived in our building.

"When did this happen?"

"Right before I knocked."

I ran to the window. The building's single elevator was notoriously slow, and our view not only gave us a grand sweep of the Golden Gate Bridge but also overlooked the street from four floors up. Jenny joined me, and not five seconds later an athletic Asian male wearing baggy pants, an oversize T-shirt, and a baseball cap with the bill riding the back of his neck hit the sidewalk and headed north. Narrow airfoil sunglasses obscured his eyes.

"Is that him?"

"Uh-huh."

My jaw clenched. "Stay here and lock the door. I'll be right back."

Jenny's eyes pooled with worry. "Where are you going?"

"To have a chat with the China guy."

"Can I come?"

"No." I headed for the door.

Jenny grabbed my arm. "Don't leave me, Daddy."

She meant, *Don't go out there*, with a subtext of *Don't leave me alone*.

"I can't let this pass, Jen. That man shouldn't have been in our building talking to you."

"That's Mr. Kimbel's job, not yours."

"Once the China guy asked your name, it became my job, not the super's. Do you want to wait at Lisa's?"

"No, I'll wait here. But come back soon, okay?"

"Don't worry. I'm only going to talk to him."

I hugged my daughter, then hustled out the door, feeling guilty for leaving her but knowing I'd feel a hell of a lot worse if Homeboy reappeared later because I neglected to scare him off now.

I hoped the confrontation would end with a verbal warning, but if it turned physical I was ready. My martial arts training stood me in good stead. After seventeen years in crime-free Japan, my life on the edge of South Central had been anything but restful. While my mother worked as a freelance art curator, supplementing her spotty income with cashier jobs at Rite Aid and the like, I sparred at a pair of local dojos to keep up my karate and judo.

When the riffraff started sniffing around, I flattened a few noses with the heel of my foot and they scurried away. But I knew I'd need more to handle the big hitters, should they ever appear. Help came in the form of our next-door neighbor, a former special-ops soldier with the South Korean army. He took me under his wing to train with his teenage son, and I added tae kwon do to my skill set. Under his tutelage my awareness redoubled and my instincts grew sharper.

I trotted down the street, considering the angles, all of them bad. Double doors and quality deadbolts secured our building and kept lowlifes out. However, if you were adept, the place wasn't impregnable. Homeboy dressed like lazy street but moved like a man on a mission. When he exited our building, he'd kept his head down. His was the experienced stealth of a burglar, or maybe a pedophile.

I caught up with Homeboy two blocks later. A set of car keys dangling from his index finger told me he'd parked nearby. I grabbed his shoulder. The instant I touched him, powerful muscles shifted under my grasp and my prey slipped loose with fluid ease, whirling to face me.

"Can I help you?"

Not exactly the lingo of his look. He spread his weight in a balanced stance, his hands relaxed but ready at his side. The keys had disappeared into a side pocket.

I said, "What were you doing outside my door?"

"Wasn't at no one's door. Just passing by."

Homeboy had walnut-brown skin and shoulder-length hair. A large gold chain with a miniature Arabian dagger hung around his plowman's neck. The chain was a part of his street costume, and the stout neck went with beefy shoulders and well-toned biceps. A solid two hundred ten pounds on a six-foot frame gave me an inch in height but handed him a twenty-pound weight advantage. His face was flat, sun-darkened, and Asian. I couldn't place the country.

"Who were you visiting?"

His right eye twitched. "None of your business."

Homeboy's cap wasn't set at a cocky angle or even the subtle in-the-know tilt that broadcast attitude. His shirt and pants still bore their original shop newness. Not the clean and cool look street punks often sported but an hour-off-the-store-shelf look most sought to erase as soon as they walked out the door with their purchase. If he was street, I was the Little Mermaid.

"Nice guy that I am, I want to believe you, but if you can't give me a name, we're going to have a hard time."

"One last time—it's none of your business."

"But it is. You were talking to my daughter."

"Fuck you," he said, and turned away.

Bottom line was he was lurking in our hallway, near my door, *near my daughter*. For that alone I wanted him whipped and cowed. I wanted to give him plenty to think about before he set foot in our apartment block again.

"Not so fast."

When I reached for him a second time, he pivoted on his left foot with the same elegant fluidity, then his right hand shot out at my throat. A martial arts move. Inches away from crushing my larynx, I batted the hand away with an arm sweep.

I followed with a punch to his chin. Once he committed to blocking it, I clubbed him on his blind side, a brutal street move he wouldn't expect. Martial arts without street works on the mats, but in the real world it can get you killed. Combine the two, however, and you owned a forceful edge if your instincts were good. Something my dad clued me in to when I began lessons in Tokyo.

The blow staggered him but his recovery was alarmingly swift. He countered with a foot-and-hand maneuver that wasn't karate or judo and nearly lost me an eye.

I backed off. "Stay away from my house, scumbag."

"You're in over your head, asshole. Walk away now and I'll let you live."

My ears perked up. A faint foreign intonation edged his last remark. Not Chinese or Malay or the choppier Korean. *Japanese.*

Which meant he was neither thief nor pedophile. He was in my building for *me.* My Japan connections ran deep—right up to last night's crime scene.

"What do you want?" I said.

"I want you gone. Or mangled."

"That's not going to happen."

I heard the rip of Velcro. The next moment metal glittered in his right hand.

A knife.

Alarm tripped down my spine and adrenaline flooded my system. I hate steel. It's the favored weapon of sleaze. Homeboy's blade was double-edged and serrated on one side, with custom-molded finger grooves on the handle that spoke of special fighting skills. A serrated edge does more than slice—it chews you up without mercy.

I dropped into a semicrouch, my limbs loose, my shoulders hunched, my eyes locked on the cutter. Homeboy circled to his right and feigned a stab. Fear brushed the back of my neck. Master the fear, you might live. Discount it, you die fast. I'd seen it on the streets a dozen times.

I glided away from his feint, looping around in the opposite direction, watching the weapon and his feet.

My assailant's lips twisted in a grin. "What's the matter? Not so talkative now?"

Eyes glued to the metal, I ignored the taunt. Didn't return the sneer. Didn't toss back my own barb.

And that one act of single-minded concentration saved my life.

He was counting on an answer. Had I given into the temptation, I'd be dead.

Jenny's China guy snapped his wrist as I circled away and the weapon flew from his right palm to his left and ended up far too close to where I was headed. I'd never seen the move before. Or anything like it. It was as if the knife itself were tracking me.

Homeboy's execution was perfect. In one step, he was on me, the blade closer than it had any right to be. I twisted my upper body back and away from the sweep of the weapon, feeling the faint whisper of disturbed air under my chin, the steel tip millimeters from my throat.

His next thrust was an extension of the first, the glistening steel never slowing, the move brilliantly conceived. Flicking the weapon to his other hand had forced me to stop with a suddenness that threw me off balance and exposed my throat area, which could only be protected by whipping the upper half of my body away at the last second, as I'd done. But this left my lower limbs in an unprotected forward position, a target a blind man couldn't miss.

Even as I recognized the cunning of the maneuver, I was powerless to stop it. The knife swung harmlessly past my throat and carved an arc in the air between us, then dropped down and swept across my right thigh, chewing a long gash through my Levi's and the flesh underneath. I grunted in pain and my leg buckled. I hobbled away, putting vital space between us as swiftly as I could. Blood oozed from the wound.

Sheer genius. The secondary strike was assured if the first missed, and designed to cripple. The next pass would be the death blow.

I edged back as my assailant charged in low for a finishing gut shot. I stepped left, then feigned a half-kick with my weakened leg, an aggressive move he wouldn't expect. He hesitated and I slapped the knife hand aside, connecting with a solid jab to the jaw, managing to put some weight behind the blow. He winced and stepped away. A fortuitous strike on my part. And pure luck that I connected at all. Hamstrung, I was overmatched. I could slow his advance but not stop him.

Homeboy paused, disdain in his eyes. "You're fast, asshole, but not fast enough."

"Stay away from my place."

Indecision played across his features as he considered how much more pain I'd be able to inflict before he could penetrate my defenses. We both knew he could advance on me, given enough time and no witnesses. But he held off, restrained by an unseen force.

He waved the knife. "Cute daughter you have. Maybe I should try slicing her up."

"Leave her out of this. I see you again; you're going to pay."

"She's in it. Way in it. And so are you. More than you know."

He dropped back, the weapon covering his retreat, then disappeared around the nearest corner.

Enraged, I wanted to race after him, but blood flowed too freely from the gash in my leg. Unthreading my belt, I strapped it around my upper thigh to stem the bleeding. Had Homeboy connected with the first swipe, blood flow would have been the least of my worries. His fighting skills were unlike anything I'd ever encountered and it was a minor miracle I was still standing.

By all rights I should be dead, and in a less public place, Homeboy would have succeeded. Although my unexpected resistance had deterred him today, his threat suggested his retreat might have been tactical rather than permanent: *She's in it. Way in it. And so are you.*

A HIGH-PITCHED scream greeted my return.

Jenny rushed forward and threw her arms around me. My blood-soaked jeans had triggered her panic, the makeshift tourniquet and limp sending her over the edge. She buried her face in my stomach and sobbed. Her body shook. I wrapped my arms around her. Each cry tore at my heart.

"I'll be all right, Jen." When I tried to pry her arms from my waist, she pressed her face deeper into my belly.

She raised bloodshot eyes to my face. "Are you going to die?"

"Of course not."

"Does it hurt?"

"No. It just looks bad."

I led her to the couch, and we sat down together. Her cheeks glistened. I took her hand.

"It's my fault, Daddy."

"Why would you think that?"

"Because I told you about him."

"He's a stranger. You *should* tell me about him."

"But—"

"Listen to me. You didn't put him outside our door. You didn't cause him to attack me. You did *nothing* wrong."

"But what if—"

I squeezed her hand. "We've talked about this before. Sometimes things we don't like happen. We can't hide from them, *especially* the ones that scare us."

Jenny's tear-filled eyes clung to my every word. What I left unsaid was Homeboy's unexplained threat.

I said, "Good or bad, the world keeps on spinning, right?" I paused, waiting until Jenny acknowledged our private refrain with a nod. "Sometimes the world gives us bad, like Billy's broken arm or Mrs. Kelter's asthma. But we also get the good, like Lisa's birthday party last week or our trip to the aquarium."

Jenny nodded, pushing out her bottom lip in reluctant agreement. "And sometimes we get good *and* bad, like Mommy leaving?"

"Yes, exactly. The fire took her, but Mommy still loves us and watches over us. When the good hits us, we soak it up. When the bad strikes, we learn from it and move on."

Jenny chewed her bottom lip. "I don't want you to leave, Daddy."

"I plan to stick around for a long time, Jen," I said, addressing the hidden concern behind her plea. "Believe me."

She raised her eyes to mine. "Why do you always do scary things? Like Grandpa's work?"

I took a deep breath. Brodie Security was my father's parting gift to me, and mainly because of the wrongheaded estrangement that was partly my doing, I chose to carry on what he'd started. As a posthumous tribute to what he had created. It didn't make much money, but I liked the idea of continuing what Jake had begun. But if my work was going to brand Jenny with psychological scars, I'd have to reconsider. I already had one strike against me: nine months ago I'd been pummeled pretty badly by the yaki boys and come home with souvenir injuries that had sent Jenny into a tailspin of worry about losing her one remaining parent.

I said, "If it ever gets really bad, I can quit, okay?"

"Really?" Silence. Then: "Is your leg going to be okay?"

"Yes. Your dad's tough. Are *you* going to be okay?"

"Well, if you are, then I am too."

Jenny smiled through her tears, then flung her arms around me once more. I embraced her, soaking up the warmth of her tiny body, amazed all over again at how big a part she played in my life. I'd do anything for her. I wanted to shield her from the world's harshness, from the brutal fact that a stranger could step in and alter our lives. But I could hardly deny the limp or the blood. The world kept spinning.

"Let's get you ready for school," I said. "It's nearly time."

"Okay."

We talked as she dressed. She chatted excitedly about her upcoming field trip to Mount Tamalpais. I helped her on with a fresh pair of jeans and her favorite T-shirt with Day-Glo butterflies fluttering over Day-Glo flowers, then nudged her out the door to summer school, where I hoped playground activities would remove any last strain of the morning's trauma.

But behind Jenny's breathless buoyancy I saw hints of a lingering anxiety just under the surface. With her mother gone, she fretted about me, and this morning's incident gave new credence to her fears.

Even leaving aside Japantown and Renna, I wondered if Brodie Security and what it stood for was driving a wedge between us as it had between my parents. Wedded to his growing enterprise, Jake often neglected his duties at home, something I told myself I'd never do to Jenny or Mieko with any undertaking. Yet in the wake of my father's death, I felt a strong desire to keep his namesake firm alive. The people at Brodie Security had mattered to my father, and they mattered to me.

But Jenny mattered more.

Which only complicated things. I had my promise to Renna to consider as well, not to mention the lingering mystery of the kanji—and where it might lead.

DRIED blood had caked around my wound, the textured denim of my Levi's acting as a natural compress to stem the bleeding. Gingerly, I stripped off the pants, washed the gash, and assessed the damage. Homeboy had barely made contact, but even so, the blade had sliced through cloth and skin with ease. Had I been wearing a lighter weave, the knife would have met with less resistance and penetrated deeper and that would have mandated a hospital visit. As it was, I escaped with an eighth-inch-deep cut running across the meaty part of my quads for a good two inches. I'd be limping for a few days.

A trip to the doctor would cost me a dozen stitches and a fee I couldn't afford, so I swabbed the wound with disinfectant, dressed it with a gauze pad, and taped the leg. Next, I rang the building superintendent and alerted him to Homeboy's intrusion. He said he would canvass the residents for further information and get back to me.

I'd already asked Lisa's mother to drive the kids to school. As soon as Jenny walked out the door, I'd followed up with a personal call to the principal, giving her Homeboy's description and requesting that she keep Jenny in the classroom after school until Mrs. Meyers, myself, or my shop assistant, Bill Abers, came to collect her. Once Jenny's safety was covered from all angles, I limped in to Brodie Antiques at nine a.m., bandaged, unfed, preoccupied, and toting the tea bowl.

Bill Abers said, "Ach, early today."

"Couldn't sleep."

"You do look snookered."

"Snookered hardly covers it."

"How about the wrong end of an elephant stampede?"

Abers was born, raised, and chased out of South Africa.

"That bad?"

"Bumps and bruises, laddie. Something's knocked you cross-eyed and I'm not talking about the limp."

"There's no hiding from you trained observers."

Bill and Louisa Abers had been liberal-minded Caucasian journalists in Pretoria, South Africa, in the days of apartheid before the wet ops began. They were passionate about ending the regime's racial suppression, which made them as rare as an elephant with three tusks. Then trouble blew into town. Agents for the ruling party bombed their small press, so they went to work for a competing rag with connections and assurances of a safe berth. One day when his wife was on her way into town to buy a summer blouse, her sky-blue Chevy Jeep exploded. Most of the pieces were never recovered. The event still haunted him. Now in his late sixties, Abers had a weathered face, troubled brown eyes, and a vigorous crown of snow-white hair.

"What's with the leg anyway?"

"A minor run-in."

Abers scratched the morning stubble he often neglected to shave. "Just so you know, I shuffled the ukiyo-e prints. They've been stagnant the whole summer."

"Good thinking."

We carried a wide range of Japanese antiques: woodblock prints, scrolls, ceramics, and furniture for starters. Most of the stock was affordable and spoke of far-off lands and long-lost times in a way few items could. In a way that brought richness to my life and, ideally, to my clients'.

The ukiyo-e were a case in point. Even though the genre did not occupy one of the higher tiers in the Japanese art world, the prints were a great entry point. People loved them. To a new client, I'd mention some of the provocative highlights of the Japanese woodblock's colorful past: its dalliance with legendary sumo wrestlers, larger-than-life Kabuki actors, and graceful courtesans of the old pleasure quarters; the oppressive shogunate government it mocked with sly innuendo and veiled farce; the subtle influence the genre cast over Gauguin, Degas,

Toulouse-Lautrec, and van Gogh, among others. Along with their new possession, I wanted people to walk out the door with some knowledge, and their lives somehow fuller.

Abers said, "I framed the new Hiroshige print too. Take a look when you have a chance."

"Will do."

I made a move toward my office at the back of the shop.

"Now's a good time," he offered.

Abers had instincts I encouraged. He had a head for the business and it was only when he was absorbed in the art that the gloom that clung to him lifted. Without Louisa, he had lost interest in nearly everything. He left journalism, traveled the world looking to make sense of the anguish that continually churned his insides, and eventually settled in San Francisco, because she was a city with a "sparkle in her eye." One day he showed up on my doorstep, and before I knew it, he had taken over in the way a very determined stray cat might. He charmed clients old and new and brought in fresh ones. He knew art and he knew people.

Until last night, Abers and I had shared only an abiding interest in beautiful objects and the sudden loss of our wives. With a jolt I saw another link: my wife may have also met with a violent death. Only a few strokes of a kanji stood between us having a third biographical fact in common.

I tapped my upper thigh. "Maybe later, all right?"

"Sure, lad. But keep your eye on the ball. Our stock's stagnating."

The truth of his words struck a tender spot. If we didn't ring up some sales soon, we'd be selling from the sidewalk. The antiques business paid the bills and left me with enough spare change every month for a few pints of Anchor Steam. The PI sideline in Tokyo was nearly as lucrative—there I had twenty-three employees to pay.

Abers shrugged and turned away. I knew he would work out his frustration by polishing a newly arrived pair of traditional *tansu* I'd purchased from my main Kyoto connection on my last trip to Japan. The best tansu were hefty chests of drawers decorated with superb ironwork and lacquer, the finish drawing out the grain of the wood and giving the piece a final coloring that ranged from a soft woody beige to a dark brown, or even a rich reddish brown.

Abers got to it, while I closeted myself in the back office to tackle my email. My office was carpeted and encompassed a desk, a file cabinet, a leather armchair for guests, and an adjoining sitting room where I could close deals in private.

The shop itself was located west of Van Ness on Lombard, part of a major byway that threaded its way through the Marina District and the lower edge of Pacific Heights, then out to the Golden Gate Bridge and Marin County to the north. Everyone shopped in either the Old Town stores below Lombard or the upscale ones above it. Both were higher-rent districts. Only motels excelled on the commercial thoroughfare where I'd opened Brodie Antiques. But the affluent drove by daily, as did the moneyed of Marin and beyond. My business needed exposure and word of mouth, not walk-in traffic, so I settled on this busy thoroughfare, and slowly Abers and I were building a clientele.

By ten o'clock, I'd finished answering my email. I noted with pleasure that the owner of three Buddhist temple statues from Ibaragi had accepted my lowball bid for the lot. As Abers had a knack for selling the alluring icons, keeping him supplied with new pieces was an ongoing challenge.

At ten thirty, the apartment superintendent reported in. Considering the matter urgent, he'd contacted all the residents, either at home or work. No one had been expecting a person of Homeboy's description and no one had laid eyes on an unknown Asian, period.

Thanking him for the effort, I hung up, wondering what Homeboy was hiding. I thought about his speed and his fighting skills, and I soon found myself quivering with an undefined rage. Who the hell was he and why was he coming after us? What lurked behind the street pose? And even more troubling, what was behind his cryptic comment? *She's in it. Way in it. And so are you. More than you know.*

In what?

Aber's stuck his head in the door. "I know you have enough on your mind, but I can't hold off anymore. We had another burglary attempt."

My pulse jumped. Every penny I owned was locked up in the store, so I paid a high premium for a private security service, which I'd recently upgraded after a break-in six months ago.

"Just an attempt, right?"

Abers nodded soberly. "I didn't mention it earlier because you seemed distracted, but this one is different."

Dread edged my voice. "How close did they get?"

"Not close. *In.*"

The room seemed to fall away around me. "That's not possible," I managed in a small voice.

My head throbbed. I tried to think. After the first break-in, I'd opted for the next level of protection, which attached enough additional bells and whistles to my state-of-the-art alarm system to discourage even the most determined B&E artist. Until now the setup had been magical, scaring one potential burglar away and allowing the private security team to bag an experienced pair of two-story men while they were still tinkering with the locks.

Homeboy. During the three years we'd occupied the cave of an apartment in East Pacific Heights, I had never heard any reports of unknowns wandering the halls. The security was that tight. Double doors, top-notch locks on the entrance. Cameras in the halls and at all the exterior doors. My shop system was even better. Yet both had been breached within the last twelve hours.

"Did the rent-a-cops get here in time?"

"The alarm didn't go off."

"What? You set it, right?"

"Do bushbucks have horns? Of course I set it. The service claims there was no alert last night, but I *know* someone was here. I leave tells. Hair, bits of paper. A trick from the old days. They came, they looked, they left. They deactivated the alarm first, then reactivated it. That's the only explanation."

"You sure?"

"I've been here two years, Brodie. I'm sure."

"Did they take anything?"

"No. Which tells me they were some seriously slick intruders." He nodded at my leg. "You ready to fess up yet? My money's on a new assignment from Tokyo."

Abers was probing. He heartily disapproved of my handling any job from Brodie Security. He raved about my perfect eye for art. "You have a magic touch most would kill for," he'd say time and time again. "Why are you wasting time with the PI stuff? Think of your talent. Think of Jenny. Sell that damn place in Tokyo before it gets you killed." After the wave of violence that he'd barely survived in Pretoria, he was nothing if not protective.

"I got nothing from Brodie Security," I said, hedging my answer for Renna's sake.

Clearly confounded, Abers scratched his head. "I know I shouldn't intrude, but considering how you came slogging in this morning, I need to ask. Have you been involved in anything stroppy lately? Anything unusual?"

Japantown. Homeboy. A break-in. What *hadn't* I been involved in? The swirl of events was bewildering. And none of it made any sense whatsoever. Could this all be connected to Japantown? One part of me thought, *Unlikely. It was too much too soon.* I'd only come on board as Renna's consultant last night, and by the time I left there'd been *sixty* cops on the scene.

There should be no reason to single me out.

On the other hand I *was* the only Japan expert. And the victims were Japanese. As was Homeboy. Could that be it? Was Japan the link? If so, it raised one hell of a question: Under what circumstances would I be more of a threat than the entire San Francisco police force?

HENRI Bertrand gazed out over the moonlit ocean waves. What was it about Manuel Castore that disturbed him so? No, be *honest,* he told himself. What was it about Castore that *scared* him?

Here he was on his yacht anchored off Capri with a French-Irish supermodel slumbering in the cabin, and he was obsessing over Castore.

As the top real estate developer in Europe for the last two decades, Bertrand had a net worth north of three billion dollars. His architecture and development firm had project billings of $800 million for the next fiscal year. He owned homes in Paris, New York, Tokyo, Dubai, and Florence. He mingled with the elite and as a *favor* designed their summer homes on the Riviera.

The Riviera—that was the problem.

Castore coveted Bertrand's latest coup. The greedy Spaniard had offered him twice the purchase price for the half-mile stretch along the Italian coast, then plan-B'ed him with a proposal for a joint partnership. Bertrand had refused both offers and in an instant knew he'd made an enemy for life. But the Italian find was too precious to forfeit even a sliver of its worth—it was Europe's next Riviera in the making. When the property came on the market, Bertrand saw the potential in an instant, as did Castore a week later. After Bertrand had refused Castore's offer of a joint partnership, the whites of Castore's dark, calculating eyes seemed to flash red with anger.

Shaking off the memory, Bertrand went through a series of breathing exercises to expand his lungs, then dove into the crystal-clear waters. He sluiced fifteen feet down through the brine before arching up to the surface.

He relished his midnight swims. On the cobalt sea, the world seemed endless, the possibilities infinite. When he returned to France, he would crush that scheming Spanish rodent, and he knew exactly how. It was not his style to be so vulgar or ruthless, but instinct told him Castore was the exception that proved the rule.

As a feeling of satisfaction overtook him and he smiled to himself, powerful arms encircled his waist and then vanished, leaving in their wake a strange heaviness at his hips.

Had he really felt arms around him? In the Tyrrhenian at midnight?

Unexpectedly, his head slipped underwater and he began to sink. He stretched for the surface, managing to snatch a mouthful of air before being drawn under again by an inexplicable weight.

His hands went to his waist and what he found shocked him. Strapped to his midsection was a diver's belt loaded with weights for a man twice his size. He clawed at the buckle and pulled. Nothing. His eyes bulged in surprise.

In a pinch, Bertrand could hold his breath for as long as three minutes. He had that much time, minus what—the five seconds he'd just lost? His fingers scrambled over the buckle. The belt had been modified to include a lock and a slot for a key.

Ten seconds.

Bertrand had never seen such a belt. Diver safety required instant release. *This was a custom-made death trap.* He was now ten feet below the surface and sinking fast. His ears popped. He stretched his jaw to relieve the pressure.

Twenty seconds.

Don't panic, he told himself. There's always a way out. The cove, he knew, was thirty feet deep, no more.

Thirty seconds.

Get to the bottom, a voice in his head advised. *You know what to do.* He brought his knees to his chest, tucked, rolled, and swam downward. The bluish-gray light of the moon washed over the grainy ocean floor. The extra weight at his waist worked in his favor, accelerating his descent and saving him precious seconds. Bertrand moved along the bottom until he found what he sought.

Fifty seconds.

Obsidian peppered the sandy floor of the cove. As a builder, Bertrand knew his geology.

He grabbed a specimen the size of his fist, found a sharp edge, and began sawing the swatch of nylon near the buckle. The material was stringy, maybe an eighth of an inch thick, but it frayed easily under his volcanic razor.

Seventy seconds.

The work went quickly. He reached the halfway point.

Ninety seconds.

Maybe he could rip the material now, save a few seconds. He tucked the rock under his arm and tugged—the material resisted. He tugged again. Again, resistance—and then disaster. The abruptness of his movement jarred the rock loose from its nesting place under his arm and he watched in horror as it drifted lazily to the bottom.

One minute, forty.

Bertrand scrambled to retrieve his tool and set to work again.

Two minutes.

He should have stayed with what was working. Fool! Wasting valuable time!

Calm down. Focus.

He stilled his doubts and began sawing again.

A shadow passed overhead. A milk shark, he thought. Suppressing the urge to flee, he stayed intent on his task.

Two minutes, twenty.

He was nearly done. His chest began to ache. Focus, focus. Another half inch. He could feel the weight begin to sag off his hips, listing toward the bottom.

There! The last thread snapped and the belt fell away.

Two minutes, forty.

He crouched, paddling in reverse to force himself closer to the ocean floor, then launched himself off the hard sand with a powerful thrust, rocketing upward.

His lungs were burning now. He wanted to draw a breath. He was twenty feet from the surface.

Two minutes, fifty.

He began to choke. His mouth opened.

No!

Drawing on the steely willpower that had fueled his rise to the top of his field, he clamped his jaw shut, but immediately the physical necessity to open his mouth overrode his internal command. He swallowed water.

Ten feet.

His chest heaved from the lack of oxygen and his body snorted more water in through his nose.

No!

Five feet.

Salt water coursed through his nasal passages and he felt the sting of foreign liquid entering his system.

He broke the surface, coughed up seawater, then vomited. Once, twice, three times.

His lungs purged, he released a triumphant shout into the moonlit night and the echo rolled over the gentle Mediterranean swells into the distance. Air, fresh air! He had never come so close!

Then strong fingers grabbed his ankle and pulled him under.

He kicked but the grip held.

His head was three feet below the surface.

A second belt snaked around his waist.

Oh God, no!

He kicked, but his strength had been siphoned off by the exertions of his first escape. He needed oxygen to fuel his efforts, and he'd been dragged under at the exhale. His lungs were empty. His chest ached to draw in air. Salt water seeped in. He tried to expel the invading fluid, but there was no air pressure left in his lungs. More water shot down his throat. He gagged and kicked violently. The belt dragged him steadily downward. His lungs began to fill.

Out of the corner of his eye, he saw movement and turned his head. A diver! And behind the mask a curiously passive Asian face.

Sinking lower, he clawed desperately for the surface, his arms swinging wildly. He thrust powerfully with his muscled legs and was propelled upward. His fingertips touched air, then he felt a cool sensation near his lower ribs as his lung sacs were swamped with seawater. He lost muscle control, and when the sea brine hit his brain, he lost consciousness.

He stopped struggling, and slowly, drifting with the languid motion of the sea, his corpse sank to the bottom of the cove.

Out of the dark waters, a black shadow in a wetsuit and diving gear glided over, inserted a key into the belt, and released the weights. Bertrand's body began to rise. A minute later it bobbed to the surface while below a second diver swooped along the bottom of the cove and scooped up the other belt.

Twin bubble trails rose behind the divers as they swam away with the only evidence of murder.

CHAPTER 10

EVEN with the news blackout, he found me.

After lunch I had locked myself in the office to nail down the purchase of the seventeenth-century Buddhist temple statues. But before I could lift the receiver, Abers rapped on the door. "You're up, mate," he said, and strolled away. Usually that meant one of my regulars was asking for me.

I wobbled to the front of the shop and froze.

Disbelief clutched my chest.

Standing at a glass counter and fingering a sixteenth-century Japanese sword guard was Katsuyuki Hara, renegade Tokyo communications mogul and poster boy for the new Japan. He'd broken all the rules and still prospered, in the process becoming a local hero. He was the nail that couldn't be hammered down, the exception to a strict social code that preferred conformity and discouraged independence. As a barrier-breaking rebel, he became a public figure revered for the hope he inspired in young entrepreneurs even as he headed for the financial stratosphere. As a newly minted billionaire, he groomed himself accordingly: face tanned, skin lotioned, hands manicured. He wore an expensive French suit of charcoal gray with a faint maroon line, the kind of item ordered from Benz-owning tailors who pulled down six-figure incomes.

The choking feeling in my chest was not because the mogul stood in my parlor but because there was no plausible reason for him to pass through my front door. He'd obviously taken a wrong turn. Yes, he collected art, but on a higher plane. If memory served, he'd last been spotted at the Christie's auction in New York, where he bought a Hockney and a Pollock.

I said, "Can I help you?"

Sharp eyes scanned me from head to foot. "Are you Jim Brodie? Jake Brodie's son?"

That explained it. He knew my father. Or his work.

"Yes."

Off the mogul's left flank stood the Great Wall of China, an Asian bodyguard of Chinese or Korean descent with expansive shoulders and hair cropped to bristles in a style you don't see much in Japan anymore outside military schools and martial arts clubs. His face was round and meaty. Cheekbones pushed his flesh to the sides and made him look like an overfed Buddha. The muscles across his chest and down his arms weren't overfed, though. They stretched his brown knit shirt to the limit and spoke of strength and speed.

Hara glanced around the shop with disapproval. "Not at all what I expected. Is it perhaps an older brother who took over Brodie Security? Or a relative?"

His English was flawless.

"Nope. Just me. You've got the right Brodie and the right place."

I'd listed Brodie Antiques on the agency's website and in the phone book as the stateside contact for Brodie Security. Embedded in the wall alongside the front door was a brass plaque that announced our presence with discretion: *Brodie Security—Inquire Within*, which riled Abers no end.

Narrowing his eyes, Hara raised the sword guard. "Tell me about the *tsuba*."

The object in question was disc-shaped and about three inches across, with an elongated triangular slit at the center to accept the tang of a sword. Because sword guards formed a pivotal part of the samurai's most important possession—his symbolic soul—some of them had been decorated with silver, gold, lacquer, hammered smithery, cloisonné, and inlay work by the finest craftsmen in the land. Today, collectors around the world sought out the best pieces.

"That particular tsuba is from the late fifteen hundreds and belonged to a Tokyo family that can trace its lineage back to a samurai ancestor who served Lord Hideyoshi."

Hara nodded. "Impressive. And the motif?"

The front side of the guard showed two wild geese in flight; the reverse side showed the same pair, one soaring free, the other plummeting earthward, perhaps weakened by its attempt to crest a pagoda in the background, or perhaps wounded by a hunter.

"The motif sets off the hazards of warfare against the Zen belief in the impermanence of life."

"At least you know your art," the mogul said flatly, replacing the piece in the case. "How are you on the investigative side of things?"

Outside on the street, a jet-black Silver Shadow limousine idled at the curb. A chauffeur, capped and immaculate, swept a long-handled feather duster back and forth across a spotless hood that gleamed in the afternoon sun.

I said, "Why don't you step in the back? We can talk there."

I ushered him into the conference room adjoining my office. With its beige carpet, coffee-colored leather chairs, and walnut table, it was a class act. The table was an early-eighteenth-century William and Mary that I picked up at an estate auction. A Charles Burchfield watercolor hung on a pastel gray wall. Burchfield was a talented but underappreciated mid-twentieth-century American master. We got along just fine.

Hara took a seat and the Great Wall angled his shoulders into the room. The next instant, Abers appeared with coffee, set it down, then eased the door shut, giving me a thumbs-down behind the mogul's back as he closed us in.

Hara crossed his legs. I remained standing, an eye on the Wall.

Hara scanned the room. *"Ano e mo warukanai kedo . . ."* The painting's not bad either, but . . .

I dropped my head in a modest bow. "It's adequate," I replied in his native tongue with the proper tone of self-deprecation.

Hara was a handsome man in his mid-fifties, his picture often in the news. In person, he had the same square chin, the same glowing tan, the same piercing eyes. What was different was the shock of white hair combed up and back. The stills in *Fortune, Time,* and *Asia Today* showed him with a black mane graying with dignity around the edges.

"Do you handle any work here?"

I decided he wasn't talking about the art.

"I run stateside security jobs out of this office, but Tokyo is still the main liaison for the agency. I hire local expertise as needed, or bring people over from Tokyo."

The Wall had spread his legs, squared his chin, and clasped his hands behind his back. At parade rest, while the general spoke to the flunky.

I jerked my chin at the watchdog. "Isn't he kind of big for a pet?"

Hara smiled without merriment. "Are you any good at what you do?"

"Some people think so."

"You were involved in the recovery of the recent Rikyu, were you not?"

"Yes."

"Impressive, but in the end that's only art. Are you as good as your father was?"

What was I supposed to say to that? I shrugged. "I know how to get in and out of trouble."

In truth, I doubted I could measure up to Jake's legendary talents. Several people had lost their lives over the Rikyu and I came close to losing mine. At Brodie Security the vote was still out.

"That tells us you're clever. But are you tough?"

"Enough."

Hara moved his chin maybe half a millimeter, and the Great Wall charged.

Anticipating the move, I preempted his attack, brushing his rising hands away with a forearm sweep and plowing the heel of my other hand into his nose but pulling back enough to keep the breathing apparatus from turning to pulp. Anything less and he would have trampled me. The Wall staggered sideways and grabbed for his face. I connected with a knee kick to the stomach, eschewing the more damaging targets above and below. He went down, but it was all I could do to keep from screaming at the intense pain that streaked down my leg. From beneath the bandage, I felt skin tear and blood trickle. In the heat of the attack, instinct had overridden caution and the knife wound had slipped my mind.

Now I was going to need stitches.

CHAPTER 11

HARA stared at the immobile form at his feet.

I said, "A little less bulk, he'd make a nice doormat."

The businessman raised his eyes to mine, his expression empty of mirth, anger, or any other emotion. "The Sony people recommended your firm. Highly. I guess it hasn't slipped any."

"Guess not."

Jake had roped in high-profile clients like Sony and Toyota, and they stayed on after his death. Name clients allowed me to keep my father's loyal staff gainfully employed, but the problem was, VIP security took a lot of bodies, and each one required a salary. And a raise. And had growing families. Keeping the enterprise going was an uphill battle, but one I felt I owed Jake.

The Wall groaned.

I said, "Tell your boy to stay on the floor and play carpet until we're done."

"Surely that won't be necessary. You've amply demonstrated what I wished to know." The magnate's eyelids slipped to half-mast. "By the way, my name's Katsuyuki Hara."

"I know who you are."

"Do you?"

"CompTel Nippon. From making computerized toys in a garage in Shibaura to electronics to chips to factories in Southeast Asia, Europe, and China. Then radio, TV, cable stations, a couple of publishing houses, and one of the first Japanese to jump on the information superhighway bandwagon. Fiber optics, wireless, telecommunications.

On and on. A lone-wolf innovator in a flock of consensus-driven companies. Golden touch, never a wrong move. Except maybe in selecting bodyguards."

He grunted. There may or may not have been some pleasure in the noise. "Tell me, Mr. Brodie, do your dual occupations of antiques dealer and PI mesh?"

Skepticism tinged his tone, as if the two professions were mutually exclusive.

"They both require scrappers," I said.

"You know why I'm here?"

"No, and frankly, I can't see any reason why you would be."

"You saw my family."

I didn't understand him, so I let the words hang. The silence between us grew dark and heavy.

"Last night. On the pavement." Five words, and he had trouble with each. His voice was fresh and controlled, but the pain was fresh, too, and less controlled.

"The Nakamuras?"

"That's right. My eldest daughter's married name."

Japantown. *The mother.*

"I see," I said. "I'm sorry. You don't know how sorry."

Once more I saw the woman's death mask and what I imagined must have been a tormented end to her life. For the briefest instant I wondered about Mieko's final moment. Had a madman come for her in the night? Had she seen him? Had she known her fate in the seconds before the flames consumed her?

"I want you to find him, Mr. Brodie. The person or persons responsible."

"Me?"

"You. Your agency. I want him found and exterminated. Like the cockroach that he is. If it were physically possible, I would ask you to kill him twice, very slowly. I will pay you well in any currency you wish and deposit the funds anywhere in the world you desire."

He mentioned a fee three times our usual rate. He would know our usual rate.

"Why offer high?"

"Incentive yields rapid results."

"Try Mercenary Inc. They're on the next block."

"You saw my family torn to pieces and you can still say that?"

"Yes."

Hara frowned with regal impatience. "The money means nothing to me. I believe in motivation. I want you to put the full weight of your organization behind this investigation and I'm willing to pay you for your *full* attention."

He'd segued into Japanese though his cadence remained decidedly Western. Direct, gruff, and businesslike. A new breed. The legendary Japanese politeness had yet to surface, and probably wouldn't. I could see why the traditional power establishment disliked him.

"Brodie Security doesn't exterminate, Mr. Hara."

"Perhaps we can discuss it at a later date after you have made some progress."

"The answer will be the same."

"We shall see. I am told I can be extremely persuasive. Invariably I get what I want."

"And I've been told I'm stubborn. Though personally I can't see it."

He watched me without amusement. "Fine. Shall we double the offer?"

"My answer will be the same."

He leaned forward, in his eyes nothing but a dark void. "Do you know what it's like to see your children go before you? It's a living death, Mr. Brodie. All your life's work wadded up like so much newsprint and thrown in your face. You know that your children and your children's children will not live beyond you, will not benefit from your achievements. When you die, all your work, all your accomplishments, die with you."

His voice quavered, nearly cracking, but he managed to maintain his dignity. For most of his life Hara had soared. Now he was falling fast. Like the weakened goose on the sword guard he'd grilled me about.

I thought of his daughter on the cobblestones in Japantown. I thought of my morning after in Los Angeles, when nothing was left but dust and debris. I thought of all the sleepless nights I'd faced, all the times I'd held my distraught daughter until she fell asleep in my arms. I had lost a wife but still had Jenny. The man before me had lost children and grandchildren in one fell swoop. I relented.

"All right, Mr. Hara. We'll look into it."

I wondered if his research showed I was a soft touch.

The mogul fell back in his seat, visibly relieved. "Thank you. Can you find him?"

"Sooner or later. With enough money and man-hours. And unless the police get there first. But either way, we won't kill him. There's been enough of that."

"Use a freelancer if you don't want to dirty your hands. As much outside help as you like. I will cover the additional expenditure."

Inwardly, I winced and his words gave me pause. From his tone of voice, I could tell that the course Hara suggested was one he'd taken before.

I said, "Why are you so set on us? You could buy an army if you wanted to."

"Brodie Security has more than twenty people in Tokyo, excluding affiliates. You *are* an army. I've been assured the police department here is working around the clock. By adding private manpower and some-one who knows both Japan and America, I believe I can significantly increase the odds of success."

His thinking made sense, but I remained skeptical.

Hara read my mind. Moving to squelch my doubt before it won out, he pulled an envelope from his jacket, offering it with both hands and a bow. "Here's half of the higher fee now, exclusive of expenses, of course."

Decision time. Silently, I debated the issue. Hara couldn't force me to do what I deemed undesirable. We were not assassins. But if the Japantown kanji turned out to be Mieko's kanji, I'd follow this thing to the end for her sake, and Renna's. Two solid reasons to say yes. So I did. I stood, reached out, and accepted the envelope in the same formal manner Hara offered it, bowing and shutting the envelope in my desk unopened, as Japanese etiquette dictated, before retaking my seat across the table from him. "We'll take the case," I said, "and you'll get a report. That's all."

Hara sat and smiled grimly. "Unless I can persuade you otherwise. But let's leave that for now. What can I provide you with to start?"

"Your daughter's itinerary. Basic bios on her and her husband. A list of friends and acquaintances in the States, including Hawaii. It should include old friends, new friends, business contacts, personal enemies, pen pals."

He stiffened. "You joke about such matters?"

"It's no joke. I want all American contacts, no matter how insignificant they might seem to you."

He relaxed. "Done. You'll have it within twenty-four hours."

"Good. And Yoshida, the other male, he was a friend?"

"A distant cousin."

I waited for more but it didn't come.

"Okay," I said. "The same for him. Was he or your son-in-law involved in anything dangerous?"

"No."

"How about your daughter?"

"She was a housewife."

"Any major events in their lives recently? Death, a falling-out with a partner, lovers' quarrel?"

"No."

"Can you think of any reason why someone might want to kill them?"

"None."

"How about you? You must have enemies."

"No one who would do that."

"You sure?"

"Of course."

"Right. Why should this be simple?"

Maybe one of the victims had an unpleasant secret, I thought.

Hara drummed his fingers on his knee. "One more thing. I've asked my younger daughter to fly in from New York so you can interview her. She was close to her sister."

"Fine."

"Do you know her?" he asked casually, an odd mixture of pride and suspicion in his voice. The pride was there because Lizza Hara was a brat-pack-type celebrity in her home country, the suspicion because the ongoing feud between father and daughter made headlines regularly.

"I read the papers."

"She's not that well known in the West yet."

"Who said anything about Western papers."

"Excellent," the tycoon said, rising. "I can see I'm in good hands. I've got a full agenda this trip, so I must go, but we'll talk again soon."

With the regal formality of his status, he gave a brief bow and departed, his bodyguard picking himself up and trailing after.

As the two men wound their way between the tansu chests and folding screens to the front of my shop, I thought about how easily Hara had found me. If Hara could do it, so could others. And there was nothing to prevent a clever person from doing it faster.

Particularly if he didn't have to fly in from Tokyo.

T HE M&N Tavern and Grill squatted on the northwest corner of Fifth and Howard like a toad on a rock, compact and colorless and wallflower-perfect for a police lieutenant seeking a low profile.

"Nice table," I said, pulling out a chair.

"My regular."

"Why doesn't that surprise me?"

Staking out an isolated two-seater against a wall of dark walnut paneling, Renna had selected a roost separated from the rest of the tables by an aisle leading to the bar. If we kept our voices down, no one would be within earshot once a waitress took our order, and Renna could watch the front door while staying out of sight of any passersby who might glance in the window.

Renna caught my faint limp. "You cut yourself shaving?"

"Ran into a punk with a blade."

"File a police report?"

"No. I figure you guys have a few higher priorities at the moment."

But after Hara's departure, I had hobbled over to Dr. Shandler's on the next block, where he informed me that I'd managed the remarkable feat of reopening the wound *and* lengthening the cut. My victory over the Great Wall cost me fifteen stitches and a bill the good doctor told me he would take in trade. Shandler's tastes ran to high-end Japanese lacquerware and I had several new additions, including an elegant pair of red-and-black *neguro* trays I'd bet a month's earnings he would salivate over.

"There's one more thing," I said, and filled Renna in on the flurry of activity at my shop and home after Japantown.

"Food for thought," he said, "I'll look into it. You know the menu?"

"What's to know? Just coffee for me."

The M&N was a San Francisco relic. It serves Middle American fare with solid home fries and the occasional regional eccentricity like boiled Louisiana crawfish and corn. Otherwise you got burgers, barbecued chicken, and truck-stop omelets. One day a food critic with an itchy pen and a looming deadline would probably wander in and write the place up as a retro diner, using words like *unassuming* and *disarmingly quaint,* and regulars like Renna would have to wait out a wave of newcomers, unless a wrecking ball found the place first.

Renna's lips twitched. "What is it? Mieko?"

"Mieko, little Miki, the mother. All of them."

"Something like Japantown will burn a hole in you if you're not careful."

"A family, Frank. A whole goddamn family."

At the bar, two postmen in their summer-weight uniforms glanced our way.

Renna ran thick fingers through his hair. "Keep it down, will you? Look, you never forget, but you learn to live with it. If you're lucky, in the morning your hash browns still taste like hash browns. But hell, you know that, Brodie. You're no virgin. Otherwise we wouldn't be sitting here."

"True enough."

Survival around South Central was an endless dance, deadly and primordial. You could never let your guard down. If you got careless, you got hurt. I'd seen the battered and the bruised and the dead. But until last night I'd never seen a whole family slaughtered.

A blond waitress arrived with pen poised and I ordered coffee, Renna a coke and cheeseburger. When our drinks arrived, Renna watched me without comment.

I said, "You mind telling me why you're so hot for this case?"

"You don't think the five-count is enough?"

"I know it's not."

Last night I'd seen more in his eyes. I just couldn't decipher what I'd seen.

Renna glanced at the wall, which held framed black-and-white stills of workmen erecting towering steel beams, from a time when San Francisco was eager and proud and raising her bridges. Stout men with hard hats and T-shirts hauled melon-thick cables into position, navigating catwalks suspended hundreds of feet above churning bay waters.

"Last year we bought Christine a dress just like the one Miki Nakamura was wearing, only blue. It's why I became a cop. I won't run from this."

I nodded slowly. With a senseless killing, you never knew what would get under your skin. What might strike too close to home.

Renna leaned forward, eyes inflamed. "Listen, I'll keep you informed, but I want you to stay on it. For as long as it takes. Can you do that?"

"Easily."

"Even if the kanji's not Mieko's?"

"After what I saw? Not a problem. Till death do us part," I said, thinking of Mieko.

"Good."

Renna withdrew an envelope from his jacket pocket and extracted two pieces of paper, spreading them on the table between us. One was the scrap from the crime scene encased in a cellophane evidence bag, the other an enlarged photocopy. "The kanji cleaned up like you said."

One look at the full array of black strokes shimmering on the textured Japanese paper and I felt my heart stutter. Before me lay an exact copy of the character I'd seen on the sun-bleached sidewalk in Los Angeles. Not similar. Not off by a line or two, but a dead-on duplicate; a stroke-for-stroke replication. Designating Japantown as the fourth known strike by the same killer.

"Well?" Renna asked.

I found my voice with difficulty. "It's the same. Exactly the same."

"I'm sorry to hear that," Renna said. "You want, I could push the LAPD to reopen Mieko's file."

My breath caught in my throat. For the longest time, I'd hoped for just such a scenario, but now that the offer was on the table, I hesitated. More than two years had passed. Down south, the evidence was nothing but cold cinders. Motivation would be lacking.

"Will anything come of it?"

He shrugged. "My guess, the ball's in our court. We catch the perp, we wrap up your wife's case too."

"Sounds like a plan."

"Good," he said again, his voice dropping half an octave without losing clarity, "then here's what I want. First, the Japantown shoot cranks things up a notch, so I need you to look for the kanji under new rocks. And this time I need answers. Lots of answers."

I rubbed the paper with the J-town kanji between my fingers. "Well, for starters, the stock is standard Japanese calligraphy parchment. Mass-produced. Machine-made. Not a local handmade *washi*."

Washi is the traditional Japanese paper you expect to see with calligraphy. It also features in scroll paintings, lanterns, and shoji screens. The best-quality paper is still made by hand in a way that has survived hundreds of years: a tray lined with wire mesh is dipped into a vat of pulped plant fiber suspended in water. The mesh captures a layer of pulp, then the papermaker hauls it up and allows the captured pulp fiber to solidify into a textured sheet.

Renna cut me a look that suggested I'd have to do more than recite a few cultural nuggets to earn my keep.

I said, "I take it your lab rats already told you that."

"Hours ago."

"Try this, then. Commercial washi is sold all over Japan and in many stores here. Handmade washi is made in limited quantities by individuals and is easy to trace by its style, which varies by region. Your labbies tell you that?"

"No."

"So if this paper was intentionally left by the shooter, then using commercial washi suggests caution."

"Okay. What about the character?"

"Your boys can't make any sense of it either?"

"It's being handled through channels. I want answers before the next ice age sets in, global warming permitting. Tell me *why* you can't read the thing."

"It's not *joyo* or *toyo* or recent historical kanji."

"You want to translate that into English?"

"Means the character isn't current, immediate pre- or postwar, or anything commonly used as far back as, say, the mid-seventeenth century."

"You call the seventeenth century recent history?"

"When you're talking about a culture that traces its roots back two thousand years, yes."

"Don't like the sound of that. What else you got?"

"The writer is a male in his sixties or seventies."

Renna shot up in his seat. "You sure?"

"Very. The hand is masculine and mature."

"Is it Japanese?"

"It's a Japanese character written by a Japanese, if it's anything. Not Chinese. But the writing's off somehow."

"Maybe it's a forger or an imitator."

"No, it was written by a Japanese. The lines are full and well proportioned and that's impossible to do unless you're Japanese or studied in Japan for years *and* from a very young age."

"Why?"

I brushed the strokes in the air with my finger. "Because writing kanji with all the components properly balanced takes practice. And then there's the stroke order that's got to be memorized. The order here is correct, and the balance is as it should be, which means the kanji wasn't copied or traced cold from an existing manuscript by an imitator. This was written by a Japanese with a special brush or brush-tipped pen."

"Then how is it off?"

"The writing is shaky. Uneven in places. As is the ink."

"Maybe the old man had a few too many."

"No, the style's tight. I'm thinking that whoever penned the kanji doesn't write it often. Or he has arthritis or some other age-related disability."

Renna brightened. "That's good too. Anything else?"

"That's all for now."

Renna leaned back in his chair, hands webbed over his belly, momentarily sated with the crumbs I'd fed him. "You know, we catch a lucky break, we might close this quick."

I gave him a doubtful look. "What's that? The party line?"

Renna's face collapsed. "It's what I thought last night. Now I think Japantown is going to get a lot worse before it gets better. I'm still going to bag the bastard, but the thing's already tail-spinning. People are spooked."

Renna's voice nosedived as he spoke, startling me. He never talked doomsday.

"This isn't witchcraft, Frank."

"Late-night murders and unreadable ciphers? You know how suspicious cops get. They're saying J-town's one to steer away from. They're saying the case's gonna sink in forty-eight, taking everyone down with it."

"What do *you* think?"

"I'm going to ride it out no matter what. Now tell me what the hell I'm looking at and why this goddamn kanji's got my people squirming like they've seen the devil. I need to crawl inside this bastard's brain."

CHAPTER 13

ZURICH, SWITZERLAND

HELENA Spengler was disgusted with the pair of creepy Asian men lounging uninvited in her sitting room.

"Christoph, do you know these gentlemen?" the Swiss banker's wife asked. Serena, that worthless heifer, had shown them in ahead of her master's return, then vanished into the back rooms.

"Vaguely, dear. I met one of them last week."

The older Asian, with funny orangeish skin and narrow eyes, sat erect on the Louis XV settee with the Aubusson tapestry. He, at least, showed some respect. The one with the ponytail slouched in Christoph's easy chair as if he owned it, long limbs hanging over all the wrong places.

"Should I have coffee brought or . . . ?" She left the sentence unfinished, the implication being that she would have no qualms about ringing the local constable.

Which was when Lawrence Casey, the younger Asian, appeared behind her without warning. Slinging one arm across her chest, he locked her in a hold while his free hand curled around from the other side and pressed a handkerchief to her face. As she struggled, Mrs. Spengler found herself mystified.

When had he moved?

Twisting her matronly body in protest, she resisted for another second or two before her eyes drooped and the drug lulled her into a peaceful sleep. Casey dragged the wife to the settee and laid her across the cushions, the older Asian vacating his seat with a mock bow.

"So," said Keiji Ogi, whom Spengler knew as Kevin Sheng, "as I explained last week, I need you to hand over the wine."

The sixth-generation banker was rosy-cheeked and sated after a late-night feast and ample drink with friends at Haus zum Muden, a restaurant that had served Swiss noblemen since the fourteenth century.

"The issue is closed, sir," the banker said, blinking his eyes to stop the room from spinning.

"Consider it reopened." Ogi tossed a stack of bills on a side table. "I'll still pay for a single bottle. The other two I'm confiscating as a penalty."

Spengler caught a flash in Sheng's eyes that seemed as dark and peculiar as the fellow's clothing. The two uninvited guests wore clinging black suits. Underneath their jackets were black turtlenecks made of the same curious material. But even distinctive haberdashery did not give them the right to manhandle his family.

"Mr. Sheng," the financier said, "I hope you will not take offense when I say I cannot, at present, bring my full attention to bear on your request." Spengler fidgeted with the left cuff of his heavily starched shirt until his monogrammed cufflink reflected shafts of light into Sheng's eyes, a ploy the banker occasionally used to remind those of a lower station whom they were dealing with. "Perhaps if you could call at my office during regular business hours?"

At which time I shall have the security guards throw you out bodily.

Ogi turned away from the glare. "This is the last time you will be able to comply without consequences."

"I really must insist you withdraw, Mr. Sheng," the moneylender replied in turn, in his disdain finding a reckless courage. "Do so immediately and I'll welcome you tomorrow."

Before last week, Christoph Spengler had known nothing of this uncouth Asian philistine. Their paths crossed over three double magnums of 1900 Château Margaux from the long-forgotten cellar of an Austrian prince who had fled with his family from advancing Nazi troops. The prince possessed the foresight to brick up his wine cellar but not the perspicacity to survive the war himself. Four owners of the house came and went before the outstanding crop of wine, closeted all these years in perfect condition, was rediscovered in renovation work by the present owner and sent to auction, drawing connoisseurs from around the globe.

Nine contenders participated in the initial phase. Bidding opened at $40,000 for the trio; at $60,000, only five men remained. By the time the figure soared to $90,000, all but Sheng and Spengler had dropped out. When the price leapt another $30,000, Sheng had had the effrontery to approach him directly.

"Rather than compete against each other," Ogi-Sheng had said, "why don't we stop the bidding here and split the bottles?"

"I do wish I could accommodate you, but unfortunately I've already promised to unveil the wine at my fifty-fifth birthday party. People will be flying in from around the world and I couldn't disappoint them."

"A compromise then? Two bottles for you, one for me? At seventy-two, this may be my last chance to sample this vintage in such superb condition."

"Sadly, I require *three*. So if you are unwilling to bid, sir, please retire. I think the next lot is nearly as suitable." The banker showed Sheng his back, repressing an inexplicable shiver he felt building at the base of his neck.

Now the financier said, "The answer I gave you at the auction stands. For the same reasons I mentioned."

"Take the money."

"Don't be crude."

"Then I'll need the combination to your cellar door."

"I think not."

"Casey. Persuade the man."

Without warning, Casey jammed a fist into the obstinate financier's stomach. Spengler crumpled into a chair with an *omphf.*

Ogi-Sheng swept an arm across the room. "We cannot be intimidated like common bank clerks, monsieur. Without the combination, things will only get worse."

"No one does this for three bottles of wine," Spengler managed to squeeze out through teeth clenched in pain.

Ogi looked bored. "Last week it was a request. Now it is a demand. That is all."

There is the maid, the banker thought. She must have noticed the altercation and had surely called the police. But come to think of it, Serena had not emerged from the back rooms to take drink orders from the visitors, and with that omission he understood that their live-in servant had been disposed of earlier, probably in the same manner as his wife.

Casey's cell phone rang. He stepped away from the dazed banker to answer the call. "Speak," he said in Japanese. Only top government agencies in South Korea, the United States, and Israel had the same encoded communications gear.

Spengler saw his chance. He leapt from the chair and ran. Without taking his ear from the phone, Casey whirled and his heel caught the banker in the back of the head, sending the moneyman sliding unsteadily across the carpet on his rotund stomach. Despite himself, Casey chuckled. *Ridiculous.*

"No, nothing important," Casey said into the phone, still in Japanese. "Go on."

He strolled over and planted a foot firmly on Spengler's spine. "Yes, I got it," Casey said. He turned to Ogi. "Sir, it's Dermott."

Dermott was leading the Japantown follow-up team in San Francisco.

"I'll take it." Ogi snatched the lobbed phone from the air with the ease of a man decades younger. "Yes?"

"The civilian at the kill site could be a problem, sir."

"The art dealer who sells knickknacks? I think not."

"Remember, he's Jake Brodie's son."

"Yes, *and* he sells hand-painted crockery to white-haired old ladies. Forget him."

"The lieutenant heading the case just met with Brodie across town, and Hara came to see him."

"Hara?"

"Yes."

Ogi grew thoughtful. "All right. The art dealer *is* the only direct channel to Japan. Watch him a little longer. *Just him.* The police are no threat."

The operation had been sanitized. Casey and his team had vacated the area within minutes of the kill while Dermott's crew swooped in, their task to monitor the local investigation and guarantee nothing went wrong *after*. The rest was covered, including any official inquiries the SFPD might send to Tokyo.

Ogi asked, "Why are you bothering me about such minor matters?"

Ogi's eyes narrowed as he listened to the answer. Defying orders, Dermott had attacked Brodie, which meant the art dealer was already dead and Dermott was calling for permission after the fact. Their best hand-to-hand man had a short fuse. *Patience, patience. Always patience.*

Ogi cut him off. "I *told* you no more bodies in San Francisco. The job's too important."

"Brodie's not dead."

After Dermott finished his description of the encounter, Ogi said, "You were right to retreat. When's the last time someone deflected your advance?"

"Never, sir."

"I didn't think so. Now, *that* could be a problem."

"That's what I was thinking, sir. I want a 'priority clear.'"

Priority clear was their code for immediate extermination by any means possible.

"I'm sure you do, but the answer is no. The kill was perfect. The police know nothing and they'll find nothing. Their investigation will die if no new developments draw their attention. *Make sure* there are no new developments. No more contact and no more bodies for the moment or I shall be extremely displeased."

"Yes, sir." Dermott hesitated. "Did you say 'for the moment'?"

Ogi knew when to dangle a carrot. Dermott and Casey were his finest field agents and required special maintenance. For Dermott, that meant feeding his bloodlust from time to time, and Ogi sensed he would have to allow him the art dealer once the Japantown affair cooled down.

"You heard me," Ogi said, and hung up, returning his attention to the financier. "Have you reconsidered?"

Casey removed his foot from the banker's back.

Spengler rolled over, tears leaking from his eyes. "Yes."

"Excellent. Now, the combination, please."

"Then you will leave us in peace?"

"You will have no complaints once I am done here."

Spengler relayed a string of numbers.

In English, for the moneyman's benefit, Ogi said, "Casey, bring the wine. Only those three bottles. Leave Mr. Spengler's other valuables alone."

Then in Japanese, he added, *"Moyase."*

Burn the rest.

In two minutes, Casey returned with three double magnums.

"Excellent," Ogi said again, his eyes glowing.

"You have your prize," Spengler said, his shoulders hunched in defeat. "Now go."

The first wisps of smoke wafted up from the lower floors.

Spengler jumped up. "Idiot! My cellar's on fire!"

He heard the soft whir of metal against fine cloth and could have sworn a wire loop passed before his eyes. He felt Sheng's hot, moist breath at the back of his neck.

The ends of Ogi's garrote were coiled around two small wooden pegs that functioned as handles. Ogi's fingers were curled around the pegs. Behind the banker's neck, Ogi crossed his wrists, closing the loop, and pulled.

Spengler clawed at his neck, his eyes wild in shock, not quite comprehending what was happening but understanding all too well the spurt of red liquid cascading over his hands and down his chest.

One by one, Ogi felt the vital structures of the neck collapse. The trachea, the carotid arteries, the jugular veins, the vagus nerves—the wire sliced through all of them like a butcher's knife through suet. When the wire hit the spinal column, Ogi uncrossed his wrists to open the loop, and with a practiced flick of his raised hand, whipped the garrote free of the victim's throat.

Eyes bulging, Spengler flailed about as crimson arcs of blood shot across the room. He attempted to stem the flow, but his fingers slipped and slithered around his neck. Gurgling sounds percolated from the throat area. Red air bubbles formed and burst. Then his arms went limp, his eyes rolled up into his head, and what was left of the sixth-generation financier flopped to the floor.

Ogi wiped the wire with a handkerchief, rolled it up, and stowed it in his jacket pocket.

Casey contemplated the blood-spattered floor. "That was not in the plan."

"I know," Ogi said. "I didn't care for his attitude." Smoke billowed from the basement door. "We haven't much time."

With practiced hands, they carried the bodies into the master bedroom, laid them out on the bed, and swiftly dressed them in their nightclothes. The fire would erase all evidence of their visit. "Accidental deaths" made up the bulk of their business. Direct assaults like Japantown were increasingly rare. Most jobs called for subtler forms of extermination—a drowning, a suicide, a high-speed collision. The list was long and inventive.

"We've overstayed our welcome, Casey. Bring the money. I believe our dimwitted friend no longer has any use for it."

I TOLD Renna what he wanted to know.

"Kanji are the characters that form the bulk of the Japanese writing system. The language also has two alphabets, each with about fifty characters, but kanji number in the thousands. They evolved from primitive symbols and ideographs. *Eye*, for example, was originally written more realistically, but over time became a vertical rectangle divided horizontally. You have a pen?"

Renna produced a ballpoint. I peeled a napkin from the steel dispenser on our table and drew the character for *eye*:

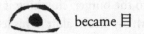 became 目

Renna studied it. "Interesting. It still resembles the original."

"Yes, just formalized. *Mountain* went from a lumpy triangular shape to a simple abstract." I added a second line of figures to the napkin:

 became 山

"I'm liking this," Renna said. "There's an internal logic."

"True. As people assimilated these early symbols, they began to combine them. A field 田 was set on top of the symbol for *strength* or *power* to make 男, or *man*, who they saw as the 'power in the field.' This happened over centuries, much of it in China, some later in Japan."

Our waitress glided up with Renna's burger and a lot of hip movement. She craned her neck at the Japanese on the napkin. "You moving up to secret agent, Frank?"

Renna raised his eyes. The waitress was around thirty-five, with abundant honey-blond hair piled on top of a shapely head. A loose strand dangled artfully to one side of a determined chin like a trawl line. I wondered if she ever caught anything with it.

"Night school, Karen. I'm studying to be a linguist in case the city decides to sack me."

"You, sweetie? They'd never dare."

The eyes behind the banter were far less cheerful.

I watched her walk away, hips swinging gently. "She casting a line your way?"

Renna nodded. "Just broke up with hubby. She brings me home, she'd be delirious because she'd know I could beat hubby to a pulp when she let it slip and he came after me."

"And she'd let it slip?"

"Count on it."

Renna drenched his half-pounder with ketchup, plopped the upper half of the toasted bun on top, then bit into the burger, clutching it in his right hand while holding the napkin with my scrawl aloft in his left.

Renna waved the napkin at me. "Okay, so if we're talking building blocks, why can't you take this one apart?"

"Two reasons. First, abstraction. As more and more elements were added, combinations divorced themselves from their simple base meanings. Combine *mountain* 山 with the character for *high*, 高, and you get 嵩, the foundation for more abstract words like *kasaru*, which means *to swell* or *increase in volume*. Then you have the historical filter: wood from a *mountain* 山 treated with *fire* 火 under a *roof* gives you 炭, or *charcoal*. The roof represents the kiln used in the old days to make charcoal."

"So it's messy."

"That's one way of looking at it."

"Guess simple was too much to hope for." Renna snagged another chunk of his half-pounder. It was maybe his third bite and the burger was about gone. "How much time do you need to check with your people in Japan?"

I considered the time lag. "Their workday started an hour ago. I put an 'urgent' tag on it, they'll send me preliminary findings by the end of the shift, but don't expect miracles."

"I'm counting on it."

I eyed my coffee sourly. "Be warned. Most things Japanese are vague to begin with, even to the Japanese."

The sentiment sat at the core of my being. Though I was an American born of Caucasian parents, my history, my work, and my personal life were partially bound to Japan. I'd passed much of my childhood playing in the back streets of Tokyo. My wife had been Japanese and my daughter shared her mother's birthright. My father had spent most of his adult life in Tokyo building up Brodie Security. Japan held a special place in my heart, lending a richness to my days I'd always be grateful for.

Yet, like an aloof friend or lover whose guard never comes down, Japan keeps her distance. For years I believed my status as a *gaijin*—the eternal outsider in an exclusive society—accounted for her fabled elusiveness. But that was only part of it. Over a few bottles of *junmai* saké with some Japanese buddies in Shinjuku, I discovered they suffered the same slights. With my language ability and my knowledge of the people and the country's traditions, I was enough of an insider to penetrate the surface, they told me. It was simply that every quarter was guarded. Layers upon layers of secrets had piled up over the centuries. Those inside the circle knew; those outside were excluded. And there were circles within circles. That's when I fully understood Jake's job, and the one I'd inherited: the calls for help came when the secrets impinged on those outside the circle.

Renna looked disgusted. "I don't have weeks, so you'll have to hustle. How many kanji are we talking about?"

"Let's put it this way. The average person can read about three thousand, and college-educated adults know between four and ten. A typical dictionary holds ten to fifteen thousand characters, but the thirteen-volume *Dai Kanwa Jiten*, which holds all of the historical characters, lists fifty thousand."

"*Fifty* thousand? Jesus. This thing could turn into a black hole. How many characters do *you* know?"

"Including the historical ones, maybe six, seven thousand."

Renna clenched his fists. "And you *still* can't read this one? I don't need this. I really don't."

"Welcome to the Orient."

"It'll keep for another couple of days but not much longer. Light a fire under your people. Swing by the station tomorrow morning around ten with what you got."

"Sure," I said with a neutral expression, knowing that only disappointment came down the pike when you expected too much too soon.

Renna stood. "Good. Got to go. And thanks."

"For what?"

"If nothing else, you've established that the kanji's not ordinary."

"So?"

"Neither was the shoot."

We stared at each other for a long moment.

A shade of concern flickered across the lieutenant's face. "One other thing. While you're looking, watch your back, Brodie. Someone's out there and we want to find him before he finds us."

His words stopped me. My heart fluttered like it does when it recognizes a kernel of truth. Again, I considered the flurry of activity in the eighteen hours since I'd set foot in Japantown: the bogus homeboy, the shop break-in that wasn't, Hara's unexpected visit.

Renna must have too.

Suddenly I knew what the handiwork at my store was about. Nothing was taken, because the B&E artist had come for something other than art. Which could only mean information on me, the shop, or my movements. Or all three. And maybe he'd even left a souvenir behind. One that could listen in.

Maybe he'd already found me.

DAY 2

THE TELL

CHAPTER 15

AFTER dashing off an email about the kanji to Brodie Security in Tokyo, I'd dispatched a second message to a dealer I'd met last summer who had already become a friend. It occurred to me that he might have a new perspective on a trail that had, for me, gone cold years ago. My long shot paid off early the next morning with an incoming call of some urgency.

Kazuo Takahashi was a high-powered art dealer in Kyoto. As far as I could tell, he was a near genius when it came to any aspect of Japanese culture. He had a brilliant eye and a deep understanding of his country's roots back to the beginning of the Nara period, in the eighth century. But more important, he was impeccably honest, an equally hard quality to find in our field.

When I lifted the phone, the amiable voice of my Kyoto friend greeted me. "Brodie-san? Takahashi. I hope I didn't wake you or little Yumi-chan?"

The question was phrased in the familiar-polite form of Japanese. Takahashi spoke only Japanese, and used an affectionate suffix with Jenny's middle name.

"No, she's at a friend's," I said, "and I was already awake."

"That doesn't surprise me if you're working on something related to the kanji. But before we get to that, can we talk business for a minute?"

"Sure."

"I need your assistance with the Sotheby's auction in November. Are you available?"

"I've nothing planned."

"Good. A client wants a Lichtenstein. A pivotal early piece. The work fills a hole in his collection and he insists that someone be on hand in Manhattan to guarantee the acquisition. We'll keep an open line during bidding. The usual fee?"

"No problem. Now, what can you tell me about the kanji?"

He cleared his throat. "It's a curious specimen."

"How so?"

"First off, I think you know the character is not listed in the any of the major kanji resources, but that's only the beginning. Did my email arrive? I rewrote the kanji so we could make comparisons as we talk."

"Hold on."

I walked into the other room, booted up my computer, and printed the file Takahashi had sent. Aside from a small kitchen, our apartment had a breakfast nook, two "petite" bedrooms (the real estate euphemism for "standing room only once you put in a bed and a dresser"), one bath, and a family room with two elegant bay windows. Beige carpet ran through all the rooms and I'd hung framed posters on the walls from art exhibitions at Tokyo's Nezu and Goto museums, and "loaners" from the shop graced one select spot on a rotating basis. In front of the northernmost bay window, I set up a small workstation, with laptops for Jenny and me, where either of us could pound a keyboard and still be social.

I grabbed the paper rolling onto the receiving arm of my printer, laid it on my coffee table, and sat on the couch. From my workstation, I snatched the photocopy Renna had given me at the M&N and set it alongside Takahashi's new version.

ORIGINAL   NEW

"Got it," I said into the extension.

"Is it clear?"

"Very."

"Good. First, the awkwardness you so correctly noted suggests that the writer does not pen the character frequently."

"So when he does write it, it's probably for a specific purpose?"

"That would be my assumption. Moreover, the inconsistent hand and dullness of line point to a limited education, probably ending in the sixth or seventh year of schooling."

A new thought occurred to me. "Could it be someone who had no need to write Japanese regularly? Say, a Japanese living abroad?"

Takahashi answered with noticeable hesitation. "Specimens I normally review do not enter that realm, of course, but, yes, a distancing could account for worsening skills. In which case, perhaps your penman may have had another year or two of schooling in a, um, more primitive environment. In either case, clearly he shows no advanced calligraphic training nor a sense of a deeper understanding of penmanship."

Traditionally, artists, scholars, and Buddhist monks penned poems or axioms for display. To this day, historical works provide partial psychological portraits of some of Japan's most noted luminaries.

I said, "How about a nisei educated in a Japanese boarding school?"

Nisei are the children of Japanese parents, born abroad. They would have less exposure to the traditional education system.

"Possibly," the dealer said, "*if* he received some classical education. It would explain the curious combination of familiarity and gracelessness."

"It would, wouldn't it. What else?"

"I suspect the kanji might be constructed. Several characters seem compressed into one, as if the creator was less concerned with meaning than with merging elements to make a symbol. A logo, if you will. The key to unlocking its meaning may lie along those lines."

"Can you read it?"

Takahashi hesitated. "I have a list of obvious and obscure interpretations, but I'll need two or three days to confirm my ideas. In the meantime, we can deal with the psychological implications. To an experienced eye, this is a disturbing piece."

I was afraid of that. The foreboding I'd carried since my chat with Renna hit me with redoubled force and a feathery fear tripped lightly through my extremities.

"To you of all people," the Kyoto dealer was saying, "I need not explain how I know what I know, but there are overwhelming undercurrents of arrogance, and an additional element I find very disquieting."

I felt my pulse spike with his last words. Calligraphy came with psychological baggage if you had the ability to read it. A string of characters could reveal a number of all-too-human traits: playfulness, joy, sorrow, pride, shallowness, longing, kindness, cruelty, anger, spiritual depth, or a lack of it.

"What do you see, Takahashi-san?"

The art dealer shifted uneasily. "Since you expressed some urgency in your note, I'm going to go out on a limb: there is a restrained manic energy here. Something brutish and uncontrolled."

He hesitated.

I said, "Which means what?"

"If I were you, Brodie-san, I'd be in no hurry to meet the man who wrote this. In fact, I should be strongly inclined to move in the opposite direction as fast as I possibly could."

T HE next bombshell arrived by email from Kunio Noda, a man of few words and also Brodie Security's best detective.

Hit with twenty-nine-year-old boy wonder at Waseda U. Kanji listed in his database. Only known appearance linked to town of Soga-jujo, Shiga Prefecture. You want it tracked, means a trip out there. Waiting reply.

Noda

I stared at the computer screen in astonishment. First Takahashi, now Noda. How had he found it so fast? Discovered in one day what I'd failed to turn up in two months of intensive searching four years ago? I'd spoken to a dozen linguists. Two dozen historians. Having pursued countless antiques with no more than old receipts or the foggy memories of a previous owner, I knew how to follow an obscure trail, yet I'd been unable to unearth more than the terror-stricken testimony of an old man. Once again, Noda had proved he was no slouch.

While I ran over the disturbing implications of Noda's message, a sleepy-eyed Jenny unlocked the front door and drifted in. After yesterday's run-in with Homeboy, I'd insisted she carry a key. I didn't want her forced to wait outside even for a second. When I looked over, Lisa's mother waved from the hall and headed back upstairs. Another adjustment. There would be no more unescorted trips between apartments for the foreseeable future.

"You're up early again, Daddy. Is your leg still hurting?"

"The leg's fine. I just couldn't sleep."

Jenny dragged a chair over to the stove, hopped up on it, and stared into the frying pan. "Are you making your special pepper-eggs?"

"Yep, but with Tabasco this time."

"Can I have some?"

"Swap you half for a kiss."

She gave me a peck on the cheek, then bounced excitedly on her toes. Jenny was buoyant this morning, the unsteadiness of yesterday nowhere to be seen. An additional night with Lisa had done the trick. Relieved, I hoped the mood would hold.

As my daughter grew, echoes of Mieko had begun to emerge. In the lilt of her voice. In her smile. In the way she carried herself. I was beginning to notice what I'd seen in her mother at the local karate dojo when we first met. I was seventeen and Mieko was a year younger. Even though I had a girlfriend and no plans to stray, my future wife attracted notice. She had buttery skin, dark brown eyes, and the otherworldly calm of someone who knew things.

She also spoke Japanese, which I found a refreshing reminder of what I'd been yanked away from with my parents' recent divorce. Indeed, Japanese was all she spoke, so I became her unofficial translator during practice sessions at the dojo.

Mieko's English improved rapidly, but we stayed friends, our common bond Japan. At eighteen, we both enrolled at the local two-year college. Once she'd taken a semester's worth of classes to bolster her English ability, Mieko returned to Japan to finish her education.

After my mother died, I cleared up the odds and ends and headed for San Francisco, where Mieko tracked me down one summer when she returned to see her parents. She offered solace I didn't know I needed, and slowly the weight of my loss lifted.

During our separation, Mieko's steadfast self-assurance—the quality I'd been attracted to at our first meeting—had ripened into a profound sense of knowing. A deep stillness now lay at her center. In those almond-shaped eyes I discovered a light I wanted to crawl into. We stayed in touch, grew closer than I would have thought possible, and after the closeness matured, we eventually married.

"You don't mind sharing your eggs?" Jenny asked, dragging me back to the present.

"Not with you."

Accepting my gallantry as a given, Jenny plopped down on her beanbag chair, arms and legs strewn about in indolent abandon. "I *love* your pepper-eggs," she said. "They taste good."

"What if I said you like them because they make you sneeze and then you giggle because your nose itches?"

She wrinkled the organ in question. "That too."

I gave the food a final stir and said, "Breakfast is ready." I split the eggs between two plates, buttered the toast, took the plates to the table, then returned to the kitchen for Jenny's milk. My daughter bounced into her seat with impatience, pigtails flying. She ate her eggs and sipped her milk.

"Like 'em?" I asked, while I was thinking, *How had Noda found the kanji so fast?*

Jenny smiled and nodded and shoveled in another mouthful of egg, holding her fork in a close-fisted overhand grip. As she lifted the next mound to her lips, she said, "Uh-oh," and sneezed twice. The yellow mass flew from her fork as if launched by catapult, smacked against the far wall, and dribbled down onto the carpet.

Eyes wide with apprehension, Jenny said, "Oopsies," leapt from her seat, dashed into the kitchen for a rag, hurriedly wiped up the egg, rinsed the cloth, then charged back to the table and wiggled into my lap. "Sorry I messed up the place, Daddy."

I said, "What mess?"

The comment yielded a nervous smile.

"In fact," I said, "that part of the room is now the cleanest spot in the whole place. Could you do the rest of the apartment too, please?"

Jenny laughed and snuggled deeper into my lap. "You're a good daddy most of the time."

Before I could probe that gem, Jenny hopped off my lap and raced into her small cubbyhole of a bedroom at the back of our apartment to prepare for summer school. After she washed and dressed, I combed out her hair, rebraided it, and escorted her upstairs to the Meyerses'.

Back in the apartment I faced a hard truth. Unwittingly, I was re-creating the same harmful cycle Jake had foisted on me when he left at night for an assignment both my mother and I sensed was dangerous. Jenny's smile was still bright, but a fretful note had crept in after the skirmish with Homeboy. I would have to keep a close eye on her.

I shook off my domestic troubles and scanned Noda's email with renewed amazement.

Somehow, the chief detective had leveraged Brodie Security's resources and given the elusive kanji a home. Not in the dictionaries or history books. Not in folkloric traditions or any of the musty archives I'd rummaged through, but in a little town in a distant prefecture hundreds of miles west of Tokyo. No wonder I hadn't found it. Noda had latched on to the slimmest of slim threads.

I sent the detective a congratulatory email and asked him to hold off on a trip to the village. Then, bearing secrets of a far-off kind, I set out to keep my third appointment with Lieutenant Frank Renna in the last thirty hours.

GUESS it's not a candy wrapper," Renna said.

"Guess not."

We were in Renna's office behind closed doors, drinking bad coffee and discussing Noda's find. Wrestling with the implications, Renna grew thoughtful, while I wondered how best to broach the subject of my new client, a clear conflict of interest. In the squadroom on the other side of Renna's glass-paneled door, three detectives on the J-town task force had gathered around a ten-foot-long whiteboard with all the latest leads. The most senior of the lot was shaking his head.

Renna snapped out of his reverie. "What you're telling me is the kanji's so rare, chances of its being at the crime scene accidentally are about as good as my waking up next to Miss Universe?"

"Or Mister Universe."

"So what's the name of this place again?"

"Soga-jujo. I checked the map. It's a small farming village in a little isolated river valley. We're talking real backwoods, Frank. Good old boys. One or two surnames. Radish and rice growers for centuries. Probably twenty, thirty generations. You could go out there and film *Deliverance Two*."

Renna made a decision. "Send your man. The city will pay. Any way I can get a handle on this thing works for me."

This is where I drew the line. I wouldn't jeopardize our friendship over a conflict of interest, and in accepting Hara's case, that was exactly what I had. Having access to the Japanese mogul gave me a handle on the case I didn't want to relinquish if it wasn't necessary. Renna would see that too. But it was still a conflict.

"The city won't have to foot the bill," I said. "Katsuyuki Hara came to see me. Wants me to work the case. Turns out he's the grandfather of the kids."

Renna's head snapped up. "The telecom guy? You?"

"Yep."

"You say the word, I'll dump him."

We were silent. In the squadroom, the three detectives were now at their desks, working the phones. Pinned to a bulletin board on the far wall were a rotation roster, a pair of wanted posters, and under a CRIMINAL OF THE WEEK sign, a photograph of the mayor, his eyes masked with a black bar of kraft paper. As I gazed out on the scene, I wondered how far my friendship with Renna could stretch under the strain of the case. With his career on the line, he would have to wend his way through the labyrinth of city and police politics with caution.

Renna leaned forward. "Hang on to Hara, but you clear everything out of this office with me first."

"Hara wants results, not details, so he won't be a problem. But I'll need to brief my boys in Tokyo. It's the only way they can work."

Furrows creased the lieutenant's brow. "Okay, but keep it in-house."

"Done. Can you hold off City Hall?"

"No telling, but at the moment they need me more than I need them."

"And if that changes?"

Renna's whole career rested with the SFPD. The alternatives were not appealing.

"Without results? The boot downstairs or worse. That happens, you can bet the mayor will act. Have you met him?"

"No."

"You're about to."

I heard a tap on the door behind me. Renna waved to a figure on the other side of the glass. Mayor Gary Hurwitz stepped into the office, followed by a suited entourage of three, including city councilman Calvin Washington, deputy mayor Robert DeMonde, and Gail Wong, the mayor's spokesperson and head tiger shark of his support staff.

"Gary," Renna said, standing. Following his example, I also rose.

"Sit, Frank. I hope I'm not intruding."

"No, good timing," Renna said, remaining on his feet. "Let me introduce you to Jim Brodie. He's the guy I told you would be consulting on Japantown."

The major gave me a bright smile. "Yes, of course. My visit was fortuitous, then. I want to stay on top of this one, so I'm glad we have a chance to meet." He wore a gray herringbone suit, white button-down shirt, and powder-blue tie, an ensemble that complemented his wavy black hair and piercing gray eyes.

We shook hands and Hurwitz introduced the other three. I exchanged quick handshakes with them, Gail's assessing gaze lingering the longest, then the mayor said, "I was down the hall at Judge Taylor's, so I thought I'd stop in and preview any new developments you might have."

It was clear he expected nothing, so I watched with masked satisfaction as Renna rolled out Noda's discovery.

"We've located the kanji."

The mayor seemed stunned, then pleased. "Have you now? Well, that's great. Just great. I heard it was a dead end."

"Not from me, you didn't," Renna said.

"From other sources." He looked at me, his smile dazzling. "Was that your work?"

"An associate's," I said.

He pumped my hand again. "Frank said you knew your way around the Orient. I'm delighted. Well-done, gentlemen. Keep it up. I'm looking for a swift resolution to this tragic affair."

"We all are," Renna said.

"Fine, just fine. I'm going to have Gail or Bob stop by a couple times a day for the latest, if you don't mind."

"Not a problem," Renna said.

"Excellent, excellent," the mayor said, and shook my hand again, then the entourage departed as quickly as it had arrived.

"Expressive guy," I said.

"Yep, but don't be fooled. He has sharp teeth. They all do. Gail in particular. She's a former VP from a Silicon Valley startup, Bob's a sales yak and self-made millionaire, and Calvin made his bucks with a chain of barbecue joints in the East Bay, mostly in Oakland, Fremont, around there. Birds of a feather, the lot of them. Rumor has it Hurwitz is grooming Gail and Bob for the election after next. Her for deputy and By-the-Book Bob for the mayor's seat after Hurwitz vacates. Keep it in the family."

I shrugged. "It could be worse, I suppose."

"True." Renna tossed down the rest of his coffee like he wished it were something stronger. "That reminds me. The lab boys dug up a tidbit."

"What?"

Renna's face dimmed. "It's not going to improve your appetite any."

"Can't get any worse."

"Oh yeah," he said. "It can. You know anything about spatter?"

"No."

"A.k.a. *blood patterns*. With all the firepower on the streets these days, it's a ballooning science. Almost an industry."

"You don't say."

"I do. When each bullet exits the body, it sends out a spray trail. Multiple entries produce multiple trails. The sprays fall in a precise progression, later over earlier. Directions are different. Blood types are different. Water on water blends, but blood on blood layers because it's thick like oil. When new drops fall on old, they make circles or half-circles, and don't mix completely because blood begins to coagulate the instant it hits the air. By charting the location of the sprays and taking enough blood samples at the points where the spray trails intersect, the lab jocks can determine who was shot first."

My heart seemed to slow. "And?"

"All five victims were gunned down in seconds. Probably five or six. Seven, tops. Good groupings. No wasted shots. But there's *always* an order, even if you're splitting seconds. The shooter stepped in close and caught the big male in the back first, raked high for the adults, father followed by mother, left to right, then swung back low, right to left, for the children."

Seven seconds, tops. We were silent for quite a bit longer than it took for someone to eradicate the entire Nakamura family. I felt the embers of a smoldering heat jump-start my blood flow.

"Very, very cool," I said softly.

"You got that right. Knocked out the biggest threat first."

"So what's that tell us?"

Renna took a long deliberate breath. "Two things. First, any way you look at it, it was an execution."

I hesitated before asking the unavoidable: "And the second?"

"We have less time than I thought. So get a move on."

I nodded guardedly. "Sure thing."

As it turned out, acceleration would be the least of our worries.

SPOTTED him on the afternoon of the second day.

With lunchtime approaching and my leg on the mend, I curbed the Cutlass in front of the shop, then hoofed it the five blocks to Sweet Heat, a feisty Tex-Mex restaurant on Steiner. I ordered my usual chicken burrito with extra salsa and actually came close to finishing it, despite my lackluster appetite since Japantown. I paid the bill and ambled up Steiner toward Lombard, luxuriating in the fine summer weather.

I soaked up the bright noonday rays, working the leg, the muscles flexing pleasantly. A light-afternoon breeze with a slight saltiness was blowing in off the bay, and a sporadic mist hinted at the approach of a cooling fog. But for the moment the toasty Californian sun was out in full force, warming my shoulders and bleaching the sidewalk a custard yellow.

That's when I felt him. My body tensed. The skin over my forearms rippled with gooseflesh. In my old neighborhood they called this the South Central early-warning system. Heightened under the watchful eye of my Korean neighbor, it kicked in now.

Someone was following me.

I strolled down the street, my gaze steady and serene, catching sight of him out of the corner of my eye, across the street, ten yards back. His gait was purposefully casual. Smooth, liquid, but not languid. He didn't get it—the mist, the sea, the fleeting afternoon warmth. And because he wasn't attuned to the vagaries of San Francisco and her fickle weather patterns, he stuck out.

At a leisurely pace, I found my way back to the shop, occasionally snatching an oblique image of a man in a beige sports coat. On Lombard, I turned left and he tagged along directly behind me for two blocks before passing over to the other side of the avenue and trailing me from across four lanes of traffic.

Abers greeted me as I reentered the store. "Back so soon?"

"Yeah. I eighty-sixed the idea of a stroll down Chestnut."

"Ach, too bad. Nice day for a walkie."

There you go. Even Abers, a South African transplant, got it. Though, cheerful as his rejoinder was, underneath he was still simmering about my taking Hara's case and then refusing to discuss it with him. But we had come to an unspoken agreement: he would wait me out, and I would mention the unmentionable when I was ready.

"Watch the front for a minute, would you? I need to make a call."

"Afterward, let's have a talk-to about rearranging the back."

"Good idea. Time permitting."

The tenor of my voice caught Abers's attention and he backed off.

Once in my office, I shut the door, pulled out a prepaid cell phone I used for Brodie Security business, and then stepped out into the alley because I'd yet to have the security people scan the shop for listening devices. I punched in Renna's number.

"Homicide."

"Renna, please."

"Who's calling?"

"Brodie."

"Ah, the Japan guy. Hang on." A hand muffled the sound. "Anyone seen the Loot?"

"Down the hall."

The detective came back on. "Loot's so busy he needs a body double. Be a minute."

He put me on hold and "When the Saints Come Marching In" oozed from the speaker. The city's public relations stiffs were getting subtle—if you thought a sledgehammer brass section was subtle.

Renna picked up and, mercifully, the saints vanished. "You got more?"

"You having me followed?"

He snorted. "I got thirty-five badges out on the J-town job following any shred of a lead we scrape up and another fifteen pulling double overtime to check out every freak in town. The pols are chewing on my ass and the newshounds are snapping at the parts the pols missed. I don't have the manpower or the time to follow you around. Unless you're planning to confess."

"You sure one of your jokers isn't trying to yank my chain?"

"I'm sure. He look like cop?"

"He's a pro of some sort."

"Maybe your client's checking up on you."

"Why would he?"

"Why *wouldn't* he? I'll send some boys by to pick him up."

"I could brace him myself but with my leg I figured I'd give you first crack."

"I'd like that."

"Thought as much. He's on Lombard, maybe twenty yards west of my shop. If your people split up and come at him from both ends, they should be able to box him in."

"I'm on it. Might get some answers."

"Be nice to have some of those before I forget what they look like. Guy you want has black hair, beige sports coat, light pants. You want *maybes*?"

"Yeah."

"Caucasian with a tan or a brown-skinned Asian, Hispanic, whatever. Couldn't get a straight-on look without spooking him."

"Got it," Renna snapped, and disconnected, the dead line buzzing in my ear like an angry bee. Clearly, Renna was being harassed from all sides.

I moved to the front of the shop and stood behind the counter where I could be seen from the street. I listened with half an ear to the radio Abers kept stashed under the counter as I gazed with seeming disinterest out the window.

Five minutes passed, then five more. I occupied myself with minor chores at the front counter while keeping my antenna pointed toward the street, alert for any activity. I couldn't see the tail, but I felt him out there for those ten minutes, then nothing. He was gone. The cops must have nabbed him.

As time ticked by, doubt distracted me and presented alternative scenarios, none of them good. A half hour after the tail had faded from my radar, two rookie cops sauntered in, one rectangular and sturdy like an upended tank, the other tall and slim and thoughtful-looking.

The tank said, "You Brodie? The point man for the loiterer?"

"Yeah."

"We caught the squeal from Lieutenant Renna. I'm Dobbs." He jerked his head at his partner. "This is Sayles."

"You catch him?"

Dobbs said, "We came at him from opposite directions, as advised, but he crossed the street and turned the corner before we could cut him off. We followed but couldn't close. We figured we'd wear him down, then hit him with a sprint and tackle. But the dickwad vanished."

"Don't really see how," Sayles added quietly.

I frowned and stared off at the far wall, disgusted.

Dobbs panned a look my way, then glared at his partner. "Damnedest thing we've ever seen, right? Alley's a dead end. A fuckin' titmouse couldn't hide in there. Buildings on both sides, cyclone fence with razor wire strung across the back."

The comment got my attention again. "The alley off Chestnut?"

"Yeah."

Dobbs had a point. It *was* a dead end. The alley ran between two converted Victorian shops fronting Chestnut before grinding to a halt thirty yards in, where the flanks of the Victorians smacked up against the rear of a third home with front access on the next street over. There were maybe two side doors opening on to the passage from the Chestnut units and a high chain-link fence running across the back of the third Victorian. There were no walkways between buildings. It was a walled-in enclave of wire and redwood.

I said, "Maybe he just outran you and ducked around another corner?"

"No," Sayles said. "We chased him into that alley. We were half a block behind and closing. The alley doors were locked. He must have found a cubbyhole somewhere."

"Or flew," Dobbs said. "Fucking sprouted wings and sailed over the rooftops."

"Dumpsters?" I asked.

"Checked."

Abers brought coffee for the patrol boys and a sharp look for me that said *This is more about the unmentionable, isn't it?*

I said, "Either of you get a look at him?"

Sayles reddened. "Never got close enough."

I took a deep breath to still my frustration. They'd blown it. Completely. A dull ache built at the base of my skull. What was Renna thinking? Sending virgin badges to cage our first potential lead? I should have tackled the tail myself. With my limp, maybe I wouldn't have nailed him, but I wouldn't have squandered the chance to catch a glimpse of the suspect. These rookies came away with less than zero: they showed our hand but gained nothing in return.

I shot Sayles a probing look. "How did he react when he saw your approach? Did he jackrabbit on you?"

Dobbs's nostrils flared. "You bet your ass the bastard hightailed it out of there. Otherwise he *knows* he's dogmeat."

Mild disagreement suffused Sayles's expression. "No, that wasn't quite it. He reacted to our presence, but smoothly, calmly. I'd say he moved carefully away and led us down Octavia."

I said, *"Led?"*

"Well, it almost seemed that way."

"Into the impossible alley?"

"Yeah."

Sayles and I exchanged looks.

Dobbs caught the shared glance and said, "What?"

Sayles paused to compose his answer. "Maybe he *wanted* us to follow him into the alley."

"Now there's a shit-for-brains idea. Where would that get him?"

I said, "The best escape route is one your pursuers can't follow."

Dobbs squinted at me. "You mean he reconnoitered the area, then fucking crawled up a wall?"

"Yeah, something like that."

Sayles nodded, vaguely troubled eyes straying absently to the back of the room. "Mr. Brodie, I don't know who that guy was, but I'll tell you one thing, he's got one tasty bag of tricks."

Looking back, I would see that, despite fumbling the pursuit, it was this thoughtful blond rookie who first sensed the unparalleled threat we faced.

CHAPTER 19

THE typhoon struck, as the Japanese are fond of dubbing an abrupt eruption of activity, while Abers and I pored over his new arrangement of the woodblock prints.

A blue truck from TV Tokyo screeched to a halt in front of the shop, and a newscaster with a scruffy crew in tow spilled from the back. On its heels came a gray four-door sedan with *Yomiuri News* scrawled across its side, reporters and photographers tumbling from its interior and jockeying for position on the sidewalk in front of my shop. Next, a white van from Asahi Broadcasting appeared. In less than a minute, a dozen Japanese press hounds had gathered outside my show window.

I had no clue as to the cause of the commotion until a black stretch limo double-parked alongside the van. An elegant Japanese woman in an amethyst silk day dress with silver belt and shoes stepped from the car and waved. Film rolled and cameras clicked.

Abers raised an eyebrow. "A lady friend of yours?"

"Not that I know of."

"Well, there's always hope."

Approaching the shop, the woman paused to allow a camera op with the store sign in the frame. A clutch of microphones sprouted up in front of her, and she graciously answered a few questions we couldn't hear.

Abers squinted at the car. "Nice wheels."

Waving at the reporters, the woman turned her back on her admirers and pushed through the front door—and suddenly I understood.

"Bill," I said, "let me introduce you to Ms. Lizza Hara."

Abers lit up with understanding. "A pleasure, ma'am."

After Sayles and Dobbs had departed, I'd fed Abers all the gory details of Japantown, telling him about the Nakamuras and Hara, then highlighting the connection to Mieko. During my recital, Abers's face had displayed a kaleidoscope of emotion: disbelief, outrage, disgust, sadness, and—when I confirmed the kanji connection—a sorrow so deep his eyes widened into what seemed like endless tunnels.

Lizza Hara nodded in satisfaction. "And you're Jim Brodie, of course. Father said you'd know me."

"I do. By reputation."

In person, Hara's daughter was more stunning than her publicity stills, which was saying something. The violet dress, though bright, was suggestively regal yet accentuated her long legs and the curve of her hips. She seemed to wear everything well. For her latest album cover, she'd posed in tight bicycle shorts and virgin-white stiletto heels. The photographer had caught her long black hair whirling above skin-tight electric blue spandex as she glanced back over her shoulder, round hips set, impish breasts thrust forward, full lips pouting and painted a ruby red—the same components she exhibited in abundance now, but coming together in a more mature fashion.

Coloring slightly, Lizza waved dismissively at the air. "Anything I can do to help. Besides, California is so *fab*, and normally I *adore* coming here, but this time I . . . I . . ."

Her eyes clouded and tears flowed. Camera flashes exploded from the sidewalk as she brought out a handkerchief. Abers escorted Lizza to the conference room in the back while I locked the front door, flipping the sign over to CLOSED. Several reporters snapped my picture. I could only guess the headlines those shots would engender in tomorrow's papers.

In the sitting room, Lizza said, "I saw Miki and Ken just three months ago, over the summer. We drove out to the beach in my limo."

A misty look fought a tremulous smile. Then the tears returned. This time her shoulders shook and a muffled sound of grief passed her lips. Her mourning continued unabated for several minutes, the sound of her weeping fading in stages to intermittent sniffles. Eventually, her shoulders ceased shaking. She dabbed at her eyes with the handkerchief.

"Excuse me. I'm sure my makeup is utterly ruined but I don't care. I'm safe with you gentleman, right? You'll keep the press away?"

"Already a done deal," Abers said. "We locked them out."

Relief smoothed her features. "Thank you. You're a sweetheart. The plane ride was so dreary. All I could do was think about my little darlings. It was simply unbearable."

Her voice was soft, but each word emerged sonorous and musical. She spoke English with an engaging Japanese lilt that bounced along on its own, peppered with the melodramatic vocabulary of movie starlets and pop personalities she obviously favored.

Her voice had launched her career. Now everyone in Japan knew who she was. Her debut album had sold nearly a million copies after she happened to be photographed with male heartthrob Noriyuki Sawada. Daddy hopped on board and his golden touch sold another million. Grateful girlfriend and daughter that she was, Lizza wasted little time in calling a press conference to throw her boyfriend over because he did not appreciate liberated women, and denounce her father for meddling in her career. This move was timed with the release of her second album, which promptly outsold the first, even without Daddy's help. She was offered movie roles, and a serial drama was written around her. Five years down the road and firmly established in Japan as a singer and actress, Lizza threw another public fit, this time to announce her emotional exhaustion and a decision to expand her career internationally by moving to New York, where the Japanese paparazzi soon snapped her clinging to Justin Timberlake's arm at an Italian restaurant in the Village.

In America, she continued to nurture what would never be more than an incipient music career, but her prowess on the party circuit was legendary.

I said, "I'm sorry about your sister and her family, Ms. Hara."

"You're so kind." She squeezed my knee. "And it's Lizza, *please*. Both of you. If either of you turns out to be a stuffy old thing I'm going to be disappointed. I was *so* thrilled when Father said you were helping out on this, Mr. Brodie."

"You were?"

"Yes, silly. Everyone in Japan saw your picture in the glossies when you found that lost Rikyu thingy. You're a genuine hero."

I said, "Kind of you to say so, but—"

"Father said to fly out here," she said, switching to Japanese, "to tell you everything I know, so I've come. I don't really know much, but for as long as you want me, I'm yours."

"Yes, well, would you mind a few questions?"

"If you think I can be of help."

"I'm sure you can. Were you close to your sister?"

Lizza pushed out her lower lip. "Yes and no, you know? I loved her and I'll miss her and Hiroshi, but we've led such different lives."

"When did you last talk to her?"

"Ages and ages ago."

"Could you narrow it down a bit?"

"Say, six or eight weeks ago?"

"Did she have any worries, any concerns?"

"You mean something that could have got her . . . her . . . like that? Oh my God, no! She would have told me. At least, I *hope* she would have told me. I certainly *hope* . . . I mean . . . what if . . . ?"

Her composure crumbled again. She covered her face and her shoulders shook harder this time. Abers gave me a look of censure. I pleaded my case silently. I needed what Lizza knew. Abers patted Lizza's shoulder.

"It's all right," my assistant said. "Cry it out."

"We could do this later," I said.

Blinking, she gave a rapid, limp-wrist wave. "No, no, now. Just give me a moment."

She drew a compact from an impossibly small black leather clutch and we waited as she retouched her makeup. Once finished, she tucked her compact away, snapped the bag shut, and gave me a brave smile.

"I'm ready."

It was a fragile front, so I tiptoed in. "Let's move on to your brother-in-law. Was he involved in anything risky?"

"I wouldn't think so. He was a gentle creature. That's why my sister loved him. The total opposite of Father. So kind, so quiet. He was a cutie-pie but he sold shoes. I mean, his company did. He was management but, I mean, men's *shoes*? Honestly, can you imagine in your wildest dreams anything duller?"

She had a point.

"Tell me about your father's bodyguard," I said. "Has he always had one?"

"That's easy. No."

"Recently?"

"About three months ago. Ever since Teq QX."

"What's that?"

"Some Taiwan chip maker he took a fancy to."

"What's so special about it?"

"Who knows? Everyone was making a fuss over it, that's all."

"Do you know why?"

"Of course not."

Right. There was a limit to what I could draw out from the effusive Lizza. I changed tack again. "Back to your sister. Is there anything either she or her husband might have become involved in that could have put them in danger?"

"My sister? Never." Lizza's tone was adamant. "You have the wrong side of the family. My father and I are the risk takers. Hiroshi and Eiko were so modest."

"Well, your father seemed to think you could tell me *something*."

My frustration must have seeped through because her voice dropped half an octave and the party girl disappeared. "No one ever really knows what Father thinks. That is the one thing you should understand about Father."

"I see."

"But don't worry. Do what I do. Ignore him and you'll get along just fine."

"Thanks for the advice."

Lizza studied me, suddenly solemn and focused. "Do you have any ideas yet about what happened, Jim-san?"

"I'm just getting started, but I'm committed. And the police are on top of it. A lot of police."

"Good. But remember. Father chose *you*. And if there's one thing Father knows, it's people. He expects *you* to find the killer, and I believe you will."

Then, abruptly, the interview was over. Without warning, just like her father. She stood and extended her right hand, thumb straight up, hand cocked at that peculiar, self-conscious angle women use when they want to project a businesslike image.

Abers and I rose. We shook the outstretched hand in turns and we escorted her to the front of the shop.

When she saw the limousine, she paused. "You know, I may never be able to look at a limo again without thinking of my afternoon at the beach with my sister and the kids."

Again the tears fell and the paparazzi clicked. To her credit Lizza ignored the shutterbugs, striding through the front door with her head held high and sliding into her sleek black machine with her dignity intact.

As the limo pulled into traffic, an uneasy feeling overtook me. Without knowing why, I was suddenly certain I'd let her go too soon. That I'd missed something. Or worse, that she'd skillfully danced around my probing.

Lizza had arrived with press hounds fawning over her. I dashed an email off to Noda and set a different sort of hound after her.

Noda's response was immediate and chilling—but came from an entirely new direction.

AROUND midnight, I was staring out my window at the Golden Gate Bridge silhouetted behind a wispy veil of fog when the phone rang. I spent a lot of time gazing at the bridge. It was a touchstone. Something in me vibrated to its unspoken promise, which was why I took the apartment, despite the cramped bedrooms and high rent.

The phone rang again. With Jenny upstairs, I had no need to worry about the noise.

"Brodie here."

"*Noda desu.* Got news," he said in Japanese.

Kunio Noda always spat out his words in short, clipped tones. Even over the telephone, Brodie Security's chief detective bristled with the heightened energy of a vigilant pit bull. He was as lovable as your garden-variety boulder, and talked considerably less. He had a flat face, shrewd eyes, and a barrel chest on a five-foot-six frame that people gave way to instinctively when he walked down the street. Below a hard, unforgiving forehead was a segmented eyebrow where a yakuza pimp had once connected with the edge of a blade in a failed attempt to carve up the detective's face. The resultant scar did not soften Noda's image. He could pass for a local thug if not for the eyes, which had some give in them.

I said, "What kind of news? About Lizza?"

He snorted. "*Chigau. Mondai da.*"

No. Trouble.

"Let's hear it."

"The linguist disappeared," he said, without wastage, as if his verbal efforts cost him in coin. On occasion, when he was feeling frisky, the terse detective strung together a dozen words.

Disappeared? A shiver of fear brushed the back of my neck. "You mean the whiz kid who had the kanji on his database?"

"Yeah."

"Where'd he go?"

"Soga-jujo."

The town connected with the kanji.

"Didn't you tell him to stay away?"

"*Mochiron,*" he snapped. Of course. "Went out there on his own anyway."

My questions grew urgent. "He call anyone after he got there?"

"His wife. Once."

"When?"

"Yesterday afternoon."

"From a cell phone?"

"No, a *ryokan*." From a Japanese inn. "When he checked in."

"You ring them?"

"First thing."

"And?" Sometimes extracting answers from Noda was like trying to coax a mole into sunlight.

"Went for a walk and never came back."

I cast a last line of hope. "Are you sure? You can't get any more harmless than a linguist."

"I'm sure."

"We're talking about a Waseda professor, dammit."

"A Waseda U professor openly asking around about a kanji linked to a multiple murder in San Francisco."

When the testy detective did muster his verbal faculties, he could be hard to argue with. He had voiced one of my worst fears: Japantown was too violent, too bold, to be a one-off event.

"You just may have a point."

"Yep." I heard him shuffling papers.

The case was growing stranger by the hour. The SFPD had nothing, I had nothing, and the street had nothing. A linguist at Waseda attaches a location to the kanji, I am shadowed by an unequivocal out-oftowner, then the linguist skips off to Soga-jujo and promptly vanishes, giving us in the process what could turn out to be our first lead.

The kanji and the linguist both pointed westward—toward Japan.

The crackle of papers on Noda's end rose to the pitch of heavy static.

I said, "Guess I'd better get over there. I'll call for a flight."

"Did that. Japan Airlines out at nine a.m."

I said, "There is a definite upside to dealing with a pro."

"Confirmation number's here somewhere." More papers were scrambled. "You got anything for me?"

I filled him in on my talks with Hara, Lizza, and Renna, then asked him to check Hara's movements around the time the mogul became interested in Teq QX, the high-tech chip company. As an afterthought, I threw in the story about my shadow and *his* vanishing act.

Noda came alive. "This alley, you've seen it?"

"Many times."

"Tell me."

I sketched the no-exit abutment of the three Victorians.

Noda grunted in displeasure. "You got a gun?"

"Yeah, why?"

"Carry it."

"I can handle myself. You know that."

"Brodie, you're fast and you're good. Pack the gun. Might give you a chance."

My chest tightened. "Want to give me a reason?"

"'Why' can wait until you get here. If you get here."

"If?"

"Don't play hero. Most people never see them coming."

A shudder shook my whole body. What the chief detective said felt right, even if I couldn't understand why.

"Get to Tokyo, Brodie. They don't kill in their own backyard."

"You got something?"

"What I'm *thinking* could get us killed. Get to Tokyo. You make it in one piece, then we'll talk."

He cut the connection.

CHAPTER 21

OGI'S cell phone chirped. He was at home, sipping a ten-year-old saké from Nara. Adjusting the collar of his indigo *samue*, a traditional Japanese men's garment with a kimono-like top and loose-fitting pants in the same rich blue hue, he reached for his handset. The three double magnums of 1900 Château Margaux from his recent Swiss excursion stood on a side table. Soon he would slot them into his wine cellar but for now he enjoyed watching the way soft light played off the bottles.

Ogi hit the encode button and said in Japanese, "Speak."

"It's time to take Brodie out."

Dermott was getting trigger-happy again. Pinching the bridge of his nose, Ogi said, "I doubt it. Tell me what happened."

Muscled, swift-footed, and unstoppable, Dermott was a brilliant fighting machine. His mental agility was another matter. Allowing him to lead his own team had been a logistical miscalculation that would not be repeated. Superb soldiers did not always yield good field commanders.

Now his top soldier shocked him for the second time in two days: "The art dealer made our tail. I put Gus on it."

Idiots! Patience, patience . . .

In their hometown of Soga-jujo, Gus Harper had been born Hideo Hattori. He was their finest shadow man, having studied with the Israeli Mossad for eighteen months by special arrangement. *Nobody* spotted him, just as nobody fended off Dermott, Ogi's best shooter and hand-to-hand combat man after Lawrence Casey. With the string of high-tech listening devices in place at Brodie's home and shop, tail jobs were kept to a minimum. Whenever possible, Ogi preferred his people to arrive ahead of time. The meet at the M&N with the police lieutenant was a prime example. A parabolic mike in a vacated office across the street captured the whole conversation. Someone must have fumbled the changeover if Brodie caught Gus in the act.

"Who missed their switch?" Ogi asked.

"No one. Brodie was smooth. Gus didn't know he was blown until the cops showed up."

Ogi was at once exasperated and intrigued. Not impossible, he thought, considering the art dealer's lineage. *Kaeru no ko wa kaeru.* The spawn of a frog is still a frog. *Yappari,* Jake Brodie's son had inherited a large measure of his father's talent, which he was squandering in his present occupation. Unless the art shop was a cover. Could it be? No, impossible. The kid inherited half of his father's business, so he dabbled. Posted a small brass plaque outside his pottery shop. But he had no training.

Though masked, Ogi's fury was unmistakable. "Keep your distance, then."

"If you say so. But the activity here is like the rush to Meiji Shrine at New Year's, sir. Cops, Lizza Hara, the Japanese press, calls from Tokyo."

Lizza Hara? Tokyo? Those would need checking. But later. For now, patience was essential, and Ogi possessed more than enough to counter Dermott's eternal edginess. Which is why so few men were qualified to lead. They panic or overreact. With the right motivation, willing trainees could be molded into precision killing machines, but leadership— that was another matter entirely. From his tenth year, Ogi had been groomed by his father, and his father by his grandfather. In fourteen generations, stretching back three hundred years to the general himself, the Ogi clan had built an invisible dynasty because leadership had been instilled from the earliest years. They came from hardy samurai stock. They were the shadow's shadow. The Ogi clan bred men of strategy, men of vision, men who knew the hearts of their fighters. Who knew when to yield and when to be ruthless. Utterly ruthless. Only a handful of outsiders had ever come close to penetrating Soga's core and each had been eliminated without fuss or trace when the time came. Dermott's excitability was premature, to say the least.

"Brodie's going through the motions for his police friend," Ogi said. "Calling in a Japan hand—the lieutenant's a little smarter than most. But so what? When all of the police leads dry up, Brodie's friend will be demoted and reassigned and Brodie will return to selling prints and pots."

"He's going to be in our hair for a while. He's flying to Tokyo."

"Why?"

"A phone call. He's been warned about us."

Dermott relayed the essence of the conversation about the missing linguist. Ogi listened, neither alarmed nor surprised. Brodie was shrewd enough to know who to ask, and reach out to someone clever enough to ferret out the kanji on short notice. Ogi recognized talent when he saw it. Maybe they'd have to deal with Brodie in the end after all. But for the moment, maintaining the status quo was paramount.

"They don't know much but I'll notify the village," Ogi said.

"Let me take him out."

"No. *Not* in San Francisco. The police would notice and our client would not appreciate the extra attention."

"Tokyo then? I can catch an earlier flight."

Ogi reminded himself that Dermott's eagerness was a trait he cultivated in his people. "You know that's taboo."

"Do you think he'll go to the village?"

"I don't know."

"Couldn't I just—"

"No. Your job is to watch. By now you must have uncovered some leverage."

Three thousand miles away, Dermott smiled for the first time.

"Yes, sir. He has a daughter."

Ogi could hear the smile in his loyal soldier's voice and returned the sentiment. "What could be better?"

*G*ET *to Tokyo, Brodie. They don't kill in their own backyard.*

That night I couldn't sleep. What did Noda know? And who the hell were "they"? I considered calling the grumpy detective back, but in a previous incarnation, Noda had taught ornery to mules. He wouldn't budge until I arrived in the Japanese capital. More telling, though, was his tone. Underneath the chief detective's professional calm, I discerned fear. Not for himself, but for me. Noda was as solid as they come. If he insisted I raise my guard, it would be unwise to ignore him.

But why?

Don't play hero. Most people never see them coming.

What kind of people couldn't you see? The story about the fleet-footed tail had triggered his warning, so at the very least we were talking about people who possessed the ability to vanish down dead-end alleys. And people who could murder a whole family without leaving behind the slightest trace—except an obscure calling card no one could read.

A shapeless anxiety enveloped me. How much danger was I in? Or Renna? Would any of this lead me to my wife's killer?

I walked to the window. A slow steady drizzle fell like a gauze curtain over the city. The Golden Gate stood proud and erect, a dusky apricot orange no less distinctive under the swaddling influence of the rain, but now its calming magic proved ineffective.

An unsettling dread trickled down my spine. *They were out there.* That much was certain. But between my earlier foraging in Asia after Mieko's death and the SFPD's distinct lack of progress since the J-town slaughter, I held more dead ends than I could stomach. And it frustrated me no end that I stood here clueless while every nerve in my body was telling me I needed to do something.

Anything.

I cast my thoughts back to the beginning. Japantown. Might be a good idea to take a last look before I left for Tokyo.

Throwing on a windbreaker, I slipped a Browning in my jacket pocket, then drove back to where it all began.

Bathed in a reptilian silver-blue moonlight, the streets of Japantown were deserted. Kanji, ancient and spiderlike, crawled over darkened storefronts.

Wishing the brick could talk, I slogged across the mall to the place where an entire family had been cut down. An oppressive hush reigned, as if the city itself mourned the Nakamuras.

All five victims were gunned down in seconds. Probably five or six. Seven, tops. Good groupings. No wasted shots. But there's always an order.

During the ride over, an upsurge in the prevailing winds had swept away the rain clouds, leaving behind brooding skies, a glittering wetness, and a concourse dotted with puddles.

Little remained to mark the kill spot once the blood had been scrubbed away. From a respectful distance, I stared at the scoured brickwork, and after a time I could make out where pools of vital fluids had worked their way into the cracks and fissures and left faint shadowy outlines.

Faint shadowy outlines. The phrase all but summed up the J-town case to date. The whole of the SFPD was grabbing at shadows and I had what? More shadows. When you pared things to the core, we had five bodies and a single kanji character. No fingerprints. No trace evidence. No witnesses. No suspects. The bodies gave us names, and the kanji gave us an AWOL linguist in a Japanese hick town more secluded than an Appalachian holler.

We had nothing.

Blowing out my breath in frustration, I trod the length of the block-long concourse. In the one hundred fifty yards from Denny's to the hotel, I counted a dozen darkened doorways, a few of them deep enough to hide in. The alley chosen by the killer was the best of a half dozen spots the mall had to offer. It was draped in absolute darkness. Streetlight couldn't penetrate it, moonlight fell prey to the balcony overhead, and the walls on either side headed off any ambient light.

What was an innocuous walkway in daylight became the perfect killing blind once the sun went down.

I strode down the chosen passage. It led to a public parking lot behind the shops. On a rise to the right, I saw shingled townhouses. A half dozen windows glowed even at this late hour. To the left, steeped in shadow, I could make out the ragged boxlike backs of the shops that lined Post Street.

A solid hide and an escape route emptying into a deserted parking lot. I tried to imagine it. . . .

It's past midnight and the family is giddy with excitement after the day's activities. Since jet lag still holds sway, they hoof it to the twenty-four-hour Denny's a block away. Like the last two evenings. It's a pattern, nearly a tradition.

Any way you look at it, it was an execution.

But what kind of execution?

When the Nakamuras head for the Denny's yet again, the shooter moves into action. He has laid the groundwork because he's stalked them for most of their trip. Maybe all of it. He retrieves his weapon, most likely in a nearby car, and sets up in the alleyway. He presses into the darkness and waits. He's confident, prepared. His weapon is cleaned and loaded, his escape route planned.

But no witnesses?

No.

The shooter would wear dark clothing. No, make that all-black attire. Black clothes, black shoes. Black ski mask donned once he settled into his hiding place. Nothing to draw notice as he walked from his car. Then nothing to separate him from the night once he stepped into the shadows.

Fiber's old. Doesn't think it's from the shooter.

No fiber. His garments don't shed. They are special, high-grade, perhaps made to order.

We got footprints in the passageway alongside the restaurant. Soft and padded and probably silent.

Add treadless shoes to the wardrobe. Carefully selected footwear. Nothing traceable. Possibly custom-made.

Well positioned, well dressed. Leading to a well-planned execution. But what kind? And why?

At the coffee shop the Nakamuras are enjoying their cake and sundaes. Chatting happily. The shooter double-checks his gun, his guise, his escape route. The post-midnight pedestrian traffic is sparse. Maybe young lovers meander by, hands clasped. They don't see him. Maybe a pair of drunken Japanese businessmen lurch into the mall from a bar on the next block, overloud voices breaking the night calm. They are oblivious to his presence.

The Nakamuras finish and leave the restaurant. They turn into the concourse, heading back to their rooms at the Miyako. The children are jacked up from the sugar rush, their voices echoing down the corridor of shuttered shopfronts. Their cheerfulness is infectious. Their banter alerts the shooter. The family can see their hotel sign. It's a two-minute walk. They feel content, safe. A chilly breeze reminds them of warm beds only a moment away. The cousin leads. The children follow languidly after. Then the parents.

Now! The shooter steps out behind them. The men are too far away to retaliate, too slow to turn in any event. They never hear the shots that take them down. The shooter levels his weapon, its heft rising smoothly in his hands. He locks on to the large male and pulls the trigger. The first target drops. He sweeps the gun left to right. A flick of the wrist, controlled bursts, and the parents fall. Husband, then wife. Blood is spraying, bodies are dropping. The shooter is in the groove, he feels the rhythm. Smooth trigger action, precise hits. No wasted time. No wasted ammunition. He swings back and catches the children. His control is spot-on. They are his. Completely.

Seven seconds, tops, and they are all dead. Is he a psycho? A local gang member on a rampage? A gun nut? An ex-military renegade?

He downs the men first, so he's a planner. Methodical. Clinical. Too clinical to be a gangbanger on a tear. Could still be an unhinged personality of some type, though. Or, as my witness in Kagoshima believed, a serial killer. Some of them were methodical to a fault, if newspaper accounts are to be believed. And they sometimes worked with a second person.

Is it a gun fanatic or ex–armed forces personnel with schizo tendencies, then? Someone who suffers from feelings of inadequacy? Inferiority?

If a well-trained former soldier or a neurotic would-be military hero wanted to prove something to the world, he would select a tougher target, not a family of tourists. No, the shooter is not suffering from minor mental anxieties. Borderline disorders are out. He's either a full-blown psychotic or nothing.

Were the killings racially motivated?

Every race crime I'd run across in South Central involved some form of degradation or disrespect. Beatings and murders both. Whether against black or white, Hispanic or Asian. But insults were absent, while the kanji suggested a Japanese connection of some sort.

Then why such an unlikely target? A helpless family is an empty conquest . . . unless . . . unless what?

Unless the target was chosen for him. Unless it is an assignment.

If so, then a clean takedown is a *must*. Which he does. With precision. Striking the two biggest threats first.

Does that eliminate the mentally deranged? No. Does it "prove" anything? Not quite. How about the escape?

The killer stashes the weapon in a bag of some sort. Dark or black to blend. A carry bag to disguise the shape of the gun. He retreats down the alley and emerges in the parking lot behind the mall. Immediately, he turns left and trails along in the overhanging shadows of the mall shops, then of those along Post Street. He moves swiftly but not so swiftly as to draw the glance of a pedestrian or someone uphill looking out their window.

The clock is ticking.

In ten seconds he's across the lot, a block away from the kill. The car is there. On the street somewhere. Parked under a tree no doubt, an urban canopy shielding the killer from private eyes uphill and the revealing rays of the streetlights overhead. He glides into a darkened vehicle, cabin light disengaged. The engine purrs. He shifts into drive and rolls off, headlights extinguished until he rounds the first corner.

Twenty seconds and counting. He's two blocks away, then three. A minute later he's six blocks removed and fully divorced from the crime scene, with only the moon overhead to witness his passage.

Japantown would have unfolded like that. Give or take a minor detail or two.

Still doesn't eliminate the all-out nutcases, though. And then it hit me: the tell is in the *lack* of evidence.

Dozens of apartments and renovated Victorians line the hillside overlooking J-town. All it would take was one peek from a window, one barking dog on a walk with its master, one late-night returnee. But we have nothing.

Nothing.

It didn't take a genius to choose the hunter's blind and escape route, but to drop all the targets and escape without being spotted or leaving a single sign of your presence suggests more than just professionalism. It suggests *supreme* professionalism.

No fingerprints, no trace evidence, no witnesses.

In the middle of a vibrant, densely populated urban district.

It wasn't a psycho. Disciplined or otherwise. Because the workmanship spoke of more than weapons competency. It screamed of some kind of rarefied training that encompassed camouflage, expert planning, and precision timing. The shoot wasn't the work of a dabbler or a talented amateur, either. Or a hopped-up gangbanger. Or an ex-military renegade. It was the work of a higher order, say special ops. Maybe higher.

Whatever that might be.

Renna and I had set our sights too low. The evidence was there in what we *couldn't* find. I spooled the idea out further and considered what followed the Japantown atrocity: *Homeboy . . . the "nonburglary" of my shop . . . the tail the rookie cops missed . . .*

All three events were clustered in the same thirty-six-hour time frame.

All three happened seemingly out of the blue.

All three exhibited similar elements of expertise.

They must be related? But how?

I'd gotten closest to Homeboy, yet no one other than Jenny and I had seen him. If we were the intended targets, then it was another case of no witnesses. A chill crawled up the back of my neck. And what was it Abers had said about the break-in? He called them "some seriously slick intruders."

Massaging my forehead, I sifted through it all one more time and the pattern hurtled into focus with devastating clarity: the string of incidents since Japantown was a containment maneuver.

Of me.

I was being tracked.

Watched.

Managed.

For some inexplicable reason they had hit my home, broken into my shop, tailed me. Classic stalk and contain. Homeboy's words weren't simple talk-back or slap-down. He *was* checking out Jenny.

Jenny.

For a moment I floundered. Then the rage built. My face grew hot. The veins along my neck bulged. And Noda's words echoed in my ears with new clarity:

Get to Tokyo, Brodie. They don't kill in their own backyard.

DAY 3

KINGBREAKER

| WASTED no time.

Standing in Japantown with cell phone in hand, I woke Renna from a sound sleep and fed him my interpretation of Noda's warning. It was all inference. Indirect linked impressions. But it felt right. Solid. I'd be foolish to ignore it. Especially with regard to my daughter.

Before I'd finished, Renna had devised a plan. For the days I stayed in Tokyo, Jenny would be sheltered in an FBI safe house the SFPD had access to on occasion. Renna would arrange for a policewoman to keep Jenny company during her stay. Sequestered in a secret location with a twenty-four-hour watch, Jenny would be secure and I could operate overseas without distraction. The precaution might turn out to be far-fetched, but I refused to come down on the wrong side of safe, and thankfully Renna was of like mind.

So, under cover of darkness, and with apologies to Kerry Lou and Lisa Meyers upstairs, I whisked Jenny off to the lieutenant's house. Renna emerged before I'd cut the motor.

Miriam led Jenny indoors for some hot chocolate, and Renna pulled me aside. He explained that an unmarked car would arrive in half an hour to take Jenny to the FBI house, with a second car as backup. For security reasons, it was best if I said good-bye now.

On the drive over I'd prepared Jenny for the move. I told her that she was going to stay at a "secret fun house." She could play games all day and watch as much television as she wanted—not the usual one hour a day—*but* in return she would have to skip summer school and avoid all contact with her friends while I was away in Japan, except Renna's kids, Christine and Joey, who would come to visit every other afternoon. Almost immediately she began tugging on my free arm, wanting to know why I always had to go away.

"I have to travel for my work, but I'll be back as soon as I can," I said, relieved she hadn't asked why I wanted her to stay at the fun house instead of Lisa's, as she usually did.

"How long is *soon*?"

"About a week."

Jenny wilted. "That's too long."

We went through a variation of this conversation before each trip. An answer of "two days" would have elicited the same response.

"Can't you stay? It's my summer vacation."

Knowing she was spinning out excuses, I gave her a broad grin and dragged her into my lap so she sat behind the wheel, looking out at the same rain-slicked blacktop I navigated.

"You want to drive?" I asked.

"Don't change the subject."

"You're too smart for me. I promise to make it as short as I can. And I'll call."

"And promise to be careful of China guys?"

"Promise."

Then she unveiled a mind-bender that rivaled the email Hara slung my way about the same time.

Running late, I rushed back to the apartment, finished packing, uploaded Hara's communiqué to my smartphone for later reading, and dashed out to SFO in the Cutlass. Abandoning the car in long-term parking, I boarded my JAL flight to Narita and settled in with a cup of green tea and airline rice crackers to read Hara's notes on his family.

Sent on CompTel Nippon digital stationery with the motto *Ears and Eyes to the Future* splashed across the top, the dispatch was filled with nothing more than names, addresses, basic vitals, and a short list of American acquaintances, everything the SFPD already had from the passports and the Tokyo Metropolitan Police Department. Forty-plus hours for a man who owns Japan's largest communications network and I get name, rank, and a PR blip.

I recognized the Japanese stall when I saw it. The immediate question was why? The ways of Japan were rarely linear and the whys often went unexplained. When the Great Hanshin Earthquake devastated Kobe in 1995 and hundreds were trapped in the rubble, a Swiss rescue team arrived at the scene from Europe sooner than Japan's own prime minister, who was an hour away by plane.

Why? Because career-minded public figures ducked for cover. In a country where good work is expected—but not praised—enemies pounce on any blunder, so pols and bureaucrats alike occupied themselves with minutiae surrounding the event. Inaction protected careers, my Japanese sources told me. If you didn't *instigate* anything, you couldn't be *blamed* for anything later.

So, on the heels of the quake, fires raged unchallenged. Pinned under rubble with the clock ticking, hundreds of Japanese died needlessly, and hundreds more lingered in makeshift aid centers watching their own vital signs weaken because medical supplies were locked up in red tape no bureaucrat was willing to stick his neck out to expedite. Doctors, volunteers, and key units of the Japan Self-Defense Forces sat on the sidelines, waiting in vain for deployment orders. With the phone lines down, I could only speculate about the well-being of Kiyoshi Tanaka, one of my elementary school buddies in Tokyo, who had married his high school sweetheart and taken a job in Kobe. Their only child, Shoji, was my godson.

Shoji and his mother died from a fire that overtook them fifteen hours after the quake, long after rescue workers could have pulled them from the wreckage, their neighbors told me, if the proper equipment had been deployed soon after the earthquake. Kiyoshi died waiting for a blood transfusion to be shipped from a nearby medical facility that was tied up in paperwork by the Ministry of Health and Welfare.

That was the classic Japanese stall on a grand scale. The world had seen it in various permutations before, saw it again with the Fukushima tsunami and nuclear disaster, and would see it in the future. As if that were not enough, life and death were secondary to the nation's face, all the more so when the citizenry in question was considered second-class, as the residents of Kobe were. The unspoken policy went like this: with the world watching, an unseemly rush to the scene suggested panic, immaturity, and weakness. It was also undignified, an even larger faux pas.

Turbulence jiggled my teacup in the hollow of the tray table. A glance outside showed a line of brooding storm clouds in the distance. Hara wasn't hiding from the disaster that was Japantown, but as usual he was going his own way. I wondered why. I had no clue, but since I would see the communications magnate in Tokyo, I gave up trying to unravel his behavior for now and returned my attention to the knotty problem Jenny had unveiled as she helped me steer the Cutlass down the deserted streets of San Francisco toward Renna's front door.

"This will keep you thinking about me," she had said.

"I always think about you, Jen."

"Well, now you'll think about me *more*."

"That's not possible," I said. "But what do you have for me?"

"A best-ever joke. What kind of bees give milk?"

"I don't know. What kind?"

"No, this is a best-ever. You have to guess."

"Okay, how about honeybees?"

"Wrong."

"Digger bees?"

"Nope."

"Great big old South American milk-pail bees."

"That's silly. No."

"Okay. What?"

She pouted. "No, no. It's a best-ever, so you have to think about it until you guess the answer. And if you're thinking about it, you're thinking about me. See?"

––––––––

I did see. And it hurt. My heart ached at such transparent need I couldn't quench, and I promised myself I'd spend more time with her on my return.

When the plane shuddered again, the flight attendants suddenly suspended activity, hurriedly returned their serving trolleys to the galley, and were strapping themselves in by the time the pilot made the requisite announcement of rough weather ahead.

If he only knew.

Wind chop plagued us all the way to Narita Airport. Even on firm ground, the turbulence continued unabated—they hit us twenty minutes after I pushed through the doors of Brodie Security.

TOKYO, 5:15 P.M.

G ET in here, Brodie."
    A large, thick-fingered hand forged from ten generations of
fishermen slapped me on the back as I arrived at Brodie Security. Shig
Narazaki, my late father's partner, was an early hire. Talented, shrewd,
and fast on his feet, he became indispensible and was soon helping Jake
expand the business. He'd also been the closest thing I'd had to an uncle
when I lived here as a child.

"What happened to you?" Narazaki asked. "You're as soggy as day-
old rice."

"George's limo service."

Narazaki grinned. "The Viper with the top off?"

"That's the picture," I said. "George figured he could outrun a summer shower."

Joji "George" Suzuki, a longtime friend and car aficionado, had
picked me up at the Narita airport in his latest acquisition—a 1992
Viper convertible, the inaugural year. Before leaving home, he'd removed the top to accommodate my luggage, exposing us to an unexpected downpour as we sped from the glittering rice fields of Chiba into
the urban chaos that was Tokyo. Fifty minutes later, his sleek machine
glided into the city's sprawl of high and low, old and new. Wherever you
looked, you saw tangled masses of narrow apartment blocks, needle-
shaped office buildings, and kanji-spotted storefronts.

But that was Tokyo. You either loved it or hated it. The city's architectural bouillabaisse fell somewhere between Singapore's neat and proper and the junkman's jamboree that was Hong Kong. Old wooden homes were overshadowed by towering apartment complexes alongside convenience stores in garish neon next to crumbling neighborhood ma-and-pa shops, maybe a tofu maker with gleaming steel vats in the kitchen and living quarters upstairs. But somehow the urban gumbo worked. Everything found a place and everyone knew where to go. The streets were clean, the people were courteous and purposeful, and the countless subway trains running underfoot were plentiful and on time.

Brodie Security plied its trade in a neglected byway of the fashionable Shibuya district in west-central Tokyo. Its offices were located four stories above a soba shop and a few doors down from a fourth-generation herbalist, whose wooden shack, a remnant of hard times after World War II, had begun to list southward. Inside, the business that Jake built was all activity. Twenty desks crammed into a forty-by-fifty-foot area, with private offices running along the back. A quick scan tallied fifteen bodies. I knew each of the full-time employees by name, as had my father. A long-haired Japanese youth I'd never met, either a freelancer or a new hire, had his head buried in the innards of one of our servers.

Jake's old partner chuckled. "Count on George. But the Viper's fast, no?"

"Very."

"That's the *big* picture. If I understood Noda's grunts, we have a lot to hash out."

"You understood."

He stared at my feet. "You wouldn't have to leak on our newly waxed floors if you berthed your boat with us."

Narazaki continued to push me to take a permanent chair at the agency in Tokyo and run the antiques business from afar. One day he would relinquish the reins of the company, but he felt obliged to stay on as long as I remained an untested quantity. "When you tracked down the Rikyu piece, you faced the yakuza and lived," he'd snipped, "but that was more about art and luck than anything else. Before you take up Jake's post, you need field training, otherwise you'll be as useless as spent moxa."

During my childhood, Narazaki had come for dinner twice a week, bringing gifts on the holidays. If my father were away on an assignment over the weekend, Uncle Shig would drop by and give me pointers on my karate and judo, sparring with me and then beaming with pleasure when I mastered a particularly complex move. The Brodies were his city family. In a common scenario for the extended family culture of Japan, he left for the big city while his own brood—a wife and three sons—stayed behind in the countryside, saddled with aging grandparents, rice paddies, and a fishing boat, run with a brother, and as they grew, the sons. Narazaki returned home four or five times a year for conjugal visits.

"It's a hard life," I said. "Maybe this will help."

I tossed him a bottle of Johnnie Walker and his fisherman's hands snatched it from the air with a quick sureness.

"Liquids from every pore, huh? Doesn't buy you fish bait in these waters, but wet or dry, it's good to see you."

"It's good to be back. Five minutes in my office after I dry off?"

"You got it."

Once ensconced behind the closed door of my father's old post, I drew the blinds, dipped into my suitcase, and slipped on a fresh shirt and jeans. Then I took a seat behind Jake's onetime desk.

I kept my workspace at Brodie Security pretty much the way my father had left it: same wooden desk, same bookshelves, and same paraphernalia. There was an old Japanese army short sword Jake had confiscated during his days as an MP, a three-hundred-year-old ceramic saké carafe presented to him when he opened Brodie Security, and a first-place trophy for marksmanship from his LAPD days, a talent the gene genie had graciously passed on to me and I'd polished on a shooting range in Los Angeles with my South Korean neighbor and his son.

To the bric-a-brac I'd added a photograph of Jenny and a certificate for Honorable Service in the Recovery of an Invaluable National Asset awarded by the Agency of Cultural Affairs for my role in unearthing the long-lost Rikyu masterpiece.

As a courtesy I placed a call to Hara's office to let him know I was in town, but caught him in a meeting, so I left a message with his secretary. A minute later Narazaki knocked, entered and, after shutting the door firmly behind him, he slapped me on the back again as I struggled to my feet.

"Damn good to see you, boy. You hooked your first big one. He check you out?"

Recalling the bodyguard's attack, I nodded solemnly. "That he did."

A wide grin split Narazaki's face. "The monster catches always do." Then the grin vanished and he grew serious. "You snagged this one yourself, but why don't you hand it off and let us reel her in?"

"Can't do that. I'm consulting for the SFPD."

Narazaki scratched the back of his head. "You could step away from the investigative work and just report our results."

"Not this time. Besides, you're the one who's always on me to get more involved in Brodie Security. This seems a good place to start."

Narazaki frowned. "I was thinking something smaller."

I shrugged. "Hara came to me."

He looked skeptical, then acquiesced. "True. If you're sure."

"I'm sure."

"All right, then I'll just have to give you plenty of backup. I've put Noda on point. He's the best we got. You work with him, you'll learn fast. Just keep your head down."

"Not a problem."

"And I want George to handle support duties. He's itching to do more than keep the books. That work for you?"

Last October, I'd suggested George take a part-time position at the firm. We needed new blood and George needed to step away from the family-owned multinational without straying too far from home. Both of us had been born in Tokyo in the same year to fathers who were best friends, their rapport one of those rare and fully ripened blends of East and West. After sharing some good childhood memories, we'd floundered in the rough waters of my parents' divorce before George came through in a pinch when I needed him, and our friendship was reawakened.

"Sounds good."

"Then it's settled. Noda leads and you'll assist, with George as non-critical support. Noda was a great friend of your father's. He'll show you the ropes in, ah, his own way."

Reopening the door, Narazaki called for Noda and George, and seconds later they drifted into the room. The chief detective dropped his bulldog frame into a chair with a thud, nodding in my direction. George settled in with genteel grace, crossing his legs. The slash cleaving Noda's eyebrow was prominent. The office grapevine had it that the pimp who attacked him never got a second chance with the knife. Noda relieved him of the weapon, then left a few scars of his own.

Narazaki said happily, "Japantown is the biggest case of the year. Rich, famous, plenty of headlines."

"We don't solve it, that'll make headlines too," Noda shot back.

In this land of oversize rose-colored glasses, the scowling detective was an advocate of the no-nonsense school of thought. The Japanese staff saw him as a crude but necessary evil. Americans found him refreshingly straightforward.

Narazaki, as the silver-haired patriarch, coddled his employees, pincushion personalities included. "Kei-kun, you old grouch," he said, referring to Noda in the affectionate form of a superior addressing an underling, "what would it take to make you happy?"

"To be happy is not in his nature," George said. "*I'd* take a hot springs trip to Tochigi and twenty-one-year-old twins."

Born into an aristocratic family with mounds of money and a lineage dating back to a powerful samurai clan, George sported an arrogance that stopped just short of intolerable. Echoing his status, today's wardrobe consisted of a light blue Givenchy sports coat, a starched white shirt with a faint marine stripe, and a mint-green Gucci necktie. For a Suzuki, he harbored something of a wild streak, which meant he occasionally went without a tie.

Ever tolerant, Narazaki chuckled. "Who wouldn't? Brodie, you want to bring us up-to-date?"

I sketched the murder scene in Japantown, then supplied a brief recap of the major events, including my suspicions about Homeboy, the break-in at my shop, and the connection between Mieko and the kanji. Last, I added my impressions on the seriousness of the threat.

Narazaki shifted in his seat. "Hold on. You sure it was the same kanji?"

"Positive."

He looked doubtful. "What are the chances?"

"It's the same," I insisted a little too loudly.

The room grew quiet and Narazaki became pensive. "I'm sorry, Brodie-kun. Let's hear the rest."

In closing, I mentioned the delicate balance we had to maintain with the SFPD, as well as my last-minute decision to spirit Jenny away. Expecting fireworks, I wound up the recital with the tail's vanishing act down the no-exit alley and nodded at Noda. When all eyes swiveled in the chief detective's direction, he merely grumbled incoherently about friends having run into some pros down in Soga-jujo a long time ago.

I grew still. What happened to *Get yourself to Tokyo, Brodie?*

Before I could decipher what lay beneath Noda's reticence, there was a soft tap on the door and Mari Kawasaki, our in-house computer expert, shuffled in. Fresh-faced and apple-cheeked, she wore pink farmer's overalls cascading over a blue denim shirt, and sported hair teased with orange highlights, this month's color. In the inexplicable way that many Japanese women have, her twenty-three years looked like sixteen and belied, in her case, an innate talent for all things software, Internet, and IT.

"What is it, Mari-chan?" Narazaki asked.

"I'm sorry to interrupt but I think you should, like, see this."

Confused, Narazaki asked, "Do we have a walk-in client?"

"No, it's the computer. And it looks like trouble."

Amid scraping chairs being pushed aside as we stood, Narazaki and I traded looks. Then Noda grumbled vague words under his breath that sounded suspiciously like "It's started."

CHAPTER 25

THE staff had gathered around a large computer console. As we approached, I saw commands scrolling up the screen unbidden. The seat before the monitor was unoccupied, the keyboard unmanned.

>Open system op.
>*Manager password?*
>TokyoBase.
>*Access denied. Manager password?*
>BrodieSecurityCentral.
>*Access denied. Manager password?*
>Open file: Correspondence—Tokyo

George squinted at the screen. "Isn't that the Brazilian affiliate's account?"

Eyes glued to the rising text, Mari gave a curt nod. "Yes. He's in their system and found some old passwords. He knows a third failure will lock him out, so he's shifted to joint correspondence."

Brodie Security shared a secured network with affiliate agencies in Asia, Europe, and the Americas. All accounts required passwords that were changed twice a week, and all messages between offices were encrypted. As we watched, the entrant called up a past-due notice, read and discarded it, then rummaged through a file of internal memos. The manner was probing, of someone unfamiliar with the system.

One of the detectives said, "Not good."

"Yeah," a long-haired Japanese man I'd never met chimed in.

"Techno scum. Don't recognize his op style, but he's absorbing your system at warp speed. Way uncool."

The speaker looked to be about Mari's age, maybe a year or two older.

"By that you mean a hacker?" I asked.

"What else? I give him eight to ten hours online before he cracks your network unless we act."

Narazaki said, "Brodie, let me introduce Toru Namikoshi. He's the outside contractor who set up our computer system."

We shook hands. Toru wore jeans and a black Bathing Ape T-shirt with a self-mocking retro design. A red bandanna above a thin, pale face kept his long wavy locks in check.

One of the women in the crowd said, "He's one of the top computer hands in Japan *and* Mari's boyfriend. Heavy input."

Rolling chuckles echoed through the office.

Toru looked sideways at me through a hank of hair that had slipped forward. "You know much about computers?"

"A little more than the next guy."

"I'm the next guy."

"A little less, then."

He gave me a wry smile and cocked an eye at the monitor. The hacker ran a search function, then opened and scanned several more files. Seeing an unguided cursor move across the screen made my skin crawl, and a sense of violation and outrage welled up inside me.

Noda asked, "Does he know we're watching?"

"No, this is a default monitor. It's inactive by system standards."

"How'd he get in?" I asked. "Don't you have firewalls?"

"The best, man. Dynamite watchdog software, too. But he signed on with a low-level password that gets him into the server space we share with our Brazilian counterpart. He only has a foot in the door, but he's trying to access our main server by inserting a Trojan horse program that'll capture other passwords as people log on. Once he has enough he'll gain access to our secure files."

From an overhead flat screen hanging on the far wall, a CNNJ announcer was reporting on the impressive exodus of Japanese banking executives heading to Zurich to attend the funeral of sixth-generation financier Christoph Spengler, who had tragically perished in a fire caused by a faulty electric socket in his wine cellar. "Spengler worked with all the megabanks in Japan, making frequent trips to Tokyo and Osaka. The bank's connection to Japan goes back to the late eighteen hundreds, when a Spengler representative based in Hong Kong paid a . . ."

"Mute that damn thing," Noda snapped, and one of the staff rushed over to the remote and turned off the sound.

In front of me, the computer screen went blank. Mari said, "He's gone."

"Good," Toru said. "I'll set up a node for his return."

Narazaki said, "Do you think he'll be back?"

"Yeah, man. Once they're in, they keep coming at you like a boomerang from hell. Usually it's just for the high of cruising a new data stream, but not this black hatter."

Toru flopped into the seat in front of the console, cracked his knuckles, and hit the up arrow on the keyboard, scrolling back through the hacker's commands. He stared at the initial string of commands for a long moment, then winced, touched a finger to his lips to silence us, and rose. Stepping behind the computer, he toyed with the wires, then curled his fingers around the main cable and traced it all the way to our central server in a back room. Without a word, we all followed him. Frowning, Toru pulled the blinking box away from the wall, crouched down, and ran his fingers over the length of cable behind the server, and finally allowed himself a private smile. He waved us closer.

We all shuffled forward and peered over Toru's shoulder. Along a vertical cable climbing from the junction box at the base of the wall to the innards of the server was a hairline slit about a quarter inch long.

Toru scribbled on a piece of paper: "Do you scan for listening devices?"

Narazaki read it and wrote, "Every morning."

More hurried scribbles followed:

"Anything today?"

"No."

"Recently?"

"Not since last February."

"Good," said Toru, breaking the silence. "No audio, then. See that?"

he asked, pointing to a slight swelling in the cord above the slit. "Some-one's spliced a capacitor into the line. Never seen these babies before but I've heard about 'em. Watch."

With a screwdriver he parted the plastic coating to reveal a small wafer less than an eighth of an inch in diameter.

"Cool, isn't she? State-of-the-art Dutch tech. Nobody gets them without big connections and bigger money. It copies and stores signals, then transmits them through your target's own computer system on command. It was the first sequence the hacker ran. You've been *trashed*."

Narazaki scratched his head. "You can't bug our system. We have safeguards."

Toru chuckled. "Most people can't. I can. These dudes did."

"How?"

"Righteous techno gear. No bullets, no spies, but they cop your moves, man."

"How come the sweep missed it?"

Toru's tone turned reverential. "It squirrels away information. Sucks it in and hoards it. Your run-of-the-mill bugs are miniature transmitters that send a continuous signal anti-bugging scanners home in on. This new tech sleeps during the day like a cockroach, soaking up the data. It only transmits when activated from an outside signal. That's why it crawled under your daily sweeps."

After the break-in at my shop, I'd finally called the security company to scan for wiretaps and bugs. They'd found nothing, but even they probably weren't equipped to search for devices of this sophistication.

Narazaki said, "So what's the damage?"

"Minimum, they've captured your email transmissions and any attached files. Keep vital info offline until Mari and I set up a mirror system to contain the hacker."

"Damage is already done," I said, recalling Noda's email to me about finding the kanji.

Toru's fingers hovered over the keyboard. "You want, we can scare him away."

"No, don't," Noda said.

Toru looked to Narazaki, who concurred. "Kei-kun is right. We'll have to play catch-up. Can you trace him to his base?"

Toru and Mari traded looks. "Sure. Give us a couple of days, maybe a week. But we'll need to go sumo. Charge ahead. Pound the mats."

Noda grunted. "Do whatever it takes."

Narazaki gave the go-ahead nod. Toru returned to his workstation and unzipped a leather-encased laptop. He connected some cords and fired up the machine. Then the wizardry began. Fingers flashed across the board, his concentration complete and unwavering. He typed and read and typed some more. We watched, fascinated, as his fingers punched keys and produced a fast-scrolling string of commands.

Three minutes later, he flicked a stray lock behind his ear. "Okay. I updated your ware so it'll retard his Trojan horse without his knowing it. Next, I'll shadow his op footprints and flame this byte skipper. Just need to snatch some cals and a z-pad."

Narazaki scowled. "Can you give that to me in plain language, son?"

Toru laughed. "First, we hamstring his password-trapping software. Then we follow his electronic footprints and fry his circuits. We need nourishment and a bed to crash on so we're set to handle him twenty-four/seven. What you real-time dudes call a stakeout. A stakeout in cyberspace."

Narazaki squinted at Toru. "Mari, get the kid whatever he wants. He finally said something this old man understands."

Another wave of chuckles rolled across the room.

Narazaki said, "One more thing. Can you track him so he can't see you? Electronically?"

"What I can do is provide a tetrapile of camouflage. We better think worst-case scenario because their gear is high-powered."

Noda growled under his breath. "How high?"

"High as it goes. These guys dangerous?"

"Very."

"How dangerous?"

Noda said, "Brodie?"

"Let's put it this way," I said. "Aside from slinging the high-tech bug and the hacker at us, they've killed nine people that we know of."

"Maybe ten," Noda said, thinking of the missing linguist.

The color drained from the keyboard jockey's face, and I turned back to the screen, pondering what I'd just witnessed. Not only had the people we were hunting slipped in and out of my apartment building and shop without tripping either of the commercial alarm systems, they'd also effortlessly compromised Brodie Security's state-of-the-art safeguards—which only underscored the conclusion I'd reached on my midnight revisit to Japantown.

These people were leagues beyond good. They were treacherous and thorough, guaranteeing, among other things, that they would come at us again soon enough. But from what angle?

WHEN Noda, Narazaki, and I regrouped in my office, we found George frowning at a freshly minted notice of some kind.

"More bad news," he said. "Not five minutes ago I received an email from Tokyo VIP Security. And get this, gentlemen—Yoshida, the second adult male body in Japantown, was not Hara's cousin. He was a bodyguard."

Before boarding my flight to Tokyo, I'd also dashed off an email requesting confirmation of Yoshida's identity. I finally remembered what I'd neglected to ask Lizza about—the cousin. Not only had Lizza not mentioned him, but well into the second day of the case, his vitals remained elusive, even in the Japanese press. Now we knew why.

Noda said, "Jiro Jo's place."

Narazaki nodded. "One of the best in the business. I've tried to lure him away for years. Good call, Brodie."

"Wish I'd made it before I took the job."

"No way you could. The only question is why the cover-up."

I didn't like being lied to, but I'd been warned that clients fudge their stories more often than accountants get creative with tax returns, and if we rejected everyone who spun half-truths, we'd have a thin case-load. Still, the lie left me uneasy.

"He's playing us," Noda said. "Money's too big for the work."

"His family was massacred, Kei-kun. Show some compassion."

"No reason grief should make us his favorite charity."

Noda's point struck a nerve. I'd faced Hara's grief head-on in San

Francisco. He was hurting, no doubt. But now he was stonewalling, which had me wondering what form his hurt would take.

George scoffed. "He's throwing money around to stir up some action. Big money does it all the time."

Another point. And George knew the territory. His father ran one of the largest private conglomerates in Japan.

Narazaki grew thoughtful. "Afraid I agree with Noda *and* George. So here's the plan—we follow in the wake at low throttle."

George's eyes glazed over. "In real Japanese, please."

"Simple. We stay close but not so close as to rock the boat. Hara's paid us good money, so we funnel some of it into covering our back. Noda, call the Ito brothers and ask them for a work-up on Hara's recent activities. Look for connections between Hara, Teq QX, this Soga village. Anything out of the ordinary. But *just* background. They're to be discreet and not ruffle Hara's feathers."

Noda acknowledged the order with a grunt.

"Good. Meanwhile, Brodie and Noda will head to Soga as planned. Stay alert, boys, and watch yourselves."

"I want to work the field this time," George said.

"You're support, George-kun. That's a step up."

"But I could contribute more. Accounts receivable won't gallop off in my absence."

With his business background, George filled a gap in accounting, but he was making the push I knew would come. It was only a matter of time. To set himself apart from the rest of the well-heeled Suzuki clan, he'd mastered karate, judo, and an ancient form of jujutsu. When I'd mentioned the Great Wall of Hara, a predatory gleam had flickered across my old friend's face.

"Noda, what do you think?" Narazaki asked.

Brodie Security's chief detective charged in with an abrupt *no*, once again stepping out of character. *What was going on here?*

George exploded. "Just no? That's it?"

Noda said, "*No* training, *no* basic skills, *no* field experience. I'll go alone. Don't need Brodie, either."

Narazaki said, "That's not a bad idea. I think—"

"I'm going," I said. "I promised Renna."

"And what about me?" George said. "How do I get any experience if I'm sitting in this dump all day? Let me drive down to Soga-jujo with Brodie. We can take the Viper."

Noda's look was dark and disturbing. "Not a good idea."

"I have no intention—"

Their argument was cut short by a knock. The door creaked open and Mari's orange highlights appeared once more. "An electronic money transfer was, like, sent to our bank account moments ago from Mr. Hara. I thought you'd want to see the notice."

Narazaki stretched a hand out and Mari passed it over. Looking at the sheet, Narazaki frowned before handing it around. Hara had just deposited the balance of our fee.

I searched my memory for a sensible explanation but came up blank. "It's far too early for another payment. He left a check with me in San Francisco."

Noda frowned. "Great. Another satisfied customer. That can't be good."

CHAPTER 27

RIE Mori, the linguist's wife, lived behind Sengakuji, the temple where the forty-seven *ronin* were laid to rest in 1703. Three centuries on, visitors still lit incense in their honor, and clouds of scented smoke still hovered above their tombstones before drifting over the temple walls into the surrounding neighborhoods, a reminder that past treachery was not so far removed.

Half a block short of the house, Noda eased in behind a brown Mazda land cruiser and cut the engine. We sat silently for several minutes, in darkness. Neither of us relished the chore ahead, but it needed doing in case there was something to add to our meager stash of evidence.

"Quiet tonight," Noda said.

"Too quiet."

The detective grunted. "Like a slap in the face."

My stomach knotted.

As we gazed through the moonless night at the linguist's house, blue-gray incense trails wafted across our windshield. In 1701, when a corrupt shogunate official taunted the young Lord Asano by demanding a bribe before teaching him the correct protocol to receive an envoy from the emperor, Asano drew his sword in anger. Although he didn't strike the shogunal bureaucrat, the law of the day automatically classified even an implied threat against a government representative as treason, so Asano, a popular but inexperienced leader, received the death sentence. And with it the several hundred samurai in his employ lost their lord and livelihood and were relegated by a single act to a life of hardship as masterless samurai, or ronin.

Angered by the official's callousness, the loyal forty-seven bided their time for two years while shogun spies monitored their movements, then one night stormed the bureaucrat's luxurious residence and claimed his head. After the ronin marched across town to deliver their trophy to their master's grave, the samurai became overnight heroes for their courageous strike against an unjust authority in an increasingly corrupt age.

Which was bad news for the shogun.

He was trapped.

His emissary had grossly abused the power of office. But first Asano, and now his former retainers, had attacked the shogunate.

So, in a peculiarly Japanese compromise, the shogun praised the virtue of the loyal samurai and accorded them the right to honorary warriors' deaths rather than execution like common criminals for their treasonous strike.

Even today, people revere the faithful forty-seven for their stand against overbearing authority. And with good reason. After the fall of the shogunate in 1868, adept samurai autocrats stepped from one bureaucracy to the next, perhaps why present-day ministry officials enjoy a similar lock over the average Japanese citizen. Modern Japanese life is riddled with mind-numbing regulations and bureaucratic tollgates at every turn.

Noda watched a wisp of incense creep across our windshield. "You ready?"

"Your call."

"Remember, you're taking the lead."

"I remember."

"You can't handle this, no way you're going to Soga."

"Got it."

"So?"

"Let's do it."

We stepped into the night and approached the house, a newly built two-story with a fresh coat of white paint. A short walkway hedged with poppies led to a door of varnished wood with a brass knocker in the shape of a cherry blossom. I rapped the knocker against its metal pad and we soon heard the shuffling of slippered feet.

The door swung open and Rie Mori invited us in. We abandoned our shoes for guest slippers waiting on an elevated landing, then Mrs. Mori guided us past a small kitchen into a parlor. We sat on a white sofa. She took up a position on a matching chair and poured green tea for both of us.

Noda cleared his throat and said, "This is Mr. Brodie. I mentioned him on the phone." Then he sat back and green-lighted me with a nod that said *Let's see what you got,* narrowed eyes signaling his doubt.

Mrs. Mori bowed a second time. She had a long nose with a high bridge and an extended jawbone that gave her a horsey look you sometimes saw in old woodblock prints. For our visit, Rie Mori wore a beige linen skirt and a light brown silk blouse with flowers in a faint plum tone. Her hair was black and dull and pulled back with a dark brown band. A black cord cinched her waist, accentuating a soft swell underneath.

"We're sorry to barge in on you on a Saturday night," I said.

"Anything to help," she said in a curiously flat voice.

The apartment was appointed with sparkling appliances and pristine living room furniture. Nothing had the markings of wear. Japanese newlyweds start their life together immersed in newness. On the shelves of polished cedar cabinetry were a stereo, TV, digital recorder, and laptop computer. All new. The lowest shelf held books and photo albums. On the spines of the albums someone had painstakingly delineated the contents in charmingly naïve English lettering: OUR WEDDING, OUR HAWAIIAN HONEYMOON, OUR HOUSE. Women's magazines were fanned out on the coffee table in front of us.

"Could you tell us when you last spoke to your husband?" I asked.

"The day he went down there."

"When he checked into the ryokan?"

"Yes."

"He called at what time?"

"A little after three."

"You talked about what?"

She ran her hands over her lap to smooth out her skirt. "His trip on the bullet train, the village, his excitement."

"His excitement?"

"After he spoke with Mr. Noda, he discovered that the kanji was not in any dictionary. He'd always assumed it was."

"How did he happen to have it on his database?"

"He found it in an old communiqué."

"How can you be so sure?"

"I update my husband's database in my spare time, although I've fallen behind of late." Her fingers hovered over the slight roundness of her stomach.

"Did you input this kanji?"

"Yes."

"So you saw the source?"

"Yes. It was a memo from a minor *daimyo* warrior lord to a person of standing in the Soga-jujo area announcing an impending visit. A typical letter of the day. The writing was difficult to decipher in places. Until Mr. Noda showed up with his sample, my husband wasn't sure he had transcribed the kanji correctly."

"Do you have the document?"

"Oh, no. It was simply one of thousands of routine letters my husband habitually sifted through. Nothing of scholarly importance itself."

"So he didn't know what the kanji meant?"

"No. Only that it referred to something in Soga-jujo."

"Would you have a picture of your husband?"

"I've prepared one. This is the most recent photograph I have. It was taken two months ago."

Mrs. Mori handed me a color snapshot. In it, she stood beside a handsome man with fine black hair swept back over a firm brow. Ichiro Mori looked beyond the camera lens with the expectant air of someone planning to rush out into the world and bring it down with a full-body tackle.

"Is there anything else you can tell us?"

"I don't think so. Nothing has changed."

"We will find him or the men who . . . took him."

Mrs. Mori inclined her head with quiet grace. "I'm sure you'll do your best, but I draw comfort in knowing that in his last days my husband was in pursuit of what he enjoyed most in this world. Our time, if over, was brief, but enough."

Her eyes met mine, then Noda's.

Brief, but enough. The phrase fluttered painfully in my chest.

From her perch on the edge of the chair, Mrs. Mori bowed deeply to us. "From the bottom of my heart, I thank you both for your concern. I know you'll do what you can, but understand that my husband was his own master. He was that way in college, and had been that way ever since."

Was. Had.

In her eyes, I saw forgiveness for all we might have done, or imagined we had done, to bring her husband to his end, whatever it might turn out to be. I saw a deep serenity. A profound otherworldly knowing. She lived at once in the present and already beyond her husband's disappearance, and would keep him alive in her own way.

Under her artless gaze, Noda grunted and blinked.

"Thank you for coming, both of you," Rie Mori said.

"Good-bye, Mrs. Mori," I said. "We'll do everything we can."

She inclined her head once more. "It will be as it will be."

Noda stood and bowed deeply. I followed suit. Then we left, stunned by our brief audience. In a few modest words, Mrs. Mori had offered release without hesitation, bitterness, or blame.

As we walked down the poppy-lined path to the car, I reminded myself that there were those who lived on higher planes, and I couldn't help but make a comparison between the Moris' life and my own. After Mieko's death, I'd longed for one last chance to say all the things to her I hadn't found the time to say while she was alive. To this day, late at night, misgivings kept me from a sound sleep more often than I liked to admit. The Moris, on the other hand, had lived their life fully, a day at a time. Rie Mori was at peace because they had told each other all those things Mieko and I had left unspoken. And what they had not shared directly, she intuited with uncommon insight.

As Noda pulled away from the curb, he stomped on the gas pedal, mumbling incoherently as we tore past Sengakuji temple and the graves of the forty-seven ronin.

With newfound clarity, I suddenly understood their driving compulsion to avenge their lord.

A N insistent ringing echoed in the near distance as I padded down the hotel's carpeted hall toward my room. I covered the last ten yards in a rush, hurriedly slipped my key in the lock, and charged toward the sound, dropping my suitcase en route and flicking on the light as I went to reveal a Western-style room with a mauve carpet, a bedspread in a cherry pattern, and a papered shoji grid over the windows.

Lunging for the receiver, I offered a breathless hello, my thoughts drifting to a scene eight years earlier . . . *Mieko with a dreamy smile . . . a swelling midriff . . . glowing cheeks . . . anticipation in her eyes.* Rie Mori glowed with the same anticipation. She was expecting. With her husband nowhere to be found.

"Brodie?" my art dealer friend from Kyoto said. "I'm glad I finally reached you."

"Takahashi? How'd you find me?"

"A young woman at your office. She giggled some."

Mari and Toru on their sleepover. The cyber stakeout.

Takahashi said, "Welcome back to the *civilized* hemisphere."

"Only by a couple thousand years."

"Some of us do count. Will we have the honor of your company in Kyoto this trip?"

"Unlikely, I'm sorry to say."

Along with neighboring Nara, Kyoto ranked among my favorite Japanese cities. A visit to Takahashi's guaranteed not only a preview of his latest acquisitions, most of them shining examples of Japanese art, but several excellent meals at five-star hideaways and a stroll through one of the city's more beautifully groomed temple gardens. A garden enthusiast and amateur shutterbug, he would snap photographs while waxing poetic on the subtle and ingenious design elements concocted by renowned Japanese landscapers of centuries past.

The art dealer shifted in his seat. "Disappointing, but plainly you have more pressing matters."

My ears perked up. "You have something new, then?"

"Yes. You can add this to our earlier discussion: I believe the kanji to be symbolic."

"So you've deciphered it?"

"After a fashion. The experts I discussed the problem with agreed that my final interpretation was the best of a bad lot. From a connoisseur's perspective, the composition is clumsy and amateurish, so I dropped the idea of an artistic approach and attacked the meaning from the most rudimentary angle. What emerged was irresistible in a morbid sort of way."

"How so?"

"Well, if we give the upper element some weight and read it literally, what do you have?"

"*Ruler* or *king*. Maybe *royalty*."

"Exactly. And if we read the lower section as a cohesive element?"

"You mean as *kowasu*? *Destroy*?"

"Yes. *Break, smash, obliterate.* Does that suggest anything to you?"

"No. Should it?"

"Not a real word, no. But to a cruder mind, possibilities present themselves."

"Such as?"

"The intended pronunciation is unclear, but the image is potent. The closest I can find in your English is the mirror image of the word *kingmaker*."

"Mirror image?"

"Yes. Not a builder, but a destroyer. A king*breaker*, if you will."

"Do you have any idea what it means?"

"None whatsoever."

"You found no past references at all?"

"None. But tell me, does my interpretation fit the situation?"

"I'm not sure. What does it imply?"

"Well, again, it suggests violence, but on a larger scale. It suggests the tearing down of powerful institutions or powerful men."

Hara.

"It fits," I said.

Takahashi fell into a troubled silence. "You worry me, Brodie-san. You're in over your head again, aren't you?"

"Again?"

"Need I remind you that last fall you were dodging the yakuza and death threats? Well, this portends to be worse."

My knuckles tightened on the receiver. Somewhere inside the device I heard plastic crack. *Death threat. Damn.* Takahashi had been ringing up his contacts throughout the country, asking about the same kanji that led to the linguist's disappearance. It never occurred to me to warn my dealer friend after Mori vanished in Soga.

"Who did you talk to about this?"

"Four or five experts. Historians, linguists, scholars. Why?"

"You have to go back to each one of them and swear them to secrecy. Under no circumstances are they to make any further inquiries."

"These are men I trust, Brodie-san. I've dealt with them for years—always in the strictest confidence."

"Make them *promise*," I urged.

"I risk offending them with such talk."

"Better a bruised ego than—"

"Than what? What *aren't* you telling me?"

"People are dying, Takahashi-san, and we don't know why."

OGI glanced fondly at the gleaming metallic garrote he had designed. He delighted in its natural arc and silvery sparkle. To maintain the fine cutting edge on the inside curve, he had adapted a sushi chef's sharpening stone for the first phase of the shaping process, then a gem cutter's delicate file and eyepiece for a final honing of the nearly invisible, double-sided cutting edge he sought. The customized blade trimmed the kill time from twelve seconds to seven, a 42 percent improvement that brought him undreamed-of results. Where once the victim had a brief moment in which to struggle and strike a counterblow, now the neck was severed before the target had any inkling of an attack. For a man of seventy-two who still relished the kill, the five trimmed seconds were vital. In its improved form, the garrote offered the perfect solution for a proud fighter of samurai lineage desiring to keep his hand in.

But his prized blade needed sharpening. Disengaging the wire from its wooden handles, Ogi passed each end through the jaws of a vise and drew the thread taut. Six men and three women had succumbed to the sleek blade since he took up the weapon on his sixty-fifth birthday, seven years ago. Unfortunately, he was forced to use his toy sparingly, as near decapitation left a distinctive impression with the authorities. Ironically, it was for this same reason that the garrote endeared itself to him. The steel wire's immediacy rivaled that of every other killing tool he had ever employed. By necessity, the razor-sharp blade brought him to within a hair's breadth of his victims, and the power he felt as he claimed their lives rejuvenated his aging warrior soul.

His phone rang. Reluctantly, Ogi stepped away from his workbench and dug out the secure cell phone from the folds of his samue. "Ken Sheng," he said.

"Brodie and Noda are headed down to Soga."

"How fortunate. We'll give the Iroha team a workout. Make it a priority clear. I want them eliminated."

"Sir?"

"You heard me."

The man on the other end spoke with a respectful hesitation. "I've been instructed by our mutual acquaintance to let them pass unharmed."

"I'm overriding that. Full weapons and camouflage."

Late last night, after Dermott's second call, Ogi had decided to remove the pesky art dealer if he should be foolish enough to present himself gift-wrapped at the gate.

"Are you sure? My orders were quite firm."

"Are you questioning me?"

A fearful intake of breath. "No, sir."

"Good. Then proceed."

"Any special disposal instructions?"

"Generic will do."

Surrounded by undulating waves of forested mountains in every direction, the isolated valley in which Soga rested offered dozens of sites where bodies could be buried—and stayed buried—for centuries.

"As you wish, sir."

"And let's keep this between ourselves. Do I make myself clear?"

"Thoroughly, sir."

Ogi hung up and returned to the task at hand. A pang of regret tugged at him as he considered Brodie's demise. Earlier, he had mulled over the idea of killing Jake Brodie's son himself. After dispatching a tenth victim—an admirable milestone for such a piece of equipment—he planned to frame the weapon in his den, and Brodie would have made a worthy subject for such a milestone. Unfortunately, Ogi wasn't in Japan at the moment, so he forced himself to put personal ambition aside for the greater good of their client. By this time tomorrow, Jake Brodie's only offspring would be lying beneath a carpet of summer ferns deep in the Japanese countryside.

DAY 4

THE VILLAGE

O N Sunday, George and I piled into his Dodge Viper, sans top, and a mere two hours later, after breaking most of the laws on the books, we found ourselves two hundred miles west of Tokyo, cruising down the highway toward the village where the linguist had vanished.

"You are part owner of Brodie Security," George shouted over the steroid horsepower of the Viper's roar. "There's no need for you to tolerate him. You ought to let him go."

"Are you mad?" I shouted back. "Noda found the kanji in a single day."

"But he undermines your authority. Think how it *looks*."

"Only in your imagination. Besides, he's too good."

Against Noda's growling protestations, George had succeeded in nosing his way further into the Japantown case by pressing the softhearted Narazaki. But as the summer sun radiated off the swoops of the Viper's apple-red exterior and scorched the black leather interior, I was deep in thought about an unsettling early-morning conversation I'd had with the seasoned detective in the soba shop on the first floor of our building.

———

Sitting at a varnished pine table, Noda nodded at the empty wooden bench across from him, dipped a half dozen strands of soba in sauce, and lifted them to his lips. The brown pasta traveled from plate to sauce to palate and disappeared with that swiftness the Japanese are able to muster for noodles. Murata Soba officially opened at 11:30 a.m., but served Noda any time Chef Naoki Murata was on duty.

With grim determination, I slid in opposite him and posed the question that had troubled me all night. "Why didn't you speak up at the meeting yesterday?"

Before he could answer, the kitchen door flew open and the master of the shop strutted in. Murata's kitchen whites were starched and spotless, the apron at his waist drawn taut. His face was round and jolly, with an underlying tiredness that showed itself in the clustered wrinkles at the corners of his eyes and mouth when he smiled.

"Oh, it's you, Brodie-san," he said. "Wondered why no one came back to the kitchen. Mornings we get only deliveries. Deliveries and Noda."

His voice softened when the chief detective's name passed his lips.

I said, "How's Junko?"

"Doing well. She finishes dental assistant training next spring." His plump red cheeks parted in a broad smile. "You want something?"

"No thanks."

"You sure? No trouble."

"Maybe next time."

"Holler if you change your mind. I'll be in the kitchen preparing for the lunch crowd."

He snapped his apron strings and breezed back the way he'd come. In a moment we heard the soft, even rhythm of large grinding stones cracking grain for his handmade noodles.

Noda had come into a lifetime supply of soba after Murata's daughter, Junko, had dipped a toe into Tokyo's darker waters and been sucked under. She had signed up for a telephone dating service and earned a thousand dollars in easy money for a few afternoons' work stroking the egos of lonely old men. "Just egos," as she put it. Promised more if she would upgrade her wardrobe, she borrowed money from the service, whose manager encouraged her to buy Chanel and Dior and Versace, first one a week, then two, until she grew accustomed to the feel of fine fabric against her skin. When he suggested pearls and gold to complement her upwardly mobile clothing profile, she accepted a fistful of crisp new bills. As an afterthought, he presented her with a state-of-the-art monogrammed cell phone to add a touch of elegance when she called her friends from a nightclub or a department store. Her beauty and coy smiles brought more easy income, but the bills on all three fronts mounted up faster than the assignments came in.

One morning, Junko woke to an insistent pounding on her front door. The monthly 10-percent interest on her $30,000 new lifestyle had ballooned to $9,000 and was demanding attention. Which is when the manager stopped cooing and offered Junko a choice: a private interview with a yakuza friend of his who slashed pretty young faces, or a plush apartment near the Ginza suitable for entertainment more involved than the verbal stroking of attention-starved men. Too ashamed to admit her folly to her parents, Junko vanished into the throbbing hive of Tokyo's water trade. Once Murata lost contact with his daughter, he approached Noda. With 35 million people in the greater Tokyo area, it took Noda five weeks to locate Junko, after which he confronted her yakuza pimp, torched the apartment, and brought her home with all strings severed.

The detective's bisected eyebrow dated from that encounter, as did the soba chef's gratitude.

With Murata once more out of earshot, I repeated the question. "Why didn't you tell everyone what you told me? About the danger you warned me about in San Francisco?"

"Might discourage them."

"They're pros."

"This is different."

"How?"

"They've never run up against a group like this before."

"Have you?"

He shook his head. "Only heard about them."

"You think it's the same guys?"

"Unless someone only wants us to think it's them."

"And we'll know if we go down there and they pay us some attention?"

"Yep."

In one sinuous motion, his chopsticks snatched more noodles, dipped them in sauce, and shoveled them into his mouth. A loud intake and the soba vanished.

"What kind of attention?"

"Won't be a dance party."

The laconic detective was holding out again. "What else?"

"Some friends ran into trouble down there."

"When?"

"About five years ago."

"And?"

"It was dark."

"I take it it didn't go well."

He studied my face. *"Shinshutsu-kibotsu."*

My heart plummeted. The expression translated roughly as "Only when God comes out does the devil slink away." Noda was talking about phantoms. An elusive, undesirable presence. As in Japantown. As in the superstitions swamping the case at the SFPD.

"How bad?" I asked.

A flicker of pain came and went. Understanding dawned. "Which is why you tried to discourage George?"

He grunted.

"You didn't want to watch your back and his?"

Another grunt. "One's enough."

Meaning me. It would take a lot to fill Jake's shoes. In my teens I'd soaked up every scrap of information I ran across at Brodie Security, turning it all over in endless fascination. I'd served an apprenticeship of sorts during those five years, and even though my current tenure at the firm was short, Japantown filled me with a new determination to master the game, regardless of the learning curve.

In spite of that, my father's best man in the field had just expressed doubts about my ability, though he seemed on the verge of giving me a chance. Unless I pushed him the wrong way.

I asked, "But George persuaded you too?"

Noda shook his head. "No, Shig. I'll keep George behind with the second car."

"And my role?"

"In his prime, Jake was the best I've ever seen."

"Better than you?"

"Yeah."

"How?"

"Good thinker, good fighter. Quick on his feet."

"What's that have to do with me?"

"You're street smart and fast like Jake."

"So you have no problem with me?"

"I do. But you handled the interview well."

"Hardly the same thing."

He shrugged. "You controlled the situation. Yourself. At the wrong time emotions can get you killed."

"Was I good enough to convince Narazaki?"

"No."

"But?"

"I'm lead. It's your case. Be good for you. An acid test."

I didn't like the sound of that.

"Time to go," Noda said.

Without warning, he stood and turned away, but not before I caught another shadow cross his face. Brodie Security's chief detective was a stoic's stoic, and fearless. Seeing another flicker of pain brush his features raised alarm bells.

There was more.

And I wanted it.

I said, "You sure you're not overreacting?"

"Hope I am."

"Can't be all bad. They made it back, right?"

The scar above his eye flared. "One of them did. Two of them didn't."

ALONG a deserted stretch of road two miles from Soga-jujo, George palmed the steering wheel of the Viper and coasted into a turnout, edging to within three inches of a silver Nissan Bluebird. Inside the Bluebird, Noda leafed through the afternoon edition of the *Yomiuri News,* quite comfortable in the air-conditioned confines of his rent-a-car. When the chief detective rolled down his window, a welcome blast of cold air swept past.

"This the place?" George asked.

Noda nodded. "Other side of the mountain."

George glanced around pointedly. Rice fields carpeted the view in every direction. Fifty yards down the road was a solitary thatched-roof farmhouse with a small rice-planting combine parked out front. Neither the home nor the surrounding fields exhibited any signs of life.

"I should think the place a bit backward," George said. "Folksy and quaint, but hardly menacing. Unless you fear ambush by backhoe."

"The deal was, you sit with the car."

"And I submit gracefully—this time. To show you there's no hard feelings, my offer stands. Take the Viper into town. You'll look *good.*"

Noda shrugged. "As long as you stay put."

"Why?"

"After dark we'll need you here, close to the river."

Two hundred yards below the road, between slender bands of cedar and pine, cool running water glittered in the orange-red rays of the setting sun. Road maps showed the river running through a steep gorge straight out of Soga Valley. Vehicles were forced to circle around to an access road over the mountain, but the river ran straight.

"A deal. Are you expecting trouble?"

"Nen ni wa nen o ireyo," the chief detective replied, quoting an old Japanese expression that translated as *Pile caution on caution.*

George's eyes sparkled. "Will I see some action?"

Noda frowned. "Only if our luck's bad."

"Well, I'm ready."

"'Course," said Noda dryly, "if our luck's *real* bad, you'll never see what hit you."

Twenty minutes later, Noda and I crested the mountain approach to the village.

From our elevated perch, we looked down on Soga-jujo—a forgotten town in a forgotten valley of a nearly forgotten prefecture. We saw a harmless-looking cluster of traditional wooden homes with enchanting blue-tiled roofs on one side of the road, and on the other lush green rice paddies stretching to the far end of a fertile basin.

Pastoral tranquility *à la japonais.*

As I shifted into low gear for our descent, pressure mounted in my chest. I thought about how an unseen force thousands of miles away had reached out and slaughtered an entire family in San Francisco. The same force had caused me to cleave my daughter from friends and school and all that she cherished. Four days ago, I was living in ignorance of such a force. Now, connecting the dots had brought me to this distant outpost. To make matters worse, I hadn't talked to Jenny yet, as Renna hadn't been able to set up a safe protocol with the FBI liaison.

Road kill spotted the blacktop as we navigated the downhill switchbacks into the valley. After the third snake I said, "Think we'll find the linguist?"

Noda winced as if he'd taken a blow to the gut. I knew how he felt. Chances were the overeager boy wonder was dead. He'd disregarded Noda's warning to stay away. We might never discover whether professional ambition or youthful curiosity led him to ignore the chief detective's words of caution, but knowing could not disguise the fact that Noda, at my request, had started Ichiro Mori down a road of no return.

The same one we traveled now.

I said. "I just thought that maybe—"

Noda bristled with anger. "Yeah, and maybe the world's made of rice balls and mother's miso."

We took the rest of the descent in silence. At the valley floor, we pulled up at a crossroad. Thirty yards on, the main avenue was barricaded with sawhorses and striped tents. Beyond the barricade, women wrapped in blue-and-white summer kimonos flitted by. Children sang and skipped and played jump rope. The next instant, strings of red and yellow festival lanterns flickered to life.

The village was gearing up for Obon, the Festival of the Dead.

"*I* RASSHAIMASE,*" the *okami-san*, mistress of the inn, sang out from the entrance as we stepped from the car. Welcome. "You must be Mr. Johnson, and you are Mr. Kuroda, the one who called?"

She wore a powder-blue workaday kimono, her hair pinned up in elegant artlessness. From the entryway, she beckoned us with a delicate hand gesture to shed our street shoes for the comfort of the inn's cushioned slippers.

Doubt assailed me. The okami-san looked enchanting and perfectly harmless. Could someone like this live side by side with the kind of men capable of planning Japantown?

Our hostess said, "It's always a pleasure to welcome foreigners, though I cannot speak a second language myself. Can you speak Japanese?"

"A little," I said, returning the expected reply.

"What a wonderful accent you have. Very Tokyo."

Noda turned his attention to the wattle-and-daub walls with exaggerated interest, and the innkeeper took the hint. She smiled engagingly and showed us to our quarters, a ten-mat room with shoji screens at the window and a short-legged table in the center. With the shoji parted, the view gave out onto a bamboo thicket at the back of the lodge. The sound of water cascading over rock reached our ears.

Tucking her cotton kimono under, the innkeeper knelt on one of the square throw cushions around the table and poured tea for both of us, then produced a pen and a registration card from the folds of her kimono. Noda and I set our bags in a corner and joined her.

After filling in the registration form, I slid it across the table with the photograph of the linguist and his wife. "Would you mind taking a look at this?"

"*Koko ni tomatta no wa wakatterun da,*" Noda said in his gruff drawl. *He stayed here. We know that much.*

The matron glanced at the snapshot obliquely. "I remember him. Mr. Mori. Also from Tokyo."

"Did he say where he was going?" Noda asked.

"No."

"Mention meeting anyone?"

"No."

"Could you recommend someone to talk to?"

"I am sorry, no."

"Can you tell us anything," Noda said, "besides 'no'?"

I nudged the photo forward. "That's his wife in the picture. Twenty-three years old."

"I'm sorry."

Regret and resignation resonated in her voice as if she were apologizing for a continually wayward relative.

Gently, I asked, "Did he return?"

"No."

With each negative reply, her head dropped a notch and my hope dimmed further. We could no longer see her expression, but at the edge of her hair the skin was pale and the corners of her eyes had narrowed. She was hiding something.

I said, "Has this ever happened before?"

Eschewing eye contact, the okami-san cast a final glance at the photograph. "What I wonder is if the wife is as kind as she looks."

"More than kind," I said. "That is the glow of a newlywed and a mother-to-be."

"I see."

The innkeeper reached for the pot of tea, a white-glazed vessel decorated with supple cobalt brushstrokes of bamboo alongside a thatched hut, and replenished our cups. She performed the ritual automatically, her thoughts elsewhere.

"You are fortunate to be with us for Obon," she said eventually, her voice subdued. "Why don't you take a stroll?"

"I would wager this is not the first disappearance," I said.

The okami-san set the teapot down, bowed, rose, and retreated to the door. As she slipped the registration card into the folds of her kimono, she eased the sliding door aside with a practiced hand, glided through, and bowed once more in a graceful motion while she shut us in.

When her face grew to a sliver behind the paper-sheathed door, she said, "Join the festivities. Everyone will be there."

L IKE the rest of the land, Soga-jujo was preparing to welcome the dead.

The Japanese believe that the departed souls of family and ancestors watch over the living, guiding them in unseen ways and returning to visit once a year in midsummer. For Obon, ancestral graves are cleansed and dressed with fresh flowers. When night falls, attention turns to entertaining the incoming spirits. Song and dance and ceremony follow, and throughout the land the chugging engines of music, mirth, and grog collide in a celebratory fashion.

Tonight in Soga-jujo the engines were in full swing. A sea of sun-darkened faces bobbed before us as we entered a corridor of village shops. Everywhere we looked we saw the gentle, ruddy visages of country folks. But when wandering eyes inadvertently met ours, they grew guarded and swung away.

A coldness bloomed in my chest. That was *not* the usual reaction. The Japanese are a shy people, but during public events like Obon their generous side emerges and they willingly play host. Yet in Soga we were clearly unwelcome. Customs vary by region, but at worst our reception should have been distant but polite, with the occasional embarrassed smile or nod. Here we were received like carriers of a contagious disease—the villagers' expressions a mixture of worry, suspicion, and aversion.

I looked at Noda. "You feel it?"

"Yeah."

"They're here."

"Looks that way."

"Can you make anyone out?"

"No. You?"

"No."

The crowd grew thicker, and the deep-throated rhythms of *taiko* drums erupted up ahead. Vendors in tented stalls along both sides of the road dished up grilled soba noodles or fried squid, or sold toys or chits for games.

We were swept along in a stream of bodies. In the general merriment people bumped up against one another. Chatter and revelry filled the air, but I felt claustrophobic, vulnerable. Shouldering our way through the throng, we heard the whisper of a bamboo flute join the primal percussion. Gongs began to toll. A harvest song reared up.

Noda and I walked on, our glances flashing across the crowd but spotting nothing. Three men in white summer shorts, *happi* coats, and front-knotted headbands gauged our approach behind narrowed eyes. Passing around a bottle of spiced saké, the trio squatted in the doorway of the village furniture maker.

"Gaijin da," one of them said, flicking ash from a cigarette into the road. Foreigner.

"Big and strong."

"Handsome, too. Better hide your daughter."

"Wonder where he's from."

"Met me some Russian crabbers once. Don't look like them."

"Looks American or British."

"You eyeball his friend? Wouldn't mess with him."

"The pug-faced one? He's nothing."

The three farmers spoke in loud, exaggerated voices, as if they belonged to an exclusive club and nonmembers couldn't hear them.

"Meet him on a dark night in Osaka, you'd be saying different."

"Wouldn't be no tougher than the one we rolled that night. What we get—five big ones?"

"He was old. Those two'll rattle your pachinko balls quick enough."

Noda and I exchanged a knowing glance and agreed to ignore them. In winter, with their fields fallow, farmers sometimes journeyed to the big cities for seasonal odd jobs. If these three were to be believed, they had deprived a weaker soul or two of their surplus cash. Whatever they were, or pretended to be, they weren't the type of man we were hunting.

Noda and I reached the center of town. Overhead, a crosshatch of red lanterns cast a crimson glow over the crowd. Faces floated by— grinning, openmouthed, and shouting across the sea of heads for a friend, a brother, a child.

As we rounded a corner, an elevated platform decorated with bunting swung into view. Erected in an empty lot between a rice merchant and a tofu maker, the platform provided an impromptu stage for musicians and performers. On it, women danced in a tight circle under the flickering orange flames of torches tied to the corner posts of the stage, while men clad in loincloths and knotted headbands beat the darkened skins of the giant taiko drums with sticks as fat as sugarcane.

In a low voice, Noda intruded on my thoughts. "Can you handle things here?"

My heart ticked up a beat. Something was brewing, but the chief detective wasn't dealing out any clues. "Yeah, sure."

"Good." Then louder, so others could hear: "Johnson-san, I'm bored. Always the same damn dances, the same tinny tunes. You look around. Enjoy yourself. I'll wait this out in our room." Noda flashed me a questioning look, wondering if I could handle "the hunt" on my own, then he veered away into the crowd.

Normally, I enjoyed Obon. The ancient festival supplied a sense of continuity. It spoke of troubles endured and victories won. Of loved ones lost but remembered. It was humbling and exhilarating, and if you immersed yourself in the festivities, a palpable sense of connectivity larger than the self emerged.

However, *normal* and Soga no longer presented a balanced equation.

A new song began. A litany of drums, shamisen, and flutes pumped up the joviality. The music churned, and the villagers danced. The women trotted their circular path with a willowy grace, arms waving, smiles slight and dreamy. *Step, step, back, wave, clap.* Their movements were hypnotic, their rhythms infectious. The dance was one of serene confidence. The way of generations of mothers. It was the picture of restrained abandonment.

Step, step, back, wave, clap.

I had always found the dances spellbinding. I recalled the neighborhood festivals of my childhood in Tokyo when I danced with my mother and netted goldfish with my father. Great times before the divorce. When both my parents were alive and together . . .

Focus, Brodie. Old memories didn't belong to the here and now. Tonight I was searching for what Noda's friends had found in the dark.

Or whatever found them.

To wash away the country dust collecting at the edge of my throat, I bought a beer, then settled in to study faces and postures of the celebrants.

I took in the sun-burnished forearms and leathery necks of men who worked the fields. Their skin was a dark, woody brown. They wore hardy, resigned expressions. On the women, I noted a placid but fixed look of endurance, of long hours toiling in the home, then beside their husbands among rows of rice stalks and cabbage. I could easily imagine them shielded by scarves and straw hats as they moved steadily across a field weeding, prodding, trimming.

Among the villagers, some faces were better fed and pale in a way the farmers' were not. They, I concluded, were the merchants. The shopkeepers and tavern owners. Sometimes plump, sometimes slim, but always eager to serve.

Eventually, I noticed a third type. Not hardy or servile but predatory, with the rigid, calcified brows of hunters. They were few, but as I learned to divide the villagers by occupation, their number grew.

A bead of sweat skittered down the back of my neck. *I'd found them.* By my calculations, five or six hundred people milled about. More moved in and out of shops and taverns. The hunters mingled with the celebrants but they could not disguise what they were. Not from me.

I stumbled across a tall monument of black granite at the foot of a large oak. Strings of ancient kanji carved into its dark face eulogized one General Kotaro Ogi, samurai to the shogun and a rescuer of the village from a famine in the 1700s. Though erected in 1898, thirty years after the shogun system fell to a modernizing Japan, the carved stone memorial was spotless, clearly someone's pride and joy. I scanned the inscription twice but the Japantown character was not to be found. At the foot of the marker, more than a dozen bouquets of chrysanthemums, gladiolas, and valerians had been left for the hometown hero.

Three hundred years on, the general remained a popular figure.

Roaming the streets for another thirty minutes, I bought a plate of grilled noodles and more beer. I played tourist to the hilt, gazing in delight and curiosity at everything traditional while watching *them* obliquely.

Their gait was silky and they held their shoulders in a way that allowed them to glide through the crowd without wasted motion. There was a smooth floating quality to their movement. I counted ten certainties and three contenders. Most were young and two were female.

Only once did I detect a sign of their attention. When a schoolgirl giddy with excitement plowed into me from behind, I turned abruptly to steady her small body and caught a glance shifting hurriedly away. In that brief moment I locked onto eyes so cold and unyielding in their appraisal, a tremor slithered through me.

With that look, the illusion of Soga-jujo as a quaint country hamlet evaporated forever, along with the possibility of an unchallenged retreat.

Our stalkers were merely waiting for their chance.

WE were back in our room. Noda swallowed two pills, then thrust the meds at me. *"Nonde."* Take these.

"What are they?"

"Keep you from sleeping."

Drowsiness and jet lag *could* slow my reaction time. I tossed down two tablets with water and blind trust. "Think they'll come?"

With fear and disbelief tugging me in opposite directions, I was having second thoughts.

"If we seem a threat," Noda said.

"Or they might ignore us."

"Might."

"You worried?"

"About the *how*, yeah."

That, indeed, was the question. We could only watch and wait. With the medication, we removed surprise from their arsenal, but they still had the night. How would they use it?

During our absence, the low coffee table had been conveyed to a far corner of the room, and two sets of Japanese futon bedding had been laid out. Starched and folded, a crisp blue-and-white *yukata* lay on top of each futon. Noda and I bathed and changed into the kimono-like sleeping garments, wrapping indigo belts around our waists.

Before extinguishing the lights, Noda extracted a 9mm gun from his bag, jacked a cartridge into the chamber, then screwed on an eight-inch suppressor. He set the weapon by his right leg, within easy reach.

"That's some silencer," I said.

"Need to be very quiet."

"Preparation is all."

"It helps," he said. "Sometimes."

Ten minutes later, Noda extinguished the overhead light, steeping our room in a deep-country darkness. Soon I was drifting in and out of a light sleep.

Noda's pills kicked in gradually. As the minutes passed, I felt myself growing more alert. There was a prickly sensation in my extremities. I felt vessels pulse in arms, legs, and torso. My muscles flexed.

Anticipation and concern occupied equal shares of my thoughts. I became aware of noises inside and out: Noda shifting his legs, a soft breeze tickling the windowpanes. Somewhere in the ryokan, the plumbing hiccupped. A midnight current rustled the leaves of the bamboo grove behind the inn.

Noda's breathing was steady and unlabored. The hours passed. My edginess waned to a soft medicinal glow.

As the last revelers found their way home, I heard celebrants' drunken caroling, mothers shouting after children, a dog howling in the distance. The noises of nature slowly usurped the revelry and the town grew silent. Cicadas and frog song grew louder. The cicada's lament was as vibrant as a shamisen. Male frogs called to prospective mates, the louder, more resonant song attracting the female. A shade too loud and a winged predator would swoop down on them.

Our predators also came from above.

A ceiling panel slid back and a man dropped to the floor soundlessly, his knees flexing to absorb the shock of the plunge. Padded footwear stifled all sound of his descent except the small *sphhut* of tatami compressing to absorb the sudden impact of an adult male.

My heart slamming against my rib cage, I feigned sleep, my eyes narrowed to slits, seemingly closed, lashes splicing the room into segments. I hoped Noda was doing the same. This was where I found out if I had any chance of making the grade. I kept my breathing low and steady, realizing Noda's pills had saved us: had we succumbed to sleep, we would have died a quiet, slumber-filled death, without struggle or knowledge of our passing.

Sleek and dark, the intruder fanned left, looking upward for a partner whose legs were already coming through the aperture overhead. His companion descended with an identical *sphhut* on the matting. *Female this time,* I thought. Both of them stood motionless for nearly five seconds.

A light sweat bathed my body. These guys were good. Extraordinarily good. A voice in my head screamed *Run!* I ignored it.

I peered at the two intruders. They were sheathed in black. The moonlight filtering through the shoji caught the shiny surfaces of the room fixtures but sank deep into the blackness of the intruder's clothing. I could just make out a tight belt with loops and snaps and hanging objects at their waist. None of the objects looked heavy or bulky or gave off the telltale glint of metal, but most of them were surely hard, maybe forged from a blackened titanium alloy. Lightweight state-of-the-art tools and weaponry. Like the bugging device Toru had found at Brodie Security.

On my side of the room, a black-gloved hand glided toward the belt. Instinct and training took over. I watched the hands and hips. My every nerve and muscle tensed. The man's motion was swift and fluid, and as his hand rose—holding something long and slender—I rolled away from it. A slender tensile form smacked into my bedding where I'd lain a moment before.

Noda shot the attacker twice, bullets closely grouped to the right of the sternum, and he crumbled. Reacting to the sound, the woman tucked, rolled, and, keeping herself small and hard to hit, retrieved a knife from her body suit and slung it at Noda.

Fanning left, the barrel of Noda's gun tracked the tumbling figure and spit two slugs at the coiled mass. The shots struck a half beat before the female intruder launched the blade, their impact altering the course of the projectile, which embedded itself in the tatami matting inches from Noda's foot.

Noda never moved. He had dispatched both attackers with the gun tight against his leg, the weapon hidden, the dark mouth of the silencer nudging the top of his thigh. He'd made no telltale movement to give away his attack, to catch their eye and set them off. Very shrewd and very professional.

One of them did. And two of them didn't.

A shiver crept down my spine. Even forewarned, the ploy had given Noda less than two seconds' advantage. I rose cautiously, a sense of dread seeping into my bones.

Noda said, "Don't turn on the light."

"Wouldn't think of it. But Christ, what *are* these guys?"

Noda held a finger to his lips. "Keep your voice down. We're supposed to be dead."

Deep in my chest, primal shadows stirred. I'd traveled to Soga with the outrage of a hunter, but the terror of the hunted now consumed me. Only now did the full weight of our predicament make itself felt: we stood in a small room of a small ryokan in a small Japanese village completely isolated from the rest of the world—with who knew how many black-suited killers waiting for us outside.

We were trapped. The Viper would be guarded. They would cut us down the second we hit the parking lot. Our only means of escape lay with a rental car miles away on the other side of the mountains.

Stepping forward, Noda shot each fighter through the head.

In a low voice I said, "So what are they? Mercenaries? A private army? What?"

"They're cockroaches."

"You know what I mean."

"There are two less of 'em for us to deal with."

I said, "Would have been nice to get some answers."

"Not now. No way to touch them without getting pricked. And one prick . . ."

"Says you."

Noda jerked his head toward the steel shaft of a knife piercing my futon. "Says that. Poison on the blade. One near me has poison on the handle."

I squatted for a closer look. The shaft of the weapon in my futon glittered with an oily substance. The weapon was double-edged and serrated. My chest hammered with recognition. Homeboy's knife was of the same make.

I said, "The guy who drew on me in San Francisco packed the same blade. Looks hard to use."

"So he was Soga. They like one-way weapons."

"One way?"

"Can't throw it back at them."

"Why not?"

"Knife's got a one-of-a-kind balance."

"You could stick them, though."

"If you got close enough. And if the poison didn't get you."

The blade excreted a sweet fragrance. "What's that smell? Magnolia?"

"A local scrub extract. Kills in seconds."

I didn't have to ask how he knew.

I examined our would-be assassins.

Black body suit, black head covering, and black padded toe socks thickened at the soles.

They wore black from top to bottom.

They used poison.

They fought with one-way weapons.

The Nakamuras never stood a chance.

And neither would my daughter.

"I need to get more protection for Jenny," I said.

Noda grunted. "Next on the list. After we get what we can here."

"We can start with their uniforms. Looks like SWAT blacks, only better."

Noda pinched the material on the woman's calf, then at her ribs. "It's thin. Ultralight. Special order."

Around the openings in the face mask, lampblack covered the exposed facial area. The whites of their eyes were blackened by almond-shaped contacts, the centers of the lenses clear. An involuntary shudder rocked me. No simple mercenaries, these. They were more evolved, more carefully conceived.

In a low voice I said, "You did the right thing."

Under the black body suits, the flesh was firm and robust and possessed the muscular resilience of professional athletes. I wondered about the faces behind the masks. Had I seen them earlier tonight? Was the man the one I had caught glaring at me when I'd turned without warning?

I said, "They weren't going to bother with threats and intimidation, were they?"

"Nope."

"I think we've outstayed our welcome."

"Like a mother on a wedding night."

"Back door's through the kitchen."

"Grab the luggage," Noda said. "We'll change outside. You did good."

"How do you figure?"

"Didn't get yourself killed."

I shouldered the pair of duffel bags, thinking that our lives had hinged on instinct, a sliver of advance knowledge, and four pulls of a trigger.

What had we stumbled into?

I still had no answer as to *who* or *why*, but I now knew *what*—and wished I didn't.

Any way I sized up the scene before me, I had no doubt more of the same—or worse—waited for us beyond these walls.

WHEN a board underfoot creaked as we descended the stairs, the mistress of the inn cracked open her door and stared at us in astonishment. She took in the duffel bags and asked, "You're leaving?"

"We had visitors," Noda said. He held the gun by his side, out of sight.

Wonder filled her eyes. Then fear. "But you're alive?"

"Yes."

"Who are you?"

"That's not important."

As if to confirm something to herself, the okami-san nodded. "We call them the invisible ones. Mostly guests just disappear. Sometimes, when I clean up, there is a spot of blood on the futon. Like a feeding mosquito had been swatted."

"Is that what happened to Mori?" I asked.

Her lips trembled. "Yes. During an afternoon nap. I was out shopping."

Her words struck me like a physical blow. I stumbled back half a step and felt a wave of nausea roll over me. "You told us he went for a walk."

"What else *could* I say?"

Noda said, "You don't mind, we'll use your back door."

A determined look firmed the lines of her mouth. "No, not the back door."

"Why not?"

"They'll be watching. Go through the delivery entrance on the opposite side, away from the parking lot."

"Is the car usable?" I asked, dreading the answer.

The innkeeper shook her head. "No, it'll be booby-trapped. You'll have to leave it behind." She took a step toward the front door.

"Where you going?" Noda said, his gun rising and tracking her movement.

"Shoes."

The gun slipped from sight.

After scooping up our footwear, she led us down a dark corridor toward the rear of the inn. We turned several times, our way lit by moonlight seeping through the occasional transom window. She turned on no lights. In a passage beyond the bathing quarters, she set down our footwear and reached for the side door.

Noda grabbed her wrist and twisted hard. A muffled a cry of pain. I felt a stab of guilt, but it needed doing.

In a brusque whisper Noda said, "Why are you doing this? *Hayaku!*" Quick!

His tone was sharp and accusing. If he didn't believe her answer, or detected a false note, he would shoot her. Blind trust in our newfound guide was not an option. Why should she befriend us at this late stage when earlier she had been so evasive? Why couldn't this be a fallback trap? We were certain of only one thing: a single wrong move and we would be slaughtered like pigs.

Alarm flickered across the okami-san's features, but it was nearly impossible to determine the origin of her fear. Was she frightened of Noda or afraid of *them* if she didn't lead us into their trap?

"Answer plainly," I said. "Now."

Nervously, eyes darted to her captured wrist, then to the gun in Noda's other hand. "They have my son."

"His name?"

"Ryo Nagayama. He's my *only* son. There are some of us—mothers mostly—who fight them in our own fashion. Centuries ago, we were a poor farming community. Samurai ruled the country, and the Ogi clan ruled our town."

I recalled the well-attended monument to General Ogi in the center of the village.

"They found a way out," she said, "but not a good way. There was a great demand for people willing to do dirty work. It always came from the authorities. That was the clan's genius, and our village has been caught up in their scheming ever since. Even today the Ogis are revered. We live better, but not freely. We are cared for, but watched. And they entice our children with money and games we can't compete with."

Noda scrutinized the innkeeper closely, as did I. Her expression was dark and solemn, her tone sincere. I could detect no false flicker. She was either trustworthy or an actress of immense talent.

Noda released her.

The innkeeper said, "Who *are* you?"

I said, "Doesn't matter."

"No one survives an attack."

"Things change."

"Not here. Not for three hundred years." She hesitated. "May I ask if you have an escape route?"

Noda and I were silent.

"You are right not to tell me. They could force me. But I guess you have prepared one."

We remained silent.

"No matter. Go," she said, giving me a gentle shove toward the door. "They will come, and when they do they'll find me sleeping soundly. They'll have no reason to disturb me or suspect me. But I will tell you this: the river is the best way out. You cannot be seen in the shallows along the left shore because of the high bank and the trees overhead. Stay in the water. It is not deep this time of year and there are many nocturnal snakes in the rocks along the banks. Even *they* fear the snakes. Now go. Quickly."

NODA crouched in the doorway for a long beat, scanning the darkness before us, then dashed across three yards of open ground and vanished into the bamboo thicket. Attentive to every sound and shadow, I waited for a response to the chief detective's foray into the night.

Registering no movement, I left the safety of the inn and sprinted in Noda's wake, hauling our gear, wondering if unseen eyes tracked me, visualizing a bullet zipping toward my back. I entered the foliage without incident.

"Change farther in," Noda whispered. "You first, I'll watch."

"Got it."

I pushed deeper into the stand of giant bamboo. The stalks were taller than houses and fatter than summer squash. In the grove, the air was damp but cool despite the heat that hung over the valley. Noda's call to slip into street clothes outdoors was a shrewd one. The bamboo provided more options than the confining walls of the inn room.

Screened by the stalks, I stripped off the yukata. Crickets chirped nearby. "Think we can get out of here in one piece?"

"That's the plan."

Noda was tense and attuned to every shade of the darkness around us, as was I. He sounded confident but I didn't share his conviction. For one thing, we were too deep in their territory. For another, only an orderly and silent retreat could save us. A headlong rush through the mountains assured a quick death. By rigging the Viper, Soga had cut off our main escape route and limited our options.

I pulled on jeans and a dark blue T-shirt, laced up black Reeboks, then spelled Noda on watch while he changed. After he finished, the chief detective came to the edge of the grove, squatted by my side, and said, "We follow the river out."

"That's it? Your whole plan?"

"Yeah."

"Tell me you're going on more than the innkeeper's word."

"Am."

Great. I couldn't push the master of laconic without irritating him, and I didn't want to irritate the man who held my life in his hands.

On the roof of a three-story farmhouse some hundred fifty yards away, I caught a glimpse of an incongruent shadow that didn't follow the contours of the roofline. I kept an eye on it. The shadow moved and glided on to the neighboring two-story, then slid down the steep slope of ceramic tile, taking the drop to the ground noiselessly before turning away.

I said, "You see that?"

"Yeah. Stay alert."

We plunged into the forest and travelled at an even clip, our advance swift but silent. I left the reassuring shelter of the bamboo with reluctance, an adrenaline charge propelling me forward as I calculated our chances for survival. The sky, glimpsed through a canopy of pine and cedar, was coal black and distant. Stars were icy blue points that shimmered and blinked and seemed to shift if you tried too hard to get a fix on them.

Noda pointed to a path in the distance. "You see the left fork? Two hundred yards down is a ravine, maybe twenty or thirty feet deep, river at the bottom. Go down. Wait five minutes, out of sight. If I don't show, go on without me. Two miles, the river bends to the right. Climb the far embankment. George is there."

"What are you going to do?"

"Make sure we're not being followed."

"You sure about the route?"

Noda gave me a look. "Walked it today."

"While I was at the festival?"

Scanning the forest, Noda nodded, and I heaved a silent sigh of relief. We weren't traveling blind.

I said, "You never expected to get any information, did you?"

"Only what we've got."

"They knew who we were, didn't they?"

"Yeah."

"Didn't matter that we used false names."

"No."

"Which means they were involved in Japantown and now we know it. And they know we know it." The sudden realization sent a chill through me.

"Sorry. It was the only way."

"They'll be looking to get even."

"No, they're pros. They'll regroup and watch."

"If we get out of Soga."

"Yeah. If. We get to Tokyo, they'll pull back."

"Why?"

"Because they know we don't have squat."

"So they regroup and kill us in Tokyo."

"Not there."

"Why not?"

"City's off-limits. Don't know why."

We heard the sound of a scurrying animal and listened intently for a moment.

I said, "You sure they weren't watching you this afternoon?"

"I'm sure."

"And if you're wrong?"

"We'll be dead shortly."

I shut my eyes to steady my nerves. Sometimes I wished the chief detective were a little less forthright.

Noda whispered, "Time to go," and we split up, Noda reminding me to wait five minutes, no more. I followed the left fork. Underfoot the deadfall was brown and spongy. Ferns and moss edged the path. Cedars with trunks as wide as small cars formed the canopy overhead. Cricket and frog song erupted from all sides.

I was edgy. I didn't like leaving Noda alone. Not one bit. It went against every instinct of self-preservation I possessed. You never split up. In South Central there was safety in numbers. It wouldn't be any different out here. Noda was good, but the terrain was theirs. The home advantage was too great.

Keeping to the trail for two minutes until it turned, I took advantage of the bend to leave the path and circle back. I made good time on my return trip and spotted Noda a dozen yards away, crouched behind a tree. I followed his lead, stepping behind a tall cedar for cover.

Noda's gun was drawn and tracking a target I couldn't see. The next instant he fired and missed, but the flash of the muzzle illuminated a dark silhouette fleeing into the thicket without a sound. Seconds later, a knife smacked into the tree trunk above Noda's left shoulder. He inched around to the other side of the tree for protection. He listened and looked, and I did the same.

A minute passed, then two more.

There was no sign of the attacker, but we remained alert. With the gunfire, silencer notwithstanding, cricket and frog song had ceased, and had yet to resume.

A moment later Noda let out a muffled yelp and I stared in astonishment as his feet were wrenched off the ground, a jet-black noose looped around his neck. *Jesus.* Without looking up, Noda sighted along the line and unleashed three shots.

A body plunged from the tree, but the rope had been secured and Noda dangled ten inches above solid ground. An insignificant height in the larger scheme of things, but plenty to die from. Dropping his weapon, Noda clawed at the cord. His body flailed about as he tried to wedge his fingers between noose and skin.

Before I could move from my hiding place, a black figure wearing night-vision goggles separated from the trees and regarded Noda's thrusting legs and twisting torso with fascination. Noda pumped the air with his legs and leveraged the strength of his powerful shoulders to pull down on the line and gain some space under his chin, then wedged his fingers between the noose and his jaw and sucked in air noisily.

"Impressive muscle, old man," the figure said. "I'll give you that. But it's wasted effort. I'll take you now and your partner when I catch him. It was dumb to separate."

The speaker pulled a gun from his equipment belt.

With an abrupt burst, I charged over the remaining few yards in a rush that gave me away.

Noda's assailant wheeled, weapon swinging around.

The scrimmage took only seconds but played out before my eyes in the elastic time of a stop-motion replay. Frame by frame. Instant by instant. I sprang, then brought my foot up. Saw that the trajectory was accurate, then heard jawbone snap as the heel of my foot connected just before the gun barrel flared. A flash, then I watched my adversary fall backward. The sting of a bullet grazed my ribs, then I saw the shooter's head bounce off the cushioned ground of the forest floor. Then I found myself hoping the bullet was untreated, and *just* a bullet. And in a disengaged place in my mind, I marveled at the Soga mystique that had me wishing I'd *only* been shot.

The shooter's spine hit a fist-size stone and I heard a sharp crack of bone. His body arched in pain, then fell back, limp.

I landed on the forward padding of my feet and was on him in one bound. He tried to rise but couldn't. His spine had snapped. I ripped off his night-vision goggles and tossed them aside. No wonder they had found Noda so easily. Underneath a black hood, watchful eyes glittered.

"The linguist," I said, "where is he?"

"Our farmhouse," he whispered.

"Brodie, keep your distance," Noda called in a choked voice.

Noda had worked his fingers more fully under the cord, his chin now resting safely on the knuckles of both hands. He countered the drag of his own body weight with the force of his biceps, which bulged under the strain. He began to maneuver his head back and forth, easing the hangman's noose fractionally forward with each movement.

"If there's any chance," I said, thinking that the okami-san hadn't seen a body.

"We took him alive," the man in black said.

"They don't take hostages," Noda said. "Stay back."

His warning was steeped in everything there was to fear, but images of Mori's wife, her stomach rounded and swelling, smothered my resistance.

I stooped down to hear the reply.

"Where?" I asked again.

"Dead," he said, grinning. "Like you."

With what must have sent spasms of pain rolling down his spine, he tried to raise his arm. It twitched and a gun I hadn't seen rolled away from his paralyzed fingers.

"You did this," he hissed.

I picked up the gun and pointed it vaguely in his direction. The linguist *was* dead. The fragile thread of hope I'd held on to snapped. My soul sagged and something inexplicably sad dropped into my heart.

The gunman laughed coldly. "And we'll get you too. Sooner than you think."

I ignored him, thinking only of the horse-faced Mrs. Mori with her forgiving look and her otherworldly demeanor. The gunman opened his mouth to speak again, but Noda pressed the barrel of his gun to the man's head.

"Stay very quiet," the chief detective growled through clenched teeth. With his free hand, Noda rummaged through a duffel bag and came up with a pair of socks. The socks went into the fallen fighter's mouth. Next, Noda wound a shirt around the man's head, knotting it to secure the makeshift gag. He used a second shirt to bind the hands.

"I was hoping to talk to this one," I said.

"No time. Gotta go."

The words echoed in my ears. I stumbled sideways.

"Brodie?"

I fell forward onto my knees and felt the dampness of the ground cover seep through my pants. A wave of nausea rolled through me. I began to shiver.

"Something's wrong," I heard myself say.

"Drop the gun," Noda said.

"What?"

Noda kicked the weapon from of my hand, then knelt down and smelled it.

"Poison," he said. "One-way weapons, remember?"

He pried open my hand. A blue ointment streaked my palm and fingers. The fragrance of magnolia drifted by. Clawing the ground, Noda grabbed a fistful of damp soil and ground it into my palm, brushed it off, and repeated the action, using the earth as a blotter to suck the poison from my pores.

"Brodie?"

A cold sweat wrapped itself around my body and hot flashes raced up my face and neck. Blinking and shaking my head to stave off dizziness, I vomited into a clutch of fiddlehead ferns.

"Look, Brodie, there's no time. Hold this and whatever you do, stay conscious."

He slapped a handful of moist topsoil into my palm and curled my fingers around it.

Fired up on adrenaline, Noda strapped on the night-vision goggles I'd slung aside, grabbed a second pair from the body he'd shot out of the tree, then slung me over his shoulder and began running down the path faster than I would have thought possible.

He left the duffel bags behind.

NODA hauled me down the steep bank and cooled my fever in the river. He made me drink a lot of water, but the moist soil is what saved me. It leached away the residual poison before a full dosage could seep through my skin. Still, the potion took its toll. I felt drained. Depleted. And equally damaging: humiliated. I'd failed. Despite all I'd learned before, during, and after the attack in our room, I'd been duped by the very man I took down.

We rested a minute, then donned the night-vision goggles and moved silently downstream, listening for the slightest ripple, the faintest break of water ahead or behind. We scanned the ridges of the gorge overhead for more attackers, all the while hugging the bank as the innkeeper advised.

With the goggles our world took on an eerie, electric green glow, enlivened by the occasional green-white hot spot when an owl or other night creature came within range. But more than high-tech accoutrements, we relied on Mother Nature. As long as the crickets and frogs on the overhanging banks sang, our safety was assured. So, an ear cocked to the fauna's late-night revelries, Noda and I moved silently through the shallows. Any cessation would signal Soga's arrival and, in my weakened condition—our quick death.

As we waded forward the crickets continued to saw, and the frogs to croak. The forest canopy, layered now with birch, covered our retreat. Underfoot were water, mud, and stone. Up ahead, a night bird plucked a small trout from the water.

I cringed. That could have been us earlier this evening.

The ravine was sculpted from granite and sandstone. In places it towered thirty feet above the river. Among the boulders on the banks, the snakes, nocturnal and venomous, protected our flanks.

In my diminished state, our progress was torturously slow, but each bend in the river took us farther from the village. As I trudged through the knee-high water, my movements were listless, and my thoughts plagued with imaginary scenarios of Mori's last moments. Twice I stumbled and fell, and Noda had to backtrack and haul me forward, a steadying arm at my waist.

Before long the mosquitoes found us. They flew at our cheeks and eyes and ears, buzzing with an eagerness in proportion to the potential of their unexpected feast. Without thinking, I swatted one and the sound of my hand slapping flesh echoed down the corridor of stone.

"Don't do that," Noda hissed. "The noise carries."

"They'll eat us alive."

"There's worse ways to go."

And right on cue, the worst materialized. Simultaneously, the cricket and frog song ceased. Noda and I heard the deafening silence at the same instant. Noda brought a finger to his lips and pointed down. The next moment, he slid into the water without a sound until all but his face was submerged. Following suit, I immersed myself in the shallow flow, lying on the riverbed, my body absorbing the chill of the water with a shiver of revulsion.

Seconds later, a head peered over the edge of the ravine. Through the night-vision goggles we watched him scan the river. With incremental head movements, he parsed the night scene before him.

His search was methodical and efficient. Anchored to the riverbed with a clawlike grip, I held my position under the Soga fighter's steady inspection as frigid water rolled over me, draining off my body heat. To counter the numbing chill and encroaching drowsiness, I periodically loosened my right hand from the muddy bottom and dug a fingernail into my thigh.

Three minutes after the head appeared, it withdrew. Noda whispered, "Wait," and a minute later the head reemerged twenty yards downriver and repeated the process. His glances were briefer this time, his head movements more rapid. Clearly, he was culling the landscape for two vertical figures. The hazy green light of his night goggles was an imprecise filter, but it was the cold water damping the telltale warmth of our bodies that saved us.

Once more, the head withdrew. Loosening my grip, I allowed my body to float alongside Noda and pointed downstream. When he nodded, I withdrew my fingers from the mud, and the current tugged me gently forward, feetfirst. Using my hands as rudders, I directed my course. When the soles of my feet nudged up against a submerged boulder, I flapped one hand or the other and floated around the obstruction.

Noda followed my lead, and in this manner we traversed the next half mile. After the first three hundred yards, I veered toward the center of the river and picked up speed. Five hundred yards farther, we redirected our course to the side until we were once more in the shallows, where we sat up and paused to listen. The songs of the forest were hearty and confident.

Noda rose and signaled me to follow him. Again, we dragged ourselves forward through knee-deep water as our bodies slowly thawed. This time I let the mosquitoes bite. Though noticeably subdued with a cooler fare, they nevertheless feasted on arms, neck, and face. They preferred the fleshier parts, but there were those that did not make the distinction. One settled comfortably on my forehead above my right eyebrow. I flicked it away and three more took its place.

We remained tense and watchful, constantly monitoring the cricket and frog song as our eyes roamed back and forth across the ravine's upper reaches.

Two hours later, our nerves frayed, our bodies shivering, and our reserve strength nearly depleted, we scaled the steep slopes of the ravine and hiked through scrub to the darkened Nissan Bluebird, where a sleeping George and civilization as practiced by the rest of the world waited.

THE visit to Soga had opened a whole new world of pain, and I thrashed around in the Nissan like a trout in a net. Some of my discomfort was the residual poison working its way out of my system. Most of it was not.

My heart slammed against my ribs with the insistence of a Soga drum, its message bleak: *What the hell are we going to do?*

In the murky backwaters of Shiga Prefecture, we nearly perished— twice. Now, hurtling back toward Tokyo in the relative safety of our car, I could not get my mind around what Noda and I had encountered in that isolated river valley.

Knives were one thing, but *poison and hanging*?

Nothing Noda had told me prepared me for what we had witnessed. It was beyond fathomable. We had awakened the devil. There was no denying it. We'd escaped this time, but now what? Soga was out there. And we had no way to evade its next attack, or even identify a potential assailant until he or she or it was upon us.

Beside me, Noda handled the encounter in his own way, driving with fierce intensity, racing over the unending blacktop, eyes glued to the narrow tunnel of brightness the headlights carved from the dense country darkness.

We spent the first hour of our return trip in silence, after which Noda said, "We've seen the worst there is."

I stared out the window, muddy rice paddies throwing back the gleam of the headlights as George slept in the backseat.

"Wish I hadn't."

"You can drop it, you want to."

"You mean head back to the States, take my daughter away for a while?"

"Yeah."

"You don't think I'm up to it?"

"Most people aren't. And you're green."

As usual, Noda called it as he saw it.

The chief detective added, "Some people would say leaving now's the smart move."

I leaned back against the headrest and closed my eyes. *The smart move.* When I'd wrapped up my apprenticeship at Bristol Antiques to open my own shop, I'd drawn a line. Based on values instilled long ago, plus lifestyle decisions about independence and not buckling under. About being able to stand my ground and look at myself in the mirror every morning with a free and unbridled conscience. When I'd committed to Brodie Security, I'd brought along the same ideals. It was also how my father had conducted his life. Fought for every case, for every inch of freedom. In my formative years, when we showered together, he showed me how he "scrubbed off the grime" and told me about the day's cases. The good, the bad, and the slimy. "No matter what," he'd say, "stand tall. For the little guy—and for yourself." It wasn't until he died last October, still estranged, that I fully understood that my underlying code came from a fiercely independent man who made a new home for himself halfway around the world on his own terms, against the hardest odds.

All of that mattered to me. Noda might see similarities, but he knew nothing of my personal preferences as I never spoke of them. So he was testing me.

To move forward on the case, we'd taken what we believed were acceptable risks. We'd underestimated the situation to the extreme, yet survived. But what we uncovered threatened to destroy us—utterly and without prejudice. Yes, we had escaped, but we were in deeper than ever. Inescapably entangled. We could no more turn away from Soga than we could turn our backs on a snarling lion into whose cage we'd accidentally stepped.

Even if dropping the case were an option, I couldn't do so without reneging on the promise I'd made to Renna. And then there was Mieko.

Soga had taken her from me. Stolen her, and in the process ripped my life apart. All the days of anguish, all the sleepless nights, all the ongoing loneliness—I owed to Soga.

For me there was no smart move, or dumb move.

There was only one move.

On the far side of Shizuoka, I said, "Not going to drop this one."

A flicker of a smile crossed Noda's lips. "Didn't think you would but had to ask."

"And now you have."

This time Noda tempered his glance. "Time like this, there is only knowing and instinct. Your instincts were good. Very good."

A wave of pleasure swept through me, though I kept it to myself. "Why didn't you kill the fourth guy?"

"Not a threat anymore. We're not them."

"So now what?"

"Now we know more."

"And the more we know, the easier it'll get?"

"Yeah."

"If we survive."

"Point still stands."

"Not a lot of flexibility in your plan."

He shrugged. "That's all there is. Do or die."

There was a darkness to Noda I could never penetrate. "When your friends went down, did they know what they were up against?"

"Not a clue."

"Did they know about the kanji?"

"No."

I sensed a hesitation in his clipped replies. What was he holding back?

"Noda?"

He tightened his grip on the wheel. "I lost a friend . . . and my brother."

There it was. Like the rest of us, Noda had scars. In the Oriental mind, revenge was a timeless entity. Going underground, the forty-seven ronin had bided their time for two years. Noda had subdued his urges for five.

"I'm sorry," I said.

Noda grunted.

Mieko, Hara, Mrs. Mori, the innkeeper's son, and now Noda. The victims living and dead were piling up.

"Your brother, was he good?"

"Taught me everything."

"But he went in cold?"

"Yeah."

My head began to throb. *As good as Noda and he ended up dead.* We might not be able to dig ourselves out of this one.

SOGA COMPOUND, UNDISCLOSED LOCATION

SET at the back of a heavily wooded plot of land, the gymnasium was equipped like no other in the world. Inside along the north wall, three men and a woman flung knives with supreme accuracy at human-shaped silhouettes twenty feet away. In the center staging area, Casey directed four people in scrimmages combining karate, judo, Indonesian silat, Shaolin kung fu, and original Soga fighting techniques.

This week, twelve men and women attended the private training session, some flying in from as far away as London, Los Angeles, and São Paolo, where they made their homes. Twice a year they arrived in shifts of sixteen each, minus those on assignment, to maintain their skill levels.

In total, Soga had thirty-two full-time active field operatives. A group of eight handled a kill, four to carry out the assignment, four to sweep in afterward to monitor post-strike events and deal with any complications: witnesses, slipups, persistent police.

Each assignment was managed with a meticulous professionalism that eliminated mishaps during execution and allowed for the subtle suppression of any disruptive postoperational issues. Put an overactive detective in the hospital after, say, an unfortunately severe case of food poisoning and his investigation tended to stall. Threaten a witness's family or career, and nine out of ten grew forgetful. For the prideful few—like the Swiss banker—the carry-through was swift and irrevocable.

Japantown was an example of a perfectly executed operation. The client wanted a very public, very violent display, and Ogi had obliged with a spectacular show. Casey carried out the kill with the other three members of his crew strategically posted to secure the site. Then Dermott's group slipped in for post-kill surveillance and containment.

Rarely had a Soga operation failed, and never had any of their people been caught alive. Under Ogi's reign, only two men had taken a fall. One in Africa, a freak death, and the other, well, he would rather not think about that one.

The Soga leader waved Casey over. "Run them through Sakov again. Crank it up a notch."

"Yes, sir."

A technique developed by the KGB in the early 1970s, the Sakov maneuver was a series of three swift hand movements used to disarm an opponent at close quarters. Soga had uncovered the technique in its never-ending search to upgrade its repertoire of advanced combat methods.

Along the south wall, a woman hurled the hook end of an ultrathin cable at one of a series of rooftop replicas sixty feet above her head, snagged an outcropping on the first try, and clambered to the top, pressing a button in the handle of the hook to retract the telltale cable in 1.8 seconds. Her spotter called out her time: "Thirty-four-point-seven plus cable."

Ogi peered up at the ledge. "I need to see thirty-five flat with cable, Bonnie."

"Yes, sir."

Ogi's eyes ran over every part of Bonnie's body. "You've put on a few pounds too. Lose them before the next session."

"Yes, sir."

The cell phone in Ogi's hip pouch vibrated. Snapping it open, he said, "Speak." After listening to the response, he asked, "What do you mean *escaped*?"

Patience, patience.

He turned his back on the trainees and swiftly exited the back door of the gym before giving rein to a volcanic annoyance that distorted his features. Pacing under the forest canopy, he swore softly. The art dealer and his friend had burned three of his people and put a fourth in a wheelchair. They had wiped out the entire Iroha team. All were still first-year trainees, only a third of the way through the mandatory three-year program, but the assignment should have been a cakewalk.

"Are you sure there were just two of them?"

"Yes, sir."

"Tell me everything."

Ogi pressed his ear to the phone. *They'd had information beforehand,* he thought as he listened. But even forearmed, they should never have left Soga alive. Brodie and company had strolled in and out of the village like it was a goddamned temple garden.

Ogi said, "They knew something. Have research run a full profile on both men. Somewhere along the line we've met one or both of them before and I want to know where."

Very little else, Ogi thought, could account for such an outcome.

"Hara hired them, remember."

"But *he* only suspects. Get me what I don't know. It's there. I can feel it."

"Yes, sir. Anything else?"

While considering his response, Ogi reentered the gym and watched Casey demonstrate Sakov to perfection. His chest swelled with pride. One day the boy would make a good leader. Into the phone, Ogi said, "Finish the job in Tokyo. Usual procedure."

"Could you repeat that, sir? Tokyo?"

"Yes, Tokyo."

Nearby, Bonnie's spotter called out, "Thirty-six-one, with cable."

The voice said, "Understood," and disconnected.

Ogi surveyed his people. An elite group. The best in the world. They operated with impunity in fifty-seven countries. Varying methods, target areas. Never too often, never repeating kill scenarios in the same city. Sometimes disabling, sometimes kidnapping, sometimes killing. Secrecy was the key. Brodie and his bunch now threatened that secrecy. Every four or five years someone mounted a challenge, but most challenges were dispelled with little effort. Brodie had the backing of the police and a detective agency, which called for circumspection.

Ogi was irritated. Why did he have the feeling that his primary source in Tokyo was holding out on him? After collecting more information, he would crush this outbreak.

"How many times have you been up the rope today?" he asked Bonnie.

"Five, sir."

"Well, you stay on that station until you get back down to thirty-five. You understand?"

"Yes, sir."

Patience, patience.

Jake Brodie's son was a clever one. And he had a "wide face." *Kao ga hiroi.* He knew people. Too many people. If he turned up dead under suspicious circumstances, those people would come looking. If he met with an accident, they would examine every aspect of the event.

The art dealer needed to be eliminated.

Soga would handle damage control.

DAY 5

SHADOW SHOGUN

WE arrived in Tokyo at ten the next morning. Back at Brodie Security, I searched my desk for a message from Hara, but there was none to be found, so I dialed the mogul's direct number. The same secretary answered.

"This is Brodie again for Mr. Hara."

"I'm afraid he's flown to Taiwan, sir."

"Did you pass on my message?"

"Yes, sir. He appreciates your checking in."

"Does his trip have anything to do with Teq QX?"

"You'll need to ask him."

"Did he say anything else?"

"Yes, sir. He said to keep on as you've been doing and he would be in touch shortly."

Keep on as I've been doing? He couldn't know what I was doing. Or could he?

"Anything else?"

"No, sir."

"Wonderful," I said, and hung up.

Next, Noda took me aside. We had to stay alive long enough to gather what we needed, but in the meantime he wanted to remove Brodie Security employees from the equation. Otherwise, Soga would feast on them the way a grizzly feasted on a riverful of salmon.

"Can we protect the others if we keep them out of the loop?" I asked him.

"Probably."

"Sounds like a plan."

"Then no one but George and Narazaki here. And Renna and his people overseas. Fewer people to protect'll make our lives easier."

So we drew the line and some of the weight lifted.

For the debriefing, the Japantown team gathered in my office. Noda filled in Narazaki, who agreed we should keep the encounter at Soga-jujo to ourselves, then we called George in and swore him to secrecy. No sense in spooking the troops. Narazaki congratulated me on my first successful assignment, and when I protested that it was Noda's show from start to finish, my father's partner smiled knowingly.

In the broad sweep of Noda's strategic readjustment was a review of Toru and Mari's work. Narazaki decided to continue the computer probe as long as we could keep our pair of keyboard jockeys out of the line of fire. The two of them had taken up residence in the southwest corner of the office, where Toru presently snoozed on an army cot. In shifts, they tracked the intruder with high-grade antihacker software. As Mari explained it, the program shot down the lines the way a fiber optic camera was thrust down a human throat, illuminating the hacker's digital tracks. By monitoring the software, they knew within two minutes when our digital "black hatter" logged on anywhere on the Net, and while he surfed forward, the software blazed his "back trail," untangling the maze of sites and electronic bottlenecks used to disguise his base of operation. Last night, they had backtracked him through the Brazilnet exchange to Istanbul and Morocco before losing him to interference.

While we were closeted in my office, an EU operation swung into overdrive and Brodie Security cleared out. After our meeting broke up, I rang Renna, hoping he'd put me through to Jenny, but Renna advised me to leave her be. All was well, and Jenny and Detective Cooper were getting along famously. I asked him to put extra people on Jenny and he told me the department would never allow it. "Yes, they will," I said, "when they hear my end of the story." I fed him information on the kanji, the hacker, and our narrow escape from Soga-jujo. After his initial shock, Renna told me he would station a two-man crew outside the house but I'd hear the chief's howl in Tokyo. He inquired if I had any proof. I said no. Witnesses? No. Anything at all he could show his superiors to indicate progress and justify a three-person team on Jenny?

Soon, I said. We discussed the case for another minute, then hung up, Renna clearly frustrated with the lack of anything concrete.

I returned to my hotel, showered, shaved, snacked, and slept. The rest rejuvenated my brain cells, and they reciprocated by shuffling the pieces of the Japantown puzzle. Over and above the threat of Soga, I worried about Jenny. I couldn't talk to her yet, and I knew her anxiety must be building. She'd been in a fragile state when we moved her to the safe house. At least by tomorrow morning, a team of three would be watching all flanks.

Wanting to run some new ideas past Noda, I called the chief detective on his cell phone and he suggested we talk over noodles at Murata's around five, just before the dinner rush. I agreed, and at the appointed time I strolled into the soba shop, slid onto a wooden bench across from Noda, and asked if he'd come straight from the office.

"Yeah."

"Toru and Mari making any progress?"

"They're getting a little ripe. Bought them a bar of soap and chits for the local public bath."

"Any *other* progress?"

"Traced the screen blip backward to London, Madrid, and New Zealand."

"Toru say when they'll have results?"

"No."

Murata appeared with two trays of *zaru-soba*, glistening handmade brown pasta cooled in ice water and then perched on a red lacquer tray with an inset bamboo grate that allowed the noodles to drain. As the chef set the food before us, I could detect the faint scent of freshly ground buckwheat.

"One thing still puzzles me," I said once we were alone again. "When you called me in San Francisco, you told me to get to Tokyo because they don't kill in their own backyard. You said it again in Soga."

"Yeah, so?"

"How do you know that?"

"The third guy."

"The one who made it back to Tokyo?"

"Yeah."

"What did he say?"

"Not *say. Did.* Flew to Sapporo three weeks later. Got dead real quick."

His reply left me speechless. Noda, however, with his usual nonchalance, dug into his meal.

I scrambled to unravel the implications. Were we trapped in Tokyo? Alive only as long as we breathed the smog-tinged air of the Japanese capital?

Tamping down a rising panic, I asked the obvious question: "How did he die?"

Eyes locked on his pasta, Noda hesitated for the first time. Immediately, I knew that he'd been protecting me. And that I would not like the answer.

"*Kaji,*" Noda said. "In his hotel room. He never woke up."

Fire. The same MO used to kill Mieko and her family. My heart bucked and vertigo blurred the corners of the room. I felt queasy and disoriented, and as if the world were disintegrating around me. No wonder Noda had stayed mum. With this knowledge beforehand, I would have gone ballistic in Soga and gotten us both killed.

Noda snagged another clutch of noodles. Fighting back dizziness, I tried to focus my thoughts. I felt a new rage building and wondered how to come at these guys. I pinched the bridge of my nose. "Let me get this straight. They waited until he left Tokyo? For three weeks?"

"Yeah."

"So what does that mean for us?"

"Don't know. Open season if we leave town?"

"Jesus, Noda."

"'Course, they've been on you since San Francisco."

Meaning that after five years of operating under Soga's radar, Noda had willingly tossed himself into the mix.

I said, "What else the third guy tell you?"

"Not much."

Noda swallowed more soba. My appetite waned and the pasta Murata had so carefully prepared languished untouched on its lacquer tray.

I said, "Well, I've got some new ideas on the subject. I think I know why Tokyo's a safe haven."

"Why?"

"It's too close to home."

"Theirs?"

"No, their clients'. Big difference."

Noda tossed the idea around while he consumed another mouthful of noodles. "Possible," he said when he finished eating.

I fed him my theory: In the darkened halls of the ryokan, the innkeeper had told us the Ogi clan's genius lay in serving the ruling powers of the day. According to Takahashi's interpretation, the kanji suggested Soga eliminated kings. And as history showed us, kings fought kings. Or in Japan, warlords. Shoguns and daimyos. And would-be shoguns. Then, as now, the powers-that-be camped in the capital of Edo, now Tokyo, the center of government and big business. Tokyo was a safe haven *because* Soga's major clients resided in the capital, now and in centuries past. With a quarter of Japan's population living in the greater Tokyo area, Soga couldn't litter the place with bodies. So, to reassure their clientele and protect the longevity of their enterprise, the "kingbreakers" designated Japan's capital city off-limits. It was simply good business sense. I topped off my recital with a plum—I believed Soga's working base was elsewhere because the village was too isolated and the faces of the recruits too young.

Noda filled the several minutes he needed to mull over my ideas by polishing off the rest of his meal, then adding *soba-yu*—steaming hot cooking water that contained nutrients from the buckwheat in the noodles—to his remaining dipping sauce to make a soup. He sipped the soup and nodded in approval, a gesture I'd seen him give my father back in the days when I sometimes hung out at Brodie Security. "Makes sense."

"You think so?"

"Ties everything up. No holes."

"Which makes what Toru and Mari are working on more important than ever. If they can trace the hacker, we could locate their base."

"You're saying we wait on the blip?"

"Yeah. Unless you have a better idea?"

"Don't, but—"

"What?"

"We crossed a line in Soga. So until then, be careful."

Meaning maybe they wouldn't *kill* us in Tokyo, but there were plenty of other things they could do.

———

I strolled out into the summer swelter. After the coolness of the soba shop, the steamy heat hammered my temples while the glare bouncing off the sidewalk sent a stabbing pain to a tender place at the back of my eyes. I was heading for the side entrance of our building when a black limousine edged up to the curb.

A pair of six-foot-two neckless bulwarks with shoulders like stone ramparts stepped briskly from the lengthy vehicle and took up positions on either end.

"You Brodie?" one of them asked.

My pulse quickened. With our building behind me, I was boxed in. I said, "Yeah. Why?"

Stalling. Giving myself time. Giving Noda a chance to spot me. He'd hung back for a few words with Murata, who would be unhappy that I'd left his meticulously prepared fare untouched.

"Come with us, please."

Please. The rear guard reached out and flicked open a back door. My mind raced to make sense of the scene before me. The two men wore dark suits and dark turtlenecks. There was some sense of agility to these hulks—maybe they'd dabbled in a martial art or two—but impressions of dark alleys and midnight thrashings were more prominent than late-night acrobatics in black.

Private bulwarks?

My throat tightened. Even if they were only hired security, an unannounced excursion in an anonymous car could still be unpleasant. In Japan, there were always unseen powers in the shadows.

I examined the limo. It had tinted windows and a miniature Japanese flag anchored to the far corner of the front hood. There was stateliness there. I glanced at the suited bulldogs and saw the same lofty pride. My apprehension gave way to expectancy. Their owner's identity remained cloaked but his status was loudly trumpeted.

Someone was reaching out.

Inside the restaurant I saw movement. Noda was up and about.

I put some distance between myself and the soba shop, then stepped toward the automobile. Noda came out a few seconds later, saw the lay, and without a word headed in the opposite direction.

As I slid into the car, I cast a discreet glance back. Palming his cell phone, Noda was punching buttons.

The way I saw it, maybe it was time to take a calculated risk.

HE was a hundred ten pounds of brittle bone and sagging yellow flesh bundled up in an Italian suit and a chrome-plated wheelchair that seemed to swallow him whole. His hands lay like dead fish under a scarlet lap cloth.

Fifteen minutes after my abduction, the limousine had rolled up to a redbrick neoclassical edifice built in the early 1900s and I was handed over to a more presentable pair of private bodies in blue suits, silk ties, and cologne. The second guard ushered me into a gloomy, high-vaulted room lathered in textured wallpaper, plush carpeting, and floor-to-ceiling velvet drapery—all in scarlet. Overhead, a silver chandelier added the final touch. It was a concept of Old Russian or European elegance that Japan's powermongers of generations past had embraced for their parlors.

"I hope you'll excuse the dimness of the room," my unknown host said. "Bright light hurts my eyes."

Not knowing whom I was dealing with, I remained silent. All interior lighting had been extinguished in favor of a dim illumination courtesy of a north-facing window overlooking a shaded rock garden. I'd been in midnight power outages with more light.

"Please have a seat, Brodie-san."

"Thank you, ah . . . forgive me, I don't know your name."

"All in good time."

Though evasive replies were second nature for men of his make, the answer displeased me. It was cagey and heralded anything but a fruitful meeting. With reluctance, I dropped into a stuffed armchair across the room, the only seat in the spacious parlor not on wheels. Between us lay an oversize coffee table chosen, no doubt, to maintain distance. Seeking a clearer view of the man before me, my eyes struggled to adjust to the daytime dimness.

"I apologize for the suddenness of my summons. Allow me to offer you some refreshment. Fresh juice? Coffee, beer, whiskey?"

Two female attendants hovered nearby, attentive to my answer. Their kimonos were silk and expensive, their manner solicitous but lacking the effortless grace of the highly trained.

"Nothing, thank you."

Hearing my reply, the kimonoed servants bowed and retreated. The scented watchdogs settled by the exits at either end of the room. I wasn't going anywhere without permission.

"I am told you are conversant in our ways," the old man said. "Do you know the expression *No aru taka wa tsume o kakusu?*"

"'The clever eagle hides its talons'? Sure."

"Good. For that is what I wish to discuss."

The phrase embodied a way of life for many Japanese: Never show your real power. A faceless form in the shadows is a position of strength. It is how Japan deals not only with its own but the world at large. The pose has the additional benefit of being hard to attack. Targets are tough to zero in on if they can't be pinned down. The most influential men in recent Japanese history were the hidden kingmakers who shied away from the limelight. These powerbrokers were sometimes called *kuroko,* after the nearly invisible Kabuki stagehands dressed in full-body black who assist the actors during onstage costume changes in full view of the audience. These behind-the-scenes movers were also known as shadow shoguns. Most Japanese know that shadow shoguns exist, but few know who they are. Before me sat one such phantom.

"Do I leave you speechless, Brodie-san? Come, come. I've heard so much about you."

Alluding to one's own strength broke the cardinal rule, so his reference involved a different power center.

I cast the only line at hand. "Japantown?"

He nodded encouragingly, a bony hand flicking once beneath the scarlet lap cover.

"The kanji?"

I watched him as I said it. He evinced no surprise, no puzzlement, no curiosity. *He knew.* Back in San Francisco, no one outside of the SFPD task force and a few select insiders were aware of the calligraphy's existence. In Japan, only a handful of highly placed sources within the government had been informed of the kanji. Which told me just how influential the wheelchair-bound man before me was.

My host said, "And should the eagle choose to show interest?"

"It might display its claws. The sight of talons is often enough."

The skin around his eyes crinkled. "I am pleased you understand the distinction."

I digested the distinction. He was offering one of several possible interpretations for the Nakamura killings. I chose the most likely one: "Japantown was a message?"

"An able comment."

"Meant to strike fear?"

"A penetrating remark."

I threw him a curve. "If these are men who do not willingly reveal themselves, they must have extracted a heavy price to leave a signature of their work."

"Your understanding gains in breadth. And?"

Eagle . . . kanji . . . message . . . "This is intimidation at the highest level, so only those in top positions would know the kanji's meaning and fear it."

My host brought gnarled hands from under the scarlet lap spread and placed them on the padded armrests of his chair. Patient. Attentive. Expectant.

I gazed up at the unlit chandelier. *The murders . . . a message . . . Hara's foot dragging . . . son of a bitch!* Was I deaf, dumb, and stupid? It was as obvious as batter on shrimp tempura: Brodie Security was fish bait.

The attack *was* directed against the maverick businessman, who in turn deflected the assault, setting us up to draw Soga into the open.

No wonder Hara was avoiding my calls. No wonder his secretary told me to keep on doing what I was doing. Having taken the offensive and set me in motion, her boss had ducked for cover. He was leveraging Brodie Security's manpower and my connection to the SFPD to force Soga into the open. He lured us into Soga's sights by jetting over to see me then directing his famous daughter to visit my shop while the Japanese paparazzi, predictably, did what they always did: recorded her every tear and flourish. An unwitting pawn in her father's plans, Lizza had even *posed* in front of the shop. "*No one ever really knows what Father thinks*," she'd told me in confidence. How right she was. I flushed with anger at Hara's betrayal, only to cringe a moment later at my gullibility.

Hara had orchestrated the setup to end all setups.

A noose into which I'd obligingly slipped my neck.

HATE welled up from a dark region low in my gut. It was not a pleasant feeling. Across the room, my host's eyes glittered with unmasked glee. He was feeding on my loathing with the relish of a rodent rooting through entrails.

Barely containing my repugnance for both men, I hissed at the powerbroker through clenched teeth. "We're pigeons for the eagle, then?"

His Gray Eminence presented a stoic front as ageless and impervious as the stone ramparts of Osaka Castle. Except for his eyes. They were enlivened with a gleam of amusement. My consternation was proving to be first-rate entertainment.

A half-smile flitted across his lips. "Have you been followed?"

"Yes."

"Since when?"

"San Francisco."

"They are monitoring your movements. If they feel you are a serious concern, they will strike. You, Brodie Security, even your family, if necessary."

Jenny.

"That's a lot of people," I said.

"Numbers present no obstacle to them, as you've seen."

Quite clearly, the man knew everything about Japantown. "But the Nakamura family was defenseless. We're not."

"Hara expects the pigeon to find claws. Out of necessity."

"What are the chances of them considering us a 'serious concern'?"

His lips parted in silent mirth. Three brackish stumps studded gray-black gums. His rotting dark hole of a mouth sent waves of revulsion through me that I managed to hide only with great effort.

"Have no worry on that account. Hara has been very thorough and"—knowing what was coming, I felt my stomach convulse—"if he hadn't been, I would have."

In the village, I'd been attacked with knives, shot at, and poisoned. Now, in a gilded parlor, a man of power and privilege tells me—without pretense—that he would have gladly set me up if my client hadn't already done so. It took me a long moment before I found my voice again. "I'll take that drink now. Whiskey, straight up."

My host raised a finger and a watchdog moved to the side bar.

In a distant part of the building, a clock chimed seven times. As I waited for the liquor, the old man's bony hands slithered from the armrests back under the protective covering of the red lap cloth, and he was once more as motionless as the lichen-encrusted stones in his garden.

The decadence of this ancient salon was wearing me down, as were the powerbroker's riddles. I dreaded his next words but craved them too. In the meantime, the liquor provided a welcome warmth and numbed my misgivings.

"Personally," the old man said, "I think someone miscalculated."

I stared at my host and tormentor without expression. "How's that?"

"They took everything from Hara. With no family remaining aside from his errant daughter, he's fighting back."

"So you also think it's an attack on Hara?"

"Almost certainly. They want him alive but tamed."

"Why?"

His tone turned glacial. "Who knows? But surely, if whoever hired Soga sought Hara's money or business, Hara would be dead and they'd deal with the heirs."

Closing my eyes, I let my head fall back against the chair. I'd had enough of the slime. "So why am I here?"

"I want to help."

My eyes snapped open. "*You're* offering to help *me*?"

"Against Soga, yes."

"What have you got?"

Eyes boring into mine, the old man leaned forward. "I can open doors."

"Okay. Who are they?"

"They are what you've seen."

"Where are they based?"

"Maybe Soga-jujo, but most likely elsewhere."

"How many are we talking about?"

"The size of their organization is unclear."

"You give all-too-familiar answers."

"You're asking the wrong questions. Names and locale we don't have, but useful information we do."

"Can you give me an example of their handiwork?"

"Sanford Smith-Caldwell, the Boston businessman eight months ago."

"Really?"

As the CEO-elect of a major East Coast financial firm with global interests, Smith-Caldwell's death had been paraded across world headlines.

"Believe me, it's true. Before him, a Bonn broker in Hong Kong slated to return home to the company presidency. Australian businessman Howard Donner, whose family sold his clothing empire to a large Asian conglomerate within days of his death. Also likely, but not yet confirmed, a French developer who had just purchased a large block of neglected seafront property in Italy."

"I heard about the Frenchman. The radio said he fell overboard from his yacht and drowned. Also something about a high number of summer fatalities among late-night swimmers in that part of the Mediterranean."

The powerbroker gave me his open-maw grin. "Soga would play to the statistics."

"Were all of the deaths 'accidental'?"

"Yes. The Frenchmen drowned, Smith-Caldwell fell down a flight of steps at his vacation home, the German's BMW collided with a semi, and Howard Donner's private jet crashed in the outback."

"No suggestion of . . . other hands?"

"Not to the investigating authorities."

A frown signaled my displeasure. Maybe his claims were valid, or just maybe he was tossing around prominent headlines for me to soak up. Since he offered no verification, he could pitch whatever he wanted my way and I had no chance of substantiating his claims. The only thing I knew for certain was that the nameless man before me was one of Japan's shrewdest political minds—and one of the most dangerous.

I said, "Japantown wasn't subtle."

"They tailor assignments to the client's needs, but I assure you an act as blatantly brutal as Japantown is as rare as a flawless black pearl." Noting my skepticism, he said, "Not unexpectedly, you are a hard man to convince. You want something for nothing, but diving for pearls comes not without risk."

I stiffened. Was he threatening me? Desiring nothing more than to be finished with the old manipulator, I spat out a challenge. "Bowl me over, then."

A low growl escaped his lips. "You may regret those words."

I sunk back in my chair, wondering what I'd unleashed.

"Four years ago," he began in a low rumble, "there was a string of murders in Los Angeles, Salt Lake City, and Chicago . . ."

Four years ago . . . Los Angeles . . .

He knew something about Mieko.

T HE spiteful gleam in the old powerbroker's eyes told me he would extract payback for my verbal scrappiness, as players in his circle invariably do.

"Soga is usually extremely subtle. That is how they've stayed in business for so long. Four years ago they spread a series of killings over half a year. No American law enforcement agency ever connected the crimes. Not the local authorities, the FBI, the U.S. Marshals. No one caught the common link. Since we unofficially monitor all unnatural deaths of Japanese nationals, we pieced it together."

My breath caught in my throat. This wasn't going to be another list of headlines.

"Seven people died. Four in Los Angeles, two in Chicago, one in Utah. In each case, at least one victim was wealthy and owned car dealerships in prime locations. Of the three primary victims, two were Japanese nationals."

No wonder I never turned up a motive. The target was not Mieko's parents but her uncle. Through a Japanese cousin in the trade ministry, her uncle had locked up pivotal Nissan franchises early in the game, building a successful string of outlets on the West Coast from San Diego to Seattle. After his death, his heirs sold the business to the first bidder and retired young.

I said, "So Soga camouflaged the automotive connection by killing the uncle away from his home. Are you sure about the dealerships?"

"There can be no doubt. The lots of all three owners were swept up by two shell corporations based in the Balkans and sold to a third in Costa Rica."

Sickened, I sprang from my chair, needing to stretch my legs, needing to think. My abrupt movement triggered a reaction from the bodyguards, and they charged in at a fast clip. At the last second, the old man shook them off.

"Let's avoid sudden movements in the future, shall we, Mr. Brodie?" said my withered host.

Pacing back and forth in front of the oversize table, I ignored the comment, instead wrestling with the new puzzle pieces he'd provided, while, with undisguised glee, he watched me squirm on the pin he'd thrust into me. I ignored that, too.

At his death, Mieko's uncle possessed an annual pretax income of three to four million dollars a year. An orchestrated grab of the three businesses from the bereaved at a hefty discount that offered instant financial independence without the next-of-kin having to lift a finger would be a win-win, allowing someone to build an empire on the cheap.

The old man asked derisively, "Have I swayed you this time?"

My breathing was ragged, and my chest heaved. Had I lost my wife to some hustler's ambitions for steel on wheels? Was Jenny growing up motherless because of blind greed?

My response was terse. "Did you follow up on the shell companies?"

He shrugged bony shoulders expressively. "My people tried but failed. Nothing but dead ends. That is where you come in. You and your organization."

I collapsed back into my chair. From deep within the corridors of Japanese power, I'd been gifted with a credible nugget of information about the Japantown killers no one else could possibly uncover. And with it, I'd also been given a believable motive for my wife's death. Knowing I could backtrack his story, the powerbroker couldn't stray too far from the truth. But when all was said and done, as with his earlier examples, he offered no hard evidence.

I needed more. Much more.

At once heartened and frustrated, I ran my fingers through my hair.

"Exactly what kind of service does Soga provide? Clearly, they can't go around killing people at will."

"Anything in Japan can be explained if you trace it back to its roots. In the first two and a half centuries of their existence, Soga was involved in spying, strong-arming, blackmail, and kidnapping, as well as the not-infrequent assassination. They worked first for the ruling shoguns and daimyos, then for the new Meiji government, and finally for our budding war machine as Japan sought overseas territories before and during World War Two. After the collapse of the war effort in 1945, Soga expanded overseas, and judging by their assignments slowly acquired clientele in Asia, Europe, and the Americas."

"Why go abroad?"

"After Japan's surrender, work here was scarce. The Allied Forces occupied the country for more than five years, so Soga went searching for additional income sources and found a demand for their services in the private sector abroad. First with some of the high-powered Japanese who escaped from Manchuria and other places and then with foreigners."

"Which part of their service?

The old man gazed up at the unlit chandelier. "The same types of machinations, with an emphasis on sophisticated, high-level 'accidents' of a permanent nature. For equally high-level fees."

I stared at the powerbroker. "Can you prove this?"

"Of course not."

I shook my head. "Let me rephrase that. How do you know?"

"Research. They don't kill tatami makers, Brodie-san. Victims are prominent citizens of their prospective countries, often globally active."

"Go on."

"After years of probing, I now know to look for the Three Ps— property, promotion, power. If one or more of these change hands with the death of a major principal, the incident becomes a candidate for further research. Soga's fee starts at half a million dollars American, and escalates according to degree of difficulty and what they see as the resultant benefits to their client. Soga offers a premier service at premium prices. For that, it delivers a clean job. No hitches. No loose ends. An error-free rollout of their plan. Viewed against assured future earnings for the client, the price is cheap. Through the tax filings of the Japanese car dealers' next-of-kin, my people determined that by offering quick cash on the heels of the tragedy, the buyer—Soga's client—picked up the businesses at two-thirds of their market value, a savings of nine-point-seven million dollars on those two deals alone."

"You're telling me they sell death to grease business deals?"

"To 'smooth over' a buyout or merger, yes. Or to secure a promotion. Or protect their client's already lucrative position. Soga eliminates obstacles or threats when a carefully planned accident makes economic sense. Some would argue that such an idea is a logical extension of your American-style free market."

The man was insane. "You may not be in the best position to pass judgment on such practices," I said, knowing that his dirty tricks were probably just as devastating.

My nameless host's eyes flashed, giving me the first physical sign of how dangerous he could be should he choose to flex his muscles. But then he rattled me with the candor of his next comment:

"That's all the more reason I understand them."

Suddenly, I felt soiled and depressed. Repulsed. But you couldn't hunt in the swamp without slogging through the muck.

"So who hires them?" I asked.

"Businesspeople who share the same worldview. Soga is only doing what they have always done. To be frank, from the days of the shogun, there has always been undesirable work that needed doing. Today, the thriving capitalist system—whether in the U.S., Europe, Asia, or the Middle East—is simply another power base, and it too has undesirable work that needs handling. Soga has always filled that need. Sound familiar?"

"Disgustingly so. Why haven't you . . . ?"

"Availed myself of their services? Not from lack of trying, I assure you. My competitors found Soga first. And if there is one thing Soga upholds, it's loyalty to their client base. That and their guarantee to tidy up annoying loose ends."

That stopped me. "Are you saying Brodie Security's become a loose end?"

Frosty eyes regarded me. "At the very least. Despite your rudeness, I'm going to give you some advice, Mr. Brodie. Advice that could save

your life. Continue on as you have been but be discreet in your movements. Discretion in the extreme is required if you desire to survive
this ordeal. Any other regimen will bring Soga down on you like a
sledgehammer."

I closed my eyes and inhaled deeply. That horse had already left the
barn. "Too late. We've been to the village."

My host's eyes widened in astonishment, maybe for the first time in
years. "*What?* Did they approach you?"

"They did more than that."

I gave him a short version of our visit. By the time I finished, his
distaste for my presence had reshaped itself into unbridled admiration.
Then he wagged his head in despair. "Such a waste. You had so much
promise. I thought that this time I would have a shot at Soga."

"Maybe you will."

"I wish it were true, believe me. But it's not possible now. Had I
known of your trip to the village beforehand, I would never have initiated contact. There's no point doing business with a dead man."

"We're not out of the game yet."

"On the contrary, you're in far too deeply. By now, if they don't
know everything about you, they will in short order. If there's one mystery here, it's why you're still walking around."

The cold certainty of his analysis curdled my blood. At the instant
I opened my mouth to reply, I saw the bodyguard at the front door
slump to the floor.

Was the powerbroker a psychic as well?

I leapt from my seat and, finding no cover in the room, instinctively
crouched behind my armchair before the unconscious watchdog's body
had settled, waiting to see how the attack would unfold, hoping to
shield myself from any gunfire. The next moment, unseen hands pulled
the guard at the rear entrance into the darkened doorway behind him
and we heard a muffled grunt as he too collapsed to the ground.

But still no sign of the assailants.

Just silence.

Swiftly scanning the dark chamber only confirmed what I already
knew: I was cornered in a large room with no weapon and no cover
worth a damn.

Adrenaline electrified me, and my body tensed. In seconds, I'd be facing them. I clenched my fists, set my shoulders, and readied myself. Then I rose from behind the overstuffed scarlet chair. Any bullets would soon penetrate its soft cushioning. Better to face them head-on and take my chances.

Looking frailer than ever, the old man's glance swung nervously from his fallen servant to me while we waited—unarmed and unprotected—for men in black to charge into the room.

IT was not my time to die.

Noda eased into the room with a snub-nosed Smith & Wesson leveled at the old man's chest but his vigilant eyes focused on me. "You all right?"

"Am now."

With a grunt, Noda scanned the room. "Need some light in here."

He flicked on a switch by the doorway and the overhead chandelier sprang to life, spraying soft white beams into every corner of the room.

"Scenic," the laconic detective said, gazing at the powerbroker with unvarnished curiosity.

Our host was completely hairless. Face, arms, and pate were bare. Incredibly, his eyebrows had also vanished with the rest of his body hair. His facial skin was dry and yellow-gray and had caved into eyesockets and cheeks like a farmer's field into a cluster of sinkholes. Revolted, I looked away.

"Darkness suits me," the old man said without any outward sign of uneasiness.

Strolling in through the back door, George asked, "You okay?"

My old friend was in top form today in a chic blue blazer and collarless black silk shirt buttoned to the neck.

"Yeah, fine."

"Good. Noda figured this to be a milk run. Kept his promise down in Soga and let me tackle the two thugs on the back door. Strapped on the plasti-cuffs." To the powerbroker, George offered a harsh censure.

"You need to learn how to make appointments, sir. We don't tolerate people strong-arming one of our own."

My host grinned. "I am pleased to see that. You don't know how pleased."

George shot him a dismissive glance, then turned to Noda. "Who is this clown who doesn't know how to pick up a phone?"

"Kozawa," Noda said.

Despite what I'd already surmised about the withered powerbroker, my pulse jumped. *Jesus.* How had I missed the signs? Goro Kozawa had an ego larger than the Imperial Palace. People walked away from a summons one of four ways: richer, poorer, their career boosted or destroyed. Make that five ways. Sometimes they left pummeled.

Goro Kozawa was the patriarch of powerbrokers. Believed to have hooks in the ruling party and the opposition, as well as backdoor ties to yakuza from Hokkaido to Okinawa, the ruthless industrialist-turned-shadow-shogun had built his fortune from a small trading company importing oil, minerals, and luxury goods before expanding into construction, railroads, and retail. His companies held many monopolistic import licenses, and since he had more politicians in his pocket than crocodiles had teeth, his interests remained monopolistic. After erecting his power base, Kozawa had delegated the top positions in his enterprises to the shrewdest of his loyal underlings and slipped underground. He attended VIP functions, yet was never photographed. If he showed up unannounced at a major gala, rumors circulated but were never confirmed. He was as much of a ghost as Soga.

George raised an eyebrow. "*You're* Goro Kozawa? We've heard about you."

"And I of Brodie Security. A treasure of a crew, if ever there was one." He glanced at Noda. "You . . . distracted all four of my men?"

Noda's nod was brief, his expression neutral. There was no sneer, no smirk. No sign of smugness or self-satisfaction.

"Excellent."

George raised an eyebrow. "No doubt your people will have a dissenting opinion when they come around."

"As they should. I warned them to expect a visit." He gazed at a fallen guard before zeroing in on me. "I think you're overexposed, Brodie-san. Your chances of living out the month are less than those of a Kabukicho whore walking through San'ya without being accosted. But assuming you somehow manage to stay alive, perhaps we can work together. I've got nothing to lose."

George snorted. "With an attitude like that, why should we?"

"Young man, whoever you are, let me enlighten you. In my more naive past, I dispatched two of my bodyguards to Soga-jujo to dispose of what I thought a minor nuisance."

"And?"

With hard, dark eyes he stared at George, then me. "Mr. Brodie, if you and your people are to survive Soga, you must be better informed." To George, he said, "In answer to your question, young man, I am here. We are conversing."

I bit my lip and dropped my gaze to the scarlet carpet, but George snapped up the bait: "The men you sent, how good are they?"

"*Were,*" Kozawa corrected, "*were.* They failed. They are dead. At least I presume they are dead. They never returned."

Annoyed, I stepped in. "That's a touching tale, Kozawa-san, but how do we know we can trust you?"

"They are old enemies. They have nipped at me in many ways over the years."

Noda said, "Still doesn't answer the question."

Kozawa considered us for a long moment before making his next revelation. "Three years ago, my adopted son—the man I'd handpicked to carry on after my retirement—was found dead on the streets of Karuizawa, his neck sliced clean to the spine. Garroted. The police wrote off the attack as a casualty of a Chinese triad flare-up in the area, but I knew better. The man who hired Soga has paid for his arrogance, but I have a long memory and have made it my business to learn everything I can about them. But it's not easy. Even for me."

I didn't like what I heard between the lines. "You come with too many strings. Why should we help you?"

"I believe you know Inspector Kato of the Tokyo Metropolitan Police?"

"You know I do."

Last fall, Kato had saved me from a fifty-four-story plunge off the top of the Sumitomo Bank Building in West Shinjuku. Between Inspector Kato and myself was a bond stronger than anything Kozawa could summon up to break it.

"Will he do?"

I nodded and the powerbroker retrieved a sealed envelope from his jacket. I made the long trip around the immense table and took the proffered letter, from which I extracted a single sheet of paper.

To Brodie-sama,

This letter will introduce you to Mr. Goro Kozawa. While his name registers in very few foreign circles, I am certain it will mean something to you. In the matter of a certain village—and only that matter—you may accept my assurances of his reliability and eagerness to achieve the same ends you seek.

Respectfully,
Shin'ichi Kato
Inspector, Tokyo Metropolitan Police, Shibuya Station

Kato would not write a recommendation lightly, nor would he submit to any pressure of the kind Kozawa could apply. I passed the note to Noda, who read it and handed it to George. Neither of them voiced an objection.

Kozawa said, "Satisfied?"

"Yes."

"Then let's go for a ride. There is someone I want you to meet."

"Who?" Noda asked, his eyes narrowing in suspicion.

"Were I to tell you certain things, would you believe me?"

"No blind trust," Noda said flatly.

"Then understand this, Noda Kunio-san. I reached my position not by pleasing men but by knowing them. To my mind, your answer was a given. You need more information, so I'll take you to where the big fish swim."

A note of alarm chimed in my head. Neither George nor I had referred to Noda by his full name, yet the powerbroker had used it. He knew exactly who our chief detective was and wanted us to know it.

"Time to go, gentleman," Kozawa said, indicating the front door while the chimes of a sonorous clock in a back room struck eight times.

Late-night machinations.

The way of Japan.

CHAPTER 45

THE old man led us to an exclusive *ryotei*, the favored haunt of people in power where the decisions of the ruling elite were finalized. Sometimes, in a single night, the course of the whole country's policy in a certain business or political sector might be settled on, with the cost for a single session's libation running into thousands of dollars.

Four kimono-clad women swooped down on our two-car entourage with beguiling smiles and bows of welcome. Once we were off the street, a suited man in his thirties stepped from the shadows and Kozawa said, "Let me introduce Akira Tejima, one of the brightest young stars in the Boeisho firmament."

His words sent a tremor of anticipation through me. We were about to receive rarefied information of the highest order. The Boeisho was the Ministry of Defense. They wielded tremendous power in their sector, as did all the other ministries in their spheres of influence. The agency's umbrella covered any program or institution involved in defending Japan's borders, including the national defense budget, the training academies, and all three branches of the Japan Self-Defense Forces—air, ground, and maritime.

Tejima gave me the standard Japanese greeting followed by a slip of a bow that ungraciously put me in my place as a low-level guest. He would not expect a Caucasian guest to know the difference.

I was predisposed to dislike Tejima, and first impressions only reinforced what I already knew from previous dealings with Japanese bureaucrats. Most of the fast-track civil servants were arrogant and full of themselves. They were handpicked from the best universities and brandished the country's power with smarmy self-confidence, keeping every aspect of the people's daily lives under a tightly reined legal stranglehold. And if new hires weren't overbearing by nature, it was instilled in them as a matter of policy. Except for the eyes, Tejima oozed the same sort of bloated self-importance, but it was tempered, at least tonight, by a haunted look.

We followed two kimonoed women down a string of dimly lit corridors, then through a darkened courtyard garden. Frail bamboo lamps set at ground level illuminated the stone footpath we trod but left faces in the shadows, our procession tasteful and discreet in the inimitable Japanese manner.

The women drew up at the entrance to a secluded cottage in the farthest corner of the garden and bowed us in. A large, low table laden with liquid refreshment and an overflowing buffet of fresh seafood and choice meats awaited us.

Kozawa's bodyguard nudged the powerbroker's wheelchair up an access ramp, while two female attendants delicately pressed damp towels against the backs of the rotating wheels so any dirt, seen or unseen, would not be tracked into the twelve-mat tatami room, an intimate yet suitably spacious dining area by Japanese standards. After propelling the kingmaker to the table, the watchdog hit an unseen lever that started a built-in mechanism and lowered the wheelchair seat to floor level.

I sat on the indicated throw cushion and immediately a woman in a powder-blue kimono knelt and offered me a hot hand towel for my face and hands. Declining seats, George and Noda took up positions in the corners of the room, where they could watch the proceedings and the front door at the same time. On the way over in our own car, Noda suggested I continue to "be the face" of the investigation since Kozawa had reached out to me. As soon as the powerbroker was comfortable, his watcher settled in a third corner, crossing his arms and frowning at Noda and George.

The attendants pressed drinks into our hands, then rose, bowed, and departed. Noda and I exchanged glances and my heart kicked up a beat. Normally, the room would be bathed in alcohol and the liquid laughter of the hostesses until parties bonded. Tonight, though, the customary ritual had been suspended.

"This evening," Goro Kozawa began, lifting his drink for a toast, "in deference to our American guest, let frankness and informality rule."

We raised our glasses and drank. On the table, abalone sashimi, spiny lobster, and Russian caviar spilled from porcelain platters.

"Kozawa-sensei requests frankness, and I approve," Tejima said. "Should our goals be the same, circumstances would dictate full cooperation. I would like, first, to have some indication that we are indeed discussing the, uh, same party. What can you tell me?"

I had no desire to reveal any of our hard-won secrets to this man. We had so little and I knew nothing of Tejima's reputation, nor did I have any inkling of who was looking over his shoulder.

While I debated the issue, Noda stepped forward and produced a photograph of the digital interceptor Toru had discovered at Brodie Security.

With an eagerness that clashed with his aloofness, Tejima reached for the snapshot. His fingers were pink and plump and trembled slightly. After a moment's examination, he passed the photograph back to Noda with a nod of satisfaction. "We are pursuing the same course. There can be no doubt."

I studied the bureaucrat coolly before saying, "And why is that?"

With the habitual condescension of his breed, Tejima expounded for our benefit. "What you've uncovered is of Dutch manufacture by the Skoss Corporation out of Amsterdam, a high-tech firm with an exclusive clientele. Their product is very rare, made to order, and extremely expensive."

I said, "So you know *who* we're after, then?"

"Three years ago, two of these bugging devices were found in the possession of a Japanese national in the middle of the Sahara Desert. He was killed while trying to cross tribal land. Fifteen poison arrows took him down, but not before he had killed *seven* tribal warriors. We have reason to believe he assassinated a local chieftain with large land holdings who refused to lease oil rights to certain powers."

"Western or Asian?"

"I am not at liberty to say, but I can tell you this. When the body was repatriated, we discovered it belonged to a man who went abroad

twenty years ago as a teenager and never returned. The grandson of
a special officer who had disappeared in Manchuria near the end of
World War Two."

"'Special'?"

Eyes darting to the one empty corner of the room, Tejima grew
evasive. "A military officer."

I stood without preamble. "Kozawa-sensei, time is short, we are
in danger, and your friend is playing the slippery games of his breed.
Thanks for the offer of help, but I think we'll go elsewhere."

"Don't be so hasty, Brodie-san. It is quite natural for Tejima-kun to
guard his secrets. That is the nature of his job."

I felt my face redden. "If we're going to have to fight for every scrap
of information, we have better uses for our time."

A hand twitched under Kozawa's scarlet lap cloth. "Tejima-kun, he
does have a point. I wonder if you would mind—"

"But . . ."

Kozawa's brow darkened. "You will answer Brodie-san's questions
without holding anything in reserve."

"But my superior—"

"Your superior presents no barrier. He will accept everything without knowledge or question. Momentum is building. This is the closest I
—or your committee—have come in decades. If we lose this opportunity because you did not provide us with all the essential information
in your possession, I will hold you personally responsible. *Wakatta ka?*"
Do I make myself clear?

His complexion paling to the shade of the porcelain platters before
us, Tejima bowed deeply and mumbled, "As you wish."

Making an enemy of Goro Kozawa was tantamount to career suicide. If Tejima did not tread carefully, by tomorrow morning the recal-
citrant bureaucrat would be holding transfer orders to one of Japan's
Siberian outposts.

"I am pleased you have returned to tonight's program. Now, Brodie-
san, you were saying?"

I retook my seat. "What kind of special military, Tejima-san?"

Eyes downcast, Tejima murmured into his lap, "The Kempei Tai."

A current of fear roiled my blood. This thing just got worse by the hour. First Kozawa, then Hara's betrayal, and now state secrets of the dirtiest sort. In Tejima's pond, there would be sharks who would feel threatened by what we were about to learn.

Trading uneasy glances, Noda and I shared the same thought: yet another way to get ourselves killed.

TEJIMA had just mentioned one of Japan's most securely closeted skeletons.

Wartime Japan swarmed with police agencies that regulated every aspect of domestic and military life, such as the Special Higher Police (known as the Thought Police), and the Secret Military Police, a.k.a. the Kempei Tai—the most feared of them all. Espionage and counter-intelligence was their territory, and their eventual leader, the legendary Tojo, gave them the power to terrorize at home and abroad, which they did with unshackled fervor. Comparisons between the KPT and Nazi Germany's Gestapo were frequent, but after the Japanese surrender at the end of World War II, the Allied Occupation authorities played down the KPT's murderous reign in a bid to remake Japan's image as a new and humbled American ally in the East. With the eruption of the Korean War five years later, America needed Japanese bases as a launching pad against its new ally's feisty neighbor to the west, so all skeletons were permanently deep-sixed. In world annals, KPT activity remains an unexplored chapter. There was no Asian Simon Wiesenthal to hunt down the worst offenders.

I gave Tejima a further nudge. "How many Kempei Tai went missing after the surrender?"

"Among the low- and middle-ranking KPT officers, losses were typical. However, among the elite, nineteen. More than our experts can explain. Of those elite nineteen, seven had formed part of a super-elite group. The men were born in Soga-jujo. Two of the seven were top KPT officers. What makes those two significant is that with two other top

KPT officers *not* from Soga, they controlled the equivalent of a million American dollars in gold bullion. In nineteen-forties dollars, mind you."

"How many of the four officers who controlled the funds went MIA?" I asked.

"All of them."

"You're joking."

"Unfortunately, no."

"Were any bodies ever found?"

"No."

"How nice. A war chest becomes a start-up fund for Soga."

Tejima protested. "We have no proof that such is the case."

Kozawa scowled. "Tejima-kun . . ."

"Which could, in itself, be construed as the next closest thing," the chastened civil servant added hastily.

"How many other non-Soga KPT officers knew about the secret funds?"

"Six."

"And how many of *those* men survived the war?"

"None."

I fell back in my seat and stared at the bureaucrat in disbelief. His admission was staggering. I glanced at Noda. His face gave away nothing. I wondered if the chief detective was thinking what I was: the efficiency of the disappearances was a chilling reminder of how ruthless Soga could be.

"So," I said after considering the revelation, "in a sense, you've been assigned to clean up your own backyard, haven't you? Exhuming the skeletons for more secure reburials, before they become a public embarrassment?"

Tejima grimaced. "Do you have time to listen to a recording?"

"All the time in the world, provided it's now."

Nodding, Tejima reached for his briefcase. He keyed in a combination, popped the latches, and extracted a handheld digital recorder. With exaggerated concern, he spent several long moments aligning the corners of the machine with the table's edge, as if he were surreptitiously buying time to steel himself against his next revelation.

I studied the man before me. He took good care of himself. His grooming was impeccable. His haircut was expert, his cologne discreet. His hands were manicured, with cuticles shaped into perfectly rounded arcs. White half-moons peeked from the arcs. The half-moons began to tremble as he turned on the machine.

We heard a rush of air as a door swung open. Two sets of footfalls approached over hardwood. Chairs scraped the floor.

An assured male voice: "*Ugoiteru no ka?*" Is it running?

A second male: "*Ugoitemasu*. I was testing the machine. Shall I rewind the tape?"

Subservient, lower-ranking, I thought. *The first voice belonged to the leader.*

First male: "No. Keep it going. We're ready. Let's begin."

A third voice, grim and tense: "Will you do me the honor of listening to my story?"

The first man: "We are grateful to be allowed the opportunity. Saeki-kun, you may leave us now."

"As you wish, sir."

A silence, probably filled with a bow, was followed by receding footsteps and the sound of a closing door.

The first man: "Now, if our session is to be productive, let me suggest you be as candid as possible. I shall, quite naturally, hold your comments in confidence."

The grim voice: "I will tell you everything in one sitting. Are you sure you're ready?"

"Yes. I will gratefully receive all you wish to impart."

"Good, because once we begin there is no turning back."

"I understand. Now, why have you come forward?"

"By birth, I am *roku dai*: sixth generation. The oldest families are *ju-yon dai*: fourteenth generation. My father was killed on the job, but the job made him a millionaire. My mother has no financial worries, so she resisted my enlistment."

"They let you go?"

"There is never any shortage of willing recruits. The work requires stamina and complete devotion, but after an intensive three-year training program, the pay is extraordinary. Now my mother has passed on and I never married, but I see my nieces and nephews nearing recruitment age. My sister pleaded with me to find a way for her children to grow up free."

"Won't your speaking out put their mother at risk?"

"No. Only their uncle."

A short pause, then: "By which you mean yourself?"

"Yes."

I heard firmness in his one-word answer. It was the voice of a determined man who had made a hard choice before stepping forward. Made it, accepted the consequences, and regained his balance enough to offer gallows humor. Impressive, if he was the real thing.

"I see. What makes you think your sister will remain unharmed?"

"The Rules of Soga. As long as she stays with her land, in the village, she's safe."

"Okay, so for the record, how could the secret be kept for so long?"

"Theirs is a fiercely loyal brotherhood, and almost everyone has a family member or relative involved. Soga is ingrown and there is *giri*— deep obligation over generations. The group has always watched over the village. During natural disasters, the villagers turned to them. In old times, Soga protected them from ambitious warlords and overzealous shogunate troops. As recently as four generations ago, their support during a famine kept many of the poorer farmers from selling their daughters to brothel owners in the cities. After World War Two, Soga provided money to rebuild."

During our visit to the village, Noda and I had seen that loyalty, and in the okami-san the fear it engendered.

"This brotherhood acts as a patron of the village, then?"

"Yes."

"What about the others?"

"Others went into the police, the military, the ministries. They are *kakure* Soga. The hidden ones. They lead normal lives, but form an extensive covert network of Soga natives, relatives, and longtime associates. They are all loyal, and all benefit financially. Using them, Soga has infiltrated all the important power structures in Japan. The supply of 'information gatherers' is continually replenished. Many others are simply well-paid informants who know nothing of Soga's activities but owe their careers and financial stability to a network established more than three hundred years ago. The villagers who spy for Soga don't know any details, either. I do because my father secretly started my training before he died."

"Have there been others who tried to disengage?"

"One or two, but Soga's outplacement program involves incense and prayer beads, not retraining."

Again the gallows humor.

A caustic chuckle. "Your sense of the dramatic, Mr. Taya, is impressive. However, let's stay focused on the facts."

"My name!"

"What of it?"

"You use it so freely! And on this recording!"

"Calm yourself."

"We agreed—*no names*."

"This recording is for in-house use only."

"Haven't you been listening? They *are* in-house."

"You are paranoid, I think." The bureaucrat's voice was tinged with condescension. "Let's leave that for the moment. You hinted in our previous exchange of a long history. When did it begin?"

A pause, then: "With Kotaro Ogi. He was a high-ranking samurai from Soga in the inner circle of the Dog Shogun until he was caught honing his swordsmanship on a stray mutt in direct defiance of his master's edict. Ogi was stripped of his rank and tossed in a dungeon."

The shock of recognition flooded through me. General Ogi was the man honored in the memorial monolith I'd seen in Soga.

"Is ancient history really pertinent here?" the bureaucrat asked.

"That one incident forged Soga."

"How?"

"When the jails were emptied after the Dog Shogun's death, General Ogi was also released. He emerged from imprisonment a changed man. The experience showed him how vulnerable he was, and he vowed never to put himself at the mercy of a higher authority ever again."

"I'm not following you."

"From that day forward he relied only on himself, his family, and his fellow villagers. Returning home with all the samurai from his village around 1710, Ogi assembled his own outfit, which he hired out for special assignments. He provided discretion and quality, and as a former high-ranking samurai in the late shogun's employ, he had instant respectability, since no one took his incarceration seriously once the Dog Shogun had died. Word spread and when the new shogun needed an outside agent for deniability, he tapped the general. From that point on, Ogi's group hired out to each new regime, as well as local lords on favorable terms with the regime. Work was never lacking. Beatings, blackmail, and kidnapping made up the bulk of the work, but spying and even assassination also came into play—anything that the ruling powers needed done but needed distance from was parceled out to Soga. They were samurai gone astray, yet provided an essential service. When the samurai way fell to a modernizing Japan, most of Soga's contacts made the transition to the new government. So the arrangement continued."

"Are you implying that such secret links continue to this day?"

"Yes."

Derisive laughter. "Your story is too incredible for words."

The bureaucrat was mocking his informant, I thought. *The arrogant bastard.*

"But let's move on," the bureaucrat said. "In our earlier talk, you also mentioned new methods. Tell me about those."

Taya went on to recite how they had updated their fighting techniques. They became proficient at modern weaponry of all types, surveillance, hand-to-hand, and poisons. They charged high fees from an exclusive clientele, and—above all—secrecy kept them in business. "They will do anything to protect their secret. They have done so with great success for three hundred years. When there is doubt, the source of the doubt is silenced. *Kanzen ni.*" Completely.

"So tell me their weakness."

"I know of only one. They operate in teams of four. Only one or two people at the top know the whole operation. If you kill the leaders, it would be like killing the queen bee. The workers would be unable to do anything but buzz around aimlessly."

"I bet they store illegal weapons in Japan, correct? If we could catch them with a stockpile of firearms—"

"You can't crush them with a legal technicality."

"We are the Ministry of Defense, Mr. Taya, and we work within the law."

"There are only a handful of munitions in this country. But it's a minor stash and not the point—"

"Well, then, my committee's job will be a tad more difficult, won't it?"

"Listen to me! They can kill as easily with a knife or their hands, *Mr. Azuma*. Most Soga-assisted deaths appear accidental, but aren't. Forget your technicality."

"My solution would solve everything so neatly. If we could establish the location of a cache of guns, I could propose a raid, and under the Japanese constitution—"

Taya let out a weary sigh. "Listen very, very carefully. It may be your only chance. They are professionals by training, tradition, and blood, and have refined their art for fourteen generations."

The bureaucrat clicked his tongue in disdain. "No doubt, no doubt. Have you any other nuggets of wisdom to offer us?"

"Just one: If you are to succeed against them, you have to break your normal patterns. They *use* patterns, they use everything. You will be enlisting trained fighters against them. Any men you send should assume their attack to be expected no matter what level of secrecy is employed. If, en route, anything out of the ordinary attracts their attention—a small noise, a shadow, a whisper, an unexpected knock, *anything*—they must shoot first and question later. If they wait for verification, they will be dead."

"Is that all?"

"I have given your men the difference between life and death. Isn't that enough?"

Azuma burst out in unrestrained laughter. "Thank you, Mr. Taya, for this—ah—precious opportunity. But be honest with me for a moment, won't you? Don't you think you might be overreacting just a trifle?"

"Fool! *Listen to me!* Do I get anything out of this? Publicity? Money?"

"No."

"So what's my motive? What's the bigger picture here, Azuma?"

"I represent the bigger picture."

Taya pounded the table. "You can't see the bigger picture. But a day or two should tell. By week's end, if I'm still alive, then I'll know you stand a chance against them."

"Cheer up, Mr. Taya. I assure you that the Ministry of Defense is a formidable adversary."

"I hope they're not all as thick-headed as you, Mr. Azuma. Use what I have given you quickly. Waste no time. If not for my sake, for your own."

The recording ended.

TEJIMA broke the charged silence that followed.

"Until the interview you've just heard, we had been unable to confirm even the existence of this group. We logged only rumors and vague reports. Every few years a kanji like the one found in Japantown would surface with a killing, but such an appearance only fueled the rumors, elevating fear levels and creating a sort of myth."

Kozawa fidgeted. "The kanji resonates with older generations. There are stories."

"What kind of stories?" I asked.

"Stories of suicides. Of prominent men dying in their sleep."

"Accidents that may not have been accidents?"

"Yes."

I turned to Tejima. "You're a member of the committee mentioned on the tape?"

"Yes."

"Didn't the committee send anyone down to Soga-jujo?"

"Of course. They conducted inquiries, but it's an isolated community. Where the villagers weren't closemouthed, they were evasive."

Noda and I had received the same reception. "So you have a file full of dead ends?"

"Yes. All investigated by the book and—"

"—signed off on?"

Tejima dropped his eyes. "Embarrassing to admit, but yes. On paper, all is well."

A gloom descended as we considered the impotency of the whole of the Ministry of Defense, not to mention the Japanese government.

Hesitantly, Tejima sought my eye. "Let me ask you something, Brodie-san. What was your impression of the conversation you just heard?"

"Taya was informed, decisive, and convincing. Your Mr. Azuma comes off as dense, to say the least."

As had happened earlier, Tejima's hands began to quiver. This time he put his palms against the edge of the table and pushed, stretching muscle and ligament. He inhaled with deliberation, then let out the air in a measured manner, repeating the procedure until his hands steadied.

Once our host had tamed the trembling he said, "Six months ago, my boss assigned me to assist Azuma-san. That was three days before the interview. As a latecomer I was not yet directly involved in committee proceedings. I was expected to familiarize myself with the material in a method of my choosing. So I copied files and memos to review on my own time, and late one night, directly after the interview, I copied the recording. I never discussed my activities in this regard, and that single non-act probably saved my life. The original recording was gone from Azuma-san's machine the next morning. He worried that he had accidently erased it. I knew better but held my peace."

Tejima scrutinized his hands. "I practice the breathing routine you just saw every night before I go to bed and every morning when I rise. I also find it necessary to repeat it several times during the course of my workday, always in private. I do not sleep well because of nightmares. My appetite has dropped to almost nothing. Every morning I wake up relieved to be alive, then dread the day ahead because I wonder if I will live until evening. I went to a top university, Brodie-san, and joined the Ministry of Defense to serve my country. Much of my job involves shuffling papers. Important papers, but merely papers. We sit behind desks. We are not soldiers or spies. Fortunately, when I went to Kozawa-sensei for advice, I found him receptive. I am frightened, but don't get me wrong. I am determined to see this to a successful conclusion as I believe it vital to my country. Can you understand that?"

In spite of his occupation and our earlier run-in, I was beginning to like this man. "I think I can."

"You might be surprised to learn that I now share the informant's view that there are high-placed people in all the ministries on Soga's payroll. I think they are in the Ministry of Defense as well."

I sat up a little straighter. "Why is that?"

"Before the meeting, Azuma-san maintained the utmost secrecy. He enlisted the services of an unmarked car. He made arrangements from untraceable prepaid cell phones. There were no intermediaries, no lapses on our part, or on the informant's, as far as we can tell. Taya-san's sister was not briefed on his decision to come forward, nor was anyone else. Azuma-san kept his report to our superiors verbal—to only five men."

"But?"

"Early the next morning he was called away to handle a sudden emergency in Sendai. He hung himself that evening in his hotel room. A note in his own hand said he was despondent over his slovenly work."

They don't kill in Tokyo.

I said, "Suicide doesn't sound like the action of the man I heard."

"No," Tejima said. "It doesn't."

"What about the informant?"

Tejima's face crumbled. "Despite the fact that he went into hiding immediately after the interview, he was dead within forty-eight hours."

CHAPTER 48

WITH Tejima's final revelation, a wave of cold fear rolled through me. Day by day, Soga grew more invincible. I'm sure Jake faced tests of his own in the early days of Brodie Security, but I doubted they reached the degree of treachery we'd encountered in the village.

To hash things out, Noda, George, and I sought privacy away from the office and finally settled on Kongo's, a discreet saké bar in the narrow back alleys of Ochanomizu, a maze only the initiated could navigate. Even taxi drivers became hopelessly lost in this part of town.

Kongo's was a Japanese-style drinking place, an *izakaya* run by a former construction worker who had, three decades ago in his youth, saved his meager wages and slept in roach-infested boardinghouses until he scraped together enough money to buy a shack with clay walls in his old neighborhood. Now he slept above the shop with his wife and two sons; who were going to be anything but construction workers, Heizo Nishikawa told anyone who would listen. Where the walls of Kongo's had begun to wear thin, labels from vintage saké had been pasted like patches on worn jeans. There were five rickety tables, a counter that seated eight shoulder to shoulder, and a sixth table on raised tatami in a secluded nook at the back. We staked out the nook.

"Do you know how explosive this is?" I asked, tossing down my second cup of warm saké in one swallow.

We now had an unadulterated portrait of the beast—and we were shell-shocked. The reasons were plentiful, but foremost among them was the fact that we were under attack from a covert enterprise launched by a renegade samurai general three centuries ago.

Noda was glum. "Bigger than I thought."

"How much bigger?" George asked.

Tonight, Kongo's inaccessibility provided us with a desperately needed margin of safety. With the chief detective's last words, I felt a measure of that safety slip away.

Noda shrugged. "Big. We got too close."

"What does *that* mean?"

"We know too much."

I sensed a new gravity in the detective's tone. "More than your brother and his friends?"

Noda downed his third cup of *daiginjo*, a refined saké made with rice polished to fifty percent of its original size. "They knew nothing."

George's eyes widened. "Nothing?"

"Well, almost nothing."

George turned pale. "And *nothing* got them killed?"

"Pretty much."

His Ivy League gloss slipping, George shot me a wild-eyed look. The rosy glow the saké had lent him vanished. A platter of scallop and yellowtail sashimi lay before us, untouched. George tossed down his saké, refilled our cups and his, and siphoned off that one too. The daiginjo was a much-sought-after brew from a saké maker on the outskirts of Kanazawa, though the liquor's appeal tonight was not due to its rarity or taste.

"Then what took them to Soga?" I asked.

"A guess."

"So they went down there on a hunch and were wiped out?"

Noda nodded grimly. "Brodie, we need to get you a gun."

Japan had enacted some of the world's toughest antifirearms laws. It was illegal to pack small arms, concealed or open. If caught, the penalties were severe, so only the stray yakuza risked carrying. Noda's admission meant that the danger we faced outweighed the severity of imprisonment.

"What about you?" I asked.

"I got the shop Beretta."

Twenty-five years ago, Jake had pulled a lot of strings to obtain a gun permit. For a single gun. We still had it, but it was a testament to the effectiveness of the country's gun control laws that it would be the only one we'd ever get.

"There's a nine-millimeter automatic locked in the back room," Noda added.

"Illegal?"

The chief detective's brow buckled in irritation. "Of course. You'll use it?"

"Don't have much choice."

George said, "What about me?"

"You didn't set foot in the village."

George looked relieved, then guilty.

We polished off the rest of the saké and ordered more. The saké cups were in the Oribe style—splashes of green and black glaze on white clay.

Noda said, "One more thing. Best not to go back to your hotel tonight."

"That bad?"

He nodded. "Every night we stay in a different place."

"We?"

"Yeah. I'll get someone to bring our stuff to the office."

"Jesus," said George, falling back on the English word for emphasis.

"I undershot this one," Noda said. "Sorry. *Dai shippai da.*"

Big mistake.

DAY 6

BLACK MARILYN

GEORGE caught a taxi home, and Noda and I checked into adjoining rooms at a trucker's dive near Kongo's after stopping at an all-night convenience store for supplies. I bathed, brushed my teeth, and crawled into a musty futon, plunging into a long-overdue slumber. My dreams were filled with Asian men in dark suits and overcoats. Leaning against lampposts, they read Japanese newspapers from Soga-jujo, and as young schoolgirls walked by, large kanji sprang from the headlines like tarantulas and went for the jugular.

When one girl morphed into Jenny, I woke with a start, my chest thumping, my thoughts straying to my daughter and her new guards. *They work in teams of four.* Sleep didn't return, so around 6 a.m. I slipped a note under Noda's door and waited in a local coffee shop, sipping a Colombian blend and thinking about Jenny. I missed her. I longed to see her freckled face and pigtails. And I needed to call her. I'd promised to ring often, but events and gremlins in the line of communications between the SFPD and the FBI had conspired against us. Again and again, my thoughts returned to the effect my extended absence might be having on Jenny.

Noda joined me an hour later for a light breakfast, then we took separate taxis in opposite directions. I headed for Brodie Security, mindful that I also needed to contact Renna. He'd tough it out until he heard from me, but by now he must be sweating the pressure. Even on this side of the Pacific, I could feel the strain mounting. I knew my friend wouldn't be able to hold out forever without concrete facts. Not

244 | BARRY LANCET

that I had anything solid to offer, but I was willing to wager I'd dug up more than his people.

At the office, the day staff was trickling in. George had yet to show, but others had arrived. Amid the budding activity, Toru and Mari pounded the keyboards, while a silenced television overhead flashed CNN news images from a terrorist bombing in a Pakistani marketplace. I spied my suitcase in the corner.

"How's it going?" I said.

Toru glanced up from his screen. "Our black hatter came out to play last night and we were on him like code on a program."

"He know?" I asked.

"Don't insult. You making any progress?"

"Bits and pieces, all explosive. Soon as you get something solid—address, site, anything—we need to know. Badly."

Toru studied me for a few seconds before his eyes drifted back to his terminal. "Sure thing."

I said thanks and headed for my office. On my desk was the weapon Noda had promised me. I slipped the 9mm into the side pocket of my windbreaker. As an active owner of Brodie Security, I'd been required to take a government-sponsored firearms course and had passed with flying colors, the instructor telling me I was a natural. Of course, none of that would matter if I were caught with an unregistered weapon.

Narazaki knocked and cracked open the door. "Kei-kun called just before you arrived." His eyes shifted uneasily to the spot on the desk where the piece had rested a moment ago. "You found the gun, I see."

"Yes, thanks."

"I'm sorry, Brodie. I never expected this to blow up as it has."

"Jake must have tackled his share of trouble."

"Trouble, yes. Like this, no. Just stay off the streets. Noda will watch your back." He nodded once and eased the door shut.

On my desk were three messages from Renna and one from Abers. I dialed Renna's office number and my call went to voice mail. Three messages and now unreachable. That couldn't be good.

Abers's message was less than an hour old. It said he'd talked to Jenny. I dialed the shop.

"Brodie Antiques. Bill Abers speaking."

I said, "Where's that delinquent boss of yours?"

"Question of the hour, my lad. Everyone's asking for you—Lieutenant Renna, Jenny, and a reporter from ABC. The reporter's a cherry. Blond hair and blue-green peepers. Favor blondes myself, heh?"

"How's Jenny?"

"Things are hotting up on this end, ja? The lieutenant's called a half dozen times. Says he can't get you in Tokyo."

"Tell me about Jenny."

"Your daughter came by with the lieutenant's family and a tough-looking 'maid.' Jenny doesn't know the story?"

"No. Do you know what she's doing there?"

"Going stir-crazy. Miriam took her and the kids to the movies. But don't worry. There's an unmarked outside. And—*oops*. Look what just ran up. Who's this wee little thing jumping up and down right here by my side? Where'd you come from, buttercup?"

Abers passed the phone and a breathless voice said, "Daddy?"

Her familiar child's lilt sent a wave of warmth through me. After knocking heads with the powerbroker and the bureaucrat, the simple pleasure of hearing my daughter's voice seemed the world's greatest blessing.

"Hey, Jenny. I've been trying to call you. How have you been?"

"Okay, I guess."

It almost didn't matter what she said, as long as I could hear her speak. Almost. "Come on. Just *okay*? All those sleepovers at the secret house. That's got to be loads of fun."

"It was at first. Now it's *boring*. I can't go to school and you're not here. I've played all the games with Christine and Joey and Ms. Cooper a zillion-billion times. Did you think about the best-ever? 'What kind of bees give milk?'"

"Of course."

And I had, but not in the way she meant.

"Did you figure it out?"

"How about an Italian queen bee? She can make gelato, too."

Jenny giggled and the warmth surged through me again. "No way."

"Cow bees?"

"Nope. When are you coming back, Daddy?"

"Any day now."

"Are there any China guys with knives over there?"

"Japan, Jenny. This is Japan, where your mother came from."

"Well, are there?"

She slung some hard ones. "There's some tough guys, but your father's tough too."

"Watch out for them, okay?"

"I will."

Jenny's voice dropped to a whisper, her hand obviously cupped around the mouthpiece. "Ms. Cooper is really a police lady, Daddy. They don't think I know, but I do. She's in the shop now. She's pretending to be a maid for where I'm staying, but I saw her badge in her purse."

Great. Undone by a six-year-old. How good could the woman be? My worry level ticked up a notch.

"I know about her, Jenny. She's there to help."

Jenny fell silent. "Then who's watching you?"

"Everyone at Brodie Security. Mr. Noda, George. You know them."

"You're in a lot of trouble, aren't you, Daddy?"

What could I say? I didn't want to lie, but Jenny's anxiety levels had already shot beyond healthy. I opted for the truth, albeit gently laid out. "I've found more than I expected, but I'm surrounded by pros, Jen. The good news is, I also found out more about Mommy. You just let the police lady watch you and my friends'll watch me, okay?"

"No, it's not okay. The police lady is *terrible. TERRIBLE.* If I saw her badge, anybody can. What if your friends are terrible too?"

Jenny slammed the phone on the counter and dashed off, abrupt sobs trailing her into the distance. Mentally, I kicked myself. The formula was simple: my daughter felt threatened when I was threatened. I knew that and still misjudged the effects of what I'd meant as reassuring comments. Jenny's crying became a wail. Her high-pitched lament mauled areas inside me I didn't know could hurt. I heard Abers trying to calm her and failing.

All Jenny wanted was a nice home. A safe nest. But the world kept on spinning in ways she couldn't comprehend. She had pleaded with me to stay. She had laid down her best-ever. And she held on with all her heart. I recalled earlier times when similar anxieties had creased her tiny brow. During each of those times, I'd offered reassurance and was there to hold her. This time the stakes were higher, the danger more acute, and I was six thousand miles away. I sighed and faced a larger truth. I had to find a way to give her a lasting sense of security. If I couldn't, I'd have to give up my father's business. In the background, I heard Abers working to assuage her fears, but Jenny was inconsolable. Cringing with self-rebuke, I set the handset back in its cradle.

The Japantown case had seeped into every aspect of my life, and I wasn't sure how much more I could take—or how much more I could subject my daughter to. The events rang an all-too-familiar bell. A long-forgotten memory bubbled to the surface. My parents were bickering as usual when my mother laid down an ultimatum. "Choose, Jake. Between your damn company and us. Choose!" "You can't ask me to do that," my father had said. "I built it from scratch. For us." "Well, we 'built' this family, too. *Together*. But it's on its last leg. So which is it going to be?" Would Brodie Security drive Jenny away from me as it had my mother from Jake? Could I really hang on to Jake's shop without causing my daughter irreparable psychological damage—or worse?

Still wading through the tangle of my daughter's fear-driven tantrum, I was reaching for the phone to call Renna when the television screen out front caught my eye. An image of the Golden Gate Bridge with the caption COLOR IT RED—AGAIN filled the screen. Rushing into the main office, I snatched the remote and punched up the volume. Everyone turned to watch. A local San Franciscan announcer I'd seen from time to time spoke breathlessly into the camera while footage showed a flurry of ambulances and squad cars racing past. Late last night in San Francisco, sometime during the period when I was playing cat-and-mouse with Goro Kozawa in his scarlet parlor, a German family had been gunned down near Ghirardelli Square.

This time it was a mother, father, and eleven-year-old boy.

From everything I'd learned in Japan, I was certain the second attack couldn't be Soga's doing. Japantown had spawned a copycat. But even so, unless Brodie Security came up with proof real soon, Renna wouldn't be able to tough out this new setback.

Maybe none of us would.

M Y next call to Renna found him locked behind closed doors in an emergency meeting with city officials. I left an urgent request with the detective who picked up the phone that Renna track down the purchaser of the car dealerships previously owned by Mieko's uncle, a trail left by one of Soga's clients I hoped he might be able to follow.

After hanging up, I scrolled through my address book for the *Mainichi Newspaper* and dialed Hiroshi Tomita's direct line. Tomita was a Japanese journalist in his mid-forties who, in his early days, had taken down a dirty Liberal Democratic Party politician, a sleazy real estate baron, and a backroom loan shark company secretly funded by a major bank. After his third scoop, the foreign press tagged him with the nickname "Tommy-gun."

"Tommy? Brodie."

"Brodie-san, *hisashiburi*." It's been a long time.

"Over a year. How's the news business?"

"Dull as August in Tokyo. Why?"

"I have a few questions about Katsuyuki Hara and a company called Teq QX."

His voice grew cold. "You're talking to the wrong guy, you know? I'm not covering any of that."

"But—"

"Working on a piece about the *glorious* new monorail. Ultramodern design. World-class technology. Stu*pen*dous stuff!"

It was hard to miss the artificial enthusiasm in his voice.

"Tommy?"

"Sorry, Brodie. Jenny-chan okay?"

"Fine," I said in a flat voice, waiting.

"Well, give her my regards. See you next trip, if there's time. Sayonara."

The line died and the dial tone buzzed in my ear. Well, you couldn't send out signals any clearer than that.

Replacing the receiver, I webbed my fingers behind my head, leaned back in my chair, and contemplated Jenny's framed photograph, my father's Bizen saké flask, his Japanese short sword, and the LAPD marksmanship award. Then I stared at the ceiling and let my mind wander. Ten minutes later, Mari patched through a call. When I lifted the phone to my ear, Tomita said, "Hey, monkey brain, you trying to get me fired?"

"Now that you mention it, don't know why they haven't axed you yet."

"You keep asking sensitive questions over the office line, they might. They listen in."

"Never been a problem before."

"It is now. You like shogi?"

Shogi is a traditional board game often referred to as Japanese chess. Rectangular wooden pieces with pointed triangular tips were moved across a varnished checkerboard, captured, reincarnated, and moved some more until the Jeweled General was checkmated.

"Never had time for it."

"Make time. West Gate Park in Ikebukuro. Come alone. No one riding your tail, okay?"

"Got it."

"No you don't. Not by half."

Once more, Noda and I took separate taxis in opposite directions. This time his driver circled around and hung two hundred yards behind mine. Staying in touch by cell phone, I arrived at the west exit of Ikebukuro Station, tailless, as God intended, wondering what Tomita was raving about.

I paid the driver and plunged into the heavy foot traffic pouring from the station exits, with Noda somewhere behind me. My cell phone remained silent, which told me I still hadn't drawn a shadow.

West Gate Park lived up to its innocuous name, abutting the west side of Ikebukuro Station, a commuter hub on the northern edge of central Tokyo. The park was a slate-cobbled public square with sculpture, an amphitheater, and the Tokyo Metropolitan Art Space, a seven-story building sporting an atrium in the shape of a massive slashed cube.

As I did before starting down a street in my old L.A. neighborhood, my eyes automatically swept the scene, dove into nooks and shadows, scrutinized each cluster of park inhabitants, looking for a furrowed brow directed my way, a surreptitious glance, any sign of a ripple in the accepted social fabric. All looked normal. The homeless lurked on the south side of the park, under a clutch of undernourished poplars. Teenagers with radios and guitars staked out the stage of the park's amphitheater. Nearby, a skein of game boards sat on overturned plastic beer crates. Squatting on plastic bath stools, lanky professor types, taxi drivers, and retirees hunched over shogi boards, absorbed in the tactics of sending pieces forward into battle. No one looked threatening or out of sync or as if they didn't belong.

Scanning the crowd for Tomita, I strolled over to the players' circle. The reporter was nowhere in sight. Making my second pass through the cluster of boards, an old man with silver hair and a Yomiuri Giants baseball cap called out, "You play shogi, gaijin-san?"

Honorary foreigner. I groaned. One of *those* guys. Just what I needed.

"No, sorry."

"Sure you do. Sit."

Right. Tommy must have sent him. No one would willingly corner a gaijin player. I sat on a yellow bath stool. The old man moved.

"Your turn," my opponent said.

I nudged a piece forward, glancing around for Tommy.

"Like this," he said. "With wrist action, you know? Slap it down, manly-like."

Cantankerous and demanding. Where the hell was Tomita? Imitating the old man's gesture, I made a second move.

"You're hopeless, Brodie-san. I'll beat you in ten." The voice had clarified, losing the geezer's gravelly edge.

I shot a look across the board without raising my head. Under a gray wig and three decades' worth of makeup, I made out the reporter's visage. I didn't show the surprise I felt, but the transformation spooked me. I wouldn't have known him if I'd smacked into him at Tokyo Station. Once again, I had the feeling I was in way too deep. Only Tomita's voice, which he'd allowed me to hear stripped of age, gave him away.

"Good," he said. "Don't look at me. Just make a move after mine, doesn't matter how. From a distance, it'll look fine. Keep your head bowed and move your lips as little as possible. Can you do that?"

"Sure," I said, bewildered that my simple question had birthed such a ruse. "But what's going on?"

"You're only asking about one of the hottest stories of the year."

"I know the Nakamura killings are big news but—"

"Not that. Hara. There's a blackout on Hara. All *but* the killings."

"What?"

"You heard me."

"Tell me what you know."

"Move a piece. If you're not playing you have to vacate the seat. Rules of the park."

I pushed a wooden marker forward, more confused than ever. Hara's pain had been splashed over the front pages and still generated lead stories. Surely, Tomita was overreacting.

"Tell me what you know," I said again. "Especially about Teq QX."

"Aré ka?" That? "I should have guessed."

"Talk to me, Tommy."

"One thing first."

He removed a cell phone from his pocket and set it on the edge of the board.

"I have men on all sides of the park, watching. Anyone approaches, the phone rings once. Twice, they're coming fast. You leave fast. The best way is south, down the steps right behind you and through the lane of shops to the right."

"Jesus, Tomita."

All feeling drained from my limbs. Suddenly I was back in Soga, phantoms hovering in the darkness, every step a risk. I didn't know how much more of this I could take.

On edge and silently cursing myself for missing Tomita's people, I said, "So what's this about?"

"There is a news blackout like I haven't seen since the triple killing in Shin-Okubo. If you've got something, I want it."

"You feed me now, and I'll fill you in when I know what the hell's going on."

"Omae no motteiru joho o saki ni kure." He wanted a sample of my wares before he divulged.

"There isn't time. I have someone watching my back too. As we speak."

"So they're on you already?"

"Big time. Give me background now and the stuff I have is yours later. Deal?"

Tomita sensed my urgency. "You got it. But be warned. The pressure is intense. Any pro-Hara story gets killed. Dirt gets printed. Until the family got shot, any dirt on them saw print as well."

"When that happens, who's behind it?"

"Guesses are useless, Brodie-san. Top of the heap is your best bet, though."

"You say you have guys watching. What kind of guys?"

"Other reporters like me. We back each other up. We know who strolls through the park and who lingers. If anyone crosses the square with purpose, we'll know that too."

"You've done this before, then?"

"Not for this story, but for others just as sensitive. I write it now, I lose my job. Got to time it so they can't shut you down, or send you to terra incognita to report on the cherry blossom front."

"Teq QX. Tell me about it."

"It's based in Taiwan, founded by two whiz kids. One American computer jock educated in Israel, and one Taiwanese software engineer schooled at Stanford. They developed a number of chip improvements. Patent fees to Sapporo and back. Then rumors started: they were on the verge of the next generation chip *and* revolutionizing microprocessor design; future of computers, wireless, 'smart' everything. Pachinko central. The Double Flower Jackpot. Then the acquisition battles began. The Chinese, Dutch, and a trio of Korean chaebols all have markers in. From your country, Intel's leading the charge. But we Japanese are waging the biggest campaign, which is where you come in, right?"

Chaebols are Korean family-owned conglomerates. The Big Five control most of the Korean domestic market.

"Yeah, a walk-on part. Is Tokyo in deep?"

"Government's swinging away with the blessing of the Iron Triangle."

"You sure about that?"

"Gossip is not my business, Brodie-san."

Japan's Iron Triangle was a secret network of high-echelon bureaucrats, industrialists, and politicians. The ministries and the pols rammed through laws and funding to support the triangle's conglomerate needs and the companies returned the favors with large campaign contributions for pols and lucrative postretirement positions for bureaucrats.

"Yeah, sorry. So who's winning?"

"Game's not over yet. There are rumors that the Taiwanese government will step in to keep its native son home and more rumors that the Iron Triangle tried to buy off the chaebols with promises to share the technology, which just made the Koreans mad. At the moment, the Chinese, Koreans, and Japanese are the main contenders. In Japan, Hara's CompTel Nippon, NEC, Fujitsu, and Toshiba are leading."

Great. I was in search of Soga's client for Japantown and Tommy Tomita had just added most of Asia to the suspect list. "Aren't the Japanese companies working together on this? They usually pool resources to lock up the technology."

"Yeah, they are. The ministries forced them. But Hara's gone renegade. He's ignoring the ministries, their regulations, the whole system. The big man figures it is *the* future, or at least a major piece in the jigsaw of global telecommunications for the next few decades. Americans and Dutch don't figure it that way. They have other options."

Hara had always been a trailblazer, rising against all odds while fighting Japan Inc. in the trenches. Among the everyday citizenry he was a folk hero to be emulated, but the powers that be hated his lone-wolf tactics.

"Who's right?"

"Doesn't matter. If the Taiwanese government doesn't intrude, it's supposed to close any time now."

"With?"

"Hara's CTN."

From the moment Hara had gone after Teq QX on his own, the pressure must have been immense. Not only from the competition, but also from the Japanese government. According to Tommy, Hara had rebuffed all comers. According to Lizza, her father had hired a bodyguard once he'd become enamored of the Taiwan chipmaker.

"So Hara's a tiger or a spoiler, depending on who you talk to."

"My sources say the Japanese ministries are rabid. Foaming at the mouth."

The rebel Hara had gone against the tribe and a dozen-plus competitors, and one of them sicced Soga on him. Yet they chose to leave him standing. Why?

"Has anyone put a price tag on Teq QX's future earnings?"

"Between two and five billion dollars U.S. annually within ten years."

More than enough motive. "But you have no idea who called the press blackout on Hara?"

"None, Brodie-san. Sorry."

"Who might hate him enough to . . ."

"Wipe out his family? I don't know, but that's what you're after, aren't you?"

"That's what I'm thinking, is all. Thanks for the help, Tomita. I owe you the story if it breaks."

"You mean *when*. How about a taste now? I hear rumors you're working for Hara."

So word had spread. "Keep it to yourself?"

"*Atarimae da yo.*" Naturally.

"You heard correctly."

Tomita grinned. "You're the man, Brodie. Stay in touch, you hear? But watch yourself with Hara. You'll get burned if you don't."

Another spot-on warning delivered too late.

"One last question," I said. "What do you know about Goro Kozawa?"

Tommy's eyes glittered. "He involved, too?"

I kept my mouth shut. Tomita got the message.

"He's *hara guroi,* a black-hearted one. If you're dealing with him, watch your back, your pocketbook, and don't trust a word out of that snake's mouth."

Tension furrowed the lining of my stomach. My client was out to get me, and now Tommy was saying our latest ally was even more slippery.

Tommy's cell phone buzzed once. The next instant a single word in Japanese scrolled up its small screen. *Nigero!* Run!

"Trouble," Tommy said.

Then it buzzed a second time.

"Go! Get out of here, Brodie. Now!"

I dashed for the corridor of shops Tommy had mentioned. In my peripheral vision, I caught rapid movements off to the far right. My attackers were twenty yards away and closing. A great flapping sound rose up as a cloud of pigeons launched itself. Two men cut through the birds, charging straight at me.

I ran faster. Behind me I heard footsteps pounding the pavement. My cell phone rang. Noda had seen them also, but a beat too late.

The shopping lane was crowded with foot traffic. I looked over my shoulder. A third man joined the chase, cutting in yards ahead of the first two and taking advantage of the path I cleared through the crowd. From three yards back, he drew a gun. He aimed. I sluiced left. A woman coming toward me with boutique shopping bags on her arm crumpled. I didn't hear the shot, didn't see a wound.

I kept running.

I figured Noda was around and closing—if he hadn't lost me.

In seconds, I knew the other two would be on me. Three men would be hard to handle on my own.

I veered left down an alley and stepped into a crevice between buildings. The man with the gun raced past. I leapt out on his heels and brought the 9mm down on his skull. He folded. I ran on. The other two turned the corner and high-jumped over their fallen crony. I took a quick right, plowing between two men in gray suits. My pursuit gained. Their guns came out. I zigzagged. A pedestrian facing me wilted, his eyes rolling up in his head. I still didn't hear anything or see a wound. What were they firing?

I took another right and found myself in front of a ramen shop whose back end opened on the passage I'd just been down. I flew through the restaurant past a dozen startled customers slurping noodles from oversize bowls and charged out the back, then circled around the corner again and came out three dozen paces behind my pursuers. I'd accomplished the turnaround in thirty seconds, a counterintuitive South Central move taught to me by a middle-school-friend-turned-petty criminal now serving time in San Quentin.

The pair ran on for another half block before they slowed, their eyes scanning the pedestrian traffic rapidly but calmly.

I shifted my gun to my left hand.

The men stopped. The taller of the two spoke and turned to glance back over his shoulder. I was on him then, smashing my right fist into the middle of his face. He dropped. His partner half-turned. I said, "Lose the gun," in Japanese, the weapon in my left hand digging into his spine.

He let his piece fall and I kicked it across the pavement.

I heard another set of footfalls charging fast. I looked around.

A fourth man, gun drawn, was five yards away and closing.

Noda blindsided him from the left. They tumbled over each other and hit the pavement with a dull thud. Noda jammed an elbow in the gunman's eye. He screamed and grabbed his face.

My prisoner stirred.

"Move again, I pull the trigger."

My captive eyed me with contempt. I pistol-whipped him before the contempt sprouted into rebellion. He buckled to the pavement.

Noda was on his feet, his man motionless.

People cowered up against storefronts, warily assessing the fallen bodies and our firearms. There was a police ministation two hundred yards back. No doubt someone had alerted them to the disturbance, or was about to. Either way, uniformed officers would arrive momentarily.

Noda grabbed my elbow and shepherded me away from the scene. "Nice takedown."

"Good to be appreciated by a pro."

Noda frowned. "Stay focused."

"Am. What was that about?"

We blended into the stream of people heading for the station.

"Kidnap attempt."

Kidnapping. My chest muscles tensed. Soga was not content to wait until I left town, as they had with Noda's friend. With no tricks to lure me away from Tokyo, they'd turned to abduction—with disposal elsewhere.

"You sure about that?"

"Firing drugged darts."

That clinched it. My chest tightened some more. We were as big a threat as Noda feared.

"Got any thoughts on why the full-court press?"

"They want you dead sooner," Noda said. "Probably me too. Did you fire the Beretta?"

Translation: Noda was worried about the firearms law.

"No, but . . ."

"Good. We're safe."

I stared at him. "You've got to be kidding."

TRAILING three guards in our wake, Noda and I burst through the door of Brodie Security. Three more men stood outside the building on the street, and another four roamed the area in pairs at staggered intervals. Before returning to our Shibuya office, Noda had called ahead and Brodie Security operatives had secured the area and set up a safe perimeter in case Soga decided to make a second play closer to home.

Murmurs of relief spread through the room as soon as we crossed the threshold. Then the blinds were drawn and the front door was locked and shuttered from the inside. Furtive glances slid my way as detectives and support staff gauged how well I was handling the crisis. I resented their clandestine inspection, but it went with the job—mine and theirs.

Noda briefed Narazaki and George, and his assessment was brutal: thwarting a determined advance by Soga bordered on the impossible. They had circumvented his backup position until the last second. It was Tommy Tomita's people who saved us, because Soga hadn't expected the journalist's team—no pattern for them to follow. Even so, as in the village, the margin of safety could be measured in seconds. I placed an emergency call to Renna, and this time he broke from whatever meeting he was attending to come to the phone. I told him of the attack, implored him to alert the cops guarding Jenny, and urged him once more to track the buyer of the dealerships. Tracing the transfer of the car lots was the only fact to date that we might be able to use to unravel things from the back end.

After the conversation, I emerged from my office to find everyone huddled around Toru's machine.

"You going to be okay, Brodie?" Narazaki asked.

"Fine, thanks," I said, feeling the heightened effects of the adrenaline rush during the attack even now. "What's going on out here?"

"Toru's got a bite."

"More than a bite. We're rocking. Mari, switch to the beta version for this move."

Noda clamped a hand on Toru's shoulder. "Got me a name?"

"Not yet."

"Address?"

"No."

"Then you're not rocking. You're doing a slow waltz."

Fingers flying over the keypads, Toru cocked an aggrieved eye at the dour detective. "Should be soon." He drilled in a few more commands, then turned to Narazaki. "We're setting up for the final leg. Backtracked him through Istanbul, Morocco, London, Madrid, then New Zealand, Berlin, Hong Kong, Mexico. Now Arizona. What a ride! Cool texture in the Berlin grid."

Teased spikes bouncing, Mari nodded. "You should have seen it. Yellow-and-black chrome and rainbow fractals." A warning box appeared on Mari's screen. She typed a response. "I've got an alert."

"What kind?"

"Wait for it . . ."

Toru said, "I see it. What *is* that?"

His screen exploded in a blinding white field and then began pulsating with concentric green circles bursting forth from the center. Next, red waves flooded his monitor.

"Whoa. Green doughnuts I know, but never seen these red babies before. Mari, run a low-profile ID program. I'll do site analysis." He typed in a few commands. "This is it! We've nailed him. Our black hatter's home ground. Mari?"

"The red is his artillery, the rings his firewalls. We penetrate the green, we're in."

"Then what?" Noda asked.

Eyes glued to the digital fireworks on his screen as he typed in commands, Toru shrugged. "Hard to know until we penetrate. Those are kick-ass firewalls, though. Not one, but flanks."

Narazaki said, "What's a firewall?"

"Electronic barriers, sir," Mari answered. "Security software to protect a system. They guard a site and search incoming information packets and stuff."

In a sudden flurry of flying fingers, Toru peppered his screen with commands. The next instant his monitor froze—then a bright yellow flash exploded across it.

He let out a whoop. "We're in, man! Piggyback sucker punch."

Toru explained that he'd fooled their system by retarding an outgoing signal and riding piggyback on the return error message.

Narazaki looked astonished. "You're *inside* their computer?"

"Belly of the whale, man."

I was equally stunned. Our motley crew had done it. Outfoxed Soga's hacker. The room buzzed in anticipation.

Narazaki said, "Brodie, why don't you take this? Computers are a young man's game."

"Sure. Thanks." Feeling my own excitement building, I turned to Toru. "Find out as much as you can without tipping our hand."

"Will do. Inserting Op-Seven protocol now . . . it's . . . in . . . and . . . no one's noticed yet . . . scan going . . . there. Whoa. Firewalls guarding firewalls. More security than the Bank of Japan. See that orange grid?" He pointed at a salmon-colored crosshatch in the corner of his screen. "That's a highly classified area. Good hunting there, I bet. Want me to poke around?"

I hesitated. "Will it give us away?"

"Could."

I pointed to a shimmering blue quadrant. "Is that an unprotected area?"

"Open as they come."

"Can you dive into some basic files without being detected? Maybe find out who they are?"

"Sure . . ." His cursor approached. He read some file names. "Gas . . . electric . . . telephone bills . . . payroll. Looks like I'm in accounting. This is an operating company. Is that what you expected?"

My enthusiasm flagged. "No, just the opposite."

For three hundred years, Soga had remained a dark shadow on the fringe of society. Everything they did was off the books, under the table, out of the limelight. They moved undercover. Payroll and accounting were the last things I'd expect of them.

"Hold on, I've got a name coming . . . coming . . . here: The Gilbert Tweed Agency? Mean anything?"

I shook my head and shot a look at Noda. He frowned. Another no.

"Looks like another camouflage site," I said. "Doesn't fit the profile but check it out anyway."

I scanned the faces of the Brodie Security staff. They were all thinking what I was: we'd hit a dead end. Dejection weighed on the room. My mood blackened. So much for the blip. We were never going to unearth Soga. They'd eluded their enemies for centuries. We'd been at it for only five days. Who were we fooling? It was over. With no new avenues to explore, our investigation had just stalled. We were dead in the water, while Soga was on the prowl. They could advance at their leisure. How long would it be before they caught me with my guard down?

Noda scowled and turned away. People wandered back to their desks. I headed for my office, calling back to Toru, "If you find anything of interest, come get me."

"Hold on, Brodie-san. I'm going into general correspondence." There was a note of desperation in his voice.

I eased my door open.

"Wait," Toru said. Then: "Try this. 'Executive Management Recruiters.' Mean anything?"

"No, sorry."

From across the room, Noda asked for a translation.

I explained it to him in Japanese.

A low growl emanated from the back of his throat.

"It's them," he said.

EVERYTHING slotted into place. According to the withered pow-erbroker, Soga handled two types of deals, business and career, eliminating obstacles for both. Gilbert Tweed must feed the career side, whether catering to top-level executives slipping down the ladder of success, with million-dollar salaries at stake, or ambitious career climb-ers wishing to advance at a more rapid pace.

An adrenaline charge sent my heart racing. "Noda's right. It's got to be them. A legit office attracts clients *to them*. Soga seeds Gilbert Tweed with legitimate headhunters, then sits back and waits. Ninety-five percent of their clients are placed in new positions through accepted business channels, while a couple of Soga people in upper-management positions cherry-pick promising candidates and contact them from an independent source outside the agency."

"That's how I'd do it," Narazaki agreed. "Cast a long line from shore. Keep my distance."

With mounting certainty, I fleshed out two possible scenarios. "Cli-ents wouldn't know how the contact got their name. Could be a col-league, rumor, anyone or anything within the industry. Soga removes obstacles above, careers advance. Soga retards challenges from below, or maybe stifles an aggressive board member, and careers and multimillion-dollar salaries are preserved. Either way, Soga makes money. The client makes money or saves money. Kingmaker, kingbreaker."

And that was only for starters. As their clients rose in power, Soga probably got calls for some business deals. Someone opposes a Soga-backed executive's European expansion plan, call in Soga, and that someone dies in a skiing mishap, then the acquisition goes through and the exec pockets ten million in incentives, with Soga taking a cut. An Asian conglomerate meets resistance in its attempt to acquire an Australian clothing firm, call in Soga and the CEO's plane takes a dive. An ambitious businessman wants to increase his stake in the U.S. car market by picking up prosperous dealerships at a discount, call in Soga and he extends his business. It all fit.

Toru typed. "Here's your locations. Offices in New York, Los Angeles, and London."

That stopped my speculation cold. "The States? Can't be. It's too big an operation to function in America without someone noticing."

"Well, I got it on two letterheads." He read the addresses out loud.

I stepped up to the screen. I'd expected a site in a modest Asia-Pacific city. Someplace central but off the beaten path. Jakarta or Kuala Lumpur. Or even a notch higher, say Singapore or Melbourne. But not London and New York.

Not in my country.

It seemed inconceivable that a band of assassins could operate undetected within American borders for years. Impossible, in fact. With Homeland Security, the FBI, anything the CIA or the NSA might cull from overseas sources, the odds were impossibly high. But the letterhead suggested otherwise. And to top it off, their offices were on Lexington Avenue in Manhattan and Wilshire Boulevard in Los Angeles. You couldn't get any more entrenched.

"Can't be our guys," I said. "The locations are all wrong. Something like this, they stay out of sight and reach out from a distance."

"Brodie's right," Narazaki said. "Too high-profile."

Noda crossed his beefy arms over his chest. "It's them."

Mari said, "Here's a sample search of periodicals. 'Gilbert Tweed Agency Quietly Becomes a Force in International Banking,' 'Gilbert Tweed Scores Another Coup for CEO Search,' 'Gilbert Tweed Top Fortune 500 Recruiter.'"

Messaging my temples, I slumped into the nearest chair. "All high-level management positions. Far too public. I can't see it."

George scanned the articles. "I know some of these names. This is mainstream corporate management. Six- and seven-figure salaries. Eight and nine when you throw in bonuses and stock options. A couple of them hit hard times a while back. Made the news again when they resurfaced."

My ears perked up. In only slightly altered terms, George had just regurgitated the main thrust of Kozawa's explanation in his sleazy scarlet parlor: execs who hit a brick wall are rescued by Soga.

What if Soga had gone the other way? Decided to play the counterintuitive hand? Setting up on such prime property was an audacious move. Bold beyond measure. Who would ever look for them there? Who would ever suspect? The Soga we'd encountered was aggressive beyond measure.

I turned the idea over from all angles.

It added up.

It could be them.

And there was this: tracing the hacker back to a top-level headhunter seemed too large a coincidence. The Gilbert Tweed setup was too well crafted to be anything but a front for the predators we were hunting. Noda was right. It was them. While observing their centuries-old strategy of sticking to the shadows, Soga had moved its commercial arm brazenly into the mainstream.

Toru sat up. "Shit. Here comes their sysop watchdog."

Trading looks with Noda, I asked, "What's that?"

"Systems-op software. We have to bail. Want me to trash them? I love to fry black sites. We got ten seconds."

"If we pull out now will they know there's been an intruder?"

"No. Seven seconds . . ."

"Can we get back in later?"

"Yeah, sure . . . four . . . three . . . two . . ."

"Pull the plug."

"Okay." Toru hit a button. A yellow flash engulfed his screen and then it went dark. "We've bailed." His head drooped. "I blew it. Just a little more time and we'd have had it all."

Narazaki slapped Toru on the back. "Not so, son. You reeled in the catch of the day."

Mari said, "Toru, you better come look at this."

A neon-orange beam streaked across her screen like a meteor across a black sky.

"What was that?" I asked.

"Damn," Toru said. "It's a binary piggyback tracer. We piggybacked their ware in and they piggybacked our piggyback out. Must have disabled our rear guard."

"So they know someone got inside?"

"Yeah, man. Sorry."

"But they can't trace it back here, right?"

"No. I cut the signal."

"They'll know anyway," Noda said.

"Why?"

"They'll know."

W E hunkered down. Way, way down.

After the kidnap attempt, everything was up for grabs. We had no idea what Soga would try next. The only thing we knew with any certainty was that Soga had no qualms about killing women or children or any other innocent associated even vaguely with the case, so all of Brodie Security slipped into alert mode.

It was time for me to head back to San Francisco. Time for a huddle with Renna. And I wanted Jenny by my side. I wanted her within reach. I wanted to take my daughter home and braid her hair in the morning and cook her scrambled eggs that made her sneeze. I didn't want strangers protecting her without me around.

Before leaving Japan, I had one more rock to turn over. Early the next morning, I called Hara's office, and when I learned he was back from Taiwan but booked solid for the next week, I told the secretary I was coming over now. If Hara remained unavailable, I'd camp out on his doorstep with a dozen security people until he became available. We would not be subtle about our presence. She got the point and I got a meeting.

CompTel Nippon occupied the top three floors of a forty-five-story office tower in West Shinjuku, and the maverick businessman's quarters in a corner penthouse was the crowning touch. Cool postmodern tones of silver and gray dominated his office. Tubular steel chairs were set around a desk of oyster-colored marble the size of a wading pool, and against a far wall was a couch of undulating polyurethane foam sheathed in muted gray elephant hide. Giving the room its only nonmonochromatic coloring was a Jackson Pollock hanging on the north wall above the couch. Warhol's *Black Marilyn*, with her fine silver coiffure, gazed out at us from the east wall. Floor-to-ceiling plate glass made up the remaining two sides, offering a view of Tokyo Bay to the south and a silhouette of Mount Fuji in the distant west. Near the desk, trying not to look like an expensive ornament, was the body-guard I'd decked in San Francisco. His presence did not suggest trust and goodwill.

I said, "Keeping vertical these days?"

He watched me with cool eyes that weren't resentful or apprehensive of our last encounter but got me wondering about him.

Hara sat behind the wading pool, his hands folded. He did not rise when I entered. "Welcome, Mr. Brodie. A pleasure to see you again."

The mogul's hair was no longer the snow white I'd seen at my shop. It was black, with a gray fringe, as I remembered from his magazine portraits. This must have been his natural color before Japantown. His regal mane had whitened overnight, but in his rush to get to the States and his family, he hadn't had time to dye it. Now he had.

"Wish I could say the same."

Hara raised an eyebrow. "You have a tongue on you. But come to think of it, one of my informants did describe you as 'regrettably feisty.'"

"Helps me keep perspective."

"I'm sure. May I offer you a drink?"

I felt like vaulting over his desk and wrapping my fingers around his smug neck. Instead, I glared and said, "No. I won't be staying long."

"Have you something to report, then?"

"I have questions."

"By now I had hoped you would have answers."

"Oh, I have some of those too. Would you like to hear?"

"Yes, certainly."

"Sending your other daughter to me was a ploy."

Hara's face remained blank. "Why would you think that?"

"To attract *their* notice. She knew next to nothing about her sister's day-to-day activities."

"I didn't know."

"Yes, you did. Just as you knew Japanese paparazzi would follow her to San Francisco."

Hara's eyes narrowed at my disrespectful tone. "That is her particular talent, yes. You were well paid, were you not."

"Not to act as a lure. Not to be set up by a client who thinks nothing of using his only living daughter as a tool. The trip to San Francisco traumatized her."

Hara rose and turned his back on me, staring at Mount Fuji on the horizon. "Jo, this young man tires me. Throw him out."

"Jiro Jo?" I asked, and he nodded. The guy Narazaki wanted to recruit. "I've heard about you," I said.

We locked eyes. Jo said, "I underestimated you the first time."

"I know."

"An art dealer. Dropped my guard."

"By a fraction."

"Won't happen again."

"I know that too."

Hara whirled around. "Throw him out."

Jo ignored Hara. He continued to watch me steadily, with nothing in his expression one way or the other. But the look told me that the next time he came for me, victory would be harder.

Hara cranked up the volume. *"I want him out of here."*

"I don't see the point," Jo said.

"The point is I told you to do it."

"I don't do dirty work. You set him up. You lied to him. And you lied to me too."

"I don't pay you to listen to other people."

"Keeping you alive means thinking on my feet and thinking ahead. Brodie is working the same problem from the other side. If he's got something I think is useful, I'm gonna listen."

Hara glowered at his rebellious bodyguard.

Jo dropped his head. "And Yoshida was a friend."

The bodyguard who died in Japantown.

It was my turn to glower, and returning my attention to the mogul, I did so without pleasure. "You've put too many lives at risk, Hara."

"The kind of risks Brodie Security is paid to take," Hara countered. "I simply forced you to become more involved."

Anger suffused my face. "*More involved?* You stuck a target on my back."

"There would have been one in any event."

I shook my head in frustration. "There are other ways to tackle these things. You should have given me all the information up front."

"Would you have taken the case?"

"Probably not. It's not our type of work."

"In my judgment, you were ideally positioned."

The pent-up rage of the last week spilling forth, I lunged at the mogul. Had there been three yards between us instead of six, Hara would be hurting. As it was, Jo stepped easily between us.

"Brodie," he rumbled, his tone low and dark.

I raised my palms and backed away. *Ideally positioned.* Noda and I now sat at the top of Soga's hit list, and I'd been forced to send Jenny into hiding. The pigeon was right where Hara wanted it.

I took a deep breath. "When did you know?"

Hara stared icily. "Why should I talk to you?"

Jo refolded his arms over his chest. "Because if you don't, I walk."

Men of Jo's caliber were rare—and could be the difference between living and dying when it came down to a matter of seconds. Hara would know that, but even so I wondered if Jo's threat was enough to stem Hara's pride.

Hara said, "I could hire five more just like you in an instant."

"Nothing's stopping you," Jo said without moving.

Hara deflated visibly, looking from Jo to me, seeing his bluff hadn't worked. He knew what he had. Or maybe the fight had gone out of him.

"A source in the Japanese government told me of the kanji," Hara said. "He couldn't understand its significance, but I could."

I said, "You knew all along who they were?"

"No. That was the problem."

"Explain."

"I knew the rumors. A private army of assassins for hire of Japanese origin based somewhere overseas. 'Business facilitators,' I've heard them called. My position is high enough to allow me to have known of such stories and know the kanji was a sign of their work."

"It was a message, then?"

"So it would seem."

"For Teq QX?"

Hara's head snapped up in surprise, then a triumphant grin played across his lips. "You see, my choice was not without merit. You have come far in a short time."

I felt like ripping the smile from his face, but I held my anger in check this time. I wanted answers. I needed them if there was to be any hope of extracting myself from the trap Hara had conceived.

"Answer the question," I said, my shoulders tensing.

Hara's eyes flicked toward Jo. "I'm not certain, but I believe so."

"You were late with the bios on your family because they didn't mean much, right?"

"*Sono tori,*" he said with a faint smile. Exactly right. "I didn't want you sidetracked by useless details. I wanted you front and center, splashing around. Making waves. Sharks are attracted to irregular behavior. You performed admirably."

I said, "And the large money transfer to Brodie Security was another wave."

Hara studied me appraisingly. "You're a quick study."

"While I was drawing the sharks, what were *you* doing?"

"Making my own inquiries."

"Any progress?"

Hara wilted. "It's all I think about. All I do. I don't sleep, I don't eat, but I haven't found them. Besides my own time, I assigned five others to it. I've invested hundreds of man-hours in the project but uncovered nothing."

His words struck deeper than he could know. I thought of my bottomless grief immediately after Mieko's death, and remembered how I'd floundered in the face of such an incomprehensible loss. In the days and nights since Japantown, Hara had struggled with the same despair. His wealth had conquered mountains, but it could not undo the deed. His money was as useless as spent confetti.

All this I grasped in an instant. My fury and hatred evaporated. In that second we exchanged a look of understanding so knowing, so privy to pain and desperation and utter devastation, it startled me.

"Let's see if I can remember everyone who has an interest in Teq QX," I said, the confrontational edge in my voice gone. "The Korean chaebols, the Americans, the Dutch, the Chinese, the Taiwanese government, and a who's-who of Japanese elec-tech firms."

Hara's gaze met mine, his distress now an open wound. "Why stop there? I brushed off two Australian CEOs, a major European bank, and nearly a dozen execs from around the world."

"Why?"

"The technology is superb. I'll license it at the right time, at the price I choose. Meanwhile CTN will have a superior product."

"Was there more than one threat?"

"Just one. They said I had better learn to be more flexible about my acquisitions."

"They?"

"The ministries. Or more likely, the ministries *fronting* for one of my Japanese competitors. A gofer showed up and 'requested' that Teq QX be jointly acquired in order that Japan Inc. could share the technology. As they always do."

"Not an elite official?"

"They didn't deign to grace my office. Even the gofer was arrogant. It was more of an order."

"Which you refused?"

"Why should I deal with someone's undersecretary?"

"Would it have made a difference if someone higher up had courted you?"

"In truth, not this time."

"And when you resisted the gofer's overtures?"

"He said there'd be 'consequences.'"

It didn't compute. Even as haughty as many top ministry administrators were, it made no sense to send a low-level assistant to meet someone of Hara's stature.

"Did they contact you again?"

"Yes. Once, to ask me to reconsider."

"Top brass this time, right?"

"No. A different gofer who reiterated the request and the threat."

A chill enveloped me. They repeated the mistake after Hara's first refusal? With Teq QX developing pivotal technology for the next-generation chip, and a cavalcade of Japanese companies drooling over the prize? I didn't like the sound of that.

"Has the government threatened you before?"

Hara's tone was dismissive. "Routinely."

"Were there reprisals after your second refusal?"

"No."

I said, "The threat included your family too?"

The mogul fell back in his chair. "Yes, but I thought it was the usual hot air."

"So we can narrow the search to a Japanese company working with the ministries."

"I did that," Hara said, "with no results. When you include the major subcontractors, there are too many."

I bit my lip in frustration. I was furious. So much time wasted. How could a businessman of Hara's proven talent be so lame? There weren't too many trails if you employed time, manpower, and funds wisely.

"Anything else you want to tell me now that the sharks are circling?"

"For years I have heard whispers of these men. But they never touched my life—until now. And they destroyed it. I want revenge, Brodie-san. I paid you good money for that."

"I told you Brodie Security doesn't exterminate pests."

"And I told *you* I invariably get what I want. These men are animals. Heartless, amoral animals. They must be hunted down and crushed like cockroaches. Their last moments must be filled with disgrace, not glory. You can do that because you saw my family in Japantown."

He'd displayed the same passion when he first came to see me, but today I knew the callousness behind the passion. We had both lost loved ones to Soga, but only one of us had turned into a remorseless manipulator.

I could feel my face prickling with the anger. "My daughter is under protective custody because of your tricks."

Hara spread his hands. "You're the professional. Protect her."

Jo or no Jo, I nearly lost it then. Reading the violence in my look, Jo edged closer to his client. His hand slid under his jacket for the weapon I knew was there.

Had Jo not been armed, I believe I would have drawn the 9mm from my side pocket and put a slug through Hara's arrogant smirk. Instead, I locked down the demons and spoke through gritted teeth. "When did you make up your mind to go after them?"

"The moment I heard the news."

"And how long before you chose Brodie Security?"

"My people came up with a list of three agencies in San Francisco with the kind of organization I required. You simply had the misfortune to be invited to Japantown. What I said that day in your office was entirely true. I simply used my . . . my personal suffering to my advantage."

My jaw clenched. "You may believe people invariably do what you ask, but there's about to be an exception."

"Don't fool yourself, Brodie. Sink or swim. It's your choice."

"I'm flying out of here tomorrow."

"You're leaving? They'll find you."

"You never know."

His eyes lit up. "You've found them. Where are they?"

I turned and walked toward the door.

"Tell me," Hara said. He could not quite subdue the note of excitement in his voice, yet his pride prevented him from begging.

"When my work is finished, you'll get the report you paid for. As agreed."

"As your client, I have a right to know now."

"And *I* have a right to stay alive. Despite the best efforts of my clients."

My blood roiling, I glanced away and my eyes alighted on Warhol's *Marilyn*. I noted the portrait's hairline in surprise. There is a little-known story about an overworked Warhol shipping the master silkscreens of his Monroe portrait to his European gallery with instructions to run off prints ahead of his arrival, which he would then sign. One night, the screens went "missing" for a number of hours before turning up in a corner of the gallery warehouse, as if misplaced. Several months later, portraits with a faint, incongruous barlike shading at the hairline rather than the fine gradation Warhol intended appeared on the market. Illicit prints had been run off, but with a telltale shift of one screen at the top by maybe two millimeters.

"You know the Warhol's a fake, don't you?" I said, turning to watch his reaction.

Hara looked startled, then flushed. "I forget that behind the brawn are higher sensibilities. Of course I know."

"Now, there's a surprise. Stay out of my way, Hara, or you'll regret it. And that's a promise I'll keep, with or without your bodyguards."

I nodded at Jo and walked out.

WE had one last huddle at Brodie Security before I headed home. Attending were Narazaki, Noda, George, Mari, and Toru. The front door was still locked and shuttered. Three men stood guard on the street and another three patrolled the perimeter. A third trio had covered my back to and from Hara's office.

"How'd your meet with Hara go?" Narazaki asked.

I recounted my reunion with the communications mogul, my anger rekindling as I spoke.

Narazaki nodded in sympathy. "In this business, sometimes clients are only a tad better than what you're trolling for."

Toru nodded. "With their byte stealer, you've got more trouble."

"What kind?" Noda asked.

"He'll be tracking Brodie and anyone else who's traveling."

I said, "You mean he'll follow our travel itinerary by hacking the airline manifests?"

"His level, he'll hack airlines, credit card companies, hotel booking systems—anything and everything hooked in and juiced. If you're traveling under your own name, Soga will know when-where-how faster than you can say *trapware*."

"Then let's leave a trail," I said. "Obvious but not too obvious."

Toru grinned. "Just flash the plastic."

I turned to Narazaki. "What do you think? Time to get off the sidelines and into the game?"

"You got some sense of sidelines, kid. I like that. But this case has escalated way beyond dangerous, so I'm pulling you off."

I stared at him, stunned.

"Don't get me wrong, Brodie-kun. Your work's been up there with the best of them, but you're still a newcomer. You've only gotten this far because I paired you with Noda. Let the pros finish it. Besides, don't you think you should get back to your daughter? Keep an eye on her until things wind down?"

Noda leaned forward, scowling. "Don't see why he can't continue. He's handled himself well."

Narazaki said, "I owe it to Jake to keep his son out of harm's way. You helped spot the whale, Brodie. That's a job well done. Now let a more experienced team clean up."

Noda's scowl deepened. "Won't fly. He's got a target on his back. Like me."

"Exactly," Narazaki said. "If we remove Brodie from the front line and hide him and his daughter until this blows over, we can probably salvage the situation."

Noda uttered a low growl. "Unlikely."

I gave Jake's longtime partner an appreciative smile. "Narazaki-san, you're like a father to me and I have the greatest respect for your opinion, but I'm not hiding from Soga. These guys killed my wife."

His face softened. "I understand all that, but it's too risky. And it's not the way Brodie Security operates."

"Of which I am half owner."

Jake's old partner drank in my determination, then slumped back in his seat, exasperated. "I got that same damn look from your father far too many times. Like a mule-assed fisherman who won't haul in his nets until he's grabbed his quota, no matter how dark the clouds on the horizon." He sighed loudly and turned to Noda. "All right, you guys got your wish. But Kei-kun, I want people stateside watching our boy's back when the SFPD isn't."

Noda grunted in assent.

Narazaki turned to me. "You'll get your friend to cover you?"

"Sure."

"Good. Then here's how we'll split up the chores. London is the prestige location. Kei-kun will check out Gilbert Tweed there since he knows the city, and George can cover Los Angeles. That way we have eyes on each continent. If nothing turns up in London, it's a short hop to New York. Brodie, you head home and liaise with the SFPD and see Jenny-chan."

"New York first, then London," Noda said.

"I agree," I said. "The Big Apple's the bold move. To date, Soga's been elusive but not shy."

Narazaki resisted. "The spread's better with one man on each continent."

"New York would be my choice, too," George chimed in. "If you're asking."

Three to one.

Narazaki started to open his mouth, then threw up his hands. "All right, New York it is. You guys are closer to this one than I am."

By the end of the day I was cruising over Siberian waters on the polar route back to San Francisco. Outside my window the sun dropped out of the sky and turbulence jostled us throughout the night.

Our plan had evolved further before the meeting broke up.

For one thing, despite Narazaki's concern, I'd become the designated decoy.

DAY 7

SOGA SPEAKS

O NCE my plane touched down, I collected my bag, withdrew my ancient Cutlass from long-term parking, and hopped on the 101 going north into the city, swung west on the 380, then north again on the 280 at San Bruno. I slid through Serramonte, then Daly City, an eye on my rearview mirror. I was jumpy. I felt naked without a weapon or anyone watching my back.

Having run up against Soga twice, neither Noda or I believed we could salvage our positions by treading water. Noda was going underground, while I had to make the rounds—home, shop, SFPD. So, despite Narazaki's patriarchal anxiety, I would be exposed until my first sit-down with Renna. As aggressive as Soga was, my traveling without protection was a huge gamble. But our hands were tied. If we chose overly cautious, we risked raising Soga's suspicions and exposing our play. We wanted their eyes on me.

It was midafternoon, so the traffic was light on the freeway and surface streets. At Junípero Serra Boulevard, I eased off the 280 behind a classic Mustang convertible. Seeing the older sports car alive and on the road brought a smile to my lips.

Where Junípero Serra sluiced into Nineteenth Avenue, the driver caught my eye in his rearview mirror, then changed lanes and down-shifted until he was tooling alongside me.

I eyed him uneasily. The move was slick. I didn't know if he was an enthusiast or something more. What I did know was that he had boxed me in. Up ahead there was a gap in the oncoming traffic. If things took a bad turn, I could fishtail across the double yellow for a quick U-turn.

Mustang shouted across the lane. "You got yourself a beauty there. What year is she?"

He was Caucasian, with a red beard, a ruddy face, and a brown beret. There had never been any indication to suggest Soga used non-villagers, or non-Japanese for that matter. But nothing we knew eliminated the possibility either. Mustang steered with both hands. If one of them slipped out of sight, I'd make my move.

"'Seventy-seven," I said.

"Good year. This baby's a 'seventy-three."

"Better."

He gave me a two-finger salute, then shifted gears and the Mustang hurtled around a corner in a show of expert handling.

False alarm. I reeled in my paranoia, feeling the tension in my shoulders lessen. George and Noda had taken earlier flights but, with detours, landed after me. We'd set things up with our affiliates so both of them would hit the ground running.

I drove north for two more blocks, then turned left onto Sloat. A few blocks past Pine Lake Park, I swung right on Sunset.

Almost there.

In seconds Jenny would be in my arms, and the worry of my days in Japan would be eased, at least temporarily. Yes, Soga remained a threat, but bringing my daughter home meant more than anything to me at the moment. I wanted to see those trusting brown eyes and her gap-toothed smile. As soon as we settled in, I'd work out a new plan for her safety. Our safety.

Renna had given me the address of the safe house, since the FBI was letting it go next month when the lease expired. I turned onto the street and a feather of fear dusted the back of my neck. About where I figured the house should be, three squad cars were parked at odd angles in the street, as if the drivers had abandoned them in haste. I approached and saw Miriam Renna standing on the front lawn, arms wrapped tightly around her chest.

No!

At the far end of the street, an ambulance rounded the corner and rolled to a silent stop, its sirens disengaged, the urgency passed.

No!

Images of a bloodbath at the safe house rose in my mind. Jenny, blue-lipped and lifeless, Christine and Joey's stiff little bodies beside her. Miriam must have come to pick up her kids, who were shuffled out here by one of Renna's team every other day.

I was overreacting. Everything would be fine. It had to be. We'd moved Jenny out of harm's way. Stashed her at an undisclosed FBI hideaway. Security was top-flight. Three of Renna's best people watched over her. Soga wouldn't dare move against a whole police unit. Or would they?

I leapt from the Cutlass before it stopped rocking. While a police-woman questioned Miriam, a pair of patrol boys handled crowd control at the periphery.

"Miriam!" I yelled, dashing past a growing group of spectators and one of the attendant cops.

"Sir!" the patrolman yelled in my wake.

"Miriam!"

Renna's wife was a brunette with green eyes and a weathered but creamy Montana complexion. As her disturbed eyes swiveled in my direction, two cops stepped instantly between us to shield her, hands hovering over their gun grips. Miriam leaned left, around her protec-tors, and our eyes met. Her mouth formed a big O of surprise. Shock and dismay distorted her features.

Behind me, a cop commanded me to halt. In front of me, the two others drew their weapons.

Miriam called, "It's all right. I know him. He's the father."

He's the father. . . . Nooooooooooo. . . .

I grabbed Miriam by the shoulders. "Not Jenny," I said. "Tell me they didn't get Jenny."

She grew limp in my grasp. Tears rolled down her cheeks. The look in her usually confident eyes grew apologetic, despairing, defeated— and a dark hole opened in my chest.

IT was all my fault. At knifepoint, Homeboy had warned me away. In the village, Soga had attacked without reservation. In Tokyo, the powerbroker had cautioned me about Soga's vindictiveness. So what do I do? I charge ahead, asking only for the extra protection. From city cops. *Against Soga.*

My stomach wrapped itself in knots while elsewhere inside an untenable rage unfurled itself.

"Jim," I heard Miriam say. "I'm so sorry."

First Mieko, now Jenny. Only now did I fully comprehend the monster that was Soga. For the last seven days I'd been so intent on tracking down Mieko's killers, I'd let Soga waltz in and kill the only other living member of my family. *What have I done?*

Miriam hovered near me. "One minute we were in the garage, the next she was gone."

My head snapped up and I searched the solemn green orbs before me. "*Gone?* Did you say gone?"

"Yes. Someone grabbed her. I don't know who."

"She's not dead?"

"No, kidnapped."

"And Christine and Joey?"

"Drugged but alive."

I stopped listening. My mind kicked into overdrive. Jenny was alive. Renna's kids were safe. There was still a chance.

I drew myself up. My stomach unclenched. "But the ambulance . . . ?"

"For the maid," Miriam said. "She didn't make it."

Lucy Cooper, the undercover cop, had taken the brunt of the attack.

The policewoman who had been questioning Miriam stepped between us. She wore a black name tag with SPILSBURY etched in white. "Sir, I'm going to have to ask you to step away."

"What about the extra backup?" I asked.

"Sir—"

"It's okay, officer," Miriam said. "He's the father. He's just flown in from Tokyo."

"I appreciate that, ma'am, but we need to talk to you while this thing's still fresh, then we'll get to him. We could finish inside, if you'd rather."

Miriam hugged herself again. "No, outside, where I can see. In case Jenny comes back."

"Fine, but we do need to finish up quickly, ma'am. Sir, if you could move back."

"Answer my question," I said. "Where were the others?"

Spilsbury squinted at me with eyes as hard as any cop's I'd ever run across. "Sir, if I answer your question, will you step back and let me do my job?"

"Yes."

"Called away on a burglary-in-progress six blocks over."

Anger buzzed in my ears. "A diversion. Couldn't anyone figure that out?"

"Yes, sir," Spilsbury said in a tight, endlessly patient voice. "We're clear on that now. If you would—"

"Where's Renna? Why isn't he here?"

"En route as we speak."

"Good. But I want in. It's my daughter."

"Sir, that may well be, but you're not a witness. You can't help us with this unless you have any information pertinent to the kidnapping. Do you?"

"No, but—"

"Then I need you to join the onlookers and let us get on with interviewing the one witness we have."

I closed my eyes, thinking there ought to be something more I could do, but Spilsbury was right. For the present, I was a liability. Not that I believed the SFPD could accomplish much, either. We were dealing with Soga. They had swept in and plucked Jenny from an FBI safe house, of all things. My daughter was long gone—drugged and tucked away in a van, truck, or private jet and on her way to a destination of their choice. The steam went out of me. I stepped back to within two yards of the swelling crowd, now topping forty.

Spilsbury turned to Miriam, an unmistakable urgency in her tone. "Okay. Mrs. Renna, we need that description now, please."

Miriam wiped away tears. "I told you. I didn't see them. They just grabbed me."

"They? There was more than one?"

"I think so. It *felt* like more."

"But you're not sure?"

"No."

A new fear brewed in the pit of my stomach. How long would Jenny be safe? How long would they hold her unharmed? In most juvenile kidnappings, the victim was killed. Left alive, a child became an unbeatable witness. Any jury would convict hands down, if a minor pointed the finger.

Spilsbury asked, "Did you see anything at all?"

"No. They pushed me into the open trunk and shut it."

"You were in the garage?"

"That's right. I pulled in and shut the door as instructed. This is taking a lot of time. Can't you call someone? I gave you her picture."

"A BOLO's out, but we need more detail. Did they say anything to you?"

"No. They shoved me down and slammed the trunk lid. Jenny said, 'Mrs. Renna?' once. That's all I heard."

I realized Miriam's life had been spared only because the trunk had provided a convenient place for her confinement. Without it, there might have been two bodies. Renna and I had agreed the kids should come out to keep Jenny company, escorted by trained detectives who knew how to take the proper precautions. Now I saw we'd been mad to put his family at risk.

Spilsbury paused to digest the last statement. She too recognized how close Renna's wife had come, but a cop's deadpan cloaked her reaction. "Did you hear them talking to each other? Whispering? An accent?"

"No. Nothing."

"Muffled commands or scuffling? Sounds of a struggle?"

"No."

The kidnappers were quick, confident, professional.

"How about the hand that pushed you, Mrs. Renna? Did you see that? Can you recall skin color? A ring?"

"No."

"Footsteps? Heavy, light, hurried?"

"No. I felt someone behind me. But before I could turn around, I was locked in the car."

"How did they shove you in?"

"What do you mean?"

"They couldn't get you into the trunk of your car without a struggle. It's not that big."

"The trunk was open. I leaned over to pull out a box. A hand pushed my head down to the bottom of the trunk and held it there. I could smell the rubber from the spare tire. It's new."

"So you were bent over?"

"Yes. I tried to fight the hand, but it was too strong. Then someone lifted my legs."

"Was your head pinned the whole time?"

"Yes."

Soga had sent a team.

"So there were at least two of them."

"I guess so. Yes. There must have been."

Spilsbury was sharp. She'd just mined gold from thin air. I felt more comfortable stepping aside and letting her work.

"Now, the hand on your head, how did it feel?"

"Feel?"

"Yes. Was it a large hand?"

"Largeish, yes. But more than large, it was strong. Powerful."

"Bigger than your hand, would you say?"

"Much. But mine is so small—"

"Bigger than mine?"

"Yes."

"A man's hand?"

"I don't know."

"But if you had to guess?"

"Then I would say a man's."

"Did you feel anything? A ring? A watchband? A bracelet?"

"No."

"What about the hands that lifted your legs? Were they big?"

"I'm not sure."

"Could they have been?"

"I don't think so. The fingers felt slimmer. The ones pinning my head were large and fat. Well, not fat—beefy, strong."

The policewoman scribbled in her notepad. "Did you smell anything? Perfume? Cologne? A body odor?"

Miriam brightened. "There was a perfume. When I was lifted into the car."

"Cologne or perfume, ma'am?"

"Perfume. I don't know what brand, but it was definitely perfume."

Bingo. A man and a woman.

"Did Jenny say anything else after she called out?"

"No."

"You sure?"

"Yes."

Three people. Two people to manhandle Miriam into the trunk while a third muzzled Jenny.

Spilsbury nodded at her partner and he stepped over to the radio car to broadcast the new information.

Spilsbury snapped her notepad closed. "That's a great help, Mrs. Renna. We'll put out an APB with the little girl's description, alone or in the company of an adult couple. Possibly three adults, with at least one female. It's a start."

At least one female. It made perfect sense. Two men accompanying a small girl might draw curious looks, but a couple with a child in tow wouldn't rate even a cursory glance.

"Thank you," Miriam said. "When will I hear from you?"

"We'll contact you as soon as we have any news. After you rest, I'd like you to come to the station so we can go over this again. You might remember something else."

"Certainly."

Someone moved into the field of my peripheral vision and approached at a casual pace from the back of the crowd. In two steps, he slid in behind me and pressed a ring of steel into the small of my back. The gun would be in a jacket pocket, his body angled toward the crowd to shield his action.

"Stay cool, my friend," the stranger said. His voice sounded vaguely familiar. The bristles of a beard brushed my shoulder. Mustang.

Without turning, I said, "Where is she?"

"Don't know, don't care."

"Then why am I talking to you?"

"Damn good question. They don't usually hire me to talk." The gun dug into my back. "You understand me?"

"Fully."

"This time it's a message, boyo. They know some of your Tokyo lads have done a skip-to and they don't like it. You hearing me?" He worked the edge of the barrel into my spine until it pinched a nerve.

I arched my back. "Yes."

George and Noda had boarded separate flights to Hong Kong and Singapore, respectively. They had arrived at their Asian stopovers under their own names, then changed planes and passports and slipped into Los Angeles and New York under the cover of false identities to set our coastal affiliates in discreet motion. All local communications were being handled in person. No emails, no computers, no telephones. Nothing digital Soga's hacker could intercept. Our affiliates would, in turn, scrutinize the personnel of Gilbert Tweed Associates, looking to match any Japanese or Japanese Americans to a profile built from our trip to Soga-jujo. We were grasping at straws—and we considered ourselves lucky to have them. Toru had put us on our guard. Chances were good, he assured us, that Gilbert Tweed's computer whiz had set up a tracking program to alert him to any sudden movement on our part. Looked like Toru was right.

"Whatever you're planning, you are to cease and desist. Take a good gander at the maid. That will be your daughter, you try anything foolish."

As if on cue, two paramedics rolled a stretcher out the front door with a body strapped down under a beige canvas sheet. Murmurs rose around us. Miriam put her hand to her mouth.

"The woman cop's a message," Mustang said.

At the sight of Lucy Cooper's body, my simmering anger flared. It was a drastic move, killing a female police officer. And a game crusher. We'd hit them hard in Japan, now they'd struck back. And if they were keeping score, more bodies would follow.

"What do they want?" I asked.

"For now, you sit on your ass. They'll be in touch."

"Not sure I can do that."

"You don't, your daughter dies. Your choice, boyo."

He backed away through the crowd. I waited a beat, then glanced over my shoulder. Standing at the back to the crowd, Mustang gave me his two-finger salute and sauntered away.

They'll be in touch.

HEFTING a mug of steaming stationhouse coffee, I sat with Renna in his office. It was late. Ten at night in San Francisco, one in the morning in New York. I'd filled him in on everything since we last talked. Now we were waiting for a call. A vital call. The office door was closed. Neither of us spoke.

The phone rang. Renna snatched up the receiver and said "Yeah," listened, and shoved the handset at me. "Gotta be for you. There's a gremlin on the other end I can't understand."

"That you, Noda?" I said in English for Renna's benefit.

He grunted.

I nodded to Renna and switched to Japanese. "Any progress?"

"Maybe. Need one more day."

"Well, make it quick."

"Why?"

"They took Jenny."

Saying it out loud brought home the kidnapping with a new intensity. Until this moment a small part of me still held out the hope that Jenny might walk through my front door later tonight or tomorrow, but that wasn't going to happen. Jenny wasn't coming home today or tomorrow or any other day unless we were extremely careful, extremely lucky, or both. The realization tied me up in ways I'd never felt. My chest seemed to implode and breathing became painful.

Noda said, "When?"

The answer caught in my throat.

"Brodie? *When?*"

Noda's gruff practicality jarred loose an answer. "This . . . afternoon. Timed for my arrival."

A snarling sound erupted from the other end of the line. "They been in touch?"

"A personal warning. They know you and George skipped town but don't know where you went. That set them off."

"Just need another day."

"Fine, but stay out of sight. Make sure George does the same. They see either of you, Jenny could pay for it."

"Yeah, sure."

"Noda?"

"Yeah?"

"In the forest, you told me they didn't take hostages."

"I remember."

"What . . . about now?"

There was a long silence at the other end. "Sometimes I'm wrong."

My throat felt scratchy and dry. I had sensed Noda mentally stretching for an answer that would ease my apprehension. Problem was, he didn't sound convincing.

By-the-Book Robert DeMonde tapped on Renna's door and stuck his head in. He wore a three-piece blue pinstripe and a red silk tie. A straight arrow, down to his wardrobe. I had trouble picturing him as the city's next mayor after Hurwitz. He seemed too tightly wound for San Francisco.

Into the phone, I said, "Gotta go. You know how to reach me."

"Yeah," Noda said, and the line went dead.

DeMonde said, "Brodie, I heard what happened. I'm sorry. If anyone can get her back, our department can. Frank, are Miriam and the kids okay?"

"Yes, thanks, Bob. You want to join us?"

"No, but I'll need a word directly after. Boss's orders. And Gail wants to talk too. Something about toning down the department press releases." DeMonde gave Renna a significant look, nodded at me, and strode away with crisp steps.

"What's that about?"

"The mayor believes things have spun out of control. He wants full-time eyes inside and By-the-Book's his man."

"That doesn't sound good."

"As hard as it is to believe, I'd take him over Gail Wong any day. Officially, she's only his spokesperson, but she rules that office. Nobody crosses her and lives."

Then Renna gave me the rest of it. The only reason he still oversaw the Japantown team was because no sane person would step up to the plate. After what had happened out at the safe house, the volunteer pool had evaporated. No one wanted to put their family at risk. Immediate or extended. Everyone of consequence had read Renna's briefs of my findings, and once they grasped the vindictive side of Soga, not to mention the extent of their expertise, the career climbers went elsewhere. With public pressure building, the mayor's office opted to monitor the task force's progress close-up until the community outcries rose beyond bearable, at which time Renna would be offered up.

"Sorry, Frank."

"Not your fault. Knew this one could be tough when I took it on. If anything, I owe *you* an apology."

"How so?"

"For the idiot who yanked the boys off Jenny. That was a class-A fuckup. As big as they come."

Having revised my view on the mishap, I shrugged dismissively. "Better they weren't there."

Renna stared at me. "You don't mean that?"

"I do. Soga are pros."

Pride kindled a fire in his eyes. "What are we? Dim sum?"

"Of course not. But murder, assassination, and kidnapping are routine for these guys. If your boys were there, Soga would have run over three of your people instead of one."

"Not so."

"You ever think about what might have happened to Miriam if the trunk had not been conveniently open?"

For the first time in all the years I'd known him, Renna blanched. His steel-gray eyes teetered on the edge. The next instant the reaction was gone.

"I see your point. We underestimated them. Big-time."

"That we did."

"This thing, normal rules don't apply."

"Won't get any argument from me."

Renna leaned back in his chair. Marbles rolled. "But you know what? These bastards will go down just like any other scumbags. They're going to pay you a visit. We'll wire your place, put some shooters on the rooftops, undercover in the street, and nail their asses to the wall."

"Won't work."

"I'll put my best people on it."

"They'll spot 'em. They know your playbook."

"You got a better idea?"

"Just let Soga come and lay out their cards."

"Too dangerous."

"They took Jenny, then put a gun in my back *at the FBI safe house* in front of forty people, not to mention half a dozen cops. They don't miss a trick, and if we don't keep that in mind, Jenny will suffer."

Renna rolled his marbles and frowned. "Not how I'd handle it, but you know these dirtbags better than any of us."

"And there's Jenny."

Renna nodded. "First and foremost."

Back in Tokyo I'd promised I'd get Renna to watch my back. But Jenny's abduction called for a change in plans. Narazaki wouldn't like it, but the stakes had risen.

"One more thing," Renna said.

"What's that?"

"With an aggressive revenge kidnapping like this, chances are you'll hear from them sooner rather than later. So be ready."

DAY 8

LOST

WHEN they walked into my antiques shop the next morning brandishing identical Glocks, I gathered they weren't in the market for art.

There were two of them. Homeboy and a sleek, muscular man in his mid-thirties.

I reached for the weapon under the register. Gone. I pressed the silent alarm. Deactivated. Abers and I were penned in behind the counter at the front of the store, trapped. Fanned for three strikes in a flash. I'd called it right: the SFPD wouldn't have stood a chance with these guys.

The new man placed the muzzle of his gun in the middle of my forehead. "If you wish to live through the next thirty seconds, Mr. Brodie, stay absolutely still."

I didn't move. I didn't speak.

Homeboy raised his gun and squeezed off a round into the rear of my shop, swung the muzzle to the right, and released a second bullet.

I remained still.

The new man shifted his gun from the center of my forehead to the center of Abers's. "Look around, Mr. Brodie, but keep your feet planted."

Twisting at the hips, I examined the wall to my left then the back of the shop. With two shots of supreme accuracy, Homeboy had turned an eighteenth-century Shigaraki vase to powder and opened a hole in an Edo-period hanging scroll. They happened to be the two most expensive items in my store. Soga was pointedly demonstrating their unequivocal mastery of every aspect of my private and public life. Gun, alarm, shop, daughter. The simmering rage of yesterday unfolded itself and spread its curdled heat to every corner of my soul.

Homeboy's partner said, "Do we have your attention yet?" His hands were slim and manicured, his eyes penetrating brown disks. A holster burdened his shoulder under a black jacket.

I nodded, not trusting myself to speak.

"Good. Now, if you wish to live out the minute, you'll take seats over there. My colleague is going to handcuff you both. Then we'll talk."

He took a step back and leveled the Glock at my chest. His movements were efficient, his English impeccable. He held the weapon with a languid casualness that told me he was beyond good. There was an elastic grace to his movements that came from pursuing martial arts with a singular dedication. He'd be good at that, too. Homeboy was dangerous, and I'd barely held him off. His partner would demolish me.

Abers sat, but I lingered near the counter, watching for an opening.

"Dermott, I believe Mr. Brodie has other ideas. Please disillusion him."

Dermott pointed his gun at Abers and pulled the trigger.

A bullet tore into the wall two inches above Abers's left shoulder, and he jumped, his eyes wild.

I raised my hands in surrender and took the chair beside my assistant.

"As you seem to have a disregard for your own life, Mr. Brodie, my gun will be on Mr. Abers while my colleague handcuffs you both. Should you make a play for Dermott and succeed in distracting him for even a moment or two, I will shoot Mr. Abers first, then deal with you. Dermott tells me your reflexes are extraordinarily good. Such talent often leads to overconfidence and foolish behavior, so rest assured that a fraction of a second after you make your attempt, I will pump three bullets into your associate. My shots will be nicely clustered and his death will be instantaneous. Best-case scenario, you overpower us both and Mr. Abers will be dead. Worst case, you get a punch in and Mr. Abers will be dead. *Any* movement on your part will see Mr. Abers dead. Are we clear?"

I nodded. He spoke in the manner of someone used to dealing out orders and having them followed.

"Good. Dermott."

Dermott turned the deadbolt on the front door, flipped over the shop sign, and lowered the blinds. Then he approached, threaded cuffs through the chair spindles of the eighteenth-century comb-back Windsors we occupied and locked the metal bracelets around my wrists. He repeated his performance behind Abers's back.

"Excellent. Now, let's get the pleasantries out of the way. I'm Lawrence Casey, and my associate, whom you had the pleasure of meeting once before at your residence, is Dermott Summers."

Sneering and cocky at our first encounter, Dermott became the attentive lackey behind Lawrence Casey, which I could understand. Casey commanded allegiance. His bearing was loose-limbed and princely, as if he were above it all. Every strand of his hair was pulled back and gathered into a ponytail of inhuman symmetry, suggesting exacting precision. He wore a well-tailored black suit and matching turtleneck, each fashioned of the same material our attackers donned in Soga, only a shade thicker. Dermott wore a variation of the same suit, but with wider lapels to accommodate his huskiness. Both men wore identical black loafers that were soft-soled and soundless. Both men were Japanese.

"Dermott? Casey?" I said with lingering disbelief considering their Japanese origins.

"They're our working names." Slipping his piece into his shoulder holster, Casey shrugged to set the lay of the suit.

"Now, can we talk about my daughter?" I asked.

Casey's look was humorless. "Are you dictating the rules, Mr. Brodie?"

"No, I simply—"

"We wouldn't want to keep you waiting, now would we? Dermott, start the clock."

Clock?

Before I could respond, Dermott raised his gun and shot Abers.

ABERS rocked back in his seat, jaw plunging open in shock. His left thigh bled freely.

"Brodie," he muttered.

"Hold on, Bill." I fired an icy glare at Casey. "What the hell are you doing? You have us handcuffed."

Casey's face darkened. "You've meddled far too much in our affairs, Mr. Brodie. I've had to make a special trip back to San Francisco, which is not only a waste of my time but violates . . . our rules. It seems only fitting that we disturb you in equal measure. Dermott has grazed the femoral artery. Blood is pumping from Mr. Abers's body at a calculable rate. He will be dead in twelve to fifteen minutes unless the bleeding is stopped. With your hands cuffed behind your back, you cannot offer aid. We hold the key. Do you have any more requests?"

"None," I said, biting my lip. I glanced at Abers. The pain etched crags across his forehead.

Casey smiled. "A wise answer. *Now* we may begin. Our proposition is simple. We wish to defuse the present situation. Taking your daughter is the first step. Normally, we'd just kill you and be done with it, but your involvement with the SFPD and Brodie Security complicates matters. So here we are. The woman cop is dead so you'll know we're serious. What we require of you is one thing—drop Hara's case. You will fade away without fanfare, Mr. Brodie, like a bad sunset. If your firm backs off, and the police investigation flounders, then your daughter lives. We'd like you to go through the motions for a few more days to satisfy your client and the police. Then you will come up empty-handed. Your daughter's life depends on it."

"I'm listening," I said, thinking, *Jenny stays alive as long as I'm a threat.* But Casey scared me. He was ruthless, methodical, and intelligent. Worst of all, he was frighteningly unpredictable. Even as I strove to bolster my spirits, I felt my confidence seep away under Casey's frigid gaze.

"Good. Aimless activity should fill your hours. At the top of your list will be a second interview with Ms. Lizza Hara. You will fly to New York. Understood?"

"Easy enough."

"Next, we want you to send Mr. Suzuki and Mr. Noda globetrotting on a few unrelated errands under a pretext of your own devising. Just make it convincing."

"Not a problem," I said, glancing over at Abers. "Can we hurry this along?"

"Pardon?"

Dermott took aim at Abers's other leg, his grin far too eager. *Jesus.*

"Nothing," I said quickly. "Go on. Please."

Casey nodded approvingly. "From here on in, Mr. Brodie, neither you, nor anyone in your employ, must stray from the plan. We can and will strike at any time if we're dissatisfied with your performance. Family and friends will be our targets. *Nedayashi ni suru zo.* Do you understand me?"

Nedayashi ni suru zo. Literally, we'll cut off your roots. Meaning your entire family. Casey was talking about one of the most terrifying weapons of war in a country swimming with gruesome warrior traditions. It was the feudal custom of killing every member of your enemy's family in the belief that even small children could come after you later in life when they reached adulthood, as had happened throughout Japanese history. As a matter of honor, the survivors would seek revenge, so only the extermination of an entire clan assured safety. The implications paralyzed me. I floundered for an answer that would not trigger another violent response, and settled for a simple nod.

"Good, because we have practiced nedayashi with great success for three centuries. It has proved itself an unparalleled persuader. Know that we won't kill just you, we will wipe out your family and closest friends." He snapped his fingers. "Dermott?"

"Sandra Fandino, 1713 Fremont Avenue, Apt B, Mill Valley."

"My old girlfriend? She doesn't know I'm alive."

"She's kept a number of mementoes and still has pictures of you on her refrigerator."

"She's got dozens of photos there. Probably just hasn't bothered to weed mine out."

"Their prominence indicates otherwise."

In truth, friends had mentioned that she still carried a torch, but we hadn't spoken in years. I feigned disinterest. "It's news to me."

"Fine. Then you won't miss her. Consider her a warm-up." He snapped his fingers again.

Dermott leered. "Done. She'll be dead by tomorrow in a hit-and-run during her early morning jog."

Jesus . . . Sandra . . . My heart dropped down a black well. In an unsteady voice that betrayed me, I said, "I've seen your work. I don't need another example."

Casey peered at me through narrowed eyes. "But I think you do. You are far too argumentative for my taste."

Argumentative? After the initial hesitation to sit, my resistance had been all but nonexistent. I'd kept my words neutral and few, and still he was unhappy. These guys *liked* killing.

"Call him off, Casey."

"Too late."

"Call him off." I struggled against my restraints and heard a chair spindle crack. Casey watched me for signs of fear. They weren't hard to find. Only a fool would be fearless in this situation—fearless and soon dead.

Casey relented. "This one time *only*, I will acquiesce to your request, Mr. Brodie. But I have to know if we understand each other. Do we?"

"Yes."

"*Truly* understand each other?"

"Count on it."

"Good, because Mr. Abers is looking noticeably distressed. If there is another outbreak, I will not reverse myself. I dislike rescinding an order.

It weakens the chain of command. The next mistake, Sandra Fandino will be sacrificed to your stubbornness, *as well as* the next person on our list. And mark my word, there will be no further negotiation." Once more, Casey snapped his fingers.

"Jenny's babysitter." Dermott said. "The Meyers broad upstairs."

My face drained of color.

"A close neighbor. That sounds promising," Casey said. "Any ideas?"

"Drop her drugged and partially unclothed in a bad part of town late at night where they like white women and—"

Abers's head lulled to the left and his eyelids flickered. "Brodie, I—"

Casey glanced at his watch. "Our timepiece seems a little fast. Pity. Jenny will follow unless you deliver, Mr. Brodie. With or without police backing, we *will* take you out if we must. We can reach you and your friends any way, any time. If anyone takes a step in our direction, your daughter dies, you die, they all die."

Casey squatted down to my level.

"Mr. Abers is in a lot of pain right now. Pain *you* caused with your persistence here and in Tokyo. I trust I need not say more."

He turned and strode out the door without looking back.

Easing away, Dermott waved his Glock in my direction. "See you around, Brodie."

He dropped the handcuff key at his feet, slipping out the door with a grin. Eyes glued to the key, I scooted forward, the handcuffs cutting into my wrists, then tipped myself over on my flank. An armrest cracked in the fall and I heard a side stretcher snap. So much for a rare matched set. A third investment irreparably damaged.

Propelling myself forward with the edge of my foot, I inched up alongside the key, then rolled over on my back and felt around with my fingers. Abers groaned, his face white, a pool of blood below him expanding at an alarming rate. I found the key, wrapped my fingers around it, and rocked back and forth until I had enough momentum to flip back onto my side.

I probed the steel bracelets behind my back for a keyhole, found one, inserted the key, and heard the lock snap open. I slid free, undid the other bracelet, then uncuffed Abers. I laid him out on the ground, propped the wounded leg in the air to lessen the bleeding, and made a tourniquet of a nearby blue kimono obi, wrapping the excess around the wound itself. As I tightened the impromptu bandage, Abers let out a low moan.

After dialing 911, I stooped over my unconscious friend and slapped him, first across one cheek, then the other.

"Bill, can you hear me?"

No answer.

In the distance, the sound of a siren reached my ears.

"You hear that, Bill? They're on the way already."

His eyes popped open, pain carving up his face. "What?"

"The siren. Help is close."

"I'm cold, lad. Real cold."

I yanked a blanket from a Korean bedroom chest and spread it over him. "Better?"

His eyelids fluttered. "They tore up the place bad."

"Nothing we can't fix."

"Guess I'll have to sell a few more pieces quicklike to keep the frikkadel flowing."

"Guess you will."

"I will, you know."

"You always do."

With a faint nod, he closed his eyes and the last signs of animation drained from his face.

CHAPTER 60

I SAT in the hospital waiting room with my head in my hands. I was utterly lost. I didn't know where to turn or what to do. I didn't even know what to think. A feverish uncertainty clawed at my chest. My breathing came in fits and starts. I'd put everyone I cared about in danger.

Attendants had wheeled Abers straight from the operating theater into intensive care, where visitors were banned. Most of the internal damage had been repaired, but there were complications, and the prognosis was uncertain.

Informing me that Abers would do nothing but sleep for the next twelve to twenty-four hours, the doctor sent me home, and I went. I drove back to the shop in a daze, left the closed sign in place, and pulled out a limited edition of twelve-year-old saké normally reserved for clients. I didn't want to drink alone but I had nowhere else to go. Renna would be wrestling with his wife's trauma and guilt. At the Meyerses', I'd have to contend with Lisa, Jenny's best friend. At home, everywhere I looked would remind me of my daughter.

That left the shop.

The premium saké disappeared in record time. I poured myself a second shot, downed it, grabbed the bottle, and marched from my desk into the small conference room adjoining the office.

I swallowed a third shot, then a fourth. I stared at the beige carpets and then at the pearl-gray walls. I had always been proud of this little hideaway where I closed deals and previewed new pieces. Now it meant nothing. My eyes roamed the room and settled on the Burchfield watercolor. I drank a fifth shot to the neglected painter.

The pale pastels of the piece drew me in, as they always did. Nightfall met an orange sunrise peeking over the horizon. In the foreground, a tree in a surreal combination of pinks, blacks, and greens sprouted upward—lush, pulsating, vital—waiting for the coming day with a decisive dignity.

Dignity was something I knew a little about.

With an ever-widening sneer, Scott Mutrux threw me for the third time. I was seventeen and stubborn, and when I staggered up and faced off for a fourth round, he slammed me to the mats again without hesitation. Mutrux was a snarling blond bully three years my senior, and I was a starry-eyed, fresh-from-Japan newbie to the L.A. dojo. Until that point, I'd lost to very few people in Tokyo or L.A.

Battered and bleeding, I tried to rise. Darkness gathered at the edges of my vision. Anger consumed me. Stepping onto the mats, Mieko bent over and whispered the poem about stillness and the Okazaki Hills. In Japanese. For the first time. Without fully understanding the nuances of the verse, I sensed an inkling of a Zen ideal about peace and knowing. The full message was beyond my years, but somehow I latched on to its essence.

Mieko's breath was warm and sweet. My heart wrapped itself around the stillness she spoke of. The darkness grew bright and Mieko and I exchanged smiles.

I didn't challenge Mutrux again that day. I let Mieko help me into a corner, where I sat until my head cleared. I sat straight and tall and proud. Like Burchfield's tree.

Scott Mutrux knew something I didn't. And whatever it was, it was overpowering. But I was determined to discover his secret.

For two years, I practiced. *Kata* and *kamae* and *shizentai* and *rei* filled my days and my dreams. And in my nightmares I saw Scott Mutrux's sneer. After the first year, I began to mix in the street moves I'd learned. And some judo. Then tae kwon do. New combinations emerged. I practiced them, refined them. The stillness watched. I reached for it but caught it only rarely. I couldn't hold on. When I did connect, it brought a knowing calm. My skin tingled and an inner glow warmed me.

What Mieko taught me that day on the mats was this: *Lose a battle, but don't lose yourself.*

Two years later, Scott Mutrux and I faced off again. I was nineteen to his twenty-two. I'd grown a few more inches. I threw him to the mats twice. Mutrux slunk away amid jeers.

The night of Soga's visit to my shop was the longest of my life. Longer and lonelier than last night when I'd fretted over Jenny's abduction. Longer and lonelier than the night George had called me after a fourteen-year silence to tell me of my father's death.

Longer and lonelier because I'd never felt so helpless.

Images of Jenny and Abers and everything good and decent in my life tormented me. I didn't have the answer, but I knew the question: How could I hope to find Jenny or support Abers if I couldn't find myself? I posed the query to the saké, the Burchfield, and myself. The first soothed me, the second inspired me, and the third—when I'd dug as deep as I possibly could then stopped to listen—answered me.

I'd found the stillness again and felt the glow. The knowing. An inner strength. Then I heard my father's words, which had long ago become my own: *"Stand tall. For the little guy—and for yourself."* Soga had taken Mieko. They had taken Jenny. But I would not let them suck the life out of me as long as I drew breath.

DAY 9

DESPERATION

THE next morning my office phone rang twice and went dead.

I locked up and slid into the shop van, an unmarked white panel truck left around back. I drove east on Lombard, swung right at Van Ness, and a few blocks down eased into the corner gas station. I waved to the owner Al as I filled up my tank, then parked by the garage. Inside, Al's kid had a Safari van on the rack and was tinkering with the front axle. We exchanged nods. I slipped out the back door, through a chain-link gate at the rear of the lot, and into the diner next door. The Soga boys would have the pay phones closest to my store tapped, and recording equipment set to snatch any cell phone conversations from the air, but slipping out the blind side of the gas station into the coffee shop behind it exposed me for less than twenty seconds.

After ordering a cup of coffee and a Danish to go, I stepped down the hall to the restrooms and a pair of pay phones. A quick look confirmed that no one stood within earshot. I dialed, fed the recorded message the money it wanted, and waited. It rang once.

"Yeah?" a voice said.

"Me. Got something?"

"They're here. Don't know how many."

"New York? You sure?"

"Got to be. They wear suits, but clothing looks like bibs on bull-dogs."

"Awful fast work."

"*Mochiron.*" Of course. "I put ten men on it round the clock. I stayed out of sight. George did the same in L.A."

A chill crawled down my spine. Ten men was an army. "I told you to keep it low-key. Jenny's life is at stake."

"Extreme long-distance surveillance only. Binoc work from neighboring buildings, cars way back. Nothing closer."

"Nobody was spotted?"

"No."

Relief rolled over me. "All right. What'd you find?"

"Nothing until we started watching the alley entrance and underground parking."

"They didn't use the main entrance?"

"Maybe before but not now."

Always a step ahead, I thought. Once our hacker nailed theirs, Soga went into deep-stealth mode. "How many?"

"Five so far."

"And George's team?"

"Three. All smoked-glass windows on their cars, underground parking, up the back stairs instead of lobby elevators. Hard to nail down."

But he had, thank God. "Five's a big number for their kind. You have a home address?

"Secluded stretch in Long Island along the north shore."

"Nice place?"

"Large, wooded, on the water. High walls all around."

"What kind of water?"

"Big."

"Must be the Long Island Sound. Easy access to mainland."

"Yeah, inlets, east, west, north."

"So they can't be penned in."

"No. Got a dock and two boats. Look fast."

"Owner?"

Noda grunted. "Had someone hit the local gas station two miles down the road. Old Japanese guy lives there, with two younger ones."

Kohai-sempai. Juniors serving their superior. Typical Japanese hierarchical arrangement. A good sign.

"Let's go with it," I said.

"I'll set up this end."

"Good. See you tonight."

"Okay."

"One last thing," I said. "They paid a visit."

"How many?"

"Just two. They shot my shop assistant." Overnight, Abers's condition had not improved.

"Tell me," Noda said, and I did. He stayed silent for a long beat after my report, then said, "Nothing we can do now but wait for the doctors. Stay cool, stay quiet, and keep your head down."

"That's the plan, but someone's got to pay."

Noda grunted and disconnected.

Next I called Renna. After Soga's visit to my shop, I could no longer afford to be seen with, or overheard talking to, a police lieutenant, friend or no friend. When he answered, I told him it was on for New York, and asked if he was going to join the party.

"Wouldn't miss it for the world," Renna said. "I put in for an official leave of absence. Made this morning's paper."

"Perfect." Soga would see the article. "Catch you on the other coast, then?"

"As planned. No one but the chief and the mayor will know I'm gone."

"Good. Anything else?"

"A lot of people around here think we're paranoid."

"How about you?"

"I know better."

Next I made a collect call to Tokyo. When Goro Kozawa came on, neither of us mentioned the other's name. I said, "It's time to open those doors you mentioned."

"Just tell me how."

I did.

Then, with my bag of takeout prominently displayed, I strolled back to Al's, paid for the gas, and headed back to the shop. From my office, I did what Casey asked. I called Lizza Hara and played my frivolous card. Though she willingly agreed to a second face-to-face meeting, I felt guilty as hell. I was using her just as her father had.

He meant her to be a beacon for Soga.

For me, she would be a shield.

THREE BLOCKS AWAY

As soon as Jim Brodie started up his shop vehicle and struck out for an unknown destination, four unmarked vans, one for each point of the compass, began to roll. Equipped with GPS-tracking monitors homed in on a device attached to the chassis of the art dealer's car, each van followed from afar. While the target rolled east down Lombard, two of the tracking vehicles advanced along parallel roads to the left and right, the third ran an intercept course three-quarters of a mile ahead on the same road, and the fourth brought up the rear a half mile back.

When Brodie turned right on Van Ness, the cars front and back immediately turned in the same direction so that they paralleled the mark. The vehicles traveling on parallel tracks swung onto Van Ness and took up the rear and forward positions. As long as the target was mobile, no car made visual contact. No car approached closer than three blocks.

Once the subject reached his destination, the surveillance vehicles sped up, the trailing one accelerating as the target turned into the gas station, pulling into a shadowed driveway across the street, giving the spotter in the back of the van a bird's-eye view from behind tinted windows.

At stationary posts seventy to one hundred yards away on their respective points of the compass, the remaining three vans activated parabolic microphones capable of capturing a cricket's call at two hundred yards. The driver of the closest vehicle primed a fourth machine. Amplification software was adjusted, and Brodie's phone calls were captured by three of the four long-distance mikes.

Two of the recordings were perfect.

FROM the cabin window of my United flight, I could see Manhattan in the distance, its skyscrapers clawing at a hazy yellow sky. Once my plane touched down at JFK, I grabbed my duffel bag from the overhead compartment and caught a cab to a midtown hotel on Thirty-eighth and Ninth, where I walked through a dim lobby with a dusty chandelier, a black- and white-checkered linoleum floor, and a pair of scuffed red vinyl couches. At the far end of the lobby a doorway led to a cheesy cocktail lounge with more red vinyl. In the indistinct light of the bar, I could make out the sheen of a well-tailored summer jacket but no faces. Fine men's apparel on Thirty-eighth and Ninth?

I rode a rickety elevator to the fifth floor and knocked on a door of walnut veneer streaked with age, maybe eight decades' worth. The door opened. I entered. The door closed. Noda stood in the shadows, holding a cell phone and a gun. The lights were dimmed and the curtains drawn. The room had a double bed with a faded maroon spread with some kind of crest, a brown carpet with well-worn footpaths, and an ugly brown desk with more nicks than the expressway into town had potholes.

"Cops right behind you," Noda said. "Affiliates picked you up at Kennedy. Confirmed you weren't followed."

"That George camped out in the lounge?"

"Who else?"

Noda wore gray summer pants and a black turtleneck under a slate jacket. The break on the jacket hid a holster.

I indicated the gun. "You've been busy."

"A loaner from our associates. George is carrying and we got a third for you."

He tossed me a small Browning and I dropped it in the side pocket of my windbreaker.

In two minutes there was a knock. Noda drew his gun and nodded. I checked the peephole, then opened the door. Renna walked in with a plainclothes cop I didn't know and a dusky blond guy with wire frames, an olive green Italian suit, and pale gray eyes.

Noda holstered his piece.

I said to Renna, "You made it."

"Might be a one-way ticket. Word came down last night, this venture doesn't solve the J-town problem, I'm better off walking home."

I felt for my friend. In San Francisco, officials hid behind spokespeople and blamed Renna. Insiders labeled the lieutenant's decision to take on the Japantown case "career suicide." But I and a handful of like-minded souls saw it differently. In stepping up to the plate, Renna had done the right thing. If you let a Japantown go unanswered, how could you look yourself in the mirror every morning? Problem was it happened far too often. To all of us. When confronted with our own Japantowns, many of us fled. An unfaithful spouse, betrayal at the office, a family member with a terminal disease—whatever it was, we turned our back on the problem instead of facing it. I should know. I'd crawled into a hole for eight months when Mieko died.

Renna's struggle was different. He was being skewered for not delivering. The truth was, the breaks did not come your way on every case. If you cleared 70 percent of your files, you made the big leagues. But even big leaguers struck out. From the outset, Renna and I both knew there was a chance Japantown might slide into unsolved territory.

"Got another piece of news," Renna said quietly.

With the sinking tone of his voice, a coldness crept into my bones. Had Jenny's body turned up? Did Casey set Dermott loose?

"Abers didn't make it."

All the men in the room frowned at the floor.

Involuntarily, a moan escaped my lips. I turned my back on the others, shoving my hands in my jacket pockets and stretching the fabric to the limit. I bit my lower lip as a hollow ache opened inside.

A hand touched on my shoulder. "There'll be time for mourning him properly when this is over," Renna said. "Now we have to focus on the living."

Meaning Jenny. My head heavy and listless, I inhaled noisily and gathered myself up. "All right. Let's get on with it." I turned back to the men in the room. "These your New York guys?"

"Yeah. Jamie McCann, Jim Brodie."

I shook hands with the plainclothes cop.

"Sorry about your loss," he said. "You Irish?"

"Father's side."

"Good side." He was big and beefy and around the same age as Renna.

Renna coughed behind a fist. "And this is Luke."

"First or last name?"

"Just Luke."

"Ah." We shook hands.

McCann said, "He's the agency's contribution. Whatever strings you pulled cleared passages that haven't been opened in decades. It's a goddamn New York miracle. We got all the manpower we needed the instant we needed it. SWAT, antiterrorist squad, air cover, and Luke."

Well, what do you know? Kozawa *had* opened some doors.

"What is it you do, Luke?"

Luke focused icy gray eyes on me. His irises were small, cold disks that seemed to register everything in the room without passion or comment. He looked faintly Nordic and wore an expensive cologne. "Mostly I take out the garbage. Today I'm to cover your back."

"Noda's doing that."

"He can still do it, but I do it too."

"Unless I give you something else to do?"

"Yes."

I nodded and introduced Noda. More hands were clasped.

"A pleasure," Renna said. "You speak English?"

"Sure. You wanna have a spelling bee?"

"Jokes. You can stay."

Noda's cell phone buzzed. He flipped it open and said in English, "Talk."

He listened and grunted. "Just one? Pale green eyes, brown hair, black pinstripe, looks like a broker?"

He looked at Renna, Luke, and McCann. "Whose?"

Renna seemed puzzled for a moment, then said, "Mine. Garbage in, garbage out."

"You need out," Luke said, "let me know."

Renna grinned. "I'll remember that."

Into his cell, Noda said, "Let him pass."

In a minute there was another knock. Renna reached for the knob and Noda and Luke unholstered their weapons. Renna saw the movement, waited a beat, and eased open the door a few inches.

"You're late," he said, and the guns slipped silently into shoulder holsters.

DeMonde walked in with a firm step and nodded solemnly. "Gentlemen."

"Bob DeMonde," Renna said, "from the S.F.'s mayor's office." Renna ran through everyone's name for By-the-Book's benefit and more hands were shaken, at the end of which DeMonde announced, "I won't get in your way, gentlemen. You're the pros." His smile was open and winning.

The straightest of straight arrows, but he'd come down on the right side. Maybe he had a better shot at the mayor's job than I thought.

McCann grinned. "A pol who likes us *and* won't interfere. It's another damn New York miracle. Must be Christmas."

DeMonde shrugged agreeably. "I have to report it as I see it, but let me assure you that everyone wants this nightmare cleared up."

Renna said, "The mayor told me he was sending Gail."

DeMonde coughed into his fist. "Change of strategy. Gary's got all the confidence in the world in you guys but, ah, he wanted Gail close in case this thing, well, goes south and he needs damage control."

Renna shot me a fatalistic look.

I shrugged, then addressed the room. "Okay, introductions are over. Final check. You all know the drill. The trigger will be my phone call to Lizza Hara at nine a.m. tomorrow morning. You have tonight for making final arrangements, but by early morning you all need to be in place. I expect Soga will have Lizza's phone tapped, and another on my hotel line before dawn. Renna, any last-minute snags on your end?"

"As Bob said, they want it wrapped up."

"McCann?"

"We're set. Here and with liaison to Jersey, Long Island, and Connecticut. Whichever way it goes, we're covered."

"Good."

"We gonna need all the manpower?" McCann asked.

"I just hope it's enough," I said. "We're also going to need sea cover. Forgot to mention that."

McCann sent a mournful look Renna's way. "Damn, Frank, I'm scratching my head here. You and I go way back, but I've been on the job twenty-five years and haven't seen an operation like this one. We already got land and air and more bodies than the Chinese military. It's just hard to believe."

I said, "You want proof?"

McCann threw up his hands. "*Something* would be nice."

I turned to Noda. "You mind?"

Noda shrugged and lowered the edge of his turtleneck. Pinkish-brown scar tissue a shade lighter than Noda's natural color and about half an inch wide stretched across his neck under his jawline and swung up on both sides to a point under each ear. The line glistened with medication.

McCann said, "I'll be damned."

By now they all knew about our reception in the village.

Luke stepped forward. "May I?"

Noda gave a go-ahead nod and Luke moved closer, studied the wound, then frowned.

McCann said, "What?"

"This burn's from reinforced flexi-cable. Lightweight, thin. Doesn't snap, can't be severed without a bolt cutter. High-tech rope that costs about three hundred dollars a foot. I suggest we follow any advice these men may be able to offer."

"Your teams ready?"

"Yes," said Casey.

"Yes," said Dermott.

Good, thought Ogi. Eight of my best people on the front line. And eight more for peripheral duties. Sixteen fighters with forty-seven kills between them. With my two apprentices and myself, that means nineteen people on the grounds.

A little extra insurance never hurt. A *lot* of extra insurance constituted a sterling Soga trademark. Maybe it was overkill for an art dealer and his cohorts, but the Japantown job had provided a $2.5-million paycheck. No corners would be cut.

Ogi said, "As before, you two are to handle Brodie personally."

"Yes, sir," they said as one.

THE London NYC was a fifty-story wafer of a hotel in midtown Manhattan on West Fifty-fourth Street between Sixth and Seventh. Broadway and the theater district held court to the west, Fifth Avenue and shopping to the east. Once upon a time, when the place was called the RIHGA Royal and owned by a Japanese hotel chain, I'd been a valued customer and received a superb business discount that made staying there cheaper than all but the real dives. The present owners honored the arrangement.

The front desk was a slab of speckled olive-green-and-white Italian marble with ornamental brass lamps and tall fountain pens. Women in long summer gowns glided through the lobby on the arms of well-groomed men in dinner jackets and red ties, a few of the more distinguished men sporting flowers in their lapels. I had Tokyo dust clinging to my jeans.

Standing ramrod erect behind the front desk, a clerk in the hotel's blazer and necktie eyed me warily. I carried a black sports bag with a yellow Nike swoosh and wore black jeans, a beige T-shirt from Banana Republic under a black windbreaker, and my ever-loyal black-on-black Reeboks. Not to denigrate my image on arrival, I'd shifted the Browning to the sports bag.

"May I help you, sir?" the clerk said. His white name tag said ROBERTO.

"Reservation for Brodie."

Roberto tapped a few keys on a computer, glanced indifferently at the screen, then handed me a room card. His machine pinged and

Roberto raised an eyebrow in mild surprise. "You have a message from Ms. Lizza Hara. She asks that you call as soon as you arrive." He said the name like he knew it.

"I'll do that."

"Are you an acquaintance of Ms. Hara's?"

"She's a fan. *You* know her?"

"She recommends many guests of Japanese nationality to our establishment." He glanced at the Nike swash with distaste. "Mostly VIPs." As an afterthought, the clerk punched up some data on the computer. "In fact, Ms. Hara seems to have booked you an upgrade. I'm afraid the computer's made a mistake. A large suite has been set aside for you."

"A computer mistake," I said. "Imagine that."

Roberto reddened. "Yes, sir. Here's your new key card."

Unhappy that the Hara clan had rerouted my room assignment, I boarded an elevator to the upper reaches of the hotel with a firm frown in place, disembarking on the forty-fifth floor. The hall carpet was plush and the distance between doorways long. Slipping the card into its slot, I swung the door aside and stepped into a sitting room with deep, eggshell-white carpet and a sprawling ivory couch set in front of a wide-screen TV the size of a wall mural. Sitting on the couch and dressed in jeans and a beige cable sweater was Lizza Hara. The glitzy pop star had vanished. She looked like she might be on her way to a girlfriend's for a sleepover.

"Daddy would never forgive me if I didn't look after you, so I couldn't let you stay in an *ordinary* room."

"I see. Have you talked to your father in the last few days?"

"Only for a minute or two. Why?"

"Did he ask you to arrange the room?"

"Oh, no. It was my idea. Do you like it?"

I wondered if her answers were truthful or only half the story. Wondered too if showing up early was part of a larger scheme.

"Do you?" she pressed.

"It's very nice," I said.

"I'm glad you think so. I've been so anxious to hear the latest, I decided to wait here. I hope you don't mind. Have you made any progress?"

"Some."

Lizza had pulled her hair back and kept her makeup to a minimum. Her eyes were wide and moist. She must have been crying, or been close to it. I could see she wanted to talk. Wanted to share her grief. The pain had wormed its way inside and dimmed her natural effervescence. Unless she was flexing her acting chops, which had grown with her fame.

Normally, I'd give her the benefit of the doubt and accommodate her, but handholding would require more time and energy than I could spare at the moment. Tomorrow, I'd be under Soga's eye, with Jenny's life at stake. Lizza's needs could wait a day or two. I sought a gentle way to ease the excitable singer-starlet out the door.

But before I could make a suitable excuse, she said, "I knew you would!" and bounded up off the couch. "You can tell me all about it at the club."

"Club?"

"A place in TriBeCa I sometimes go to dance. They have quiet alcoves with enough privacy to talk, too."

"Let's not and say we did."

"Oh, come on." She tugged my arm. "I think we could both use some cheering up. It's a new spot we hang at. Very exclusive. It doesn't even have a name yet. Just 'The Club.'"

"I'm not much of a clubber. Besides, I think I have to work on my tan first."

Lizza was shifting into modest party mode. Her concern over her sister's case was present and genuine, but so was her determination to have fun. Now. Tonight. Almost desperately so.

"Well, how about the cocktail lounge at the Waldorf? Very quiet and proper. We'll have all the privacy we need, so you can tell me what you've found out. You'll need a tie, of course. Samson can pull an evening dress from the trunk for me."

I saw what she was doing. She wanted an update on Japantown, but in surroundings that would bolster her spirits when the inevitable gloom hit. If she couldn't surround herself with festive, then she wanted the cordial and comforting refinement of a luxurious setting, with the accompanying liquid refreshments to soothe her nerves. Or was it all a pose to draw me out? Had her father sent her fishing for more information?

I also saw the tension at the corners of her mouth, the bags under her eyes, and the extra layer of makeup to disguise them. Act or not, clearly she wasn't sleeping well.

Against my better judgment, I agreed to accompany her, telling her I could only spare an hour, no more. Once I'd passed on the same information I'd given her father and patted her hand a couple of times, I'd excuse myself.

But first I needed to clean up. We made plans to meet downstairs in twenty minutes after I showered and changed. Lizza left and I dove under a hot, stinging spray, emerging revived and smiling. I was slipping into a pair of dust-free jeans when the phone rang.

It was Lizza. "Don't you know it's impolite to keep a girl waiting?"

"I'm nearly out the door."

I disconnected, troubled by Lizza's impatience. As I pulled on a clean shirt and my windbreaker, dropping the gun into the side pocket, a new thought occurred to me. I called reception.

"Front desk, Jonathan speaking."

"This is room 4507."

"Yes, sir."

"I'm joining Ms. Hara shortly."

"Of course, sir."

"Do you know where she is?"

"In the tearoom, I believe."

"Did Miss Lizza meet any, uh, associates?"

"There did seem to be three or four gentlemen of her acquaintance in the lobby."

"Camera-carrying gentlemen?"

"Why yes, now that you mention it."

Lizza wanted buddy pictures for posterity and the papers back in Japan. Distraught though she was, old habits died hard. Catering to the Japanese press while she lounged about in the Big Apple was how she kept her lucrative career in Tokyo alive. I'd acquiesced for her peace of mind, and she was about to repay the favor by milking it for all she could. Those indomitable Hara genes. You had to love her, but enough was enough. I'd come to New York to get my daughter back.

"Ever seen Japanese press, Jonathan?"

"Yes, sir. On several occasions."

"Ms. Hara's acquaintances, do they remind you of Japanese press?"

"Very much so."

"I thought as much. Could you pass on a message?"

"As you wish, sir."

"Tell Ms. Hara I've had to leave suddenly on urgent business. She'll understand."

"Or course, sir."

I was combing my hair when the bell rang. Lizza wasn't going to put up with being stood up. Excuse time.

I walked across the suite and opened the door. "Listen, Lizza, I've made—"

That was as far as I got.

Casey stood at the door, wearing a sleek silver-gray suit that looked tailored and holding a gun that looked like my Browning. His hair glistened with oil and his fingernails were small white squares of perfection.

He said, "Postcoital bliss, Mr. Brodie? Sloppy, sloppy."

Then he shot me.

The weapon spit a small dart into my abdomen. I plucked it out and Casey fired two more at my chest. My vision blurred. Casey put a palm on my forehead and shoved. I stumbled back. I reached for the gun in my pocket, but my hand refused to obey, dropping like a lead weight to my side. Casey glided into the room, Dermott Summers sharp on his heels, pushing an oversize laundry cart. He wore janitor's blues with the hotel name stitched in red across the breast pocket.

Dermott said, "Surprise, surprise. Don't have the wrong place this time, do I, Brodie?"

He moved around the cart and pivoted on the ball of his foot.

I saw the kick coming in plenty of time, but neither my arms nor legs responded to the defensive posture I had in mind. I took the blow on the chin and went down.

"Been waiting a *long* time to do that," Dermott said.

"You've had your fun, now we've got work to do," Casey said, and Dermott scooped me off the carpet as if I were a rag doll and dropped me in the laundry basket. Dermott looked down at me with a sneer. "It's a New York miracle. Must be Christmas."

McCann's words two hours ago at the hotel. Soga had infiltrated our meet. Someone had betrayed us. But who? Renna and Noda were beyond suspicion. DeMonde was too far out of the loop. McCann and Renna went way back. That left Luke. He had the resources and Kozawa backed him. *Kozawa's* hara guroi, *a black-hearted one,* Tommy Tomita had told me. *Watch your back, your pocketbook, and don't trust a word out of that snake's mouth.* Luke had arrived wearing a wire, the bastard.

In another worthless moment of hindsight, I recalled the informant's words of caution on the taped interview: *Any men you send should assume their attack to be expected no matter what level of secrecy is employed. If, en route, anything out of the ordinary attracts their attention—a small noise, a shadow, a whisper, an unexpected knock,* anything—*they must shoot first and question later. If they wait for verification, they will be dead.*

The knock. It had been that simple. Envisioning a pouting Lizza standing in the entrance, I'd opened the door to Soga. They had played it brilliantly. Tomorrow's sneak attack had been preempted. The next morning, my backup would arrive and find me long gone.

We'd lost the battle before it began.

CHAPTER 64

SOMEONE slapped my left cheek. Hard.

I heard myself say "Stop that" but the sound came out as an unintelligible rumble. The rumble echoed through the darker reaches of my mind. I forced my eyelids open. It felt like someone was standing on them. Dermott Summers floated in a milky haze before me. He struck me a second time, putting some body weight behind the blow, and it rocked me. The only reason I didn't tumble to the floor was because I was already on it, secured by a thick cord.

"You are once again among the living," Casey said dryly.

"But not for long," Dermott added with a smirk.

I was in a panel van, with Casey, Dermott, and a driver. There was brown pile shag on the floor and white auto paint on the interior. The back panels had no windows. Between the bucket seats at the front, the van's headlights illuminated a two-lane country road with forest on either side. We were a long way from Manhattan. A long way from Renna, McCann, and the rest of the task force.

"We're almost there," Casey said from the passenger's seat.

"Where's that?"

This time my words were decipherable.

"Where we're going to crate you," Dermott said. He sat facing me on the carpet, leaning against the opposite side with his knees raised. "Tonight you're missing, tomorrow you're just another New York stat."

I fought back a fleeting panic. "I don't believe it."

Dermott sneered. "Believe it. You're about to be raw meat for maggots. Raw, red, and dead."

I sneered back and tested my bindings. Inches from me sat the man who had killed Abers. Hate scorched my heart but I could do nothing. My hands were tied behind my back. My legs were wrapped in some kind of cloth restraint. A rope around my midsection was secured to a metal apparatus anchored to the side of the van behind me. I wrenched the ropes around my wrists. They held firm. I ran my fingers over the hardware digging into my kidney—and found a thin metal tab with a sharp edge, on the back of the framework. It was one of those bits of metal they need during the formation process but never bother to trim away since no one can see it in the finished work. I pushed, felt some give, and began to work the tab back and forth.

"That true, Casey?" I said, glaring at the man who'd ordered Abers's shooting.

"Afraid so."

Uh-huh. First-class kidnappers, fourth-class liars. They were pushing the scare, but I knew a hoax when I heard one.

"Nice try, but it doesn't wash." I worked the metal tab some more, meeting less resistance. "You wouldn't have gone to all the trouble of kidnapping Jenny. Wouldn't have killed the cop."

"Fairy dust," Casey said. "To get you to New York."

"Still doesn't wash, guys."

The tab separated from the hardware's superstructure and dropped into the palm of my other hand. It was the size of a dime and had a thin cutting edge. I slid it into the fleshy V between my thumb and index finger.

"Ah, we're here," Casey said.

The van ground to a halt in front of a fifteen-foot tower of wrought-iron grillwork bristling with security cameras and razor wire. Ornate yet impenetrable, the gate was the construct of a moneyed owner who valued his privacy.

The driver punched a code into a control panel below an intercom and the structure swung open. We rolled through. Ten-foot-high stone walls with more razor wire encircled the compound. Inside, the grounds were densely wooded and encompassed ten or fifteen acres, maybe more. We crawled along a twisting single lane of paved drive for nearly half a mile. Around the fourth bend, the trees broke and a three-story

French manor with maybe twenty-five rooms swung into view. Flaunting an immaculate brick façade, the manor also boasted four chimneys, a large undulating lawn, and white wooden shutters on all the fifteen upper-story windows that I could see. Partially obscured by trees, what appeared to be guest cottages sat off to the right, and farther on, the shadowy forms of larger outbuildings loomed.

It took a moment before I got it. And only because I'd been *there*—to the village. A sharp stab of fear rippled my stomach muscles. I sat very still and drank in what passed in front of me. What very few, if any, outsiders had ever seen.

They were building the modern equivalent of a Soga village.
On American soil.

BEYOND the immediate grounds, everywhere I looked I saw pine and oak and dense undergrowth. Beyond the house, I saw more trees and, between them, slivers of moonlight flickering on water. The Sound.

That was the giveaway. We were on Long Island, at the house Noda had unearthed. Only it wasn't a house but a budding Soga community. A Japanese export of unique and horrifying proportions.

When Dermott released me, I wobbled unsteadily to my feet, my vision blurred, my head muddled. Floodlights bathed the manor in an icy blue brilliance. In the shadowy darkness beyond the illumination, men and women milled about in Soga black, their voices soft, ghostly whispers reverberating in my ear with drug-enhanced clarity.

We'd been outmaneuvered on every level.

With Casey leading the way and Dermott serving as rear guard, I was paraded across a gravel driveway, up the entry steps into a large marble foyer, then to a vast study with a baby grand piano on one end and a large colonial desk and floor-to-ceiling bookshelves at the other. Gleefully, Dermott prodded me from behind with a steady stream of shoves. Once in the study, he thrust me into a chair near the desk and tied my hands behind my back, weaving the rope through the chair spindles exactly as he had done in my shop with the handcuffs.

Casey whispered into the ear of a tall, limber man in his mid-seventies. He had skin the color of marmalade from a bad indoor tanning experience and a severe face: thin lips, a sharp chin, and smoky brown eyes that moved incessantly and missed nothing. He wore a black

Japanese samue with the usual roomy pants and truncated kimono-style top belted at the waist.

When Dermott had finished his handiwork, he stepped to the side and bowed.

"Well done, Casey. Dermott."

They bowed deeply. Somewhere along the line, they had picked up flesh-colored earpieces, no doubt with the prerequisite wireless transmitters hidden somewhere on their persons.

In a deferential tone, I said, "You must be an Ogi."

Dermott stepped forward and slapped my face. "Speak when you're spoken to."

"Fourteenth generation," the older man said in accentless English, his chest expanding in pleasure. "And Mr. Summers is right to caution you about your manners."

Ogi threatened with the same regal bearing as Casey, and moved with the same lightness. The final luster of Soga's training, I imagined, something that had not rubbed off on Dermott, though the lack of polish made him no less deadly.

"It was merely an observation," I said.

Dermott raised his hand but the Soga patriarch shook him off. The ploy didn't fool me. From the outset my manner had been modest, but their game was submission and terror. The first time around, Dermott would have slapped me no matter what I said, a variation of the routine at my shop that culminated in the shooting of Abers.

I would need to choose my words carefully.

"Your attitude was inappropriate," Ogi said without humor.

Dermott resumed his position alongside Casey, a pace behind his master. No one stood behind me or could see my back. I slipped the metal tab from its hiding place next to my thumb and began to rub the sharp edge against the rope.

"I apologize. The slight was unintended."

"Accepted," Ogi said too quickly, already bored. "I only regret your visit had to be an unwilling one."

"You left your signature in Japantown. That's nearly an invitation."

Ogi frowned. "The kanji was meant as a warning. One you chose to ignore."

"I didn't know what it was."

"Hara did."

"He didn't share the information."

"The fee Brodie Security received suggests otherwise."

"I thought I was dealing with a distraught grandfather."

Ogi's eyes became slits. Then he gave a spiteful laugh. "You know what? I believe you."

As a direct descendent of General Ogi, he carried himself as grandly as his noble ancestor must have. A steely condescension inflated him. No doubt commanding your own private army could enlarge your sense of self-worth. Or maybe he was simply proud of coming from a long line of blue-blooded butchers.

"It's a pity you've been so resourceful, Mr. Brodie. Had this been a social call, we might have discussed art," he said. "I have two Klees, three Brancusis, and a half dozen Diebenkorns."

I was silent. Ogi examined my face in brief, predatory flicks. His skin gave him a sickly gleam but he was fit, his muscles taut. I wondered about his coloring.

"Over the years," the Soga leader said, "there have been three or four who have come as close to our core operation as you have. Others have survived a visit to Soga. But until now no one has managed both. It is a feat to be applauded. We respect such accomplishments, especially since we work so hard to be, ah, self-effacing. It is essential to following our Way. Our tradition goes back three hundred years and requires perfection. When we meet superb execution in another, we feel honor bound to applaud it. Unfortunately, your skills failed you in the end. In our eyes, yours will be an honorable death, as were those of your predecessors."

There it was again. So matter-of-factly laid out. Given the risk they took to kidnap Jenny from under the nose of the police, it made no sense whatsoever. But, illogical or not, this time I heard the truth in the firmness of Ogi's tone, saw the finality in the austerity of his look.

The stillness I'd rediscovered late at night after Abers's shooting settled low in my stomach. I could die if it came to that. If I were alone. But I wasn't. I had Jenny to think about. Was my daughter's life to be cut short because of callous men like Ogi and his crew?

I continued to saw at the bindings, my progress slow but steady.

"What about my daughter?"

"We told you. Nedayashi."

"You told me to back off."

"But you didn't, did you? You took a risk and were caught. Face it like a man."

"There's Noda and George," I said.

The fingers of Ogi's right hand lingered at the left cuff of his samue. From the angle I had, seated and lower, I could see a glint of metal inside his sleeve.

Ogi's look was stern. "Who, you would have us believe, are on flights to Shanghai for a new assignment, as we demanded. We intercepted emails to your Tokyo office and checked the flight manifests. They bought tickets, and indeed men with their passports boarded their flights. Yet they are here in New York."

How early had they caught on to our double fake? It had been my idea to use the tapped computer terminal in Tokyo against Soga—to let them "intercept" the email—but that plan too had failed.

I sighed. "You've been thorough."

"We always are."

I didn't know how, but Soga had penetrated every aspect of our operation. Their efficiency gave rise to an unbearable arrogance. But keyhole peepers were always paranoid about missing the bigger picture.

I said, "Good habit, that."

"Pardon?"

"Being thorough."

Ogi narrowed his eyes at me. "What are you saying?"

"Maybe you're not the only one who thinks ahead."

"If you're stalling for time, you're wasting your breath."

"We know all about Teq QX, for example."

Ogi's head swiveled toward me, his eyes pooling with curiosity, the first spark of life I'd seen in them since my arrival. "What do you know?"

"It's the plum. The prize."

A grin spread across his face with the languid ease of a rattlesnake slithering silently over cool desert sand toward its prey, and I knew I'd guessed wrong. Again. I waved Teq QX around in an attempt to show him I knew too much to be silenced. His grin told me the ploy had backfired.

It told him how much I *didn't* know.

"That's why," Ogi said with relish, "it makes the perfect camouflage. Hara angered too many people with his aggressiveness."

So Japantown *was* an attack on the renegade mogul, but not because of Teq QX. I said, "Camouflage or not, Teq QX is going to generate billions going forward."

"In Japan, money is secondary to power. You know that. Once you have control, you can squeeze the money out anytime you want."

Damn if he wasn't right. On both counts.

"Teq QX was a decoy, then. That your idea too?"

"Yes." Ogi beamed with an unequivocal pride, and I drew back, repelled at his uninhibited display and what it implied.

He shared his secrets far too freely, which served to confirm what Dermott and Ogi had told me: my death warrant had been sealed.

SCRAMBLED desperately for a new foothold. The problem was this: Ogi could no more share his creative genius with the world at large than an S&M aficionado could display his whips and chains at a neighborhood block party. The Soga leader could, however, reveal his mastery in front of someone who wouldn't be taking the secret far. *Think, Brodie, think.*

"Sharp," I said, hoping my voice sounded assured, "but you killed a whole family in Japantown. Which must have fetched a hefty price tag. Not too many people have that kind of money to toss around. Either one of Hara's bigger rivals or someone in the government with a solid slush fund. I'm banking on the government."

Ogi's eyes sparkled. I'd regained some ground, and time. "Very good. But *why?*"

"Government means the ministries, right?"

"Right."

I drew a long breath, collecting my thoughts. "Hara's case is different, isn't it? Japantown says that. Hara's always been clever. They couldn't quietly chip away at his empire with audits or by changing some statutes like they usually do, because Hara would fight, and win sympathy from the people for his struggle. So they needed a new way to take him down."

Ogi was motionless against the edge of the desk, listening closely, enjoying himself.

Think. A ministry gofer shows up and prods Hara about Teq QX, then threatens him. The performance is repeated. After the shock of

Japantown, Hara starts hunting for the culprit. There are too many possibilities and it's driving him mad. He's lost his family, he can't nail down their killer, and slowly, inevitably, the tenacious rebel begins to unravel. I saw clear signs of his disintegration in Tokyo, and now I saw how it was meant to end. When Hara's downfall was complete, stories about the once great, now broken, man would begin to circulate.

Japantown was a face-off between the entrenched powers and a rebellious upstart.

I took the logic to the next level and the answer slotted home. "The killings in San Francisco will be remembered for a long time. They're a warning to Hara, as well as to others not to follow in his footsteps. That's why you left your calling card."

Ogi brought his hands together in silent applause. "That was quite a show, Mr. Brodie. Your talent's wasted in antiques. Hara is a part of a new breed of Japanese business leader who forsakes the clannishness of tradition for more selfish Western ways. He's outspoken, independent. He acts without considering the greater good of Japan, and Japan Inc."

"Which is directed by the ministries."

"Of course. Japan is a small country. The bureaucrats control the economy, the laws, the politicians, the people. All facets of life. They control who does business in Japan, and *with* Japan. They control *your* dealings. Do you deny it?"

"No. I'm very aware of their meddling."

Ogi said, "Hara's growing profile signaled a trend the ministries didn't like. Should it continue, they foresaw control slipping away. That is when they called us."

Keep him talking. "How high does it go?"

"The top."

"Yuda, then?"

His eyes flinty, Ogi brought his hands together once more in silent accolade.

My breathing grew ragged, my insides burning with rage. Shingo Yuda, as head of the Ministry of Finance, was the most powerful bureaucrat in the land. Famously, he had railed against what he called the "selfish, unpatriotic new business ethic." His was the rallying cry of the Iron Triangle, the old crony system.

"There's one other thing," I said.

"What might that be?"

Older man . . . sixties or seventies . . . arrogant and brutal . . .

"You wrote the kanji found in Japantown, didn't you?"

Ogi grew unnaturally quiet, and for the first time I glimpsed anger behind his haughty bearing. I'd made a grave mistake. The force of his displeasure pressed in on me.

Ogi glared. "I should have listened to Dermott from the first, when he begged me to dispose of you. A major blunder we'll repair tonight. But you asked about the kanji. Consider my answer a parting gift. Yes, I wrote it and Casey delivered it."

Casey delivered it. The man in question reddened, gratified to be singled out for praise by his superior. Jesus.

I shook off my disgust. "The kanji was for Japanese eyes only, wasn't it?"

"Correct. A reminder to any others who might consider following Hara's footsteps once he self-destructed. Leaving our trademark in Japantown was a low-risk proposition since channels to Tokyo had been shuttered. Until you showed up. Now, if that is all, we have other items on our agenda tonight."

This time the finality of his tone was undeniable. But I had one more question.

"What about Jenny?"

"We've already discussed that. She's to die."

"Can I see her?"

"I *could* arrange a brief reunion, but I'm not inclined to do so."

Jenny is alive . . .

I felt relief, though it was a false relief. We had lost. Utterly. I was penned in behind enemy lines while Renna and the task force were miles away, dreaming about a tomorrow I'd never see.

"Good-bye, Mr. Brodie."

Ogi's fingers crab-walked up his sleeve. I heard a whizzing sound of metal over cloth, and watched in alarm as a length of wire wormed its way from the patriarch's clothing. His fingers curled around wooden pegs at both ends of the wire and pulled it taut.

Wire . . . handles . . .

It came in a flash of understanding, the old powerbroker mourning his loss: *Three years ago, my adopted son—the man I'd handpicked to carry on after my retirement—was found dead on the streets of Karuizawa, his neck sliced clean to the spine. Garroted.*

All at once, I understood how my life would end. Mumbling a silent good-bye to Jenny, I closed my eyes. Behind the dense blackness of my eyelids, I grasped the stillness. The thief stood before me, but I was anchored in a calm he couldn't take.

I was ready.

JUST then a distant explosion rocked the manor, and a fine spray of dust sifted down from the exposed beams overhead.

Ogi shot a frown at his two soldiers. "Find out what that was."

After hurried bows, Casey and Dermott bolted from the room.

Ogi turned burning eyes on me. "You want to tell me about that?"

Explosives? Had to be Luke. McCann's reach wouldn't stretch that far. Neither would Renna's. Noda's background was limited to guns, knives, and hand-to-hand. That raised a troubling thought I had no time to consider but found extremely disturbing: if Luke willingly rigged something as destructive as a bomb, he wasn't the traitor.

"It's beyond me," I said.

Ogi scowled. "No, it isn't. And you're going to tell me."

Taking a step forward, Ogi raised the garrote. I pressed myself back in my chair, putting maybe four more inches of distance between us, for all the good it would do me.

Hurried footfalls approached and the next instant a young recruit in Soga black, his hood pushed up, dashed into the room, halted abruptly, and bowed deeply before speaking in a breathless but controlled voice. "Ogi-sensei, they destroyed the boats."

"Both of them?"

"Yes, sir." The messenger bowed and retreated. For some reason his superior did not want to broadcast the news via their headsets.

Smart, I thought. *Retreat by sea had just been eliminated.*

Ogi glared at me. "Bringing you here was a costly indulgence."

My time was up.

Another pair of footsteps echoed in the corridor, then a second soldier appeared in the doorway. "Ogi-sensei, Naito-sensei wishes to see you immediately."

Sensei. Another commander was present in the field. Soga was out in full force.

"What is it?" Ogi asked.

The fighter glanced my way. "He requests a word in private, Sensei."

Ogi frowned. "I'll contact him over the wire."

The messenger shook his head. "Naito-sensei insists his communiqué cannot go out over the public line."

"All right. Get Casey and Dermott back here. They are to guard Brodie but leave him for me."

Turning his back on us, the messenger relayed the orders softly, cupping his hand around a microphone in his ear to hear the response. "They're on their way."

"My friends are here," I said.

"We prepared for that possibility. But I am curious. How many are there?"

I held my tongue.

Irritated, Ogi cast me a sharp look. "No matter. They will not stop us. If they get too close they will die. This is what Soga does. What our ancestors have done for three centuries. We never lose."

"You lost in the village."

"Those were first-year trainees. Infants by our standards. I offered you up as a live exercise. Your art dealer background fooled me, but I won't make that mistake again. Tonight, you will die. If our Long Island base has been compromised beyond repair, so be it. It's inconvenient but easily rectified with relocation. It wouldn't be the first time. Already, Gilbert Tweed has been purged. Our men are gone, their files shredded."

Raising a hand to his earpiece, the young messenger stirred restlessly. "Naito-sensei is waiting. What shall I tell him?"

Ogi cast a look my way. "You're not going anywhere and Casey will be back momentarily." To the messenger he said, "Take me to him."

The Soga leader showed me his back, and once more I heard the sound of metal rubbing cloth and the wire snaked up his sleeve.

As soon as I was alone, I sliced through the remaining fibers of my bindings. With one shake of my hands the rope fell away. My heart thumped wildly. This was my one chance. I needed to be gone. If they caught up with me, I'd be executed in an instant.

As I dashed for the door, I caught the sound of footsteps approaching fast. *Too fast.* I changed course, flung open the window, then dove into the chair well under Ogi's desk.

From the hall, Dermott said, "Okay, Brodie, it's payback time."

"The old man wants him," Casey said.

"Doesn't mean I can't . . . he's not here."

Casey drew up short. "How did he . . . ? Doesn't matter. He's only postponed his death."

"*Now* he's mine," Dermott said.

"Only if you find him first. Escape triggers a priority clear. He'll be shot on sight."

"I'll do more than that when I catch the bastard," Dermott said, slipping out the window as I heard Casey broadcast my getaway over their wireless system.

ONCE alone, I leapt from my hiding place and searched Ogi's desk in haste, Casey's words echoing in my ears: *He's only postponed his death.*

With the issuance of a *priority clear*, at least a dozen armed Soga agents on the grounds had standing orders to shoot me on sight.

I fumbled for the drawer handles, my breathing heavy and erratic. In the bottom pullout, I found a baby Glock and a .22-caliber Beretta with a spare clip and silencer. Neither weapon betrayed the telltale coating of poison that had nearly finished me in Soga.

I slipped the Beretta into my waistband and pocketed the silencer and extra clip. The Glock stayed. Firing an unsilenced piece would draw return fire from any Soga personnel in the vicinity and get me killed. Only a silent retreat gave me a chance at survival. A slight one. I had no delusions about how lucky we'd been to escape the village.

However, abandoning a working weapon bordered on suicidal, so I wedged the pointed end of a brass letter opener into the workings of the Glock, snapped off the firing pin, then etched a faint line along either side of the barrel with the severed pin to mark the defanged gun. An old South Central trick. *Disable when you're able.*

Freshly armed, I exited the back of the manor, heading out the opposite way Ogi and troops had gone. With Soga in fighting mode, the estate lights had been extinguished. After I'd put a good fifty yards between the house and myself, I dodged behind a large pine tree and examined the Beretta. I released the clip. Eight rounds. Eight more in the spare. The chamber was empty. Sixteen shots. I replaced the clip, attached the silencer, jacked a round into the barrel, and stuck the gun back in my waistband.

Then I paused to listen. I heard nothing. No footsteps shuffling through the undergrowth. No one brushing aside branches and shrubbery. No shouts from the house at my escape. But then again, this was Soga. It wouldn't be that easy. A lucky break had given me another chance, and I wouldn't waste it. Caution was key.

My friends are here, I'd said.

We prepared for that possibility.

In the far distance, near the gate, I heard gunshots. Then screams. Then nothing.

Damn. The screams confirmed Ogi's boast. He was prepared. This might be Long Island but the setup was pure Soga: isolated location, good cover, hard to penetrate. The home advantage was overwhelming.

The screams announced that the first preliminary push by McCann and company had been repelled and there were casualties on our side.

Soga wouldn't scream.

I could only hope McCann and Renna had brought enough manpower. But in the haste with which they must have been forced to assemble tonight's team after I'd gone missing, I thought it unlikely. McCann would have only been able to cobble together a handful of city cops and Long Island deputies. I didn't see or hear anything suggesting a retreat on Soga's part, which only confirmed that McCann's team was probably bantamweight and Soga had made a sizable dent in it. Once our side took casualties, we would retreat and call for serious backup. But that would take time. Time I couldn't spare. Not if I wanted to see Jenny again.

Any way I looked at it, I was on my own. I was half a mile from the outer perimeter, separated by a forest infested with Soga's troops. But that was only the beginning of my worries. Jenny was now expendable. With the police at the gate, she went from leverage to liability. From hostage to potential witness. When Soga retreated, they wouldn't take her along. They would kill her.

I had to hurry.

I headed deeper into the woods. The minty scent of pine filled my lungs. Silver shafts of moonlight filtered through the canopy. If I were

Soga, I'd guard the front gate long enough to allow Ogi and other senior officers to retreat and put a lot of distance between themselves and the compound. I'd strike, fade back into the foliage, and wait. Guerilla tactics. With the boats demolished, a pullback became more complex. I'd have the gate detail linger longer to hold off the next push, discouraging a quick advance. Maybe fire warning shots and wound a few cops to temper eagerness. But as soon as the main contingent was safely away, I'd want the guards to vanish as well.

I was the only one behind the lines. My presence in Soga territory left me with a clear mandate: I had to cut the odds—and find Jenny. Otherwise Soga would fill the night with their victims' screams.

But time was short. I needed information fast. Which meant a live body.

Cloaked by darkness, I roamed the brush, getting a sense of the property I traversed. Ferns and light brush and deadfall composed the forest floor, but with the air laden with moisture, none crackled underfoot. Paths, mostly animal but sometimes human, wound their way through the trees.

You have to break your normal patterns . . .

Once I found a well-traveled footpath, I looked skyward. For a two-year stretch in my more reckless teen years, we took down street dealers for the wads of cash they always carried. It had been a risky enterprise, and looking back, bordered on insane. But it had worked beautifully. We'd map out a dealer's nightly routine, then *search for a perch*, a position high enough to put us above the normal sweep of pedestrian vision.

I found a suitable tree, scaled it, and made myself comfortable on a massive limb, leaning back against the trunk to wait. I was about sixteen feet above ground. For a six-foot target, that gave me ten feet of loft.

I shifted the Beretta to the small of my back.

Before long I had a chance to play jungle monkey again. Thirteen years had slipped away since my last attempt, but in my veins the itch for action pulsed.

The trick was to position yourself between fifteen and eighteen feet above ground. You came at them from behind, using their body to cushion your landing and the force of the impact to stun them. The height spread supplied momentum and was crucial. Too high and the timing became difficult; too low and the impact would not disable your target.

A male figure about my height came up the path. Perfect.

I scuttled farther out on the limb and squatted on my haunches.

He passed underneath.

I jumped.

HIT him perfectly.

My torso slammed into the back of his head, smashing him face-first into the ground. Stunned, he lay still, his eyes open but glazed. After casting a quick look up and down the path, I flipped my catch onto his back, grabbed his heels, and dragged him deep into the woods, where I straddled his chest.

He wore the same form-fitting black suit and state-of-the-art equipment belt I'd encountered in Soga. Needing him vulnerable and exposed, I ripped off his night-vision gear, then the hood. Underneath, I found his earpiece. I plucked the device from its nook and pocketed it along with the transmitter pinned to his chest.

Moaning, my captive trained unfocused eyes on my face. Before he could regain his bearings, I rammed the Beretta down his throat. "Stay very quiet," I whispered in his ear. "No noise, no talking. Unless I tell you."

His eyes widened, then his training kicked in and disorientation gave way to the same inbred cockiness Casey and Dermott had exhibited. I'd have to break that if I was going to get what I needed.

My captive was old enough to be a full-fledged Soga fighter with notches on his belt. He was forged from rough country stock, more worker bee than upper management material. If he hadn't stepped aboard the Soga express, he'd be wading through a muddy rice paddy or manning a local road crew.

I jammed the muzzle in farther. On the edge of my vision, I saw his fingers crawl toward the equipment belt. "If your hand moves another inch, I'll put a bullet through the back of your skull. Blink once if you understand."

Blink.

"You also understand that I can pull the trigger faster than you can attack—no matter what your training or any brainwashing may have taught you?"

Blink. Yes.

"Good. Now I want you to tell me how many men are on the grounds tonight. Can you do that?"

One blink.

"Okay, well?"

He blinked ten times, paused, and then nine more.

"Nineteen. Does that include women?"

Blink.

"How many?"

Three blinks.

"Are there trainees on the grounds?"

Blink. Yes.

"How many?"

Blink, blink. Two.

"Does that include you?"

Blink, blink. No.

"Which makes you smart enough to know I *will* kill you, right?"

Yes.

"Good. Don't forget it. Do you know where the girl is?"

Two blinks.

"You're lying."

Two blinks. No.

"You are. There's only the main house and the outbuildings. Each building has a function. Guesthouses, dorm, garage. Like that," I said, filling in the holes with guesswork about what an American Soga compound would require. "So the possibilities are limited. If you know how many people are here, you know where the girl is."

No.

"Then I have no more use for you. Say good-bye."

I shoved the barrel in farther until he started to choke. He began to blink rapidly.

"Would you like to reconsider?"

One blink. Yes.

"So your memory's improved?"

Blink.

"Are you sure? One more lie and I'll kill you and go find myself a trainee."

Blink.

"Very good. Now, I'm going to retract the gun enough for you to speak but not shout. Wrap your lips around the barrel. Any foolishness and I pull the trigger. Speak softly, tell me the truth, and you'll live through this. You cross me and your brains will be fertilizing ferns. We clear?"

Blink.

"Good. After you answer, I'm going to tie you up with your own rope and gag you. No one will be able to find you and you won't be able to escape. If my daughter is not where you say she is, I'll return and put a bullet between your eyes. So consider your answer carefully."

I retracted the gun barrel a fraction of an inch.

"*Hanashite kudasai,*" he wheezed. "*Onegaishimasu.*" Release me, I'm begging you.

"If my daughter is where you say, you'll go free."

"Just let me go. I got younger brothers and sisters."

"How old are you?"

"Nineteen and a half."

And a half. Not only was my estimate off but my captive was still of an age where six months mattered. Shame colored my cheeks.

I pushed the barrel back down, suppressing his tongue. "So you lied to me. You're a trainee."

He hesitated, then blinked once.

"I understand why you lied about your skill level, but the next lie sees you dead. Got it?"

Blink.

"Where's the girl?"

I ADVANCED through the green landscape of the night-vision goggles swiftly and without incident and approached the guest cottage from the rear.

According to my young captive, Jenny was being held in a second-floor bedroom of the third cottage down. Architecturally, the cottage echoed the manor. Redbrick walls, redbrick chimney, white shutters at the windows. I'd passed two more just like it and perceived the blocky shadow of a fourth in the near distance.

The night-vision apparatus allowed me to catch movement at one of the second-story windows, which confirmed what I suspected: inside, they would be waiting for me. There, and along the road, and anywhere else they thought I might turn up.

You have to break your normal patterns . . .

The Soga uniform was a miracle of garment design. Aside from a two-inch shortfall, it fitted me to perfection. The fabric stretched to accommodate minor body variations but hugged every curve and muscle. It was as thin and light as fine silk, yet breathed and retained body heat. It was also nearly weightless. Under normal conditions, clothing adds three to seven pounds of pull. This suit's drag could be measured in ounces. No wonder Ogi and Casey and Dermott oozed such confidence. Everything about Soga was supremely evolved.

As I drew up in front of Jenny's supposed holding area, every nerve in my body hummed with tension. They wouldn't have assigned many to guard her. I figured two or three. One upstairs, one down. And maybe a roamer. Which made the coming confrontation dicey.

The rear door was painted white to match the shutters and had a glass panel in its upper half, subdivided into six small panes. I unclipped a blackjack from my equipment belt and held it alongside my leg, then tapped on the glass with my free hand. Sweat collected in the small of my back where the Beretta pressed against the Soga black. A dark form emerged from the shadows of the cottage and yanked open the door.

"Any news?" the cloaked figure asked in Japanese.

"Just what they broadcast," I answered in the same language. "Casualties on their side. We'll be evacuating soon."

Nodding, the guard glanced about before signaling for me to enter and retreating to the interior. Easing the door shut behind me, I trailed after him, eyes darting into every corner for signs of another guard. We were in a small pantry. A well-equipped kitchen branched off the right side, running along the back of the lodge. No bodies there. A second doorway loomed up ahead, leading to the front of the house. No one. When I clubbed him, the crunch of packed-grain on skull sent a jarring vibration down my arm. My black-suited envoy stumbled but didn't fall, so I cuffed him again and he melted to the floor with a thud.

"Damn," I muttered in Japanese.

"There a problem?" a soft voice said from the front room.

"Stubbed my toe."

The next instant a silhouette appeared in the doorway directly ahead of me. I shot it twice in the chest with the silenced Beretta and the figure slumped against the wall and slipped sideways, sketching a dark arc of blood across the painted surface.

I stepped up for a closer look. Dead. A woman.

Teens and females. A sour taste crossed my lips. I'd shot a woman. Something deep inside me shriveled. In the village, I'd fought but killed no one. Tonight I'd become a killer, a badge of distinction I despised. I fell back against the nearest wall, slid to the ground, and let my head fall between my knees.

Get a move on, Brodie.

I felt tainted. Disgusted with myself.

You have no time to waste. What if another one walks through the door?

I jumped up, alarmed. While struggling through moral quicksand,

I'd dropped my guard long enough to get myself killed. If I wanted to live through the night and save Jenny, I couldn't fall apart now.

Hurriedly, I pulled both bodies up against the innermost pantry wall, then stood alongside them, hidden from line of sight if another guard rushed in from the front or the kitchen. With Beretta drawn, I listened for sounds inside and out. Scents of oak and pine and cleaning solvents saturated the cottage. Outside, an owl hooted. A cricket chirped. Inside, I heard nothing. Neither downstairs nor overhead. No scuffling. No creaking floorboards. No hushed preparations to counter my double takedown. I let another minute pass. The owl hooted again. Long Island pastoral. What could be more disarming?

No guards appeared, so I braced myself and stepped cautiously into the kitchen, weapon raised. Still empty. No one rushed to the attack. The kitchen fed into a small hall, which led to a bathroom and den. No new foot soldiers. Beyond the den I could make out the front door and a living room.

After pausing a beat to quell my adrenaline-charged heart, I swung into the living room, the night-vision goggles illuminating every shadow-steeped recess. There was a black leather couch with matching chairs and a vast window overlooking a well-groomed lawn and the woods. But no black-clad guards.

I scanned the room, then the exterior grounds. No movement. No glowing, green-hued human forms. Keeping to the shadows, I crossed the room quickly. A third door at the far end brought me full circle to the pantry and the two prone guards.

The first floor was secure.

I removed the guards' transmitters and crushed them underfoot, then dragged the bodies into the bathroom and locked the door. I grabbed some toothpicks off a kitchen shelf, jammed them into the keyhole, and snapped them off. While I considered it unlikely the man I'd clubbed would recover any time tonight, you never knew, so I'd followed Noda's lead and put a bullet in his head. It troubled me greatly, and there were moral issues to consider, but not now. The short version was these guys had crossed a line in taking my daughter, and for now I took comfort in the fact that one less kidnapper could come back at us.

With the lower floor safe, I mounted the stairs, holding the gun back behind my thigh, broadcasting my approach with undisguised footfalls.

At the top were three doorways along a short hallway. I figured two bedrooms and a bath. From the third door, a head emerged and looked my way. I waved with my left hand and fired with my right. The first shot went wide but I kept firing as I advanced and the second and third struck the head and throat. As the Soga fighter went down, I backpedaled quickly to the top of the stairs and flopped to the floor, planting my elbows firmly on the thick carpet, pistol aimed at a spot midway down the hall, so I could fan either way in a hurry if a fourth figure or more appeared.

I maintained the position for one minute, then another. Nothing. I crawled forward on my stomach and nudged open the first door. No movement. I went in fast and low. More nothing. I hit the middle door in the same manner. Bathroom. Empty. I approached the last room with equal caution, stepping over the body of the guard, this time going in low and slow.

There was a closet to my left and a large double bed against the far wall with a body under a dark blue summer quilt.

I edged open the closet door with the gun barrel.

Clear.

I peered under the bed.

Nothing.

I straightened to my full height.

Motionless on the bed, her face thrust into a pillow, was Jenny.

My heart plummeted. *I was too late.* Just as I feared, once the fighting began, the leverage my daughter brought to the table as a captive was moot and they'd killed her. From the looks of it, they'd smothered her with the pillow.

First Abers, and now Jenny.

I drooped against the wall, my eyes stinging, my head spinning.

S WALLOWING hard, I peered through the green gloom at the petite form of my daughter's lifeless body. A salty sting burned the corners of my eyes. Dazed and numb, I stared at what had once been my flesh and blood. A vision of little Miki Nakamura limp on the cobblestone of Japantown floated before my eyes.

Trembling, I bent down and kissed Jenny's cheek. It was warm. Body temperature. Not cooler, as it should have been. I raised the goggles and squinted closer. There! Movement! What was imperceptible in the foggy green tint of the night-vision glasses clarified itself as my eyes adjusted to the natural darkness of the room. Up close, Jenny's chest rose and fell in an unnaturally sluggish cadence.

She wasn't dead. But her breathing was shallower than her normal sleeping pattern. Why? What could explain her deathlike sleep? *She'd been drugged.* That had to be it. Soga could hold on to their ace while rendering her mute. My daughter was alive!

A second look tempered my joy. Jenny's body language revealed a more gruesome tale: under the light spread, she was tucked into a tight ball, her scalp brushed with perspiration. Her stay, asleep or awake, had been anything but peaceful.

Stashing the Beretta in my waistband, I pulled back the blue quilt and scooped her up in my arms. Her eyes fluttered open. Groggy but attentive, she stared at me with unbridled fear.

I lifted the hood. "It's me, Jen."

"Daddy?"

Her voice was a wisp of air over strained vocal cords, struggling with the tail end of a drug-induced stupor.

"Yes."

She pressed her palms against my cheeks. "It *is* you. *Finally.*"

She sighed and burrowed her face into the pocket between my neck and shoulder. I clasped her to my chest. I felt her heart beating and mine kicking back. Her body was warm and soft and frail. Her breath, moist and delicate, flitted across my neck. I was incredulous. I thought I'd lost her for good.

"I want to go home, Daddy."

"That's where we're going."

"Are they still here?"

"Not in the house. Are you hurt?"

"No. Are they outside?"

"Yes."

Her body tensed.

"But not for long," I added quickly.

"Are you beating them?"

"You could say that."

She turned her head and lay with her ear on my shoulder, her breath stronger now against my neck, her body perched on my left forearm. With my right hand, I grabbed a blanket and a sheet from the bed, flung them over my free shoulder, and whisked Jenny to the door. Drawing the Beretta, I dared a quick look up and down the hall. Clear both ways. I swept through the door, down the stairs, and out the back of the house, pausing at each juncture to check for Soga troops. There were none.

Once outside, I plunged straight into the woods, deeper into the estate, traversing the soft undergrowth, avoiding the trails. I padded silently along, past pine and oak and hickory. I checked back over my shoulder every ten paces, until I had put the guesthouse far behind us.

Then I slipped behind a towering oak and fell back against the trunk, breathing hard. We were safe, for now. I took a deep breath and let it out slowly. My breathing came in short bursts. My heartbeat was off the charts. It was one thing to be fighting for my own life, quite another to be defending my daughter's.

I pressed Jenny close. Just holding her seemed a gift beyond measure. Safe for the moment.

Once more, the corners of my eyes burned. I couldn't lose her a second time. It would kill me. But how could I protect my daughter against Soga? Even if we eluded them tonight, our escape would be temporary at best—unless the police rounded up Ogi and all his troops. Soga was already on the move. They would, as Ogi had so confidently proclaimed, simply disperse and relocate, after which they would hunt us down on their own timetable. Three hundred years of success lent ample testimony to the claim. And then there was nedayashi, the vicious but necessary Japanese tradition of protecting your own clan by eliminating your enemy's. The practice was savage and unforgiving—and allowed for only one survivor.

I'd gotten it entirely wrong.

We were nowhere near safe.

JENNY raised her head. "Why are we stopping?"

"I have more work to do."

"Fighting work?"

"Yes."

Her eyes glittered with fear. "Don't leave me, Daddy."

"Actually, I need your help."

She shivered. "You want me to fight them too?"

"No, I need you to wait for me here. Can you do that?"

She shook her head back and forth like a mechanical doll whose circuits had gone haywire. "*No, no*. No more alone, Daddy. No more alone. *Please.*"

Each word was a knife in my chest. I was asking the impossible of her. She had been abducted, and the prospect of being separated so soon after our reunion terrified her.

I hugged my daughter for all I was worth. Leaving her alone was going to be the hardest thing I'd ever done. But there was no other way.

"Listen," I began in a whisper, "the world is spinning. At the moment, badly. But *now*—right this minute—you and I have a chance to put it right."

"Daddy, please don't . . ." Her voice faltered.

"We're together again, aren't we?"

"Yes, but—"

"And that is good. So first, I'm going to make sure you're safe. Which will be another large dose of good for us. As soon as I let you down, I want you to climb on my back."

Reluctantly, Jenny slid to the ground. I slung the sheet and blanket around my neck, then crouched down and Jenny clambered up my back.

"Slip your hands around my waist." She did, and I looped the sheet over her head and let it drop down to her hips before knotting the ends at my stomach and binding her slim body to mine. "Is that too tight?"

Jenny shook her head. I couldn't see her but I felt the movement.

I said, "Okay. Now, hold on tight. We're going up."

With the night-vision goggles, I examined the tree I'd selected. It was a massive oak ballooning open overhead, with a stout base. I peered upward into the foliage, my eyes threading through the branches. When I found one high enough and thick enough for my purposes, I hoisted myself onto a low branch and began to climb.

As we ascended, leaf clusters grazed our skin and I felt Jenny flinch with each unexpected touch. Thirty feet aboveground, I edged out onto a sturdy branch, sat, and scooted backward until Jenny's back rested against the trunk. The perch I'd chosen had the circumference of a large medicine ball where it met the trunk and would support Jenny's weight and mine twice over without effort.

Instructing her to wrap her legs around the limb and latch on to it with her hands as soon as she could, I untied the sheet and inched away, putting a safe distance between us before swinging my left leg over the limb to sit sidesaddle. I found my balance, then swung my other leg over the branch so that I was facing Jenny. I scooted forward and she flung her arms around my neck.

"I *knew* you'd come," she whispered, laying her head once more on my shoulder.

We were still for a long moment. Around us the sounds of rustling leaves and humming insects soothed our nerves. I recalled the times she had fallen asleep in my embrace in just this manner. Recalled all the quiet evenings we'd spent together at home, Jenny snuggled into my lap as we chatted or laughed or watched a Disney movie. Tonight, the weight of her diminutive head on my shoulder was the most perfect burden I could imagine. If we lived through the next several hours, never again would I take a moment with my daughter for granted. Things would be different. When her breathing grew calm, I slid away. Sadly. Reluctantly. Inevitably.

Jenny raised her eyes to mine. "Time to go?"

"Yes."

Her lower lip quivered. "Are there a lot of them?"

"Fewer than there were. Not only that, Christine and Joey's father is here with a lot of police."

A note of excitement crept into her voice. "He's a big one for our side. He can arrest them, can't he?"

"Exactly."

"Then what happens?"

Recalling our disastrous phone conversation, I answered with care. "With luck, they will disappear forever and never bother us again."

"What do I do?"

"You stay up here where they can't find you and be very, very quiet until I come back for you."

"Up here? By myself? What if I fall asleep?"

I lifted the sheet and smiled. "I am going to tie you to the tree."

"And the blanket will keep me warm! I'll be camping out in a tree. I can do that!"

"Good, but keep your voice down. And after I leave, no noise, okay? No calling out, no talking, no singing like you love to do. Not tonight. Up here you're safe because there are thousands of trees around us and no one will think to look up."

"No talking? What if something happens?"

"I doubt anything will happen."

"But what if it does?"

I looked at my daughter. Her jaw trembled. "You're a big girl now, Jen. You'll have to decide for yourself. Like I've always taught you. Just make sure that it's the right thing to do."

"But how will I know?"

The eternal question from a six-year-old. Finding the right answer under normal circumstances was hard enough. With Soga lurking in the shadows, the task bordered on impossible. I thought about the stillness. I thought about Japantown. I thought about the thief and the Okazaki Hills and returning to the core. There was only one answer.

There always had been.

"Just listen," I said.

"What does that mean? I'm only a kid, Daddy."

I blew out my breath in frustration. She was right, of course. If I couldn't provide her with an anchor to ease her fears, I couldn't leave her.

"Ask *yourself* the question that's bothering you, then stay still and the answer will pop into your head."

"From where?"

I tapped her chest. "From here."

Her brow knitted as she gave my words what she believed to be mature consideration. "Is that how you know the things you know?"

"For the tough ones, that's the *only* way I know."

Then, with the greatest reluctance, I left her—and headed back into the night.

N my haste to put distance between us and the cottage, I'd left a trail Soga operatives could easily follow. Once they spied fresh tracks with abnormally deep impressions, it wouldn't take them long to figure out the additional depth signified Jenny's extra weight, so I needed to move on in order to draw attention away from my daughter's cozy nest.

I'd dropped from the tree but hadn't gone more than five steps when a shot hummed past my left hip, shearing off the top of a pine sapling.

"Stand very still, Brodie. The next one won't miss."

Dermott stepped from behind a large spruce with a .45-caliber Glock aimed at my midsection. He wore Soga black and night-vision goggles.

"You made a mess back at the cottage. Now I'm going to make a mess outta you."

Panic flooded my thoughts. At close quarters, with his weapon already drawn, I saw no way out.

"Where's the girl?"

"Long gone," I said. "To the neighbors."

"That doesn't seem likely. You stash her up in the tree, like a squirrel?"

"Daddy?"

Instinctively, Dermott eyes shot skyward. "Called that one, didn't I?"

Hoping Dermott wouldn't shoot up at Jenny, I slipped swiftly behind the broad, scaly trunk of a nearby hickory the instant his eyes left me, drew the Beretta, and stretched my arm around the far side of the tree, firing blindly at the spot where I'd last seen him, a shrewd little maneuver my Korean neighbor in South Central taught me. Spraying shots high and low, a bit to the left, a bit to the right, I emptied the weapon without giving my opponent a target for return fire. I heard him grunt and fall. I popped the empty clip, slammed home the new one, and tried to chamber a new round. The gun jammed. Shit.

I peered cautiously around the other side of the trunk. Dermott had collapsed to his knees. His Glock hung limply at his side, as if the weapon were too heavy to raise. With his free hand, he held his stomach, blood seeping between his fingers.

My gun trained on the faux homeboy, I stepped into the open, ready to dive back behind the hickory if the Soga assassin raised his weapon. He didn't. He saw me but didn't seem to care. A second round had caught him in the chest, probably puncturing a lung. His breathing had become labored.

"A kid," he said. "Taken out by a six-year-old kid and her punk father."

He toppled over.

Before I could move, a figure approached from my blind side and nudged the back of my head with a gun muzzle.

"Mr. Brodie, you are one lucky man," a voice said. "Or should I say *were?*"

Protected from sniper fire by a bend in the road, Renna paced restlessly two hundred yards from the front gate of the Soga compound. "It's taking too long, Jamie."

McCann pursed his lips. "Hang on, Frank. They're ten miles out. They'll be here any minute."

"There's no time left. Brodie's been in there too long."

"We're pinned down. Our first approach was a disaster."

Trailing fingers through his hair, Renna continued pacing. "I know, I know. But we've got to do something. Keep them focused on us and not our people inside. They got Brodie and his girl and probably Luke and Noda."

"Nothing we can do until backup arrives. No one expected so much firepower. We took too many casualties, Frank. I can't authorize a second approach without more equipment. You know that."

"We got four people in there and time's run out. There's got to be something."

McCann looked away, frustrated. "My hands are tied. I got orders to stay put until we have full riot gear this time."

"Must be something."

"Well, there isn't. We've done all we can. They're on their own."

TURNED my head carefully and glanced behind me into the well-oiled barrel of a baby Glock.

"Casey."

His look was cold and hard. "First you, then I scale the tree and put a bullet in the girl. I want you to *know* that before you die."

So close. So damn close. If only Jenny hadn't given away her location, at least she would have survived.

"Drop the piece, and turn around slowly," he said.

"How'd you find me?"

He wore no black, no belt. Only night-vision goggles. Unlike Dermott, Casey hadn't had time to gather his own gear, so he'd grabbed goggles and the closest weapon at hand.

"Once we circled the area and couldn't pick up your trail, we checked along the road then doubled back to the mansion before heading to the cottage. Knew you'd make your way there eventually. We arrived too late, but you left a clear trail. Dermott and I followed but split up a minute ago when your direction became unclear. If Dermott hadn't been so eager to bag you himself, you'd be lying in his place. But no matter. Look at me, Mr. Brodie. When I kill you, I want to see the light die in your eyes."

I turned slowly, studying his gun, then said, "And I, yours."

Before he could say another word, I whirled around and planted the barrel of my Beretta in the center of his forehead, the steel kissing his brow as his mother had probably done years ago in more innocent days.

"Too late," he said, and pulled the trigger.

There was a click but no discharge. Casey's instincts took over. Even as he fired lightning glances, first at the malfunctioning Glock and then upward to the muzzle pressed to his forehead, he slammed my gun arm aside, going for the weapon. But knowing his Glock had been disabled, and that my Beretta was equally useless, I was a beat ahead of him. He never saw my blow coming. I rammed the heel of my left palm into his nose and felt cartilage collapse.

Casey stumbled back. Normally, my strike would have triggered an immediate defensive response from a fighter of his caliber and, pain or not, years of high-level training would have kicked in. But, with the gun at his head, the misfiring of his piece, and a thrust that made porridge of his nose—I'd opened up a split second's advantage.

Which my years of training wasted no time in exploiting.

While striking him with my left hand, I'd cocked my hips for a follow-through. Now, as Casey staggered back, I unwound them, spinning around and unleashing a roundhouse kick. Providing unbeatable power, a roundhouse leveraged enough movement to stop someone of Casey's superior abilities. That was its appeal. Time was the major drawback. Swinging the leg around for the full effect took an extra second, so the blow was easy to deflect or avoid, which was why I needed Casey off-balance and distracted.

By the time he recovered, I was well into the arc of the kick and less than twelve inches from my target. I caught him in the throat and felt more cartilage cave.

Casey flopped over on his back and began clawing at his neck. His face turned red. Thrashing around among the ferns and deadfall, his body whipped itself into a frenzy. Wheezing, he tried to draw oxygen, but it was hopeless. I'd crushed the larynx and Casey was choking on his own flesh. Snorting sounds erupted from his sinus passages. He dug his nails into his throat. Then his body twisted, shuddered, and grew still, as tangled a mess in death as it had been in life.

Countless hours of sparring had guided me safely through the dual encounters. Instinctively. Automatically. But in the deep forest silence that followed, with my daughter a mute witness overhead, I cringed. *I'd killed two more men.* Once again I felt the urge to crawl into a corner, but with Jenny still on Soga soil, I had to forge on. Now was not the time for self-recrimination.

Listlessly, I retrieved Casey's Glock, stared at the long scratch along the barrel, then tossed the neutered piece into the brush.

Distant gunfire snapped me from my lethargy.

The task force's second assault had begun. I signaled to Jenny to stay put, then headed toward the noise.

B Y the time I reached the front of the estate, the assault was in full swing. Canisters of tear gas rocketed over the wall, trailing looping arches of smoke. Wisps of gas snaked through the trees. The Soga compound had taken on the look of a war zone.

A smile crawled across my face. The lively buzz of voices on the other side of the wall told me that reinforcements in numbers too large to oppose had arrived. Unless Soga had some new tricks, only the wrought-iron gate separated us from rescue.

I fanned left, well clear of the target area, then shimmied up a tree until I had a clear view of the activities on the other side. There had to be two hundred men outside the wall. In the moonlight, the crowd bristled with gas masks, riot shields, and full-body armor. Some were NYPD, others were SWAT and sheriff's department and maybe state troopers. Many of them stood well back from a front line of squad cars, which had been ranged in a loose semicircle around the gate. At the rear, more shields and masks were being handed out from police vans.

I heard a grinding noise at the base of the wall, and the next moment an armored vehicle rolled into view from behind the wall, made a sharp left, and plowed through the stout wrought-iron gate like it was a hedgerow. Police in helmets, full-body shields, and gas masks rushed in behind the vehicle. They drew fire from a treetop on the right and three men went down, writhing in pain. Two NYPD sharpshooters nestled in the trees outside the gate picked off the Soga sniper from the flash of his weapon and a body plunged earthward. Return fire from a new assailant dropped both police marksmen with consummate skill, after which a third police rifleman tagged the second Soga man with one well-placed round. Then the treetop engagements ceased.

One by one, the patrol cars peeled away and formed a caravan behind the troop of officers and armored vehicle. In under a minute, the police inserted ten cars, followed by a second squad of cops. From this point onward, McCann's forces could greet anything that moved with a shower of bullets at close range. Soga's retreat would be silent and swift now. I didn't see them, but I knew they were pulling back. No doubt Ogi and the others had vacated the property long ago.

McCann's task force had opted for a show of strength at the main gate rather than attempting to penetrate the grounds from several points along the perimeter and diluting their numbers, and the strategy seemed to be paying off. They encountered no more sniper fire. The tear gas ceased, and the police contingent headed deeper into the heart of the Soga domain, crawling along the narrow road toward the main house.

Renna pressed through with the second wave, and McCann followed. I couldn't see Noda and Luke, but George and DeMonde, as civilian observers, stood beyond the wall, at the farthest perimeter. While the main column marched slowly toward the house, two auxiliary groups swept through the trees on either side of the road. The maneuver was more military action than cop tactic, but it had to be done, and they handled it as best they could.

Renna joined the group covering the right flank. McCann headed out with the one moving left, away from my position. Time to collect Jenny. To avoid a bullet in the head, I peeled off the hood and the top of my Soga duds, tying the shirt around my waist and shoving the hood in my pocket, then quietly lowered myself from the tree.

Renna's squad had penetrated twenty yards into the trees when the lieutenant separated from the pack and moved deeper into the woods. I could see him intermittently. I adjusted the focus of my goggles. Renna stiffened and crouched. I scanned the area in front of him and saw a shadow flit across my field of vision from right to left, unaware of Renna's presence.

Stay away! I wanted to shout, but couldn't utter a word without giving away Renna's approach.

Spotting his stalker, the Soga figure paused a beat then turned away at a sharp angle.

Renna charged, firing on the run, zigzagging left, then right. Standard police training. *A predictable pattern.* Renna squeezed off two shots. The first went wide, but the second round hit the figure in the shoulder and spun him around, sending his drawn gun flying from his grasp. Renna fired again, but the figure changed course and dissolved into the trees. A moment later he reemerged on Renna's right flank, his hand snaking up from his belt with a blade.

I yelled too late.

The knife sailed across the five yards between them and glanced off the edge of Renna's protective vest, pricking him in the arm before falling away. The assailant was running again. To steady his aim, Renna dropped to one knee, his barrel swinging left as he tracked the rapidly retreating figure. I watched Frank's finger close on the trigger. He fired a single shot, high, and the Soga soldier spun and collapsed.

"Got you, you bastard," Renna said.

He stood, took three steps toward his prey, and keeled over. Hauling himself up again, Renna fought hard for two more paces, then tumbled sideways. He tried to rise a third time, and when he couldn't bellowed in frustration.

Adrenaline pumping, I sprinted up to my stricken friend. "Stay down."

Renna turned unfocused eyes in my direction. "Brodie? That you?"

"Yeah. Don't move." I shouted toward the gate: "Man down. Need a medic over here!"

Fighting against an invisible force he couldn't understand, Renna dragged his massive torso into a sitting position. "Damn if I'm going to let these bastards tag me now."

"They won't," I said, gently easing him back down.

"The scumsucker get up?" Renna asked.

"No, you nailed him. Now lie still."

"It's just a scratch."

"No, it's poison," I said. "Very potent poison." I ripped open his vest and shirt. Renna's eyes rolled up into his head.

"Medic!" I yelled again.

This time I heard footsteps and a shout. "Where?" a voice called.

"Over here. In the trees to your right."

Renna groaned. "Dizzy. Can't hear . . ."

I exposed the cut, a two-inch gash along his biceps. The knife had sliced sideways across the muscle and drawn blood. The wound was shallow but the poison had direct access to the bloodstream.

Squeezing the area around the puncture, I bent over and sucked out the flowing red liquid from skin damp with sweat, then spat out the blood. It had a muddy taste. The end of my tongue went numb.

Renna was moaning loudly now. I knew I had to hurry. Drawing out as much fluid as I could, I worked the middle, then each end of the cut.

The paramedic arrived and knelt down, flipping open his kit.

"Snakebite?"

"Man bite," I said. "Poison from the knife."

He reached for the weapon.

"Check the handle before you touch it," I said. "Is there an oily substance on it?"

He squinted and inhaled. "There's oil on the blade. Flowery smell I don't recognize. Antidote?"

"I don't know."

Renna mumbled something. I leaned closer, cocking my head to hear better.

". . . sells cars . . . owns thirty-one dealerships . . . got the uncle's lots . . ."

My breath caught in my throat. Renna had found the person responsible for Mieko's murder.

"Tell me who, Frank. Just the name."

Lips parting, he mumbled something unintelligible and slipped under. Damn. I went back to cleansing the wound. My thoughts raced. Renna had identified the owner of the shell companies used to buy the dealerships. The information must have come through in a late-night call after we'd parted.

"We're losing him," the medic said.

"Can you inject something? A stimulant?"

"Hard to do without knowing what we're dealing with. An adverse reaction could kill him later."

"Do it. The poison's killing him *now*."

"Are you his superior officer?"

"No."

Yellow bile spilled from Renna's mouth. Glancing back over his shoulder, the medic started to rise. "Need to find his superior."

I put a hand on the medic's shoulder and forced him back down. "Give him something now."

"Can't without the proper authority. His family could sue—"

"I'm a friend of the family. They won't sue."

"I don't know, buddy."

"Do it! Now! Otherwise he's dead."

Yanking a syringe from his kit, the medic plunged the needle into Renna's arm.

Renna's eyes jolted open. "Brodie. It *is* you. Thought I was dreaming."

"Who is it, Frank? Give me a name."

His lips moved, but what came out was gibberish and he slipped under again.

Frowning, the paramedic slapped Renna's face. Left cheek, right cheek. No response. The frown deepened. "He's gone into shock."

Bending over Renna once more, I repeated the cleansing routine with renewed energy until I could no longer milk any blood from the wound. When a crew arrived, I stepped away from my friend as they lifted him gently onto a stretcher. I trotted behind the procession as they raced Frank to an ambulance.

Just before they shut him in, I pressed the senior medical officer for a prognosis and he gave me the kind of sympathetic look you don't want to see.

WE'D won the battle, but lost the war.

By my count, Casey, Dermott, and seven Soga soldiers were either dead or in custody, but Ogi had slipped through the police net, as had the rest of his force. Soga would regroup and strike again at their leisure. It was unlikely I or anyone else could stop them next time. It was unlikely we'd even *see* them next time.

Tell me their weakness, the bureaucrat had said to the informant.

I know of only one. They operate in teams of four. Only one or two people at the top know the whole operation. If you kill the leaders, it would be like killing the queen bee. The workers would be unable to do anything but buzz around aimlessly.

Naturally, the opposite also held true: *Without Ogi dead or arrested, my life was worthless.*

Soga had crushed us. Abers was dead, Renna was in critical condition, and Noda and Luke were now officially missing and presumed dead. McCann confirmed that the two men had blown the boats, adding that the noise had probably drawn too much attention. I had no trouble imagining Soga swarming through the woods and pinning Noda and Luke at the shoreline, near the docks. By McCann's calculations, the pair had become victims of their own success.

I plunged back into the grounds to collect Jenny, the one good thing to come out of the assault. Maybe we could go into hiding until they caught Ogi. But for how long? Soga would never stop looking. I circled around the cottage where my daughter had been held and headed for her airy roost. In my waistband, I carried Renna's piece.

At distinct points around the grounds, I heard cops shouting out with each new discovery. Confidence among the conquerors was spreading. I wished I had a reason to join the jubilation.

Arriving at the base of Jenny's oak, I took a minute to compose myself before the climb. She could see no trace of my concern. Under the illusion of safety, I'd escort her home. But with Abers gone, Renna ailing, and Jenny hovering on the edge, how happy would our homecoming be? What would I tell Miriam if Renna didn't make it? How could I ever look Christine and Joey in the eye? And how long would Jenny and I be forced to hide from a refortified Soga? Our assault had been an unmitigated fiasco.

As I reached for the lowest branch, I heard a noise behind me.

"Hold it right there, Brodie."

I turned. A shape separated from the darkness, and I was caught staring down the barrel of yet another Soga Glock.

Held by a man supposedly nine thousand miles away.

"*You,*" I said. "What are *you* doing here?"

ENGULFED in an agonizing silence, we stared at each other from opposite ends of the gun. I didn't know why he had betrayed me, but the pain of his choice was etched across his face.

"Of all people," I said.

"I'm sorry, Brodie-kun."

Staring back from the other side of the Glock was Shig Narazaki, my father's longtime partner, friend of the family, surrogate uncle.

His appearance on the scene rocked me to the core. I'd been betrayed by *family*.

My head spun with the implications. *He* was the reason Soga was always one step ahead. *He* was the reason they found me in Ikebukuro after I took every precaution before meeting my journalist friend. Now I understood why Narazaki insisted Noda head to London when New York seemed the obvious choice to the rest of us. And it was Narazaki, not Luke, who betrayed our secret plans in New York. I caught a further glimpse into Soga's successful methodology: they covered their back from multiple angles.

"I tried to keep them away," he said.

I shook my head in disbelief. The disconnect was enormous. "What are you talking about?"

"I'm Soga born. Halfway through training, I took myself out of the program. Soga and I reached a compromise. Brodie Security was it. When Jake opened the first Western-style PI agency in Tokyo, it was thought that his place would attract some big cases. And it did."

There were legends about Jake's prowess. By the time he opened his doors in 1973, the free-for-all of postwar Japan had gone underground. Developed a good public front. Black market racketeers, yakuza, Italian Mafia, and carpetbaggers from Texas, Moscow, Paris, and a dozen other Allied cities all operated virtually unchecked by an emasculated Japanese police force in the two decades after the surrender of 1945. It was a time ripe for private enterprise—legal, gray, and otherwise. By 1973 they were still operating, had more to protect, and often resorted to the same methods of enforcement. The Japanese police were all but useless against this more evolved criminal element. For those in desperate straits, Brodie Security provided an alternative. Jake solved more than his share of headline-grabbing cases, and his enterprise thrived.

"How is this possible? You ran the agency with my father for forty years."

"All legit, too. We did some great things. Only occasionally, maybe once a year, when a case related to Soga came up, I'd assign it to an inexperienced employee and let it flounder. I'd been doing that for years, without hurting Jake or the firm. Soga would give us just enough information to save face with the client, but in truth the cases were never fully resolved. I supplied inside information on some of our clients to Soga when necessary, and with those minor concessions I got to work the *good side* of the trade. I'm sorry things went this far. I did everything I could to keep you clear of it. Twice I tried to get you to drop the whole thing."

A long speech but not one folksy fishing metaphor in the lot. Soga was landlocked.

"You let them take my daughter."

His reaction was startled and immediate. "Little Yumi-chan? Never! But no one asked me. Or told me."

"Who hired Soga to kill my wife?"

"I don't know."

I believed him on both counts. The string of killings that took my wife and her family had unwound across the water, far from Tokyo. "But you did send them after me in Ikebukuro, didn't you?"

He held the gun steady. "After you and Noda ran through a whole team of trainees in Soga, I had little choice. I could no longer protect you. I begged, but Ogi was adamant. Initially, he'd promised to let you pass through the village unharmed, but your showing up in Soga proved a temptation he couldn't resist and he double-crossed me. When I heard what had happened, I confronted him, but your very success proved his point. Hooking up with Kozawa only increased Ogi's determination to see you dead. Yanking you off the case and sending you into hiding was my last-ditch attempt to protect you. But you wouldn't budge. I came here to plead your case one last time with Ogi but it was a lost cause."

Shock, disbelief, and disgust rippled through me in continuous waves. With our client setting us up and my partner giving away our secrets, we were hemmed in on all sides from the start.

"So you were in on all of it?"

"Yes."

"The bug at Brodie Security?"

"A built-in excuse should you or Noda ever suspect a leak from the inside. Toru wasn't supposed to find it."

"The hacker?"

"Meant as a diversion. A time-waster. I wanted you and Noda distracted in Tokyo. I never imagined Mari and her flaky boyfriend would actually be able to catch our computer guy, let alone tail him to our home ground. Especially after I *warned* him he was being stalked."

"You can't shoot me, Narazaki. You know that."

Remorse pooled in his eyes. "Until tonight I couldn't. Now, if you live, Soga will come after *me*. When you escaped from the village, Ogi accused me of assisting you. In our three-hundred-year history, no one has ever inflicted so many casualties in the village. Because of that, Ogi not only refused my request to leave you alone but also said he'd hold me personally responsible if you lived through the next attack. And you did that when you escaped from the kidnap attempt in Ikebukuro. Ogi thinks I helped you out in both places. He repeated the threat tonight once you broke free."

His words drained the fight from me. Burned by the man I'd sought to emulate as I stepped into my father's shoes. This was *not* the world I knew. "You could still let me go. Pretend you never found me."

Narazaki regarded me sadly, the gun never wavering. "Even if I did, I wouldn't be doing you a favor. You're already dead. By tomorrow every

Soga operative in the world will be hunting you. This way, at least one of us lives."

"Because of the village and Gilbert Tweed? Why press it? They're exposed."

Sorrow wrinkled his brow. "No, it's not either of those. Any chance I had of swinging a last-minute reprieve vanished when you killed the heir apparent."

"I did no such thing."

"You don't know, do you? Casey. He was an Ogi. And next in line to lead."

For a moment I stood speechless, absorbing the implications. *Casey the heir apparent?* No wonder he spoke with such a commanding arrogance. Ordered the shooting of Abers with such cavalier abandon.

My old family friend was right. In killing the heir, I'd killed myself.

Narazaki's finger closed on the trigger. "Now or later makes no difference."

"Don't shoot my daddy, Uncle Shig."

No! My heart plunged. She'd *almost* made it. Tonight had been all about Jenny. No matter what happened to me, I'd taken immense comfort in knowing I'd removed her from the field of fire. She was safe—my one consolation should I take a fall. Now Jenny would die too.

Exhausted, I shook my head in defeat. Narazaki wouldn't let her live. With Dermott, Jenny's timing had been brilliant, but this time I was too far from cover, or Narazaki, to take advantage of the surprise.

He glanced up into the darkness without taking the gun off me. "You hid her in the tree. Clever. Just like Jake. I wish she hadn't heard our conversation."

"Forget about it," I said. "In a week she'll have blanked out the whole episode. Kids are like that."

Narazaki frowned. "Can't do it. Sorry."

"If not for me, then for Jake."

"Wish I could oblige, but she has to go. Big shame. If only—"

Without warning, a silenced weapon coughed behind me. Narazaki's legs buckled beneath him and he sat down with a grunt, an entry wound in his shoulder staining his clothing red.

Noda stepped from the shadows, a gun trained on his boss.

He'd survived!

Narazaki's resigned smile was tinged with gratitude. "Thank you, Kei-kun. I didn't want to shoot Jake's kid."

"I know," Noda said.

"If it had to be someone, I'm glad it's you. Finish what you started."

Noda hesitated.

"Go ahead, Kei-kun. My life's over. It's either prison or Soga."

Noda stared at his old friend. "Won't do it."

"You don't, I'll shoot Brodie." Halfheartedly, Narazaki raised his weapon. From the trees, another shot opened a hole in Narazaki's forehead and my father's longtime partner pitched over into the deadfall.

Luke stepped from the foliage.

"Garbage in, garbage out," he said.

Eyes dark with grief, Noda gazed at his fallen friend for a beat before mumbling a gruff thanks to the CIA man. Nodding, Luke holstered his gun. Noda turned away and Luke stepped in behind him, uttering a single word: "Ogi."

Brodie Security's chief detective grunted, and together they slipped through the woods in search of the Soga leader.

FERRIED my daughter from her roost, and once on solid ground I smothered her in an embrace. Jenny threw her arms around me and squeezed for all she was worth. Neither of us spoke. Despite the lifeless forms at our feet, or perhaps because they bore testimony to how far we had come down a hazard-strewn path, the silence between us was long and full and freighted with a sense of relief and renewal. Everything we had endured, everything we meant to each other, and everything that had unfurled in the last nine days spilled out in the embrace.

After a time, I said, "Let me look at you, Jen."

Lifting her head, Jenny gazed at me with her mother's probing brown eyes. They were bursting with questions. For the first time in days, I laughed. A foreign and unfamiliar sound. My daughter was beautiful, and she was mine. The thought swept over me with undiluted joy. We'd get past Ogi. Somehow. Even if it meant hiding out for months.

"Jen, I just want to tell you that no matter what—"

The bushes behind me exploded with movement, then a voice hissed in my ear: "The world's a funny place."

Even distorted with hatred, I recognized the inflection.

After all, he was the mayor's eyes on the scene.

Supportive. By the book. All of us grateful to find a pol without an agenda.

All of us suckered.

With a .22 trained on Jenny, DeMonde circled around the front, stepping back until he was beyond the range of a swift karate strike.

The man was well informed. "If your wife hadn't been at her parents' house that night, she wouldn't have died and you wouldn't have such a hard-on for this case. But she was and you do. Now Soga's on the verge of collapsing, incredible as that seems, which forces my hand. With all the bodies tonight, you and your daughter will be just two more casualties. I've always been lucky that way."

My mind reeled. What was DeMonde raving about? Had he snapped? Then revelation cleared the mist. *Sales yak and self-made millionaire*, Renna had told me the first time I'd met the deputy mayor. DeMonde must have sold *cars*. Owned *car* lots. That's what Renna had tried to tell me tonight.

DeMonde had hired Soga to orchestrate the "accidental" deaths of three car dealers whose lots he coveted, among them those owned by Mieko's uncle.

An all-consuming rage roiled my blood. The man responsible for my wife's death stood two yards away pointing a .22-caliber pistol at my daughter. I did the calculations. The caliber was small. I could absorb two or three bullets and still take him down and survive, but a single round was more than enough to kill a six-year-old child at close range.

Inwardly I was incredulous. After running a gauntlet of Soga obstacles—the village, a near garroting, Jenny's rescue, skirmishes with Dermott *and* Casey—I was going to die because DeMonde had waltzed in under the guise of an ally. The simplicity of his plan stunned me.

And with Jenny in my arms, I was helpless to stop him.

Another revelation overtook me. *DeMonde* had worn the wire for Soga during our meet at the hotel. Narazaki knew the basics but not the details of our New York operation, or the words spoken behind closed doors.

I tried laying down a stall. "Renna knows about you."

DeMonde nodded in sudden understanding. "He *does* know something, doesn't he? He was looking at me strangely tonight. But I heard he's dying. Either way, he'll never *prove* anything."

Jenny squirmed out of my arms. In an instant she wriggled from my grasp and took up a position standing at my side. DeMonde froze. Didn't shoot. Before he could respond, I stepped in front of her, shielding her and bringing me half a pace closer. I remained parental. Passive. Nonthreatening.

DeMonde shifted sideways, his gun barrel tracking Jenny's small frame as he tried to reclaim his bead on her. It was an amateur's reaction. I sluiced forward. Too late did his gun arm swing back toward me, and when his wrist banged against my ribs, I pinned the arm under mine, then pivoted away and to his rear, skewing the barrel away from Jenny and at the same time forcing the elbow against the joint and snapping it. DeMonde howled, stumbling past me with a broken, rubbery appendage. I rammed the elbow of my free arm into the back of his neck. Bone cracked, his neck snapped, and my wife's killer crumpled to the ground.

Dead.

Just like that.

A pinch of pain and his ordeal was over. It hardly seemed a fair trade for the suffering Jenny and I had endured in the months after Mieko's death. Hardly fair at all.

But, fair or not, it was finished.

Finally.

T was only a matter of minutes now.

Noda and Luke had been tracking Ogi for a good quarter of an hour and gaining ground on the unsuspecting Soga patriarch. Earlier, they had missed him by seconds. Having rigged a timer to the explosives that destroyed the boats, the pair was ninety seconds short of the main house when the explosion occurred. From thirty yards back, they saw the Soga commander exit the building at a fast clip under the guidance of a younger fighter. They noted his footprints, watched two other Soga men dash in and out of the manor, then slipped into the house themselves, hoping to find Brodie or his daughter.

They searched every room but came up empty-handed. Back outside, they picked up Ogi's distinctive tread, lost it, roamed the grounds, and eventually spotted his tracks again, which led them to Brodie and Narazaki. Ogi had lingered in the bushes near Brodie before moving away, probably vacating his position when he heard them approach. Which suggested Soga's number one was lurking nearby.

So the two had set out after the top prize. Their confidence grew with each passing minute. For some unfathomable reason, Ogi had not left the grounds, and that was about to prove detrimental to his health. In anticipation of a confrontation, both men drew their weapons.

Then the trail vanished.

Disappeared without explanation or a hint of how the feat was accomplished.

Both men froze. A quick exchange of hand signals followed, then Noda headed west into the brush and circled north. Luke turned east and then south. Weapons out, safeties off, they moved through the surrounding woods in concentric circles with consummate expertise, first five yards out, then ten, then fifteen. Then they called it off. They could find no new trail.

"Foxy bugger," Luke said. "No trace whatsoever."

Noda nodded unhappily.

Luke said, "Probably circling back. Going after Brodie."

"No other reason."

Luke cursed softly, his words indistinct. "He must have heard us and knew one or both of us would come after him, so he set the trail and drew us off."

"Worked, too. We're too far away."

"I got my cell but . . ."

Noda nodded, lips tight, saying nothing. They had found Brodie's phone abandoned on the nightstand of his hotel room.

Luke said, "He's taken us out of the game. How good's your boy?"

Noda's reply was grim. "Good, but not this good."

CHAPTER 80

SCANNING the trees for my daughter, I spied her cowering behind a large pine. As I moved toward her, I heard the faint hissing sound of metal over cloth behind me.

Ogi!

At my back, unleashing the garrote.

Too close for me to turn and attack.

Just in time I flattened my palms against my forehead, drawing in my elbows and shielding my face and neck with my arms. A split second later a wire looped over my head from behind, seeking the tenderness of my neck but finding the sinew of my forearms instead.

My defensive move kept the garrote from my neck but didn't stop it from slicing through the flesh of my arms. Howling in pain, I backpedaled and slammed Ogi into the nearest tree. A couple of his ribs popped and a hot saliva-laced cry burst from his lips, but Ogi clung to the wire tenaciously and it cut deeper. Cold steel razors cleaved raw nerves. My screams rose to the treetops. Unconsciousness flickered before my eyes.

In frenzied desperation, I smashed the back of my head into Ogi's face. Once, twice, three times I hit him with a reverse head butt until his nose caved and his jawbone cracked. Only then did the tough old warrior's hold break and the wire grow slack.

Ogi wheezed in pain, his hoarse breath hot and heavy at my ear. Without turning, I rammed the Soga boss against the trunk a second time, then brought my elbows down and peppered his torso with alternating blows from both sides, the killing wire swinging wildly from a gash in my arm.

Another rib snapped and Ogi slumped to the ground. I stepped away. The Soga leader tried to rise but couldn't. His eyes closed and he was still. No matter how well trained, a man in his eighth decade wasn't going to recover from a beating like that without assistance.

I was numb all over. Blood streamed down my forearms. The shock to my nervous system from the garrote had sent my body into a stall; it was shutting down. Shafts of pain shot through me. Jagged bolts of white light flashed across the undersides of my eyelids. I fought to stay conscious. I bit down on my tongue to keep from blacking out. The induced pain brought a jittery rush of adrenaline. I grew dizzy with the injection, but the immediate danger of passing out receded.

Gritting my teeth, I extricated the garrote from a bleeding flap of flesh and flung it into the darkness.

Only one or two people at the top know the whole operation.

To live, Jenny and I needed Ogi to die. The Soga leader lay immobile at my feet. His breathing was feeble. Hara's prophetic words came back to me: *Invariably I get what I want.* A part of me wanted Ogi tried for his crimes. Paraded in public so his string of victims could get some satisfaction. Another part of me wanted him permanently removed from our lives.

And the sooner the better.

I dug the Soga hood from my pocket and tied it around the cut on one arm, the Soga shirt around the gash on the other. Ogi should have been miles away by now, but pride and revenge had drawn him back.

From behind me Jenny called faintly, "Daddy?"

I looked over my shoulder. Tentatively, Jenny inched forward from her hiding place among the trees. Terror spilled from her eyes. I smiled reassuringly and she ran to me, her arms spreading. I turned and swept her up in a hug, and as a wave of parental relief swept over me, I felt a cold blade snake into my back the way a copperhead slides into an empty sleeping bag. Jolts of white-hot pain spread through my middle regions.

How was it possible? I'd only taken my eyes off the battered Soga chief for a second.

I staggered sideways, shoving Jenny ahead of me—back into the trees—and opening as much distance as I could between Ogi and myself. The next moment, my legs rebelled and I collapsed to the forest floor, falling forward, conscious of the rod of steel in my back.

I glanced backward. The Soga leader was on his knees, grinning, his jaw hanging at an odd angle. While stabbing me with one hand, he'd extracted Renna's gun from the small of my back with the other. He'd only feigned defeat, dragging himself forward on his knees once my back was turned.

Now, with the piece aimed at my prone figure, Ogi hauled himself to his feet. When had he moved? I hadn't heard a thing. It was inhuman. The man had a fractured jaw and three broken ribs. Then I recalled Ogi's proclamation: *This is what Soga does. What we train for our whole lives. What our ancestors have done for three centuries.*

With his nose bludgeoned and his jaw disfigured, he looked more demon than human. His eyes flickered in pain, yet they stayed focused on me.

It was then that I noticed the greasy blue streaks running across his palm.

Poison. From the knife in my back.

Ogi would have built up an immunity, but what did it mean for me? I tried to think. The blade of the knife that had felled Renna had been treated but not the handle. *Not both.* The pattern repeated itself with the knives flung at us when the Soga trainees came through the ceiling of the inn. Handle dirty, blade clean on one. The opposite on the other. For some reason, it was Soga's practice to treat one surface or the other. I suppose it gave them options. The handle of Ogi's knife was treated, which meant the blade should be free of poison. But was it?

As Ogi limped toward me, I clawed desperately at the ground, drawing myself forward. Ogi advanced. I thrust with my toes, my progress measured in inches.

Ogi was five yards behind me and closing.

Dense foliage, from where Jenny probably watched, was three yards away and unreachable.

A burning sensation rippled through my flesh.

At two yards, Ogi said, "Give it up, Brodie. It's over."

I craned my neck to look. Ogi swayed unsteadily, his feet spread wide for balance, the gun pointed at my head. At that distance, an experienced gunman couldn't miss. Even a thoroughly pummeled one. I crawled forward another couple of inches. Ogi squeezed off a shot that kicked up dust a hair's breadth from my right shoulder. I stopped my struggle and rolled onto my side and faced him.

Ogi grinned, savoring the moment. "Very slowly, very painfully, you're going to die, Brodie."

I was silent.

"There's going to be more suffering than you could ever imagine."

Still on my side, I scooted backward in small increments. Even a fractional gain could be valuable.

"I'm going to fill you with holes one bullet at a time. Near the joints."

I thought it a rock at first . . . but it was a handle . . .

Ogi's misshapen jaw wrenched itself into a sneer. "Intense pain is nearest the joints. Did you know that?" The muzzle of his weapon rose. He aimed it gleefully at my left knee. "When the first bullet tears through you, you'll—"

Reaching behind me, my fingers came up with Narazaki's weapon, the gun knocked loose when Luke had shot him. While Ogi gloated, I brought the piece up over my hip and pulled the trigger. With the first shot, an invisible force shoved the Soga leader backward.

"Noooooo!" he wailed.

He swung his weapon around and I fired again. And again.

I kept shooting.

In my mind's eye, I matched the rounds with the victims: one for Mieko, one for the Nakamuras. One for the linguist, one for Noda's kin. One for Abers, one for Renna. One for all the victims I'd never met but knew were out there.

With each shot, the kickback electrified my body with a searing pain and I screamed as if I were reliving each victim's tribulations.

But despite the pain, I fired.

Fired, then heard myself scream.

Ogi's body jerked spasmodically with the impact of each bullet. The last discharge knocked the Soga chief off his feet. He fell back dead, Renna's gun still clutched in his lifeless hand.

There would be no resurrection this time. I lay my head on the damp deadfall, my body a throbbing network of torment.

"Daddy?"

Hesitant footsteps signaled Jenny's emergence from the foliage. Straining, I raised my head. She reached over my hip for the dagger. I brushed her hand away before she could grab it.

"Don't touch the knife," I whispered, a worrying numbness spreading through my lower extremities. "The handle is coated with poison, and right now the blade is keeping the blood *in*. What I need you to do is bring help."

"I can't leave you, Daddy. You're hurting."

"I need you to get help, Jen."

"Alone?"

"Yes."

"It's too dark."

I winced. More obstacles. Would it never end? Jenny was afraid for me, afraid to venture out on her own, and afraid to face the darkness. All of her worst nightmares had coalesced in this moment.

My nerves shrieked in agony, and before I could stifle it a moan escaped my lips, escalating my daughter's panic. Keeping my voice calm and soothing, I said, "You need to find a paramedic as fast as you can, Jen. For that, all you have to do is run to the road about two hundred yards to the right. Ask the first person you come across to call for medical help. Okay?"

"But—"

Sweat beaded my brow. "I need you to go now. It's important. *They* are all gone. The only people left are our friends. Ask any one of them to—" I clamped my jaw shut against a sudden surge of pain.

Tears streamed down my daughter's cheeks. She saw my suffering. She heard the tightness in my voice. And she was immobilized with fear.

"I can't leave you, Daddy. *You'll die.*"

I'll die if you don't leave me, I wanted to shout, but couldn't. Jenny was on the edge. Any further sign of weakness on my part would cause her to shut down. Then she would hover over me protectively, watching with eyes steeped in dread and self-doubt while my life drained away, her guilt over my death in turn crushing her fragile soul without mercy. If I couldn't convince her to leave my side voluntarily, neither of us would survive.

Desperation clamored in my chest. I searched for something to ignite her confidence.

"Jen, do you love me?"

"Yes, of course."

"If you love me, go for help. Forget everything else."

"I love you but—"

"*Forget everything else.*"

"I can't."

"Try."

Her voice broke. "I can't."

I sighed, resigned. "All right. If you can't, you can't."

"Sorry, Daddy."

What did I expect? She was only six. First, the kidnapping. Next, the terror of captivity. Now, a life-and-death decision. The world was asking too much of my little girl. I shifted into protection mode while I still had the strength.

"I understand, Jenny. And you know what? It's okay. But I want you to promise me one thing. It's a best-ever from me, only a promise instead of a riddle."

"What?"

Before I died, I had to forestall the guilt. Had to give her a reason to live beyond the horrors of her kidnapping and tonight. "No matter what happens, remember that none of this is your fault."

"It isn't?"

"Of course not. It's the world spinning badly. That's all. If you're strong enough, you'll beat it. Because you're my girl. Because you're you. Have you got that?"

"Sort of."

"Don't worry about the details. It's a best-ever. Just remember it's not your fault. When you're older, you'll understand."

"Am I strong enough now?"

"Of course."

"Why of 'course'?"

"Because you have your mother's strength."

Jenny's eyes widened. "I do?"

"Yes."

Chewing her bottom lip, she stared at me for a moment, then something behind her eyes shifted and she trooped over and kicked Ogi in the knee. The leg shook with the lethargic wobble of dead weight and my heartbeat ticked up at my daughter's show of bravery. She'd make it. Maybe with scars, but she'd make it. I could rest now. I closed my eyes.

"I stomped him, Daddy," Jenny called.

"Yes, you did," I said faintly.

My voice cracked. I felt the remaining shreds of my stamina drain away, and for the second time tonight unconsciousness loomed.

Jenny saw me fading. "Daddy?"

I could summon no energy to respond.

"Daddy, can you hear me?"

Willing my eyes to open, I managed a ghost of a smile.

Jenny said, "I'm going to get help now, Daddy. Okay?"

No words would come.

"Okay?" Panic hovered behind her insistence. "Please say 'okay,' Daddy."

With the faintest of voices, I managed to satisfy her demand.

"Wait for me, all right? Promise?"

With my last breath, I did.

Jenny kissed my cheek then sprinted for the road.

Exhausted, I could hold my eyes open no longer. *Forgive me, Jenny, for a promise I can't keep.* There was no poison in my system, but it no longer mattered. Garroted and knifed, I had sustained too much blood loss. There could be no doubt: I was dying. But I'd won. Ogi was dead. His son was dead. Soga was dead. Even Mieko's killer was dead. All of which meant Jenny would live. It was enough.

In the distance, a cheer rose up from the police swarming the manor. I pried my eyes open. Helicopters had arrived en masse and roared overhead with mechanical fury, their spotlights slashing the darkness. Weary and relieved, I allowed my eyes to fall shut one final time—and I smiled. Mopping-up operations had begun. My daughter would find the police or they would find her. That's all I cared about. At six, Jenny had so much yet to do. I had lived thirty-two long, eventful years. Traveled the world. Pitched camp in Tokyo, Los Angeles, and San Francisco.

Made lifelong friends in all those places and more. Loved and been loved. I couldn't ask for more.

A new kind of darkness clouded the edges of my vision, carrying with it a feeling of wellness. The pain lessened, then dissipated. The soothing blackness spread a tingling warmth over me. The last stage before the end.

"Sorry, Jen," I whispered into the night. "I did the best I could."

EPILOGUE

I SLUMBERED for eighteen hours, enveloped in feverish hallucinations. Over and over, I saw my daughter running toward me, arms outstretched. The scene played in an eternal loop I never tired of watching. In my drug-induced visions, the world was perfect. Anguish and pain had been airbrushed from my immediate memory. Those I loved suffered no loss, no hurt, no distress, but floated in a pillowy softness that coddled and nurtured and brought only smiles and blissful looks.

But in the darker corners of my mind, reality hovered in all its brutality. Abers shot, Renna poisoned, Jenny traumatized, Narazaki dead. In the fabric of my medicinal dreams, my adopted uncle came alive, smiling and waving and slapping me on the back with his usual camaraderie. What kind of life had he led? What kind of death had taken him? What should I make of the man I once called uncle?

Hours later I clawed my way out of the narcotic sleep. Looking around, I was greeted with an unexpected vision: Renna lay in a bed across the room. His right arm was in a sling and an intravenous feed dripped steadily into the other arm. Renna rolled his head in my direction.

"How'd we get here?" I asked.

"Don't know."

"You gonna make it?"

"Looks that way."

I nodded and drifted down and away. Voices floated around in my head. Apparitions danced above me. Had I talked to Renna or was he another hallucination? Where was Jenny? Where was Noda? Where was I? Had Luke really killed Narazaki or was that another bad dream? Who was dead? Who was alive? Which was I?

Ten hours later I woke a second time.

Renna looked over. "I know," he said.

"Know what?"

"How we got here. You jinxed us. 'Till death do us part,' remember?"

"Do and wish I didn't."

Something moved under my covers, and I lifted the blanket. Jenny had snuggled into my side and was sleeping soundly.

––––––

Lieutenant Jamie McCann showed up next. It was his third visit to our hospital room, but the first one with all of us conscious. He brought Renna and me up to date and asked if the results were good enough to declare victory over the monster that was Soga. Which, of course, was the question of the hour.

Was Soga still out there or had they been defanged?

I didn't know.

McCann told us that Long Island looked like a war zone. In all, six policemen had died in the assault on the Soga estate. The number of wounded reached a staggering seventeen. Twelve men fell on the first charge, mostly leg injuries, thank God, when a pair of submachine guns operated by remote control strafed the front guard, discharging a spray of ankle-level firepower that dropped nearly the whole of the first advance and accounted for some of the most horrifying screams McCann had ever heard. *Who were these Soga guys and what the hell did they think they were doing?* he asked more than once.

On Soga's side, the police bagged the two snipers at the gate, and Renna's takedown brought the count to three. According to McCann I'd turned into a one-man wrecking crew, taking down Ogi, Casey, Dermott, my daughter's three captors, and the young trainee left bound and gagged in the shrubbery. Grand total: nine dead, one captured. Considering the expertise of the opposition, a resounding success despite the nine Soga fighters who had escaped. And then there were the civilian casualties: DeMonde out of the San Francisco's mayor's office and Narazaki from Brodie Security.

On the following day, when I could speak coherently from my hospital bed, I funneled the results of the Long Island showdown to Tejima and Kozawa in Tokyo. Both the Ministry of Defense bureaucrat and the powerbroker congratulated me but were otherwise distant and uncommunicative. Knowing a muted response meant one or both of them would shift into cover-up mode, I was saddened.

But they were what they were, so I shrugged it off and dialed a third number, where Tommy-gun Tomita listened to my account with just the right level of jubilation. After verifying the facts with McCann and the SFPD, the journalist released another scoop on the front page of the *Mainichi Newspaper,* and action by reluctant government officials followed directly because, Tommy told me later, the Soga debacle would fester for years in the international arena if the pols and bureaucrats adhered to their usual indolent course, ignoring what they could and sweeping the rest under the rug for the "good of the country's image" or some other excuse of the day.

For the first time in modern Japanese history, the authorities put a whole village under house arrest. Not since premodern times when daimyo and shogun warrior lords torched entire towns or ordered the death of a whole clan had such a sweeping action been carried out.

A special squad from the Self-Defense Forces surrounded the village. Roads were blocked, mountain passes sealed. Barbed wire was strung across the river. Soga-jujo was bottled up tight.

Three high-ranking officials from the Ministry of Finance were indicted. Then the suicides began. Shingo Yuda, the top man at MOF whom Ogi had fingered as his client for Japantown, headed the roster. There were twelve in all, seven at MOF and five more at the Ministry of International Trade and Industry and the Ministry of Foreign Affairs. Those led to more indictments. The defense ministry itself did not escape unscathed.

Brodie Security was the hero. The papers raved about our perseverance, and before long we garnered threats from right-wing groups who said we'd sullied the reputation of the *hinomaru,* the Japanese flag and all it stood for. Recognizing the gravity of their fury, we secured our doors during business hours until the heat died down but otherwise carried on as usual.

For Jenny and me, the most welcome news arrived with Tejima's last call: guided by a master list they had uncovered in the village, the Ministry of Defense was tracking down the Soga assassins posted outside Japan and offering them a onetime amnesty-and-rehabilitation package, a classic Japanese solution. Even with Ogi dead, I worried about vengeance-seeking assassins stalking us, but the offer of absolution would dissolve the desire for payback.

On American shores action was no less swift. As I looked on, Lieutenant Franklin Thomas Renna received a citation bedside in New York City from the *new* deputy mayor of San Francisco, who flew to the East Coast with Miriam and the children.

Renna could have gone either way, the doctors informed us, but my action in the field most likely swung the needle into positive territory. By the time Renna boarded a flight home two weeks later, the department's toughest cop was nearing a full return to health.

My recovery was nearly as tenuous. Blood loss and extreme shock to my central and autonomic nervous systems almost sent my body into a "permanent nosedive," my doctor said, "like a plane whose engines have stalled." Leaving the knife in place was the smartest thing I could have done, as it stemmed the outward flow of blood, although the intrusion of the steel shaft had played havoc on my sensory systems. The move also assured that the serrated edge of the weapon could not fulfill its full purpose, which was to rip open the wound upon withdrawal. But what really saved the day, the doctor confided, was the knife's shallow penetration. Because of the thrashing I meted out to Ogi, the battered Soga leader only managed to thrust the blade in a mere 2.2 inches, "luckily avoiding injury to the vital organs and spinal cord, but puncturing the stomach lining." They put me on mush for thirty days.

During my convalescence, I recovered not only my health but also the stillness Mieko worked so hard to draw from the shadows—what she assured me resides in all of us. Over the years, I'd lost it, reclaimed it, then lost it once more. At twenty-one, with my mother's death, I'd thought I'd lost it completely. But her passing brought Mieko back into my life, along with her sense of knowing. With Mieko's death it slipped away yet again, only to force its way back into my life on the bloodstained cobblestones of Japantown. In the hospital, reviewing it all, I regained my foothold and the stillness returned to stay. What I locked on to was deep and clear and offered an umbilical connection to something beyond everyday normalcy. I finally understood that it was always with me—I had never lost it, only myself.

Comforted, I closed my eyes and in the darkness behind my eyelids, I could make out a hint of Mieko's pearl-white smile.

Jenny slept in my bed every night for a month after she heard the news about Abers. But slowly she emerged from the shock. She seemed to survive the trauma of her kidnapping mostly unscathed, although I watched her closely. Her minor celebrity status at school helped. But it wasn't until she finally felt frisky enough to ask the question I'd long hoped to hear that I felt confident she would come out on top.

We were sitting at our kitchen table, sated after consuming extra-large portions of pepper-eggs.

"Daddy, you still haven't guessed my best-ever."

"'What kind of bees give milk?'"

She squeezed my hand with pleasure. "You remember!"

"Of course. In Tokyo I thought about it a lot, and I thought about you a lot, but mostly I was too busy thinking about your safety and the men who were after us."

"You did a good job there, you know. The papers said so."

"You're reading the papers now?"

"Sort of. I found our names a bunch of times. And Mr. Renna's too."

"Hmmm."

"Because you did such a good job, this one time I'm going to tell you the answer to a best-ever, okay? Only this once. And only if you promise to keep it a secret. Do you promise?"

I raised a hand. "I do."

"Really a secret?"

"You bet."

"Okay, here goes. 'What kind of bees give milk?' And the answer is . . . boo-bees."

I expected to laugh upon finally hearing her answer, but my face showed only confusion. "Ah, do you mean scary bees? Ghost bees?"

"Oh, Daddy, you don't know *anything*." She jerked my arm like she was trying to ring a church bell. "Boo-bees. Boobees. *Boobies*. Like big girls have."

"Oh. Those."

As her mother often had, Jenny covered her mouth and giggled. She was starting to exhibit the same infectious laughter. My parental shock passed and I joined in. One way or another, my daughter was growing up. And I would be here to see it.

ABOUT AUTHENTICITY

I've made every effort to render the Japanese material as accurately as possible. More than three decades of residency in Japan gives me a step up, though I am far from infallible. Here's what's true:

The background information on kanji and the Japanese language is accurate. The Soga kanji was created for the purposes of this novel, but its components were taken from existing characters.

Discussions of Japanese calligraphy, woodblock prints, and other art objects (Japanese or otherwise) are also accurate.

Settings at the inn, ryotei, soba restaurant, and elsewhere echo actual sites and my real-life experiences. While the village of Soga and its residents are fictional, the locale and the details are based on village life in that region of Japan. Historically, secret groups of assassins of various origins inhabited the area.

The Obon festival is a cherished Japanese ritual.

The events surrounding the Kobe earthquake occurred; the specific victims in these pages are fictional.

The ministries mentioned in the book are official government institutions, although the names sometimes evolve. For example, the Ministry of Health and Welfare, as it was known at the time of the Kobe earthquake, is now called the Ministry of Health, Labour, and Welfare. Many Japanese feel the ministries to be oppressive in the ways described in this story. To what extent varies with the individual, but the views expressed in these pages are in no way extreme.

Shadow powerbrokers existed in the recent past and to a degree exist today. Some observers believe they are dying out. Others think their role is merely changing with the times. In either case, the way power is wielded remains the same.

The "Dog Shogun" was the well-earned moniker of Tokugawa Tsunayoshi (1646–1709), the fifth shogun in a line of fifteen Tokugawa shoguns. The forty-seven ronin are also actual historical figures, and Sengakuji Temple, in central Tokyo, is their resting place.

Before and during World War II, Japan invaded its Asian neighbors to create what it called at various times a "new order" or a "co-prosperity sphere." A pivotal part of these expansionist efforts fell to the secret police organization known as the Kempei Tai (KPT), which committed countless atrocities.

In comparison to the standards followed in the United States and Europe, the restrictions on Japanese journalists are severe.

The Hanshin Tigers are an actual ball club, as its legion of fans will attest.

The poem Mieko Brodie recited was originally written by a Buddhist nun named Rengetsu (1791–1875) and appears in English in a short but elegant volume of her poetry called *Lotus Moon*, translated with aplomb by John Stevens. I am pleased to report that the Okazaki Hills front the Higashiyama Mountains at the eastern edge of Kyoto.

You often hear that it takes many people to launch a book. Nothing could be truer in my case. I have been fortunate in the people I've met. Many have extended a hand, advice, or insight with generosity and grace.

I owe an immense debt of gratitude to my agent, Robert Gottlieb. He "got it" from the first and has been supportive, professional, and on point throughout. I also want to express my thanks to others at Trident Media Group, including Erica Spellman-Silverman, Adrienne Lombardo, and Mark Gottlieb.

I am equally indebted to Sarah Knight at Simon & Schuster, who read this novel and then called me in Tokyo from New York, knowing as much or more about the work than I did. Her sharp editorial perceptions, enthusiasm, and great good humor have been a blessing. Also at Simon & Schuster, I wish to thank Lance Fitzgerald for his keen interest and support from the outset; Marysue Rucci for her sage advice and kind words; Molly Lindley for so efficiently taking care of additional publishing matters; Jackie Seow and Thomas Ng for a stunning jacket design; Andrea DeWerd for marketing; Jessica Lawrence and Grace Stearns for publicity; Elina Vaysbeyn for digital marketing; Kathy Higuchi for handling the production with such precision; Anne Cherry for her impressive copyediting; James Walsh for eagle-eyed proofreading; and the Internet and IT wizards in the digital group whom I've not yet gotten to know but whose work to date has been imaginative and cutting edge. And last, my deep thanks to Jonathan Karp and Richard Rhorer for their support of this project.

I also offer thanks to the following: Ben Simmons, a professional photographer with a focus on Japan and Asia, for taking the author photographs; web meister Maddee James and her crew, Jen and Ryan, all of xuni.com, for designing a superb website; and psychologist Betsey M. Olson for her insights into young girls going through trauma.

For help and encouragement along the way I also want to express my thanks to Mike and Cecilie Salo, Ann Slater, Janet Ashby, Ethel Margolin, John Paine, Jeff and Bonnie Stern, Richard Marek, John S. Knowlend, Lincoln Lancet, Margie and Mike Wilson, Linda and Bruce Miller, J. A. Ted Baer, Adrienne K. Di Giacomo, Kathleen Ireland, Fred Randolph, and Miles Kline.

Over the years, some of my publishing friends in Japan have offered stimulating conversation and general support: Shigeyoshi Suzuki (who also penned the art dealer's version of the kanji), Mio Urata, Ayako Akaogi, Michiko Uchiyama, and Michael Brase.

Family played a big role. My parent's steady presence on the other end of the Internet in California and their unquestioning support proves that blind faith has its moments. My brother Marc has also followed the years-long process with unbridled enthusiasm, plunging into the world of thrillers and mysteries with such abandon that his advice and insights were often stunning. Also thanks go out to his wife, Annette De Bow, for her enthusiasm for the project and her warm welcome during a brief stay at their home when things got rough. My brother Scott and his wife, Rosaleen, offered encouragement from the early stages of this book. As if that weren't enough, their children, Daryanna and Daniel, are proving to be a formidable cheering section. Melbourne and Teresa Weddle were early supporters, and Mel kindly offered his legal assistance as well. At home, my wife, Haruko, accepted my endless hours pounding the keyboard with amusement. My children, Renee and Michael, willingly put up with my distracted state and odd hours. They gave me inspiration on more levels than they could possibly imagine.

In Japan, my in-laws, Hozumi and Masako Horiuchi, supplied the occasional evening meal, conversation, and wonderful stories. The Chiba gang—Masaharu and Hiroko Nagase, Hirotaka Nagase, Chikako and Shinya Ishioka—has always been a kind and steady presence.

To each and every person here, and others unmentioned, I offer my sincere gratitude and profound thanks, as well as a promise to do it all again—soon.

ABOUT THE AUTHOR

Barry Lancet's first thriller in the Jim Brodie series, *Japantown* was selected as a Best Debut of Year by *Suspense Magazine* and by renowned mystery critic Oline H. Cogdill in her annual roundup. It has also been optioned by J. J. Abrams's Bad Robot Productions, in association with Warner Bros.

In his twenties, Lancet moved from California to Tokyo, where he has lived for more than two decades. He landed a position at one of the country's top publishing houses, and spent twenty-five years developing books on dozens of Japanese subjects from art to Zen—all in English and all distributed in the United States, Europe, and the rest of the world.

His unique position in the Japanese capital gave him access to many inner circles in cultural, business, and traditional fields most outsiders are never granted. However, it was an incident of an entirely different nature that started him on his present course. Early on in his tenure in Japan, Lancet was directed by the Tokyo Metropolitan Police Department to come down to the stationhouse for a "voluntary interview." The MPD proceeded to interrogate him for three hours.

The police grilling evolved into one of the most intensive psychological battles of cat-and-mouse Lancet had faced up to that point in his stay in Asia, and caused him to view many of his experiences, past and future, in a whole new light. The reason for the confrontation turned out to be a minor, noncriminal infraction. But even before they informed him of this, Lancet's initial anger had given way to a fascination with the encounter itself, and soon after sparked the idea for a thriller based on his growing number of unusual experiences in Japan. *Tokyo Kill* is the second book in the series. The third is on the way.

Lancet is still based in Japan, but travels frequently to the United States. For further information, please visit **BarryLancet.com** or look for his Twitter thread or author page on Facebook.

Turn the page for an excerpt from Barry Lancet's
next Jim Brodie adventure,

TOKYO KILL

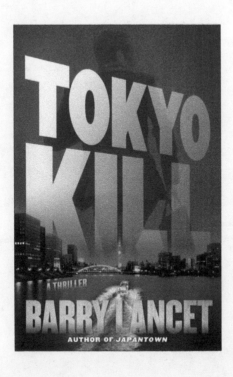

EIGHT people had already died by the time Akira Miura showed up at our door fearing for his life.

When the commotion broke out I'd been on a long-distance call to London trying to track down an original ink painting by Sengai, the renowned Japanese painter-monk of *Circle, Triangle, and Square* fame. The rumor had come out of the United Kingdom, so I was plying channels to nail down the potential gem for a client in San Francisco who would kill to get it, and kill *me* if I didn't.

People killed for a lot less. I learned this anew with each day spent at Brodie Security, the detective agency and personal protection firm established by my father in the Japanese capital more than forty years ago.

Had I been sitting in my antiques shop in San Francisco instead of behind my father's battered pine desk in Tokyo, I wouldn't have given the shouting match in the front office a second thought, but in Japan a loud altercation constituted a serious breach of decorum.

If not more.

Mari Kawasaki tapped on my door. "Brodie-san, I think you should get out here."

All of twenty-three but looking more like sixteen, Mari was the office tech whiz. When I came to town, she lent me a hand. We were a small operation and people wore multiple hats.

"Could I call you back later today?" I asked my London connection. "Something urgent has come up."

He said certainly and I jotted down his schedule, bid a polite good-bye, and stepped out onto the main floor.

Mari pointed across the room to where three hardened Brodie Security ops had herded a fourth man against a wall. The man cast indignant glares at them, and when my people didn't wither and fall back, he pelted the trio with the exasperated sighs middle-management salary-men usually fling at underlings.

That didn't work either.

Mari rolled her eyes. "He charged in here demanding to speak with you and refused to explain himself or wait at reception."

When the unexpected reared up at Brodie Security, containment came before all else. Our work brought us into contact with every manner of fringe character. Old-timers still talk about the right-wing lunatic who sprang from the elevator with short sword drawn and put two of the staff in the hospital.

"Calm down," one of the three men cooed. "If you would just return to the reception area . . ."

The salaryman was irate. "But it's urgent. My father is a sick man. Can't you see that?" He saw me and yelled across the expanse in Japanese, "Are you Jim Brodie?"

Since I was the only Caucasian in a sea of Asian faces, it wasn't a brilliant deduction. Our unannounced guest was handsome in the unassuming way Japanese men can be. He was in his fifties and sheathed in the requisite business suit—dark blue in his case—with a white dress shirt and a perfectly knotted red silk tie. The tie had set him back some. What looked like platinum cuff links sparkled at his wrists. His attire was flawless, and under normal circumstances he'd be considered nonthreatening. But his expression was frayed, as if he were unraveling from the inside.

"That's me," I said in his native language.

He drew himself up. His eyes grew watery. "Kindly allow my father to intrude. He is not well."

All eyes shifted toward the paternal figure waiting patiently at Reception. He had a full crown of silver-gray hair and the same unassuming good looks: sculpted cheekbones, a firm chin, and the deep brown eyes women habitually swoon over.

He waved a wooden walking staff in salute, then began a tremulous foray around the unmanned half-counter that passed for Reception in our no-frills office. With singular determination he shuffled forward. His hands trembled. The cane shook. He wheezed with each step. And yet, there was something noble in the effort.

He had dressed for the trip into town. A brown hand-tailored suit that had gone out of style maybe three decades ago. As he drew closer the smell of mothballs suggested his attire had been plucked from a dusty clothes rack expressly for this visit.

Three feet away, he stopped. He squinted up at me with unflinching brown eyes. "Are you the *gaijin* the papers said caught the Japantown killers in San Francisco?"

Gaijin means "foreigner," literally "outside person."

"Guilty as charged."

"And tackled the Japanese mafia before that?"

"Guilty again."

For better or worse, the overseas murders and my run-in with the Tokyo thugs had made headlines in Japan.

"Then you're my man. Got notches on your belt."

I smiled and his son, who had sidled up on the other side, whispered in my ear. "That's his meds talking. Makes him emotional. Sometimes delusional. I only mentioned coming here to calm him. I never thought he'd actually do it."

His father frowned. He hadn't heard what was said, but he was astute enough to guess the content. "My son thinks I've toppled off the train because I've put on a few years. Well, I'm ninety-three, and until last December I could walk three miles a day without a damn stick."

"A few years? You're ninety-*six*, Dad. You shouldn't be charging around town like this."

The old man waved the cane under his son's nose. "You call this charging? There are tombstones in Aoyama Cemetery that move faster than I do, but upstairs my train's still running on straight tracks. Besides, when a man my age no longer wants to shave off a couple years to impress the ladies, *then* he's done for."

I was going to like this guy.

I said, "Why don't we step into my office? It's quiet there. Mari, would you show these gentlemen the way? I'll be there in a minute."

"Follow me, please," she said.

Once Mari had shut them in, I turned to a pale-faced detective nearest the entrance. "Anything else besides their showing up without an appointment?"

"Only the last name. Miura."

"Okay, thanks. Do you know where Noda is?"

Kunio Noda was our head detective and the main reason I came away from the Japantown case in one piece.

"He's out on the kidnapping case in Asakusa but supposed to be back shortly."

"Send him in as soon as he arrives, okay?"

"Will do."

I headed back to my office, where I exchanged cards and the customary bows with the new arrivals. The father's name was Akira Miura and he'd once been senior vice president of a major Japanese trading company.

The son with the pricey tie was a *fuku bucho*, or assistant section chief, at Kobo Electronics. His company was equally impressive but his position was not, especially for a Japanese salaryman in his fifties. You didn't start making good money until you hit *bucho*, the next step up for Yoji Miura, so either he was spending beyond his means or there was money trickling in from another source.

Taking my seat I said, "So, gentlemen, how can I help?"

Before they could respond, Mari knocked and entered. On a tray she carried green tea in decorated porcelain cups with lids. Guest chinaware. In Japan, courtesy rules.

"I was in the war, Mr. Brodie," Akira Miura said after Mari departed.

When a Japanese mentions *the war*, he or she means World War II. And only the youngest soldiers—now the oldest surviving veterans—were around today. Japan fought no further battles after the big Double Two.

"I see," I said.

Miura Senior eyes zeroed in on me. "How much do you know about Japanese history, Mr. Brodie?"

"Quite a bit, actually."

My endeavors in the field of Japanese art made knowledge of the country's history, culture, and traditions mandatory.

"Did you know that in the old Japanese army you followed orders without question, or your commanding officer put a bullet in your head?"

"Yes."

"Good. Then you probably also know that my country conquered part of Manchuria and set up a puppet state."

I did, and he seemed pleased.

Japan had entered China aggressively in the early 1900s, then cemented its grasp by laying railroads, bringing in settlers, and setting up branches of its large conglomerates. In 1932 it famously resurrected the rule of China's twelfth and final Qing Dynasty ruler, Pu Yi, canonized in popular culture as the Last Emperor.

Miura said, "I was sent to the Manchurian front in 1940 as an officer. My men and I fought many battles. Then new orders shifted us to a frontier outpost called Anli-dong. Our assignment was to stabilize the region, and I became the de facto mayor of Anli and the surrounding area.

"We were outnumbered two hundred to one, but by that time the Japanese military had a reputation so fierce we retained control without incident. Although I preached nonviolence and it held, my predecessor had been ruthless. Any Chinese male offender faced a firing squad or worse, and his women became the spoils of war. Which is why I need you."

"For something that happened more than seventy years ago?"

"You've heard about the recent home invasions in Tokyo?"

"Sure. Two families slaughtered within six days of each other. Eight people were killed."

"You saw the police suspect Triads?"

"Of course."

"They're right."

Inwardly I cringed at the mention of the blade-wielding Chinese gangs. I'd run into them in San Francisco once when I lived out in the Mission. It hadn't ended well.

"How can you be so sure?"

Miura's handsome brown eyes flooded with fear. "In Anli-dong they told me they would come after us. Now they have."

CHAPTER 2

He had my attention. "How can you be so sure the Triads are targeting you after all this time?"

"Because I know what was *not* in the papers."

"Which is?"

"Two of my men are dead all of a sudden."

My men. "And you told this to the police?"

"*Uma no mimi ni nembutsu,*" he said with undisguised disdain.

Might as well read sutras to horses. Meaning the Japanese police were too dense to understand.

"But you did tell them?"

He shrugged. "They insisted the killings couldn't possibly be motivated by 'ancient history.'"

During the war years, the Japanese police became an organ of terror at home almost as much as the armed forces did abroad. After the surrender, the police were emasculated. A heavy-handed bureaucracy filled the vacuum, and to this day a cautious mind-set colors their every action, which leaves a lot of territory for the likes of Brodie Security.

"And you think otherwise because?"

"My gut."

His son smiled apologetically.

I ignored Miura the Younger but could no longer dismiss his earlier comments about his father's instability. "And what is your gut telling you?"

"That two of my men killed so close together is no coincidence."

I said, "Even assuming that what you say is true, how would Brodie Security be able to help?"

"Guard my house."

His son wanted me to humor him, so I said, "That we can do. But security takes men, in teams, and doesn't come cheap. Are you sure?"

"I'm sure."

I looked at his son, who nodded reluctantly.

"Okay," I said, "we'll put some men on you for a few days."

"I also want you to find out who butchered my friends."

"The murders landed on the front page. You can bet the police have made them a top priority."

He shook his head. "The police are idiots. I gave them a connection and they didn't even bother to check it. Both men served together because they grew up in the same neighborhood. The same place they were killed. It is not a gang of thieves targeting the neighborhood, as the police think, but Anli-dong Triads targeting my men."

There was a knock, then Noda barreled in without waiting for a reply. The chief detective was short and stout and built like a bulldog—broad shoulders, a thick chest, and a flat humorless face. His most distinctive feature was a slash across his eyebrow where a yakuza blade had left its mark. Noda's return swipe left a deeper mark.

I made introductions and brought Noda up-to-date. He grunted when I mentioned the Triads.

"What? You think Triads are a possibility?" I said, pushing the habitually laconic detective for a more revealing response.

Chinese gangs had been in Japan for decades. They could trace their roots back to the end of the Ming Dynasty in China, where they started as a political group aiding the government against the invading Manchus, and were hailed as heroes. Over time the glory faded. But the beast needed feeding. Triad leaders looked elsewhere to buttress their dwindling support and found the easy money—protection, extortion, loan sharking, prostitution, and drugs. First at home and, inevitably, overseas. In Tokyo, gangs inhabited the darker corners of Shinjuku, Ueno, and other enclaves. Yokohama Chinatown, thirty minutes by train, was a major operational base.

Noda shrugged. "Could be."

"And?"

"Tricky."

Frustratingly curt as usual.

Miura looked from Noda to me. "So you'll take the case?"

"Noda?"

He shrugged. "It's what we do."

Meaning Brodie Security had handled Triad cases before. That was the question I'd really been asking. I was still new to my father's outfit, having inherited half of the firm just eleven months ago. But showing my ignorance in front of a client was not an option.

"Okay," I said. "We can look into it. My father's people are very good at what they do."

"They'll need to be," Miura said, his eyes lingering on Noda with vague apprehension.

"How many men from your old squad are left?"

"Twenty-eight of us survived the war but most died long ago. Only seven showed up at our last get-together. Then Mitsumoto died of a brain aneurysm, and Yanaguchi caught the bird flu on a visit back to Anli last year. Before the home invasions there were five of us."

So only three remained.

"Where are the other two?"

"One left for a friend's vacation home in Kyushu. He won't tell me where. The other went to stay with his son in the countryside."

Noda and I exchanged a look. That the remaining members of Miura's troop had fled Tokyo—and one to the farthest western island of mainland Japan—bolstered the old soldier's claim.

I had a last question:

"If you ruled Anli-dong with an even hand, then why would someone want you and your men dead after all this time?"

He sighed. "It's the dirt. Whenever higher-ups came through they expected to be entertained. They invariably ordered us to 'weed out traitors' and 'set up inspections.' The first consisted of lining up any villagers in jail for target practice. The second involved examining local beauties in private. These were orders we couldn't refuse or they'd—"

"—put a bullet in your head."

Miura's shoulders sagged under an old guilt. "Without a second thought."

"I see."

"After the first VIP visit, the Triads threatened me. I told them I could only control those under my command, not above. They were unconvinced. 'If you wear the master's uniform, you can bleed for him too.' They didn't act then because they knew more villagers would suffer if any soldiers were attacked. But they told me they would come one day.

"Years later, when China finally allowed Japanese tourists into the country, a handful of us went back. We looked up the families we knew. We were shocked to see how poor they were, and still are today. We've returned many times, bringing them money and modern appliances like Japanese rice cookers. We ate together and drank together. We did what we could to make amends. But we couldn't help everyone. I think our trips triggered an old resentment. We gave out our addresses freely. That may have been a mistake."

Noda grunted. "Revenge slayings."

Miura concurred with a nod. "My future killer is in Tokyo, Brodie-san. I can feel it."

A team of six men escorted Akira Miura home.

Once they arrived, two would canvass the neighborhood, then the local shops. Two others would secure the residence. Windows, doors, and other exterior access points would be sealed, then house, garage, and yard scanned for listening, tracking, and incendiary devices. The last pair would work with Miura on safety protocol, including an emergency evacuation plan, after which they would spend the next twelve hours with their charge until two rested operatives replaced them.

However, before the team left Brodie Security, they gathered in the conference room with the Miuras to discuss procedure. Sometime during the proceedings, the son slipped away and cornered Noda and me in my office.

"Thank you for indulging the old man," he said. "The murders have rattled him, but to be frank, we are seeing signs of senility lately, and mild paranoia."

"Has he gone overboard before?" I asked.

"No, but the doctors told us to expect a slow degeneration."

Noda and I traded a glance.

"Noted," I said. "But we'll want to treat the threat seriously until we can prove otherwise."

Yoji Miura remained skeptical. "Your presence will comfort my father, so what could it hurt? But between us, you'll be babysitting."

Noda scowled. "Two men murdered is beyond babysitting."

The head detective's voice was low and menacing. Yoji looked startled until he noticed that Noda's rage was not directed at him but at what might or might not be out there, lying in wait. Even so, when the younger Miura left my office, he gave Noda a wide berth. The detective himself followed a minute later, mumbling about clueless offspring.

Alone, I leaned back in my chair and stared at the ceiling. Deep down, something primal stirred, disturbed by the undertow of Miura Senior's fears. I liked the old veteran a lot. Pulling out his musty suit for the visit. Habitually shaving three years off his age so he could still attract "the ladies."

What I didn't like was his fellow veterans abandoning Tokyo for safer grounds. Nor the triple threat—home invasions, Triads, and old war atrocities. I'd been through a lot in my life. Seen a lot. Had learned the hard way to give any early sign of danger its due.

This could be the world's wildest goose chase, or the beginning of something very nasty.

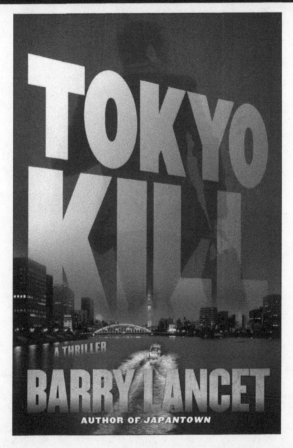